'A story of every day, that is never told. Uplifting and simultaneously heart-breaking'
ANSTEY HARRIS

'A thought-provoking and compelling coming-of-age story, with a fearless and funny protagonist in Bess'
RICHARD ROPER

'Real, raw, heart-wrenching and so wonderfully written'
JESSICA RYN

'Heroic and powerful, but also tender; this is such an important novel'
CHARLOTTE MENDELSON

'So good I'm lying in a tepid bath because my 15 minutes reading turned into 45. What a voice!'
AMY BEASHEL

'I am so proud of my super-talented former student, Kirsty Capes. I'm so impressed with how her writing has flourished with the cracking characters and energetic prose of her fantastic debut novel'
BERNARDINE EVARISTO

'I felt this book in my gut! It's funny, it's emotional, and at times definitely heartbreaking, but Bess is a hero you can believe in'
JENDELLA BENSON

Kirsty Capes works in publishing and is an advocate for better representation for care-experienced people in the media. She recently completed her PhD, which investigates female-centric care narratives in contemporary fiction, under the supervision of 2019 Booker prize-winner Bernardine Evaristo. Her first novel, *Careless*, was longlisted for the Women's Prize 2022. *Love Me, Love Me Not* is her second novel. She lives in Slough with her golden retriever, Doug.

Also by Kirsty Capes

Careless

LOVE ME
ME

LOVE ME
ME NOT

KIRSTY CAPES

ORION

First published in Great Britain in 2022 by Orion Books,
an imprint of The Orion Publishing Group Ltd
Carmelite House, 50 Victoria Embankment
London EC4Y 0DZ

An Hachette UK Company

1 3 5 7 9 10 8 6 4 2

A CIP catalogue record for this book is
available from the British Library.

ISBN (Hardback) 978 1 3987 0012 3
ISBN (Export Trade Paperback) 978 1 3987 0013 0
ISBN (eBook) 978 1 3987 0015 4

Typeset by Input Data Services Ltd, Somerset

Printed in Great Britain by Clays Ltd, Elcograf S.p.A.

Chapter One

Lucy Banbury sits down on the lip of the kitchen door, her legs straight out in front of her on the patio to better catch the sun. She thinks, *This garden could really do with some furniture.* She tells herself off for thinking about furniture again. She unlocks her iPad and closes the three IKEA and four Made tabs she has open in Safari. Her legs are pale – too pale – because she's never liked the feeling of the breeze on her bare skin. She is trying to be better at this. Today, at the ground-floor flat Lucy shares with her friend Anais and Anais's boyfriend Cam just off Lambeth Road, tucked under the curve of the Thames that serves up the City, the West End and Westminster on an awkward inverted saucer, the three-by-three-metre patch of concrete that functions as the garden is a suntrap. It's a Saturday in mid-May and the weather is beginning to turn.

Despite its proximity to some of the best-known cultural, political and financial hubs of the Western hemisphere, the Lambeth flat is shabby if clean, just like the over four hundred flats in the same brown-bricked brutalist-inspired complex, built sometime in the nineteen eighties to correspond with the population boom that hit the city during the tail end of the second-wave feminist movement, the gay liberation front and in the wake of the Brixton riots. The middle classes – the parents of Lucy's flatmates included – moved out of the city to the safe, homogenous, classed suburbs and raised kids like Anais and Cam who spent their whole adolescence crafting plans that would bring them back into town. Lucy was born and raised on a council estate in Chadwell Heath. As a sixth-former, to get as far as Liverpool Street on TfL rail, on the weekends, sightseeing and people-watching and imagining herself a city-dweller, with a swim membership and maybe some sort of penthouse flat in Canary Wharf sometimes felt like nothing short of a miracle. Her mother, Erica, works in a launderette. Her father, Daniel Banbury Senior, is a retired painter-decorator. Lucy recently learned at her cousin's wedding that these people adopted her. She is not a Banbury after all. She doesn't know her origin story, whatsoever, not like Cam and Anais, who are breaking up again very loudly in the hallway.

It is now that Lucy feels conspicuous on the back stoop of the flat. But to leave her flatmates to their break-up in peace would be to sidle past them, squeezing herself into the gaps, to get to the front door. She thinks that maybe Anais is cramming clothes into bin bags. Cam is possibly crying.

Anais and Cam grew up in Berkshire: Anais in Langley and Cam in Datchet. They went to the same secondary school and college together. By virtue of their hometowns, they both have drivers' licences and treat Sunday roasts as a religious experience. Anais has always been one of those people who can talk to anyone – and can tease out some aspect of a person that makes them want to please her. Cam is awkward, and lanky, and paints Warhammer figurines with tiny brushes under a very bright desk light on the kitchen table at weekends. It is very clear to Lucy why Anais and Cam, who has worked as a History teacher in the same classroom at the same secondary school in Peckham Rye since he graduated, are so frequently arguing.

Lucy feels that she is somewhere in-between the personality types of her flatmates. She has spent the past five years in London, since graduating, cultivating a particular type of persona for herself. Lucy appears sociable, with many friends, and fun to be around. She likes to listen to people's problems. She likes to agree with others on their political and cultural opinions. She likes to dress well and receive compliments because of it. She rarely refers to her upbringing or her family because she likes to control her narrative; to maintain a certain level of mythologisation about herself. Instead, she likes it when people call her *cosmopolitan* and *a yuppie,* on account of her job at Kube, a trendy marketing start-up where she and Anais both work as senior supplier relations executives. Lucy likes things to be clean, neat and orderly. She likes the smell of chlorine. She likes to count money. She likes to fill silences, if at all possible. She is acutely aware that she needs to be more outspoken and individualistic if her friends and colleagues are to continue to take her seriously and enjoy her company. Lucy must try on new things like clothes: being flighty, or fickle, or volatile. There is always more work to be done to make yourself a more interesting person.

Lucy squints up at the spring sunshine and listens to the bin men slowly and noisily making their way along Lambeth Road beyond the garden fence. Anais is in the bedroom now, and Cam has joined Lucy out here on the concrete. His eyes are red and raw and ugly.

What happened? Lucy asks, shielding her own eyes against the sun as she looks up at him.

Anais is moving out, Cam replies, his voice impassive.

Anais is now in the garden too, the thin plastic of her bin bags cutting angry red stripes into her knuckles. One jet-black acrylic, filed to a point, has separated itself from her fingernail and now dangles by a thread of skin.

3

Anais and Lucy, since first working together and now living together for a year, are generally quite good friends. Lucy wonders whether her break-up with Cam has anything to do with Anais's personal trainer. Josh, built like a brick shithouse, as Lucy's dad would say, meets Anais at the gym three times a week. Anais's stories at work about her sessions with Josh, told across the desk in excitable whispers, have got warmer, more animated, delivered with a deeper strength of feeling over the past couple of months.

Lucy likes to keep her personal life personal, and as a rule doesn't share her secrets with anyone.

I'm going to my parents' for a bit, Anais says. She waits for Cam to respond and when he doesn't, she looks at Lucy, expectantly. Lucy pretends that she hasn't noticed Anais looking at her.

I feel like this is none of my business, Lucy says, and she gets up to leave. But Anais is standing in the kitchen doorway, blocking her path back into the flat. Lucy shifts from one foot to the other, her heart hammering. Anais and Cam are staring at each other with indecipherable expressions. Lucy wonders if she could hop the fence. She might land in the bin truck, though, which is now directly outside the building and filling the warm spring air with the pungent stench of bin juice.

I'll start looking for somewhere to live, Anais says. Maybe with some friends from work.

Lucy tries the wobbly fence panel, but it's not wide enough to slip through.

I haven't worked the details out, yet, Anais continues, one fat tear rolling down her face, dragging a swirl of leaky mascara with it.

Aren't you going to stay with Josh? Lucy asks Anais, matter-of-factly, flailing around for some notch of conversation to dissipate the crawling second-hand humiliation she is feeling.

4

Cam looks at her – eyebrows knotted up, cheeks red and shiny.

Oh. Josh, is it? That's his name? Cam asks Lucy.

Lucy realises she has made a terrible mistake. Anais slides down the wall onto the patio slabs, as though she is melting. Lucy is not very good at saying the right thing at the right time.

It's really none of Lucy's business. But Anais is not just abandoning Cam for Josh the personal trainer. She is abandoning Lucy, too. In this flat, with her sad cuckolded boyfriend.

In any case, Anais will be back in six to eight weeks, Lucy is willing to wager. Anais and Cam have broken up and got back together at least twice in the past year that Lucy has lived with them. They have been together almost ten – college sweethearts – so the actual tally is probably higher.

Well, Anais says.

Well, Cam replies.

She comes towards him, as though she is planning to embrace him, but changes her mind at the last minute and picks a piece of lint from the collar of his shirt.

I think this is it, she says, slightly lifting her bin bags to demonstrate their presence and significance.

I'd better get going, she says when he doesn't reply to her. And he looks down at her. Everyone is waiting for him to say something, including him, possibly. But he doesn't. The tears brim over Anais's eyelids again.

Lucy turns back to the concrete garden, and stares again at the busted fence panel near the bins. She needs to call their landlady Marcy, or their letting agency, to get it fixed. She can hear Anais struggling to get her suitcases and bags out the front door.

Shall I go and help her? she asks Cam, who is staring at the wall. He blinks at her and shrugs.

Lucy does help with the last of Anais's bags, into the back of the Uber she has called. It idles on the edge of the pavement while glorious red buses heave themselves around it, hydraulics puffing out great sighs of discontent as they do so. This corner of the city is thriving with the anticipation of the Saturday night ahead: with music spilling out of the open windows of passing cars; day-drinking twenty-somethings returning from the park to their flats to get ready for a night out. The Three Stags down the road is already thrumming with the overspill of bodies clutching warm pints on the pavement outside. The life of the city is like a low-frequency vibration that laces itself through the concrete and hums up through the soles of Lucy's shoes. The nervous anticipation of something about to happen.

I can't believe you said that about Josh, Anais tells Lucy.

I thought he knew.

Well – he does now.

Anais tips over, again, into burbling sobs. Lucy mutters a quick apology and pulls her into an angular hug of the kind where their bodies somehow don't seem to touch.

Will you text me?

Yeah, Lucy replies. She is unclear of the etiquette on supporting friends who have done morally reprehensible things like cheat on their significant other (and hide it for months). It occurs to her that Anais has left her in a really shitty situation. See you at work Monday, Lucy says, trying for a reluctant cheerfulness as Anais climbs into the car. Anais doesn't reply. There doesn't seem to be anything else to say, so Lucy stands awkwardly on the kerbside and waves her off.

She returns to Flat 5, walks through the hall with its uneven shabby carpet, and the kitchen with stains on the lino that Lucy has never been able to scrub out, despite her best efforts. She resists the compulsion to clean the countertops, to fill up a bucket with diluted bleach and mop the floor. This is how Lucy copes with uncomfortable situations. The dirt makes her itch.

Cam stays in the garden, eventually sitting down on the hard concrete and crossing his legs, until the sky turns indigo-coloured and the voices of Saturday-night revellers fill the garden from beyond the fence, mirthful screeches emanating from windows and passing cars; the steaming meat smell of kebab-shop mixed doners intermingling with the remnants of the bin men and exhaust fumes and cut grass. Lucy deliberates about how she should interact with Cam. Eventually, she boils some tea and takes it out to him, with peanut buttered toast. It occurs to her that she has never really had a proper, sincere conversation with Cam in the twelve months that they have lived under the same roof together. She and Cam are (it seems) both naturally quiet people, when alone.

Lucy sits in the kitchen, feeling that she needs to stay nearby. She wonders whether Cam is in some sort of mental-health crisis and whether she should call someone. His parents? She doesn't know his parents' names, let alone their numbers or where they live, besides Datchet. She realises now that she knows barely anything about him. And thinking of Cam's parents makes her think of her own, and the knowledge she has now, of her adoption, and how she has been ignoring texts and phone calls from her mother for the past month, since she found out. It is like a stone weighing her down from the inside, this new knowledge. She can't stand it, so she avoids Cam without straying far from him – just in case – and wonders at how acutely he now appears as a stranger to her. Eventually, he drags himself up from where he's sitting and closes the back door, locks it and goes to bed.

Chapter Two

Days later, Lucy is trying on a dress the colour of egg yolk in the Zara changing rooms, overheating under the strip lights, hair slowly humidifying and remembering something her brother Danny said to her last spring. She had come home for an Easter Sunday lunch to celebrate her promotion with her parents. Her mother, Erica, and her father, Daniel Senior, prefer not to travel into town. They don't like loud noises, strangers or traffic. Are afraid of being pickpocketed on the tube. Years ago, Lucy's Uncle Marv, a friend of her father's, lived on a canal boat on the River Lea, just off the Hackney Marshes. This was the farthest west her parents would venture, except for two trips to Madame Tussauds when she was a kid and her dad got flush with a big cash-in-hand job. When they started building the Olympic Park, Uncle Marv moved out to a housing estate in Chadwell Heath, too, and her parents stopped visiting London postcodes all together.

Lucy used to go home once or twice a month, and it was always an occasion. Her parents' home is really not that far east when you think about it (though still technically Essex). But every time she gets on the TfL rail at Stratford, that monstrous Anish Kapoor public art looming over the station, it feels as though she's travelling to the end of the world. She hasn't been home since the wedding. Last Easter, she was promoted from junior supplier relations executive to senior supplier relations executive. She told herself that she was excited to take on new responsibilities and challenges at a job that she already loved: a line she also used in the interview. She repeated it again to her parents over a chipped bowl of steaming buttered new potatoes at their kitchen table. Her mother, a terrible cook but an expert at any sort of arts and crafts, had painted boiled chicken's eggs in the likeness of each of the four Banburys and placed them in terracotta eggcups in the centre of the table: a tradition that had extended well past Lucy and Danny's childhood, when they would help her stick googly eyes to hard-boiled eggshell and draw on leaking red grins with poster paint for mouths.

`At dinner, Lucy's father was talkative (a miracle), and her mother was in a good mood because she hadn't burned the special lamb chops from the butcher's. Danny was three-quarters through a bottle of red wine from the off-licence.

Lucy's parents went into the garden to hose down the deckchairs. It was a mild afternoon and there were crows cleaning their feathers on the roof of the shed. While they were gone, Danny said to her, unprovoked, Is there really any substance to you at all, Loose? He picked up the egg painted with Lucy's likeness: her mum's expert hand had daintily curled fire-orange hair around the narrow oval end. She had painted a tiny clipboard into Lucy's egg hands – symbolic of Lucy's promotion, at a job and a company whose function no other Banbury fully understood. Danny said to Lucy, holding the egg between thumb and forefinger, You're cheaper than the real thing and nothing on the inside. And he laughed, and cracked the egg with a flourish over a glass, and it hadn't been hard-boiled at all. The yolk, speared by the shell, leaked across the table.

Now, Lucy is one arm in, one arm out of the orange shift

dress, with miniature glass bead buttons on the bodice, when she gets the text from Anais. The text says that she is moving in with Josh, the personal trainer. The text doesn't actually say *the personal trainer*, but that's who Anais is referring to.

Before Lucy moved in with Cam and Anais last year, she lived in a battered Dalston house she shared with six other people, four of whom were postgraduate research students at UEL who had not quite mastered simple household etiquette like washing your own dishes and bleaching the toilet. She once went to the kitchen in the middle of the night to pour herself a glass of water and found a slug halfway in, halfway out of a plug socket. The bathroom ceiling dripped with condensation when she got out of the shower, due to poor ventilation, with blossoms of black mould crawling across the ceiling. Around the same time the slug crawled in (or out of) the plug socket, Anais started working on the desk opposite Lucy's at Kube. She mentioned that she needed a new flatmate: she seemed clean, well-groomed and not the type of person to leave cooked mackerel uncovered in the grill pan for four days. Lucy moved in a month later.

Her speculation about Anais's personal hygiene had been correct. This was significant for Lucy, who is a *very clean person*. More than one person has told her that she's *too* clean, going as far as using the words obsessive compulsive, though Lucy was in fact tested for that when she was fifteen and was told that she was just a very particular person. There is nothing wrong with wanting to be clean.

The same goes for how Lucy presents herself. Lucy is very proud of her position at Kube. Lucy loves – *loves* – her job. She loves living and working in the city, especially now she's out of the Dalston slum house and living in Lambeth, which is more central and slightly less scummy, less crawling with *hipsters* (although she herself – to her secret delight – has been accused of being a hipster more than once). Lucy likes to plan her work outfits for the week ahead on Sunday nights, carefully mulling over each piece of clothing and accessory. She rotates four pairs of sandals in the summer and three pairs of boots of varying styles when the weather is cooler. She tries not to wear the same thing twice to work within the space of a fortnight. She throws out tights after three wears without exception. She *never* does her make-up on public transport. Everything Lucy knows about clothes, and how to wear them, she learned from her mother. She likes being a *girl about town*. She likes hurrying past tourists on her way to the office in the morning, at the tube station, expertly tapping her iPhone at the barrier and breezing through, often with headphones in and the expression (bored-detachment-cum-ever-so-slightly-sneering-superiority-complex) of the busy local Londoner, perfected over many hundreds of commutes. She cannot walk efficiently up and down the escalators on the left-hand side because she finds that it gives her the most sickening vertigo. She likes having brunch in expensive Kensington coffee shops in the basements of five-storey terraced Georgian mansions.

The yolk-coloured dress, she decides, inspecting herself in the mirror under the horrid fluorescent changing room lights, is not going to cut it. The string-tie shoulder straps are too bohemian. The cotton material of the skirt slightly too thin. The colour is too stark against her skin, clashes with the red-brown shade of her hair (oxblood) which has been expertly mixed at the boutique salon near the office. This year, Lucy has vowed to take up cycling to work. She wants one of those Pendleton bikes with creamy-white tyres and a wicker basket. She cannot risk cycling in a dress. With this thought, Lucy realises that she must now rethink her whole June wardrobe.

Lucy knows, in an abstract way, that if someone were party to the inner thoughts that permeated her stream of consciousness during most of her waking moments – a constant and continuous reassessment of how she is being viewed by other people at all times – they might think her self-absorbed. Lucy knows that the way she thinks is not like how other people think. No other person she knows would be walking down Oxford Street towards the Circus, as she is now, wondering whether the couple walking behind her, who are having a mildly agitated conversation in Italian, are in fact discussing the spot of dry skin on her left ankle, or the ugly mole on her back between her shoulder blades; or whether the man across the road busking with a xylophone has noticed that her side profile enhances the appearance of the soft pouch of skin under her jaw, which – without an outdoor swim at the leisure centre on Tottenham Court Road three mornings a week – is in ever-imminent peril of turning into a double chin.

It is sometimes exhausting, being so acutely self-aware. Lucy worries a lot about whether these thoughts – the incessant obsession with her own self – indicate that she is a vain or egotistical person. Sometimes, at night in bed, Lucy wonders whether everyone around her – her friends and colleagues and flatmates – can see the mechanics of her thinking and find her repulsive for it. Sometimes she finds *herself* repulsive. Lucy knows that it is *not normal* to think like this. She also doesn't know how to stop thinking like this, because it's the only way she has ever thought. She tries to feel empathy for people, like Cam, who has hardly been out of his bedroom since the revelations of last Saturday night. But she only feels it in small, almost imperceptible wave of emotion.

Her phone vibrates in her bag. She takes it out and sees a text from her mother, Erica. It says: *Please talk to us, Loose. Come round for dinner next weekend.*

Lucy knows that she will not be visiting her parents next weekend. There are several reasons for this:

One, she has a hair appointment on Saturday at two o'clock and a mani-pedi booked on Sunday at three. With both appointments, getting to Chadwell Heath in good time and in a presentable, dinner-worthy state becomes difficult.

Two, Lucy needs to place an ad for the single box room in the flat on spareroom.com, on the basis that Anais is moving in with Josh, which is an unexpected turn of events. She was certain that Anais would be curled up on the sofa, hot chocolate in hand, waxing her arm hair and leaving the used strips on the coffee table for someone else (Lucy) to clean up, within the month.

She mentioned getting a new flatmate to Cam – in passing – this morning.

I don't want to be insensitive, Lucy told Cam, edging around him in the narrow walkway of their kitchen to get to the kettle.

Not at all, he replied, not looking at her. I can't afford to cover Anais's portion of rent.

I can, Lucy said, without thinking. But I don't want to. Is Anais *definitely* not coming back?

Cam turned to look at her.

It's just, she said, sipping coffee, I don't want to go to all this effort if you're going to get back together in, like, a week's time.

He raised his eyebrows at the wall, stiffening.

Do what you want, he said, shoving through the doorway into the hall, I don't care.

She realised, too late, blood flooding her cheeks, that she had said the wrong thing again.

Lucy will be conducting viewings all weekend, when she's not at a hair, hand or foot appointment, as Cam will be busy marking GCSE mock exams and being sad about Anais. Lucy realises once again with new clarity how badly Anais has dropped her in the shit, let alone Cam.

And three, the whole adoption revelation, which is recent and was discovered in deeply unpleasant circumstances. Since this revelation, she has felt uncomfortable about visiting home. Especially because her older brother, Danny (thirty-one, an alcoholic, and running his photography business out of the shed in her parents' back garden), is *not* adopted, and knew about Lucy's adoption the whole time, along with all the other members of her family at the wedding.

She has also recently stopped liking being called *Loose.*

She tells her friend Meredith so over lunch in Le Pain Quotidien in Covent Garden forty minutes later, after purchasing a pair of snow-white espadrilles in a boutique near the square. Meredith is very, very posh. She and Lucy met at a networking event for young marketing professionals shortly after Lucy moved to Dalston and started her first, bottom-of-the-rung, brand marketing job at a now-defunct start-up called Doughnuts. Lucy's first client was a microbrewery that had opened opposite the Dalston Curve Garden, pricing out the small radical left-wing publisher that had a tiny office on the top floor of the building. When she met Meredith at these networking drinks, Lucy told her about the microbrewery and Meredith spent a very long time, without pausing to let someone else interject, soliloquising about the perils of gentrification in East London and how the fabric of authentic community was being torn asunder by corporate interests.

Well, I think it's actually just two guys with skaggy beards, not a corporation, Lucy replied quietly, referring to the microbrewery.

I just don't see, Meredith said, how you can stomach working for them when they're destroying those neighbourhoods that have been there for decades – *hundreds* of years.

Lucy hadn't heard of gentrification and didn't really know what to say to that. Meredith's father had recently bought a townhouse on Upper Road in Islington, converted it into an HMO and now allowed Meredith to let and manage the property and take all the rent profits for herself. Meredith often discussed the pity it was that all the independent bookshops on Upper Road were now Foxton's estate agents.

I can't stand being called Loose any more, Lucy tells Meredith over a steaming plate of seafood chowder.

Who's calling you Loose? I don't call you Loose, Meredith replies, shovelling a forkful of syrupy pancake into her mouth.

My mother calls me Loose.

Lucy hasn't yet given Meredith details of the adoption news, because Meredith knows nothing about Lucy's family and Lucy prefers to keep it that way.

You're very uptight, Loose, says Meredith.

Lucy looks down at the fishy broth, the unidentifiable bits of seafood limb floating limply in it. It smells garlicky, though she asked for no garlic. She will now have to mouthwash in the toilets before she leaves the restaurant. She is itching to get up and do it now.

I think you need a boy, Meredith announces.

Excuse me?

A man to loosen you up a bit. You know.

Lucy contemplates Meredith: her naturally straight sandy-blonde hair tied into a functional ponytail; her straight teeth the result of expensive adolescent orthodontal work to correct an overbite; her short-sleeved blouse in blue and white pinstripes.

You need to get laid, Meredith elaborates.

It's not that easy, Lucy tells Meredith, I can't just speak it into existence. Not like you. You don't need to *try*. You always seem to be dating four men at the same time.

Cool, thanks for slut-shaming me, by the way.

I'm not slut-shaming. You're projecting.

Meredith narrows her eyes, shrugs and dabs at her mouth with the cotton napkin draped across her lap.

I'm not exactly meeting tons of people, either, Lucy says.

She is now at a stage in her twenties, where everyone she meets, she already knows, and she doesn't want to date any of them. She has her friends – lots of them, more than she ever had at school or uni – and she doesn't need any more. The idea of finding a *millennial* man for a boyfriend, who hasn't been coddled by his mother and previous girlfriends to the point of dysfunction, seems impossible these days. Lucy has noticed how boys are often let off the hook of performing the basic decent be-haviours and social functions of human beings because, simply, they are male. Lucy can't stand men like this. She wonders how she will ever find someone to have sex with who doesn't deeply repulse her. These things are *cyclical*; there is a *pattern* to them. Lucy is not interested in raising a boyfriend.

She doesn't meet new people; and when she does, she feels herself shrivelling up on the inside. She doesn't know what to say to them. Doesn't know how to make herself seem interesting to others. When she *does* say something, it somehow always comes out wrong. Last week, a new person started at work – Brandon, a freelance graphic designer. His sister had just given birth, and his newborn niece had a club foot.

Club feet are fine, Anais said, smiling at him encouragingly as he passed his phone around the desk.

The baby on the screen – pinkish purple, mottled, mid-squeal – looked just about the same as every other baby Lucy had ever encountered.

Anais continued, My little brother had it when he was born. They just have to get their feet stretched out, or something.

Anais is very good at this: the minutiae of social cues; the elaborate dance of conversational politics.

I'm worried she'll get bullied at school or whatever, Brandon said. She's got a birthmark on her cheek too – see – a big one.

He jabbed his index finger at the screen and Anais nodded sympathetically.

At least she'll have a really good personality, Lucy said, smiling at him, copying Anais's expression.

I'm not sure how I feel about that, actually, Brandon told her.

Anais handed Brandon's phone back to him and frowned at her computer screen, and Lucy felt the smile slip from her face. Brandon went to the kitchen for tea and stayed there for over twenty minutes.

You just need to get on an app, Meredith tells her. That's how everyone does it. It's like window shopping.

I don't like window shopping.

Yes, you're more of a *commitment to purchase* kind of person. I know.

Do you know any men I could date?

Meredith snorts into her prosecco. You don't want to date any of the toffs I know. Trust me.

But *you* date them.

Yes, but I'm also a toff. It's the world I operate in.

What, you're saying I'm not a toff? Lucy asks, aiming for a joking tone.

Lucy. Please.

Lucy wonders at how Meredith can say such cruel things and get away with it. But it's Lucy who can't make one innocuous, well-intended comment about a baby's club foot without being made to feel like some sort of supervillain.

Meredith rolls her eyes at Lucy's expression. Oh, you know what I mean. And anyway, you don't want to sleep with any of those prissy rich Eton boys. They're all wankers living in penthouses paid for by their daddies. And they've all got terrible taste, you know. They dress like they're on *The Tweenies*. You could *never* deal with that. I was at a party once and walked in on a gaggle of them with their banking apps open on their phones, comparing balances.

Lucy stirs her chowder. Meredith, too, is in the enviable position of *choosing* to work and viewing her job as something of a hobby. One day Meredith will marry an aristocrat and involve herself in some sort of charity work. Lucy sometimes wonders if she had said something that night about Meredith's questionable ethical position on the gentrification of the East End, whether they would ever have become friends.

Probably, to be fair, because Meredith seems to have skin made of reinforced concrete.

Before Lucy gets up to say goodbye and pretend to leave before circling the Square and going into the toilets to gargle Listerine, she lets Meredith download a dating app onto her phone.

You've got a text from your mum on here, Meredith says, while she's linking Lucy's Facebook to her new dating profile and choosing Lucy's most flattering selfie for the hero picture.

Lucy still hasn't responded to her mum's text about dinner. The thought of going makes her want to regurgitate all that garlic-fish-seafood-soup nonsense she's just sipped up.

They say goodbye, and while she mouthwashes, Lucy rereads the text from Erica. And then she scrolls back up to the top of the conversation thread, up to months ago when Lucy got this new phone and all her WhatsApp data got wiped when she transferred her SIM card. She reads all the texts as though they are a story. She realises her mother texts her far more than Lucy replies. To an outsider, Lucy appears a little distant and stand-offish. Even on text. Lucy reminds herself that this is not the case in real life: that she is a warm and generous person with many friends and a busy social calendar. She looks at herself in the mirror, teeth gritted, and wills herself to believe it.

Lucy runs a brush through her hair and picks at a piece of wayward nail polish on the cuticle of her thumb. She leaves the restaurant, via the fire exit, so that she doesn't bump into Meredith again.

Chapter Three

Kube is located on the fifth floor of one of the trendy brown-stones just off Borough Market. One of the things Lucy enjoys about the marketing agency office, and its location, is that it makes her feel very much like a more put-together red-headed Bridget Jones. The sensation of fulfilment that comes with being a girl-about-town type, who wears trench coats in the winter and light cotton blazers in the summer, whose heels make pleasing *clip-clopping* noises on the bricked pavements of Tooley Street; who sometimes likes to go to the falafel truck outside the post office at lunchtime for a *little treat*; all of it is entirely joyous to Lucy. It's unfortunate that rather than the roomy, well-heated loft above a restaurant Bridget has all to herself in the film, Lucy is stuck with the cramped flatshare in the arse-end of Lambeth, where there is always a strange smell coming from the micro-wave, no matter how much she bleaches, soaks and scrubs.

Some of the other things Lucy likes about working at Kube are the fancy lifts that are controlled by a touchscreen where you select your floor number and get whizzed straight up there. She likes the floor-to-ceiling industrial factory windows with slim black frames, the white walls and tessellating ceiling tiles; and with the train tracks running parallel to the building, she loves the noise of the rickety Southeastern stock rolling into London

Bridge station. She has a keyboard at her desk that lights up like a rainbow, if she presses the right button.

Things Lucy doesn't like about her office, and she supposes her job as a senior supplier relations executive, are the open-plan working arrangements (where everyone can overhear everyone else's conversations, stop by to interrupt you for an impromptu chat and peer over your shoulder to see whether you're skiving on Twitter) and the fact that she spends so much time talking to suppliers on the phone. There is nothing that Lucy despises much more than a telephone call with a stranger. Sometimes she even finds telephone calls with her close friends unbearable. This makes her job – where she spends at least forty per cent of her time on the phone with suppliers, and occasionally has to go on site visits, hard hat and hi-vis included – seem like an odd choice for her. Nevertheless, Lucy *loves* working at Kube and feels very at home among the succulents and filing cabinets, both rarely disturbed, of the Kube office environment.

Lucy doesn't see Anais at work all week. She has called in sick with food poisoning. It's the third time this year that Anais has had food poisoning, and Delilah, Lucy's boss, who takes the call, raises her eyebrows at Lucy across the shared desk as she listens to Anais on the other end of the line.

Lucy can't imagine being so devastated about something that she misses a day of work: she feels a deep sense of fulfilment at the end of each workday when she has achieved her list of tasks or delivered work that ensures the company's continued success. Lucy has heard rumours about budget cuts, but she feels the essential nature of her role as senior supplier relations executive deep within her, down to the bone. She does the same job as Anais, but her attendance record is spotless. Lucy is totally in control of her own destiny, and the carpet tiles reaffirm this for her every morning when she arrives at the office and sees that they are freshly vacuumed, the faint stripes on each of them like lines on a cricket pitch.

Anais texts Lucy three times about going out for a drink this week, food poisoning apparently forgotten. When they lived together, Lucy and Anais would sometimes have a drink or two after work before getting on the tube back to Flat 5, across the street to Flat Iron Square, or down Borough High Street to one of the sixteenth-century wonky pubs half-hidden in alleyways, always heaving with young professionals crouching under low-slung wooden beams on a Wednesday or Thursday rush hour. Anais has lots and lots of friends, but Lucy has always felt a little bit special because she *lives* with Anais – or at least used to – and consequently has her confidence more so than other people do. She knows secret things about Anais that Anais's other friends will never know, like how she still wears a retainer, and sometimes mixes up her 'r' and 'w' sounds when she's tired, and last year when she was off work for a week it was because she got lip fillers and had an allergic reaction and her jaw swelled up to three times its size. Lucy was, after all, one of the first at Kube to know about Josh the personal trainer. Before Jenna and Kerry from accounting, before Delilah and the freelancers. Being friends with Anais makes Lucy by association a little bit more interesting.

But the idea of pretending to empathise with Anais's problems feels unnatural, too. Lucy doesn't know whether she will be able to keep up a façade of sympathy and comradery through an entire charcuterie board and bottle of sav. Despite this, she still desperately wants Anais to like her, to think of her as someone with whom she wants to spend time. She wonders whether, now they don't live together, she will be able to hold Anais's attention in the same way. Whether the excuses she sends back make Anais more or less keen to be her friend. She must calculate the optimal level of rejection she must deliver, without being cruel or coming off as judgemental of Anais's behaviour. Lucy doesn't want another Brandon situation – who just yesterday moved his MacBook off her desk cluster and now works alone in a meeting room.

Lucy cleans Flat 5 from top to bottom the following weekend. The advert for the spare single box room – up to now used as storage and a sleeping space for rare overnight guests, like Cam's sister and occasionally Meredith, who spends most of her visits to the flat pointing out the peeling wallpaper and the cracks in the ceiling – has only had two requests for viewings. Lucy wants to make a good impression on the new flatmate, mainly because the room needs to be filled quickly by someone who can put down a deposit without signing anything, in light of the illegality of the sublet. Lucy is still acutely aware that if it comes down to it, she'll be the one to foot the missing rent, with her salary being higher than Cam's teacher's wage.

Predictably, Cam has had no involvement in any of this whatsoever, instead holing himself up in his bedroom to mark homework or scroll Reddit, or whatever.

Lucy has found herself wandering around the flat late at night, like a displaced child. She finds that cleaning the place – scrubbing marks off the skirting boards; poking a broom into the farthest corners of the ceiling to dissipate the spiders' webs; spraying foaming, nostril-stinging chemicals into the oven and wiping away the brown grease – gives her a bone-deep sensation of calm. Dirt and mess are problems that Lucy can solve easily. These are itches that may simply be scratched. But the smell from the microwave only seems stronger in the quiet of the night and this unsettles her. She can't find a spot to relax.

On Sunday, the first prospective tenant to view the room is a man in his forties, who arrives wearing a long dirty-green fishing coat and holding a blue plastic bag, of the kind you get in off-licences, its contents a mystery. He takes a cursory glance around the small single room, with its dated wallpaper and the wardrobe with a broken door hanging from one hinge, the cardboard storage boxes shoved unceremoniously to one side, and immediately asks for £100 docked from the monthly fee. Lucy suggests that there is lots of interest and the room is a bargain at the advertised p.c.m., and he leaves without saying goodbye.

The second viewing is with a girl who can't be more than nineteen, and her mother, both of them wearing matching pink jumpers with love hearts patterned across them and holding hands. The mother asks Lucy what the local area is like.

It's not bad, Lucy replies as the daughter looks imperiously round the kitchen. Lots of good nightlife. Good transport links.

She won't be going out after 8 p.m., the mother replies.

Oh. Okay, Lucy says.

And I'll be staying here on the weekends. On the sofa. What does the sofa look like?

Lucy shows them the living room and the mother lies down on the couch.

You're going to need a new sofa, she tells Lucy.

Well, we'd have to speak to the landlady, Lucy says.

Ridiculous.

Lucy is unsure what to say to this.

At the door, she promises to call them.

Later that afternoon, Lucy gets a phone call from Ash, whose pronouns are they/them. Ash is a musician whose friend, Bec, went to secondary school with Lucy for one year before moving to Chalk Farm. Lucy wouldn't call Bec her friend, but thanks to the curated snippets of her life that she posts on Instagram, Lucy knows lots of things about Bec that seem a little bit too intimate. Lucy knows that Bec comes from a good family: her mother a lawyer and her dad some sort of stock trader in Hong Kong. After a year abroad between college and uni, Bec moved back to London to do sculpture at the UoA. She's had reasonable success since, at some of the smaller galleries in the city. Her crowning achievement so far has been a work featured at the Masculinities exhibition at the Barbican. Someone paid £8,000 for it, according to Bec's grid post. Judging from her Stories, Bec has already blown most of that eight grand on coke and expensive trainers.

On the phone, Ash tells Lucy that Bec saw the room on Facebook and recommended it in a not-so-subtle way. Ash has been crashing on Bec's couch since moving to London from Poole six months ago to try to make a name for themself as a musician and get some sort of label interest.

It was only meant to be a couple of weeks at Bec's, they tell Lucy on the phone. She wants her couch back. And her girlfriend Cassie is sick of me. Oh – I shouldn't say that, should I? They love me. They're begging me to stay. I'm a model flatmate.

Ash sounds sensible and lively and enthusiastic. They arrange to visit that afternoon to view the room, and they arrive wearing a giant terracotta-coloured distressed T-shirt and skinny pleather leggings. They have dark, thick hair that seems to explode from their head in a silky tangle, and a small angular face with freckles.

I love the room, they say, beaming at Lucy across the kitchen table, sipping delicately from the tea Lucy has prepared.

Lucy goes over the particulars. The monthly rent and the need for the first and last month's up front. The security deposit.

Ash doesn't question the lack of contract or documents.

What do you do for work? Lucy asks, noticing that there is a small tremor in her voice.

I'm a guitarist, mostly, Ash answers. Singer-songwriter. I've been gigging around London since I got here. Got a few good ones, but a lot of horseshit too. Twenty minutes at an indie club night at 2 a.m. and then I get paid in drinks.

You do have steady work, though, right? Lucy asks. The prospect of not having a guaranteed income is horrifying to her.

Oh, yeah, Ash says, looking away to examine the cupboards. Bar work, cleaning, barista. That kind of stuff.

At this moment, Cam emerges from his bedroom and pads down the hall barefoot into the kitchen.

Cam, this is Ash. They came to look at the room, Lucy tells him.

Cam takes his glasses off and introduces himself, subdued, nodding stiffly at Ash, and returns to his bedroom.

What's up with *him*!

He got dumped.

Ahhhhh.

So, are you interested in the room? It's available immediately.

Just give me, like, a few minutes? I need to make a phone call.

Lucy lets Ash take the kitchen and half-listens at the door, pretending to examine a spot on the carpet. Ash is asking their grandad (it sounds like) for a grand to cover the first and last month's rent.

It's a bargain, Grandad, they say. And a great location.

Lucy wonders if she's made a terrible mistake. She gets the impression that Ash kind of doesn't have a plan. This is not something Lucy feels comfortable about. But then Ash opens the kitchen door and says, Okay, done, and transfers the money directly to Lucy there and then.

The following week, Ash moves in, and Lucy is able to properly appraise them as they unload boxes and bin bags together from an Uber. They are skinny, maybe just over five feet, with bangles jangling up their arms like windchimes, wrapped up in an oversized muddy-green poncho. Eyes big and dark yet bright. Overlong fringe brushing against their eyelashes so that they have to tilt their head slightly upwards, chin jutting out defiant-like, when they speak. They look young – younger than Cam or Lucy – maybe even fresh out of uni.

It's so good to see you again, they tell Lucy enthusiastically once everything has been dumped into the box room. And Lucy notes the dab of Cornish in their accent. They hug awkwardly and she notices that their knuckles are a little bruised on one hand, each one a lilac carnation blossoming across the skin. Then she notices the three guitars neatly stood up in individual stands leaning against the wall. Compared to the rest of their stuff, charity-shop-looking clothes screwed up and stuffed into bin bags, the guitars are pristine – glistening – as though freshly polished. One is an acoustic and the other two look electric, cherry red and a deep olive green respectively, but Lucy doesn't know enough to ascertain anything more than that. Ash is bare-foot, and on the side of their left ankle is a huge, angry blister. They are setting up a ring light – the kind you see vloggers use – in the corner of the cramped room.

Do you want to watch a film or something tonight? she asks them.

That's okay. I've got a gig, so I'm probably going to go to bed for a few hours. I need to get there at, like, midnight. Just so you know, my sleeping pattern's a little bit fucked up. I sleep at really weird times. I'm a night owl.

They smile kindly at Lucy, and she nods, pretending that she is not feeling some small note of panic fizzing through her. She wonders whether she and Ash can be compatible flatmates.

She chooses *Legally Blonde* for herself and curls up with a gin and tonic. She wonders about inviting Meredith or another of her marketing-type friends, Nara, over. But then she would have to get changed and put make-up on. She could invite Anais, but Cam is here still, tapping away furiously on his laptop on the other sofa.

Do you mind if I put this on? Lucy asks him, startling him.

Yeah, no problem, he says. Five minutes into the film, he gets up, shoves his feet into his slippers and returns to his bedroom, closing the door with a soft click.

Lucy hears Ash collect their McDonald's delivery from the front door before taking it into their bedroom and closing their own door, turning on Nina Simone.

Lucy watches the film without really watching it, scrolling Instagram absent-mindedly and tapping through Stories to see what everyone else is up to on a Saturday night. She sees that Anais has gone out for dinner with Jenna and Kerry from the office and feels an acute pang of jealousy before reminding herself that it's her who has been ignoring Anais. She contemplates calling her mother, again, but stops herself, again, before she can follow through with it. She wonders, abstractly, what her *real*, biological parents might be doing right now, on a Saturday night. Where in the country – on the planet – they might be. How they might be living their lives, conducting themselves, existing in the spaces that they occupy. She imagines an invisible thread tied to her and spanning a great distance, the other end of it tied to her parents, together or apart. She pauses the film momentarily to close her eyes and breathe in and out until the burning sensation in her throat subsides.

She crawls into bed at 10 p.m. and stares up at the ceiling, Ash's Nina Simone greatest hits album now on its third play. She closes her eyes and tries to sleep, but her body won't let her. She scrolls idly through the dating app that Meredith has set up for her on her phone. At two or three in the morning, when she has exhausted her mind and her eyes with Twitter and Instagram and YouTube videos about conspiracy theories, she falls asleep.

Chapter Four

When Lucy was nine years old, her parents hired a bouncy castle for her birthday. The dying leaves set fire to the fuzz of grass over soft mud, the ground a little too damp to play on, but Lucy *really* wanted a bouncy castle. She knew if she sulked enough she would get it. And she did. Her entire class came to her birthday party. Lucy was well-liked and popular among her classmates, in the uncomplicated way that eight-year-olds often are. It was only when she got a bit older, at secondary school, that Lucy shed friends as though she were shedding skin, until by the time she left college there was no one at all. In the empty garden after the party, as Uncle Marv deflated the bouncy castle, the detritus of the children was everywhere: half-empty plastic cups of Fanta spilled on the patio, discarded wrapping paper trodden into the grass. The carcass of a cake that her mum had tried to bake that morning – burnt around the edges and drowning in watery pink icing sugar – was set upon the garden table. Everyone was gone, besides Lucy and Danny and Mum and Dad and Uncle Marv.

They were going to have beans on toast for dinner, which is what Mum cooked when it came to the end of the month and Dad hadn't been paid.

Why can't we have a *McDonald's?* Lucy moaned. It was her birthday and therefore she was allowed to be a little bit more bratty than usual. She was vaguely aware that her parents had spent a lot of money on her birthday party. The bouncy castle. A big Tesco shop of cocktail sausages and Dairylea dunkers and fizzy pop, and bunting and balloons scattered all over the garden now escaping the drawing pins tethering them to the fence.

Lucy was also old enough to ascertain that her family was not well off. She didn't care in this moment.

Her brother Danny picked up a generous handful of mucky brown leaves and shoved them down the back of Lucy's T-shirt, under her collar, and cackled as she screamed, wriggling away from him.

I want McDonald's, Lucy insisted. It's my *birthday*.

We didn't get McDonald's on *my* birthday, Danny said.

Danny's voice, Lucy noticed, was starting to break: sometimes low and raspy and sometimes pipsqueak, like a character on CITV. She knew that Danny hated this because he tried to hide how deep it got by adopting a fake soprano lilt; he flushed red every time his voice cracked. Another way in which Danny was becoming less like her as he grew older. They were never much alike anyway: Danny had warm-toned skin, icy blue eyes and dirty-blonde hair that had recently started to darken. By the time he was twenty, it would be almost-black. But Lucy had always been pale: a poker-straight ginger with sharp right-angled shoulders and skin almost translucent that sometimes she could see the capillaries on the backs of her hands, meandering and wormlike. Very soon, Lucy would start to question these differences between her and Danny. Not just the physical ones, but the intangible ones, too. How Danny could command the attention of any room, even at his young age, the same way their father could, with some anecdote or bit. The way he could make anyone laugh: even the grumpiest sod at the bookies, where Dad took them sometimes on the way back from a job.

Lucy watched her parents, standing on the patio smoking and drinking tins of John Smith's, as a look passed between them. Her mother came to her in the centre of the garden and smoothed her hair down and kissed her on both cheeks.

My perfect, special girl, she said, quietly and sincerely.

We didn't have a bouncy castle on my birthday, either, Danny said loudly.

That's because you don't have any friends, Uncle Marv shouted from over by the bouncy castle, laughing. Uncle Marv enjoyed saying things like this to the children: the kinds of things that were objectively cruel but treated by adults as gentle teasing or an important piece of wisdom that the child must capture and comprehend.

Erica turned to her son and pulled his head into her chest, too. We can get a bouncy castle for your birthday next year. How about that?

I can't have a bouncy castle when I turn fifteen, Danny replied, it's for kids.

But Mum was already walking away and hadn't heard him. Lucy watched Danny watch their mother disappear into the dark of the house.

The McDonald's didn't materialise at dinner, and Lucy cried dramatically while they ate their beans on toast – the three of them – and refused to finish it. It was now that her father became short with her.

He gripped her by both shoulders and looked at her squarely in the face. We don't cry in this house, he told her. I won't have it. Banburys don't cry, Lucy. They get on with it. And you should, too.

This was not the first time she had heard this mantra from her father.

Danny pinched her on the back of the neck while they shared the job of washing the dishes.

Danny pinched me, Lucy wailed when Dad came into the kitchen to get another beer out of the fridge.

No I didn't, Danny replied, his voice earnest.

Her father ruffled her hair. Don't tell porky-pies, Loose.

This made Lucy cry even more. Her father ignored her.

Danny had taken to pinching her or pulling at her hair when they passed one another in the house. Sometimes he muttered hurtful things to her under his breath when no one else was listening. No one likes you, they're just pretending to. Everyone thinks you're weird. Mum and Dad are going to send you away. When she accused him to their parents, she was told off for lying, or for making a fuss about nothing.

Lucy couldn't make people laugh the way Danny could. She couldn't hold a conversation with a stranger without bursting into tears. No one expected her to, really. She was young, after all. But she saw how Danny did it and she wondered what was wrong with her. She wasn't like her parents or her brother, who seemed not to let the world affect them so deeply.

Danny had recently taken to going fishing with their Uncle Marv. He sometimes hid a fish – a small perch or roach – in his sleeve and brought it back home, even though he was meant to throw all the catches back into the river. Tucked it into Lucy's pillowcase or her sock drawer when she wasn't looking. Sometimes it was a whole day before she noticed, and by then the smell had got everywhere, stronger than the stale smoke from Dad's cigars that seeped into all the furniture in the house. She tried not to scream or cry when she found the dead fish because she knew that's what he wanted. Banburys don't cry.

An hour later, while they watched *The Little Mermaid* (Lucy's favourite film) in the living room, Mum had a hushed conversation with Dad in the hallway. Twenty minutes later, he returned to the house, flourishing a Happy Meal, just for Lucy.

She ate it quickly, stuffing chips and cheeseburger into her mouth all at once, half-guilty, half-smug, a little afraid that Danny would snatch it out of her hands. When he looked at her, she could tell that he hated her. But she didn't care.

On the sixth day after Ash moves in, Lucy decides that she must prepare a welcome dinner, which is not something she has ever done before. But she is trying to be a better version of herself, like the self-help podcast she listens to, featuring her favourite wellness influencer, tells her.

There is a disconnect in the flat, between Lucy and Ash and Cam. Ash sleeps all day and works all night, coming home in the small hours of the morning when Lucy is brewing her first coffee before she goes for a swim ahead of work. They cross paths in these strange twilight moments: Lucy not awake enough to make proper, interesting, entertaining conversation or to deliver the carefully tailored anecdotes that she practises in her head. Ash too strung out to stop for a heart-to-heart. Cam is either working at the secondary school, marking homework, preparing lessons or hibernating in his bedroom, coming out only for food.

Lucy wants to change this dynamic but doesn't quite know how to. It's very important to her that Ash and Cam care about the health of the flat dynamic; the necessity for community and company in the home. Lucy knows that before, when Anais was here, she was a supporting cast member. Anais was such a big personality that you couldn't help but make yourself smaller to give her more space. But Lucy wants to be the main character, now. Or at least have equal billing in an ensemble cast. Lucy knows that a household is a delicate ecosystem which must be nurtured in order to thrive. Without proper care and attention, things start to rot.

This is why she has decided to cook the dinner. It occurs to her that she is doing what her mother has been trying to do multiple times over the past few weeks; bring a group of dissonant people together using food and forced company. The way Lucy is doing it feels hopeful rather than underhanded, though. Mainly because she hasn't been keeping the secrets of her flatmates' identities from them for their whole lives, like her parents have with her. Whenever Lucy thinks about the fact of her adoption, her brain goes foggy and she can't put her thoughts into a coherent order. So she boxes it up and shoves it to some dark corner of her brain.

Lucy has made a particular point to be a much better cook than her mother ever was. It has been eight years – not since she left home aged eighteen – that Lucy has put a potato smiley face, a potato waffle, or any other type of engineered potato, or a baked bean, or a chicken nugget, into her mouth.

In order to communicate dinner plans, Lucy has to create a new WhatsApp group. Anais is still active in the old one for Flat 5, and Lucy knows, even with her own awkward social manner, that it would be cruel to kick her out. Lucy texts the new group with the date and time for the dinner.

On Wednesday at work, the day of the meal, instead of briefing flyer designs to Brandon the freelancer, she is researching kung pao pork recipes on BBC Good Food. She decides against doing a starter. She Amazon Primes a new wok specifically for the occasion. She has already prepared the lemon cheesecake for afters, which is setting on the bottom shelf in the fridge at home. She can almost feel her body vibrating with the nervous anticipation of the night ahead. Both Cam and Ash have seen her text but not responded to it.

Across the desk from her, face partially obscured by her monitor, Anais is making a point of not speaking to Lucy. It is difficult to establish the correct dynamic with Anais now that they don't live together. The difference is, they are still forced to see one another at work. In another lifetime, Lucy and Anais would meet in the toilets on a night out and hate each other upon instinct. Or perhaps they would drunkenly fall in love with one another, exchange Instagram handles and spend the next five years aggressively liking one another's selfies and re-sponding with the '100' emoji to each other's Stories. Anais is kind of loud, and she freely lets people know her opinion. She likes to tell stories and be listened to, but doesn't listen when other people speak. Despite this, she is also naturally very funny and draws people into her orbit. If Anais is making plans to be somewhere, everyone else wants to be there too. People just seem to *care* more about people like Anais. She is the kind of person whose birthday you remember without effort. She is also very beautiful, which helps. People like to be around beautiful people; it's a scientific fact.

In the bathroom, Lucy reapplies concealer and contemplates what Anais must think of *her*. Maybe a bit too prissy. Snobby and judgemental. Anais probably doesn't know Lucy's birthday. Even looking at herself in the uplighting of the bathroom mirror now – a terrible design choice which would make anyone look hideous – Lucy sees that she has this sneering superiority look about her, beneath all that dyed-red hair, like she's better than everyone else. Cheaper than the real thing and nothing on the inside. No wonder Anais doesn't want anything to do with her now. In a moment of absolute clarity, Lucy is certain that this is the case: that this is the truth of it.

Lucy locks herself in a cubicle and sits on the lid of the toilet, takes deep counting breaths, in through the nose and out through the mouth, like she used to do as a teenager. After what seems like an age, she feels the tide of panic pulling away, the threat of hyperventilation dissipating into calm waters. She feels small invisible tremors passing through her.

She smooths down her blouse – sheer and cream with a pussy bow necktie – and returns to her desk. She worries that her face will have something written across it that exposes how close to crying she is. But Anais, opposite her, doesn't look up as she sits down.

Back at the flat that evening, Lucy prepares the meal anyway, ignoring the fact that still no one has replied to her dinner invitation. She has put a lot of thought into this over the past few days. She lays out special woven place mats, lights a candle, pours out fresh glasses of red wine from the bottle she picked up from the offie by the station on the way home.

Lucy likes the prescriptiveness of recipes. She is good at following instructions. But tonight she is feeling unlike herself. Perhaps it's the wobble she had earlier that has done it. Lucy hasn't had a panic attack since she moved to London – not even when she spilled her rum and Coke on a girl in Metric when she was at uni and the girl spat in her face.

Lucy has sprayed Febreze into the microwave so the smell is sufficiently masked while they eat. She cooks the pork in sesame oil and realises very quickly that the steaming pan is not good for her skin or hair or body odour. The extractor fan does little to diminish the overwhelming smell of hot oil and rendering pork fat that fills the kitchen – spits of it all over the countertop, the hob, the splashback and Lucy's dress, which is black velvet and specially selected.

At six thirty, she hears the door slam and Cam pokes his head into the kitchen.

Oh, this is tonight? he asks, eyeing the kitchen table – set beautifully with the best of the crockery – suspiciously.

Yes, it's tonight, Lucy replies, struggling to keep a note of hysteria out of her voice as she flings a strand of hair back. She is sweating. Can feel the beads of it rolling down her spine and pooling in the small of her back.

Cool, I'll get changed, Cam says easily.

Lucy returns to the food. She is behind schedule. Something is burning and she's not sure what. The recipe she is using has no instruction on when to add the chicken stock despite demanding that she prepare it. She takes a punt and slops it messily onto the pork and carrots sizzling away on the hob. Most of it evaporates in a steaming cloud across Lucy's face, flushing her skin with heat. She knocks a plate onto the floor and it cracks cleanly down the middle. She hears Cam in the hallway: he is tapping on Ash's door and not getting a response.

How're you doing? Do you need a hand with anything? he asks Lucy from the hall.

Everything's great, thanks, Lucy shouts. She opens the back door to let some of the steam and smoke and fumes dissipate.

Eventually, later than planned, she lays everything out on the table. She looks at the arrangement: the pork a little burnt because she had the temperature too high; the rice cold because she put it on too early; the spring onions in the sauce too wilted.

Lucy smiles as Cam comes back into the kitchen, but she can feel her face going a bit wobbly, like it wants to jump off her skull and run out through the back door. Cam has changed into a different shirt, which is nice of him, because the one he was wearing earlier had a huge blue blot of ink on it from where a biro had exploded in his breast pocket. The new shirt, however, is not very nice. It's a faded pink and unironed and short-sleeved.

Lucy tries not to stare. Cam notices the broken plate on the floor and swiftly picks it up.

It looks amazing, he says, indicating the food. He sounds sincere.

I messed a few things up, Lucy replies.

They sit and wait for Ash, who hasn't yet emerged from their bedroom.

I think they might be asleep, Cam says.

It's okay. We can wait. The meat needed to cool down a little, anyway.

They wait some more. Lucy has the distinct feeling that her lungs are shrinking. She is aware that her breathing is very loud. She tries to quieten it, reduce the number of breaths she takes, but that makes it even harder to inhale. She can feel her pulse quickening.

Are you okay? Cam asks her.

Yeah, yeah. Fine, Lucy replies.

Wordlessly, Cam goes to the sink and pours Lucy a pint of water. He sets it down in front of her. She thanks him and drinks it in ugly audible gulps.

After five minutes, Cam goes to knock on Ash's door again. This time the door opens a crack and there is a hushed conversation that Lucy can't catch. She suddenly is feeling rather embarrassed.

Another five minutes go by and Ash emerges from their room in an overlarge black T-shirt with the words 'Too cute for the binary' scrawled across it in big letters and fluffy slippers. They pull up the third chair, a broad smile stretched across their face.

I'm sorry I'm late. I overslept, they say.

No, no, don't worry. It's nothing, Lucy is saying before Ash has finished apologising.

It was a late night, Ash explains and Lucy smiles placatingly at them. What have we got, then? Ash asks, and Lucy smooths her dress across her knees, conscious that she's now overdressed for her own dinner party.

Neither of them have washed their hands yet. She gets up and makes a point to wash her own – again – hoping that they will follow her example. Neither of them do.

It's kung pao pork, Lucy replies, marginally lifted now that they are both here, both prepared to show an interest in the food.

Oh god, Ash says, the smile slipping from their face, replaced with a look of sheepishness.

What is it? Lucy asks.

I should have told you. I'm a vegetarian.

There is a beat of silence as Lucy stares back at Ash, not quite sure what to say.

Cam says, Oh no, uselessly.

I'm so sorry, Loose, Ash says, and Lucy flinches. I've always lived in a vegetarian household, see. Both my grandparents are veggie. It didn't even occur to me that I should mention it.

Not even when I asked for dietary requirements on the group chat? Lucy asks quietly, gripping the edges of the table.

Honestly, I'm *so* sorry. I'm such an idiot. It looks so amazing, Lucy. And you've gone to all this effort.

Yes, I'm starving, Cam says. I could easily eat all of Ash's. Maybe we can pick the meat out and Ash can have the sauce?

There's chicken stock in the sauce, Lucy replies, setting her cutlery down very deliberately on the table.

Oh.

They sort of sit and stare at one another, none quite sure what to say now. Ash's face is painted with a look of abject horror.

Cam breaks the silence by serving up the rice.

Have you got something you can put with the rice, Ash? he asks them.

Ash gets some sweet chilli sauce from the cupboard – Lucy's sweet chilli sauce – and drenches their rice in it.

This will be fine, they say too brightly.

They eat in silence. Lucy feels as though she wants the kitchen lino to suck her down down down into the concrete underneath.

Cam tries to make light conversation. He asks Ash about their music, their reasons for coming to London, their life back home in Poole. Ash talks animatedly: about how they worked as a kayaking instructor after they dropped out of uni to pursue music and did some guitar tutoring on the side. But after exhausting all the local pubs and clubs on the south coast between Bournemouth and Truro, they realised they needed to come to London to be taken seriously.

I'm hoping I get scouted, they say, at one of these gigs I'm doing. I heard that label executives go out to these open mics and acoustic nights to discover fresh talent.

That sounds rad, Cam says, enthusiastically. He glances at Lucy, and she knows he is trying to include her in the conversation. Inviting her to participate. But she can't think of a single thing to say.

Ash gobbles up the chilli rice. Lucy thinks it looks vile, but Ash makes a big show of enjoying it. She kind of hates how unbearably nice they are both being about this shitshow that she has orchestrated and forced them to participate in. She hopes that the cheesecake can save the night.

She takes it out of the fridge ceremoniously.

This is vegetarian, Ash, she tells them hopefully.

Amazing. Looks delicious, Ash replies as Lucy cuts out generous slices.

They all dig at their portions with teaspoons. With the first mouthful, Lucy knows that she has made a terrible mistake somewhere in the creation of this cheesecake: there is something deeply disturbing about its texture, like she has used the wrong type of sugar and it hasn't dissolved properly. It gets stuck, grit-like, in between her teeth. The biscuit base is oily and over-saturated, leaving slicks of grease on their lips as they eat.

Oh god, I'm so sorry, Lucy says. It's disgusting.

Not at all. What are you talking about? Cam says. I love it. It's delicious.

He makes a point of wolfing his portion down and cutting himself a second slice. Ash is less enthusiastic, their brow furrowing a little as they contemplate each mouthful. But they manage to finish their plate too.

So what happened to your girlfriend, Cam? Ash asks after they've finished and Cam is halfway through his second helping.

Lucy's plate sits untouched in front of her. She is now barely listening to the conversation, has folded into the centre of her brain, where she replays every single mistake she has made to get to this very moment. She didn't double-check the dietary requirements. She didn't use the right sugar in the cheesecake. She used margarine, not a block of unsalted butter, in the base. She cooked the pork on the wrong heat. She added the veg too early. She put the rice on too early. She smashed that plate. She got dressed before she started cooking, rather than after. She didn't keep the door open the whole time to keep the kitchen clear of fumes. She didn't send reminder texts. She didn't get enough wine. She couldn't get that smell out of the microwave, and now it's back.

Lucy is pulled from her reverie by a look on Cam's face – one of extreme discomfort – and she realises that Ash has asked a probing question about Anais. This is not something that Lucy has tried to discuss with Cam yet. It's just that she wouldn't know what to say to him. She has kind of just left him to it – to do his seven steps of grief in peace. The way Cam speaks about Anais – their relationship – is truly like someone has died.

It was a shock, Cam tells Ash, A really big shock. Completely out of the blue. Too early, as well. Too soon.

Do you feel like you've done the right thing, leaving her? Ash asks him. Lucy realises now that Ash is an oversharer and demands the same of the people around them. They have already mentioned three exes from back home in this short, stilted conversation at dinner.

Bafflingly, though, Cam contemplates their question seriously, as though he wants to give a truthful answer. Eventually, he looks back at Ash and shrugs. I don't know, he says, anticlimactically. I don't know.

What about you, Lucy? Ash asks, their face hopeful. Have you got a squeeze?

There it is. A personal question.

Lucy shrugs non-committally. Not really, she replies.

Not really? Ash asks.

Yeah . . . well . . . you know.

She keeps her cards close to her chest, that one, Cam tells Ash. And – bizarrely – he grins at Lucy as though they are sharing a secret between themselves. Lucy doesn't understand what could possibly have given Cam the impression that she is not the type of person to *open up*. She has barely spoken to Cam in the year they've lived together. He has no right to make such assumptions.

They both stick around after dinner and insist on doing the washing up for Lucy. She watches them, tracking the slicks of food and grease that they have left on each plate placed on the drying rack with their inattentive scrubbing. Ash dries using the *food* tea towel rather than the *cleaning* tea towel, smearing more bacteria across the crockery. Lucy is already calculating when she can get into the kitchen to re-wash everything without being spotted and causing offence.

Rather than watch any more, she forces herself into the living room and mindlessly scrolls Netflix. She overhears the following in hushed whispers coming from the kitchen as she sips her wine.

Ash: . . . didn't even ask to be cooked for.

Cam: I know, but it was a thoughtful gesture.

Ash: It's like she's desperate for us to like her or something.

Lucy turns on *The Office (U.S.)* extra loud. She's never watched it before but has caught snippets when glancing at Cam's laptop.

Cam sticks his head into the living room and says, Thanks so much for dinner, Lucy.

Lucy says, Yeah, no, it was fun.

Ash has followed him and climbs onto the sofa next to Lucy, enveloping her in a cavernous hug. For someone so small, Ash's hugs are big.

I've got some work to do, Cam says awkwardly and wanders into his bedroom.

Can I plait your hair? Ash asks Lucy. The colour is so beautiful.

No, thanks, Lucy says, quickly, and Ash looks taken aback.

Oh – okay.

They stare at one another awkwardly, Ash's face stricken. After a moment, they turn away from Lucy and stare at the television.

It's just that . . . sorry, I should have said, Lucy starts.

You don't have to explain! Ash sing-songs.

No – it's just that I don't like people touching my hair. That's all.

Oh – right. That's fine.

Lucy stares at the television screen. This is one of my favourite shows, she says.

Really? Ash says enthusiastically, leaping on the conversation. I prefer the later seasons to be honest. The early ones make me cringe.

Lucy nods.

What do you like? Ash asks.

What, which season?

Yeah.

Oh, I'm not sure . . .

What did you think of Will Ferrell?

Who?

You know. Will Ferrell when he turns up as the new boss, with the basketball game.

Actually, I've never seen it before. I don't know why I said that I had.

Ash looks at her, eyes widened, troubled.

Sorry.

Ash repositions their legs on the sofa and grimaces. There is a silence that seems to stretch out across the whole summer.

I think I'm going to go back to bed, Ash says eventually. Night, Lucy.

They slither off the sofa and, moments later, the door to their room closes with a soft click.

Lucy stares at the screen, picking at her fingernails. Steve Carell's character is making a sexist remark to the receptionist. It's clear from the set-up of the scene that the audience is meant to be rooting for the receptionist rather than Michael Scott: that he is hideously out of touch and a caricature of a real-life manager, and a joke. The receptionist glances knowingly at the camera.

Chapter Five

On Friday night, Lucy has plans to go to a house party in Dulwich with Meredith and their mutual friend Nara. She *considers* inviting Cam and Ash, but decides against it. She can't think of anything at all that she and Cam have in common, and she imagines the stilted chit-chat she and Ash might have on the bus on the way to the party, wearing their best going-out clothes (Lucy in her LBD and Ash in some sort of sequinned tent, no doubt) swaying with each turn of the 176, stumbling in the aisle every time it comes to a stop. Lucy has had one conversation with Ash since the night of the dinner party, and she went on an overlong spiel about her job. Lucy does this a lot and she can always see the moment when people start to switch off, eyes glazed. Lucy knows, objectively, that supplier relations is very boring. But there's something in her that gets stuck, and she can't stop herself, even when she knows she's being boring. Lucy really does love her job.

She wants very much for Ash to like her, and to be interested in her. But she knows that there is something intrinsically unlikeable about her that cannot be switched off or disguised, by kung pao pork or cheesecake or *The Office (U.S.)*. She's too keen, maybe. *It's like she's desperate for us to like her or something.* This morning when Lucy was leaving for her swim before heading into the office, the spare room was dark and noiseless; and when she got home, she could hear Ash practising their guitar and singing softly, a glow of orange light spilling out through the crack under the door.

Having Ash around doesn't really affect Lucy in any way whatsoever. But she was secretly hoping that Ash would be her friend in the same way Anais was when they lived together. Despite being a few years older than Ash, Lucy finds them to be nervous-making. Ash, Lucy thinks, is one of these people who is *effortlessly cool*. Lucy knows that she's cool too, but in a way that is very *high maintenance*. A different kind of cool. It's very difficult to talk to people when they are cooler than you. You both know that one of you has something to prove. Lucy sees that Ash is one of these types of people. What's frustrating is that they probably don't even realise that they're one of these types of people.

They have draped the boxy single bedroom in the flat with glittering gold-threaded Turkish fabrics and a Progress Pride flag from the curtain rail, and the sorts of plants that crawl up the walls and around the window frame. They burn incense incessantly. Lucy has the impression of walking into what she imagines a nineteenth-century opium den might look and feel and smell like. Ash themself dresses in what appear to be second-hand clothes, always oversized and in muted mossy colours, with all those bracelets and big hoop earrings. If Lucy tried to dress like that she would look *try-hard*, not *bohemian-chic* like Ash does.

Lucy tells herself that she doesn't need Ash; that she is lucky that she has such a happy and thriving social life – with many friends, like Meredith who is waving frantically at her from across the road now as she steps off the 176, gesturing at the house behind her (a slim Edwardian terraced conversion).

Meredith is wearing red glittery heart-shaped nipple pasties under a loose translucent mesh vest, sandy-blonde dominatrix ponytail swinging behind her.

Lucy sprints through a gap in the traffic, clutching onto her little snakeskin wristlet bag with her phone, keys and debit card zipped safely inside, and draws level with Meredith. Her own silk-look slip dress and matching black heels seem incredibly boring in comparison, though this is the most risqué outfit she owns, mainly because you can't wear any underwear with it. Lucy even put some diamanté stick-on jewels around her eyes, following a tutorial on YouTube.

These friends of Meredith's at the house party are theatre types who are prone to doing their Tesco shop dressed as though they're at Glastonbury. Lucy can see that Meredith has already started the party, so to speak; her jaw is working overtime, her teeth loudly grinding. Pills make Lucy nervous in the same way that people do. She concluded a long time ago that she simply doesn't have the personality type to indulge in a recreational habit. She's too anxious, too high-strung. Too self-aware. Even on the couple of occasions she tried a spliff at college in some-one's back garden when the parents weren't home, she felt as though she were a tree, bearing luscious ripe fruit to be plucked away and peeled and sliced and eaten. She couldn't command the trunk of her body or the branches of her limbs. She sat in silence and steadily became aware of every single part of her body, every single involuntary movement it made, and the ways in which people stared at her as though she were a stranger who had invited herself.

Girl, you look fire, Meredith says as she lights a cigarette.

Thanks – and then, as an afterthought – You too. She has to force herself to avert her eyes from Meredith's nipples.

Where's your flatmates?

Lucy shrugs, feigning nonchalance. Busy.

You should've invited Cam. He probably needs a good night out after getting dumped.

Me and Cam aren't really on that level. How do you know these people again?

Helen works with Jordan, who's friends with Angus, who I went on a date with last year. Remember? Nara will be here soon, too. I'm going to see if Helen has tequila.

Meredith takes Lucy by the hand and leads her into the house.

Oh, is it meant to be fancy dress? Lucy asks, peering into the hall, feeling self-conscious.

Meredith laughs at *fancy dress*, though it's not clear to Lucy why she does.

As soon as they're through the door, Meredith screeches, HELEN MY DARLING! drops Lucy's hand and melts into the crowd of mid-to-late twenty-somethings in the most outrageous outfits Lucy has ever seen. There is a girl in a stars-and-stripes bikini and a silicon head mask of Trump and nothing else. Another is in full Notting Hill Carnival get-up, with neon green feathers exploding from her back and circling around her like a halo. She can't get through any of the doors unless she shuffles sideways like a crab.

Bodies, hot and clammy, smelling of sweat and cigarettes and sour alcohol and Paco Rabanne, glazed with glitter and hairspray and body paint, converge in the living room, the noise of their chatter battling to be heard over the distorted bassline of some house remix. Everyone seems to be slightly damp. Lucy realises that perhaps it was a mistake not to invite Ash. If Ash had come, and seen these people, and assumed that these were the kinds of people Lucy associated with, they might have thought Lucy interesting and creative and teeming with *joie de vivre*. Nevertheless, these people seem far too old, to Lucy, to be behaving like this. She suspects they all went to Goldsmiths, are pining after their freshers' week peak and have parents who work in investment banking.

Somehow, Lucy who is the only age-appropriate dresser in the room, has come overdressed, and now she is certain that everyone at the party, engaged in their own conversations and private jokes and screaming matches and singalongs, are in fact talking about *her*, and her cringey outfit. How stupid she was to dress like this, like she was going to a cocktail party at Mahiki Mayfair. She feels as though she is shrinking. She can't bear anyone to glance her way. Meredith is long gone.

Lucy wonders whether she could shoulder her way through the crowd into the kitchen, without getting clotheslined by a feather boa, and find a drink or a punch bowl or something. The floorboards, underneath many many pairs of shoes, are oak. There's also an ornate restored fireplace in the living room, with the original stone-carved mantel in a gorgeous white marble, but Lucy can't get a proper look on account of the inflatable sex doll that has been stuffed into the chimneypiece. Someone has pulled the light fixture out of the ceiling and bits of plaster dust the floor and people's heads in the centre of the room, like talcum powder.

Lucy shoves through the bodies, her eyes closed and 'sorry' at her lips. She can feel her heartbeat beginning to pick up as her skin brushes against the moist, hot skin of all these strangers. The kitchen leads through French doors into a glass conservatory, with wicker garden furniture, that someone has hotboxed. At the kitchen sink, pouring herself a shot of sambuca, is Nara, the third girl in Lucy and Meredith's party of three. Nara works as the sole marketing person at her uncle's family-run chain of three boutique bakeries in the West End. They sell custard tarts to tourists from stalls set up outside the theatres and sea-salted caramel shortbread to upmarket farm shops in the Home Counties. Lucy met Nara through work, four years ago at Doughnuts, after Nara's uncle engaged Lucy's company to put together a guerrilla marketing campaign that involved installing a giant cake baked in the likeness of a tube carriage on the bandstand in Regent's Park. Both Lucy and Nara were roped into walking around the boating lake in chef whites, handing out free flapjack samples to tourists.

Thank god, she says as Lucy approaches her, and sets about pouring a second shot. Did you know this was going to be the vibe? Did Meredith tell you? I didn't know this was going to be the vibe.

Meredith didn't mention anything about the vibe to me, Lucy says, noticing too late that she has repeated Nara by using *the vibe*.

It's really, truly not my scene, Nara says. I wish someone had bothered to mention it was fancy dress.

Nara, Lucy is relieved to see, is wearing a simple jumpsuit the exact same shade of scarlet red as her lipstick, with a chunky gold necklace and big dangly earrings. Like Lucy, Nara looks incredibly basic next to the blue-wigged drag queen and person-of-indeterminate-gender in a gimp suit who also occupy the kitchen. Her hair falls in thick dark waves down her back, cascading like a fountain. Nara is really very beautiful.

She seems to remember something and pulls Lucy into a tight hug, the sambuca bottle thumping her in the back. She smells of Chanel Coco Mademoiselle.

Missed you, she says, sincerely, flashing a row of perfect white veneers at Lucy. Where's Meredith, anyway?

She found Helen, I think, Lucy replies, suddenly feeling very scruffy, and Nara dramatically rolls her eyes.

Always on the hunt for new people to collect, she says, and she pours two more shots. Can you imagine living in a place like this? All on your own?

Lucy shakes her head no.

The mind boggles.

They talk a little bit about work, Nara's family, her uncle's business, which is thriving, a weird encounter she had with a teenager in the little Sainsbo's next to her flat in Shepherd's Bush last weekend. It's easy to talk to Nara. Lucy doesn't have to feign interest or force laughter like she does with the girls at the office. She feels at ease, which is rare for her. She notices that Nara intuitively doesn't ask her too many questions, but pauses plenty to make sure that Lucy has an opportunity to speak or supplement whatever it is that she is saying. While they talk, she feels her iPhone vibrate in the snakeskin wristlet against her hip. She checks the caller ID: her mother. She quickly rejects the call.

You can get that, I don't mind, Nara tells Lucy, noticing her rejecting the call.

It's all right. It's just my mum.

Just your mum? What are you on about? If I rejected a call from my mother, even on a Friday night, I'd be disinvited from Christmas.

Lucy laughs and shrugs, but a bubble of uncertainty is beginning to grow just beneath her belly button. She is already on edge from the number of people and the reckless destruction of property in this beautiful old house. Now they are talking about mothers and, as it seems to be doing a lot recently, the thought of her *real* mother, her biological mother, swims to the surface of her consciousness. What is her mother doing now? Is she thinking of Lucy, just as Lucy is thinking of her? She can't conjure an image of her in her mind, and it is disconcerting.

What would Christmas be like with her real parents? Soon, she knows, the bubble will get so big that it will have to find a way out. And it will travel up her oesophagus and escape from her mouth so as not to suffocate her.

At that moment, Meredith arrives by the fridge with Helen, the party's hostess, in tow. Meredith has acquired a sombrero since she left Lucy at the door.

Oh, hello, you two, Nara says. Thanks for the invite, Helen. I think someone broke your garden furniture.

Babes, Helen says. Helen works the front desk at a swanky gym-swim-spa in Paddington. She has what Lucy's mum would call a *strong chin*, and less kind people would call a *Habsburg jaw*. She is wearing something that resembles Angelina Jolie's costume in Disney's *Maleficent*, including the headdress. The flat, Lucy remembers Meredith telling her, is mortgaged by Helen's parents. She feels second-hand anxiety for the clean-up/repair bill after all Helen's friends have left.

Helen kisses everyone in the kitchen on both cheeks, including the person in the gimp suit, leaving lipstick smudges on their PVC face mask.

I'm going to the bathroom, Helen says to them all, and then to Meredith, Babes? her voice a question.

Yeah, in a minute, Meredith answers as she struggles with the lid on the tequila.

Once Helen is gone, Meredith turns to them both.

Girls. Not sure about the vibe here.

That's what I said, Nara stage-whispers meaningfully. Does Helen call literally everyone babes?

I think Angus has brought his new girlfriend. It's really awkward.

Lucy nods, widens her eyes, gasps softly in the appropriate places as Meredith and Nara discuss these developments. She is grateful in this moment that while she is the mutual connection between Nara and Meredith – having invited both of them to Wireless Festival two years ago when Delilah got gifted hospitality tickets by a client – it is not necessary for her to facilitate the conversation. Nara and Meredith talk enough for all three of them and are the kinds of people who can become best friends with strangers overnight. She strokes the edge of her iPhone, feeling the plastic casing warm beneath her thumb. She wonders what's new on Twitter, whether she can sneak away to sit in the toilet and find out. She wonders what she needs to google to find out who her real mother is. Whether she even wants to do that, anyway.

Are you okay? Nara asks, noticing Lucy's expression. Lucy is still smiling at them both, as though she is following their conversation, but she can feel herself glazing, the corners of her mouth twitching against the deception of it.

I found out I was adopted, Lucy tells them, blurting it out before her brain has time to stop her mouth. It is so unlike her, but she can't seem to help herself: the words come out before she can stop them. She resists the urge to clap a hand across her mouth. Quite recently, she clarifies.

Sorry, *what*? Meredith asks, and the lid of the tequila bottle pops off dramatically, splashing liquid across her see-through mesh shirt. Shit, she says.

Oh. God, Nara says. I'm so sorry. Is that the right sentiment? Well, I'm sorry, in any case.

I don't know why I'm telling you. I haven't told anyone. I wasn't planning on telling anyone.

Well . . . how do you feel about it? Nara asks, setting her drink down on the counter and leaning against it, turning her whole body to face Lucy properly, her smooth elbows propped against the draining board.

I don't know. I haven't interrogated the depth of my feelings yet. I'm trying not to think about it.

How did you find out? Did your parents tell you? What did they say? Why only now?

Lucy feels as though the room is suddenly very bright.

I found out by accident. At a wedding. My brother dropped the ball. I don't know if they were *ever* planning on telling me.

This, Lucy realises, is what hurts the most, when she allows herself to let go of the numbness for a moment and feel the strength – the full weight – of the secret.

And have you spoken to them since you found out? Nara asks her.

No. Not yet.

You should call her. Call your mum.

Lucy laughs, her body tense. For some reason, embarrassingly, she can feel tears pooling at the corners of her eyes. What. Now?

Definitely call her, Loose, Meredith agrees.

Yeah. Why not? Just pop outside and do it quickly. Before you're too drunk.

Lucy's phone buzzes again with a WhatsApp. Mum. *Please let me know when's a good date for dinner, hun.*

From the living room comes the distinct sound of something smashing, followed by a chorus of cheers.

To be honest with you, Lucy tells them, very quietly, I've been feeling a little bit adrift lately.

You what? Meredith shouts.

Don't worry, she says, laughing. It's nothing.

Helen pokes her head around the kitchen door and shouts for Meredith, who shrugs sheepishly, and disappears with her into the downstairs toilet.

Nara pulls Lucy into another unexpectedly sincere hug.

I'm going to get a kebab, she says. And watch *Sex and the City 2* in bed. Are you coming?

No, thanks, Lucy replies, careful that her face doesn't touch the shoulder of Nara's exquisite red jumpsuit and smear foundation all over it. She hates to leave anything early, to reveal to others that she's not having a good time, that she would rather be somewhere else. This is part of the version of herself that Lucy has cultivated over the years that she has lived in London and worked at Kube. She is always having a good time, always light and carefree and enjoying herself.

She can feel the slippage of her mood, the corners and edges and fringes of it almost-touching that knotted, weighty sensation of sadness that is pricking at her. She knows that she can exist numbly here: in this loud place, parallel to these vibrant people, in the company of her friends. If she leaves with Nara, the numbness will give way to loneliness. The thought of going home to the flat, where Cam and Ash will be, makes her feel inexplicably awful. She knows they both hate her.

Call your mother, Nara says.

I will, Lucy replies, unsure whether she's lying or not.

After Nara is gone, Lucy wanders through the conservatory and to the end of the garden, past the deep-and-meaningful taking place on the trampoline between a girl dressed as Tony the Tiger and a boy as a matching bowl of cereal. She passes two women drinking from tinned Southern Comfort and lemonades on the garden path, and with a flash of recognition sees that one of them is Anais. She realises that she invited Anais to this party, a month ago, when Anais and Cam were still together and Anais was still living at Flat 5. It is bizarre to her that Anais has actually turned up, and without telling her. She feels immediately and inexplicably embarrassed. Wonders whether she ought to say something. Stop for a conversation, maybe. But Anais makes the decision for her. Their eyes meet momentarily before Anais slides her gaze away and pretends that she didn't see Lucy at all.

At the back of the garden, where the Axwell remix pumping from the sound system in the house isn't so loud, Lucy leans against the fence, counting her breathing, and scrolls back through the texts from her mother. She considers calling her. She considers taking the thing she is hiding out of the box in the back of her mind and examining it. But she is afraid of how it's going to make her feel.

Instead, she gets distracted by the dating app Meredith installed for her. The first four profiles she swipes left on all have pictures of the profile owners doing indoor bouldering.

The sky is particularly clear tonight and Lucy can see an aeroplane from Heathrow crawling across the vista, leaving a trail of dark steam in its wake. Inside, Lucy can see through the conservatory, a man is naked. It's only half ten.

She traipses back through the garden, Anais now disappeared into the house, her heels sinking into the soft turf with every step, to find Meredith.

Chapter Six

On Sunday night, on the floor of the bathroom in Flat 5, waiting for the tub to fill, Lucy swipes right on Tom, five-eight, non-smoker, because he's got those glasses that she likes on a man – kind of round with thick dark tortoiseshell frames. In his profile picture, he's smiling with straight teeth, a pint of pale ale in hand. In the second picture – the more important one, in Lucy's opinion, because it's not the guy at his *very best* but he still thinks enough of it to have it as an emblem of his entire personality – Tom is standing with a group of *lads* on the South Bank at one of those pop-up outdoor bars, overlooking Tower Bridge, his arms draped across two men who are both taller and more attractive than him. That's not to say Tom isn't attractive: he is, in a sort of geeky, non-aggressive way. This is what Lucy notices about him first. His answers to the questions disappoint her in how generic they are: he likes travelling and dogs, works in finance and is looking for a long-term relationship. In the third picture, he is wearing a tweed jacket and brown leather gloves, and holding a cocked rifle, a broad grin sliced across his face. The caption: *clay pigeon shooting @ our familys farm in ascot.* This is the picture that makes her swipe right on him, despite the grammar.

He messages her 'hi' almost immediately and she taps back

a few innocuous starter-for-ten replies while she's in the bath, using her toes to turn the taps and top up the hot water – something she has perfected with years of practice and unusually dextrous feet.

As the steam rises and slicks the mirror with a cloudy film, she also replies to three other men with whom she's been having casual conversations over the past couple of days. She has been reading up on how to talk to men on dating apps online; she has been listening to a podcast about online dating, which has been highly instructive.

Dating apps make Lucy feel strange in a way that she can't quite articulate. There is the excitement of the promise of a connection; the anticipation of sex; the variety of choices endlessly stretched out before her like some sort of human flesh buffet; the thrill of composing clever and witty responses to substandard men until the novelty wears off and she un-matches them. And, of course, she enjoys the sensation of being *liked*, which gathers warmly at the pit of Lucy's stomach and sends a frisson of delight through her whenever one of these people texts her a compliment. Together with a stranger she is cultivating a shared reality: a dimension that exists only in the intangible cyberspace between them, containing the projections of the people both parties want the world to see them as: versions of themselves that don't truly exist. But then there's the mundanity of repetition; the exhausting routine of having to prove herself; the way she knows that as she is doing it too, every detail of her own photos, every message she sends, is being scrutinised for imperfections. Oh, he's wearing *boat shoes*. How can someone's whole life, their personhood, their ability to love, their hopes dreams and aspirations, be distilled into boat shoes? A collection of ten photos max and answers to a series of banal questions, like is it okay to put pineapple on pizza and what's your ideal Sunday afternoon?

Meredith has already told Lucy to stop overthinking it. Just send like three messages tops, she says, and then suggest a drink. The longer you spend on text, the more chance you have to overthink it. Pick holes in the profile, and un-match. Or otherwise fall in love with someone you've never met and don't know is genuinely the person they say they are. The whole thing – the swiping, the scrutiny, the awkward introductory messages – fills Lucy with a low-frequency undercurrent of shame that she doesn't understand. But, for some reason, she can't stop herself. In her downtime – in the bath, on the toilet, on her lunch break at work, et cetera – she's browsing them. Her thumb bent awkwardly, poised to swipe.

She has never had what her friends would call a *serious* boyfriend. Her longest 'relationship' was a few months with a boy called Georgie on the same economics module as her in her first year at uni, when she was nineteen. Georgie was into Formula 1 racing, had gaps between his teeth and was a member of the Zombie Society. Lucy was unclear what the Zombie Society actually *did*, besides dress up as zombies for house parties and final-year drama students' dissertation performances. Georgie, when not dressed as a zombie, worked in Metric, the students' union bar. Lucy met him one night in the club when she was out with some of the girls from her course. It was the early days of first year, when friends were fast-won before disappearing into the ether of university life and turning up in the news the following year having been arrested for setting up a cannabis farm in their student accommodation. Georgie, who was working a shift at the time, complimented Lucy on her hair and asked for her number. They went to Pizza Express and found that they had very little in common, but Georgie talked a lot and paid her compliments, and Lucy preferred that. She lost her virginity to him on his single bed in halls. The sheets were musty with dead skin cells and stale sweat. Afterwards, Lucy went back to her student flatshare and scrubbed herself all over in a very hot, very high-pressure shower. She felt like she couldn't bear the sight of Georgie after that, so she waited for their economics module to end before gently ghosting him.

Since then, Lucy hasn't met anyone properly. She's had a few casual things, yes. She's dated a lot of mediocre men. She's not had sex in over a year; not since before she moved out of the Hackney house. The last man she brought back there, after meeting him in Tiger Tiger on a night out with Meredith, burst into tears halfway through and confessed to her that he was engaged.

Lucy is quite happy in her own company, really. It's *easier* not to get involved with someone else. To have someone involved in her life, knowing where she is and what she's doing and how she's feeling at any given moment, to be *accountable to someone else*, feels a bit like hookworms embedded in the lower intestine.

She continues to swipe.

Her phone lights up with a call from an unknown number. Startled, she answers it.

Loose?

Huh? Yeah?

Loose? It's me.

It takes Lucy a moment to place the voice amidst the cacophony of background noise. A heavy-metal guitar and several men shouting and screaming over each other. It's Danny. Her brother.

Danny? Where are you?

I'm in Stratford. Look. Lucy. I need you to come and get me.

Lucy pauses, staring up at the mismatched tiles on the bathroom wall. The water has gone lukewarm around her. All of the bubbles disintegrated.

What do you mean, *I need you to come and get me*?

I've had an accident. Don't panic. Not a big one, all right? I've just fallen down some stairs. I need you to call me an Uber home.

Lucy can hear, now, that Danny is slurring his words. She's so used to that stumbling cadence, croaky and hollow, the vowels mixing all into one like he's swilling custard, like his mouth is moving too fast for his brain to catch up, or the other way round, that she's forgotten what normal, sober Danny's voice sounds like.

What's the problem, she asks, with calling your own Uber?

I've got no money, Loose. I've lost my bank card. This isn't even my phone.

Call Mum and Dad, Lucy replies, ready to hang up.

They'll kill me, they will. They think I'm thirty-two days.

She pauses again, her eyes closed now. How many days were you?

Thirty-one.

Lucy listens to his breathing, shallow and erratic above the static of the line. Panting. Laboured. She feels the corners of her mouth pulling her face downwards, her eyes stinging, a hot, dry throat, a stabbing sickness in her stomach.

Give me the address. Quickly.

Danny, five years older than Lucy, started drinking in parks and on street corners at thirteen, because his friends' older brothers were doing it and there were no youth groups, or sports centres, or clubs – not that the Banburys could afford those things, anyway. Danny was already checked out of school by the time he was diagnosed with dyslexia (too late) in Year 8. He had committed himself to the class-clown role instead, throwing chairs out of third-floor maths class windows. Lucy, too young to understand what was happening until much later, only wanted her big brother to like her. On weekends, he hung around outside off-licences waiting for a likely-looking person to come by, and he would empty a handful of silvers and coppers into their hands – scrounged from the back of sofas, behind the fruit machines in the bookies where Dad took them both after school, the kerbside – to pick up a four-pack of scrumpy for him and his friends. Sometimes Uncle Marv bought booze for Danny until Dad told him to stop.

By the time he was fifteen, Danny was stealing money out of drawers in the house to pay for bottles of White Lightning from the only offie in Ilford that would serve him. Mum and Dad made a point to stop leaving cash around and put locks on the bedroom doors to stop him going through their things. But then, instead, he chored bottles of booze from the big Tesco, and ended up getting nicked for that more than once. Dad tried to get him jobs and when they wouldn't stick, because of the drinking or the fact Danny didn't want to try any more, he insisted on bringing Danny to work with him after he finished school. But still, he sometimes would disappear for days at a time and turn up at home later, gaunt and pale and rotting and cracking jokes like nothing had happened.

Lucy could never stand to be around Danny, especially when alcohol made him cruel. Soon, she didn't want her big brother to like her, didn't want to hang around with him. She only wanted to stay out of his way so he wouldn't say spiteful things to her and make her cry. Surely her parents must have felt something of the same.

It's not entirely clear who the blame lies with. It was like no one noticed until it was too late. This is the story of Danny, to Lucy. She can't remember a time, except for when she was very, very young, that Danny didn't have a problem with drinking.

After she has hung up, she is in her bedroom pulling on a

sweatshirt and leggings and scrubbing her hair dry with a towel. In the living room, she passes Cam, who sits on the sofa with a laptop balanced on his knees. On the television is *The Antiques Roadshow*.

She can see Cam watching her, as she sits down and keys the address Danny slurred at her down the phone – a housing estate near Westfield – into her iPad. He closes his laptop softly.

Everything okay? he asks.

Lucy wonders whether she can get away with ignoring him completely. Before the silence becomes a rudeness, she glances up at him.

My brother, she says, he's had some sort of accident. He needs me to get him an Uber.

God. Is he all right?

I don't know, to be honest. All right enough to call me and get a taxi arranged.

What if he needs an ambulance? What has he done? Got in a fight?

Knowing Danny? Probably.

Lucy can't get the Uber app to stop navigating to her location, not Danny's.

This isn't working.

She wants to throw the iPad against the wall and scream.

Alcoholism is a disease. Addiction is an illness. Danny is trying his best, she thinks. Danny doesn't know what he's doing. You can't blame him. It is a useless endeavour to hate Danny.

Cam is still watching.

Look, he says. Maybe you should go and pick him up. Use my car, if you want.

Cam, a suburbanite by upbringing, has a teeny-tiny ten-year-old Nissan Micra, rusty red, for his commute to his secondary school job in Peckham Rye.

I don't drive, Lucy says.

I'll drive you.

He's already pulling on a pair of worn-out New Balance trainers.

Lucy stares down at the Uber app open on the iPad, the little car graphics surrounding her location pin, slowly trundling across the river on Vauxhall Bridge single file.

You should probably see if he's all right, Cam says again, looking up from where he's yanking his shoes on, one arm braced against the wall.

Haven't you got marking to do or something? she asks as she follows him, quickstep, into the underground car park beneath their block of flats. Lucy has never really bothered to pay attention to Cam's car before. Three of its four hubcaps are missing. Dents and scratches are laced across the bumper and the wheel arches. An obnoxious sun-shaped air freshener, its scent long gone, is strung up to the rear-view mirror in a stranglehold.

Cam shrugs as he sets his phone into its cradle and taps the address Lucy gives him into Google Maps. There's always marking, he says. It can wait.

The app says it will be a forty-five-minute drive. The sky outside is a darkening violet, the moon a slim curl of orange peel. Cam drives them north, through Newington and just skimming Elephant and Castle, and takes them over Southwark Bridge in stop-start traffic. The river is glittering in the sunset light, and behind them, in the rear-view mirror, Lucy can see that same orange-gold-pink gleam bouncing off the shiny angled glass of the Shard, the great corporate obelisk of it impossibly tall up close, as though it can't support its own height and might topple into the river at any moment. The lights on the Thames – their owners ferries and the Clippers and, beyond that, the yachts languishing in the tide, further toward the estuary – are little

dots in the broad brushstroke of the water. There are trains pulling into London Bridge station, streaks of white and green and
yellow, their near-empty interiors like lightboxes, each one a different tableau of domestic life. In the Square Mile, the grand old
grey banks and their streets sit silent and dark. But then driving
through Whitechapel and Mile End, life teems in all directions:
every corner shop and kebab takeaway and Polish food market
scrabbled with people. Every parked car a meeting place. They
pass Stepney Green, Mile End and Bow Road tube stations in
quick succession; each one catering to its own congregation on
its steps.

Lucy leans back and picks at the edges of her thumbs, trying
to think of something to say to Cam. She is aware that they are
not talking. Her skin is fizzing with nerves. She looks at him
sideways. He is humming along to Radio 1, which is on low,
barely audible over the engine of the car. The song is something
Lucy hasn't heard before. Cam doesn't seem to expect anything
from her: he is concentrating on the road. He catches her watching him and flashes her a quick, reassuring smile.

The closer they get to the Stratford Centre, the A11 an artery
leading to the ventricles, her pulse spikes and she is sure that
even Cam seems a bit nervous, his fingers curled around the
steering wheel ever-tighter, his eyes making darting, uncertain
glances at the rear-view mirror. She hunches over until her ribs
dig into her uncomfortably.

It's just down here, Cam says, referencing the map on his
phone.

They pull into the entrance of a housing estate, with six or
seven blocks of flats, with thin single-glazed windows, washing lines strung up precariously on small square balconies, and
1970s-style boxy architecture, all neatly laid out like a chess-
board. The sky, now, is almost black.

In the car park, several men are having a loud debate, some of them leaning against a wall by the entrance to one of the blocks; some of them sitting on the kerb, candy-striped plastic bags between their feet.

Lucy looks over to Cam. Are you ready?

He nods slowly and gives her a reassuring smile.

At the same time, they exit the car. One of the men in the group looks over to them.

You here for Danny? he asks, casually.

Lucy nods yes, gritting her teeth, and the man points at the covered alleyway leading through to a courtyard in the centre of four of the blocks. An attempt has been made at landscaping, but the bushes are dead and skeletal, their flesh fallen away.

There, in one of the fire-escape doorways, is Danny. He's on the floor, panting hard, his arms braced against the walls. There's no blood on the concrete around him, the steps or the paving slabs. But his face is unrecognisable. His lower lip three times its normal size. Both eyes puffy and blackening. His thick dark hair matted with sweat and maybe blood, clumps of it variously slicked to his head or sticking up straight as though electrified.

Lucy jogs over to him and Cam follows.

That's him? he asks, his voice coloured with disbelief.

All right, Loose, Danny says, his voice still swerving like a broken carousel.

There is one other man with Danny, who seems less drunk than him and the others in the car park.

He's done something to his leg, he says. He can't put any weight on it. I don't know if it's broken or not.

Lucy takes out her phone and shines a light on Danny. His left ankle is swollen, mottled lilac and bent unnaturally. He's not wearing any socks. She leans closer to him, and catches the tidal scent of scrumpy cider rolling off him in waves.

You should've just called an ambulance, she tells him.

Fuck an ambulance, he says.

He is the same as Lucy in this small way. A lifelong distaste for hospitals, established over the long eleven weeks they spent aged twelve and seventeen respectively visiting their father, at the Royal National Orthopaedic Hospital in Stanmore, strapped to a gurney, his face a permanent contorted mask of agony, alien noises coming out of him, while the two broken vertebrae in his back slowly fused together.

What do we do? Cam asks, nervous.

Let's get him in the car.

There is nothing new to see here. Lucy is twenty-six years old. Danny is thirty-one. As Lucy and Cam prop Danny up between them and, careful not to drag his swollen ankle across the concrete paving slabs, carry him to Cam's Nissan Micra in the car park, she thinks of all the versions of this night that she has witnessed over and over again. All the different iterations.

Lucy at twenty-four, her first week in her new job at Kube. Danny turning up in the reception area of the building and demanding to see her, swinging his arms wildly, dirty hands and face. She pretends that she doesn't know who he is.

Lucy at twenty-three, home for the weekend, when Danny spits in her rice pudding at the dinner table.

Lucy at twenty-one, graduating. Danny is drunk on the free Pimm's they've been handing out at the university party. Her parents somewhere in the periphery, here, anxious to get home. He calls her a know-it-all bitch in front of her dissertation supervisor, and vomits into a plant pot.

Lucy at eighteen. Danny is twenty-three. It seems like a lifetime ago, now. He watches her stuff her belongings into suitcases, bin-bags anything she's not taking with her into her new student flat in Paddington. She is leaving, and she feels as though her heart is going to leap out of her ribcage and fly out the open window. Danny stands at her bedroom door and says, Maybe it's for the best.

High above them, twelve floors of apartments are boxes of light, with old CDs strung on bits of twine across balconies, to keep the pigeons away, and TVs blasting through open windows. The air is mild. Down in the courtyard, the twinkling lights make everything slightly more magical. Down here, Lucy smells someone's barbecue pork chops for dinner, and the residual tang of weed, and rain on concrete and the sharp, sour smell of Danny's breath as she and Cam wrestle him into the back seat. He is like dead weight.

He leans out of the door and vomits onto the uneven concrete slabs.

Cam rests his hands on Lucy's shoulders – one on each of them, only for a moment – and squeezes gently. And she looks up at him, frowning. She is suddenly, inexplicably, furious at the look of pity writ across his face, the fact that he has insinuated himself into this secret part of her life, that he's being so nice about it.

Let's go, she says, shrugging his hands away from her.

They slide into the car. Lucy taps a postcode into Cam's phone, which is still in the cradle above the dashboard.

That's not a hospital, Cam says.

Just drive to that address, please, Lucy replies. Chadwell Heath.

Cam shrugs and pulls out of the car park, onto the main road. Danny makes miserable, self-pitying noises, his words bubbling over one another.

Are you sure we don't want to go to the hospital instead?

Lucy at twenty-six. Danny is thirty-one. Weeks ago. At the wedding.

Lucy doesn't answer Cam. She feels as though there is a low-simmering rage inside her, and at any opportunity it might boil up through her body and escape from her mouth, and she might scream, or smash a window, or throw herself from the car. She rakes her fingernails through her hair instead. Danny begins to snore.

They drive further east in the darkness, the traffic thinning out as they approach Romford. The address Lucy has navigated to is a residential road close to the train station, which is an ugly, squat red-brick building with peeling white paint and too many steps leading to the platform. Passing the station, Lucy feels a leaking sense of nostalgia. The many evenings she spent on that platform, as an awkward fifteen-year-old, waiting to catch a train into Liverpool Street, waiting to be a tiny blood cell in the vessels and capillaries of the city, part of some larger organism. As a teenager, she explored the city alone on weekends, taking buses and trains to the corners where the tourists didn't go. She so badly wanted to be a part of it. She liked hiding away in the crowds: that, in town, no one watched her the way her parents did. No one knew anything about her at all. She could be any version of herself that she wanted to, here. It didn't matter that she was friendless and broadly considered by her classmates at secondary school a weirdo, that she was what her mum liked to call overly particular and what her brother called a 'freak'. Lucy knew, from the first time her dad took her and Danny into town, to see the wax figures at Madame Tussauds when she was nine, that she wanted to live here. Away from her parents, who embarrassed her, and her brother who had recently started making her feel humiliated by the fact of her own existence.

Preferably, she would live in a box room above a bookshop in Notting Hill (unlikely) or in a new-build with laminate floors on the twentieth floor overlooking Greenwich Park by the farmers' market (slightly more achievable). Chadwell Heath, with its industrial estates that let out thick orange smog that could only be seen on clear days and she was certain was poisonous; its high-rise blocks of flats; its daycares full of screaming children; the vape shops; the Chinese dried noodle packing factory; the burger van that parked outside the builder's merchants opposite her family's house and filled her mornings and hair and school uniform with the smell of hot chip fat, so that it felt as though the airborne grease particles were embedding themselves into her pores. Lucy decided before she left school that Chadwell Heath was not where she was destined to be. She made a list of everything she wanted to achieve in the next ten years. Move to London. Have at least three best friends. Make at least *this amount* by the time I'm twenty-five. Be able to afford a haircut whenever I want one. Never eat beans on toast or ketchup sandwiches for dinner, ever again.

At college, she hoarded careers pamphlets and circled all the jobs with a starting salary of over £26,000, her biro slicing through the glossy paper. She made a list of all her best transferable skills – numbers, organisation, project management, attention to detail, Microsoft Excel – and applied to business school. When she was accepted into Imperial College to study Finance, she took out a maintenance loan and the maximum grant amount, applying as an estranged student, and rented her first flat-share in Paddington with two other girls on her course, took a data-entry job in the university admissions office, and walked to her lectures every day through Hyde Park with an umbrella in the crook of her elbow, a copy of *GQ* in one hand and a skinny mocha in the other. That first autumn at uni was the year of camel-coloured everything, and she bought a vintage single-breasted trench coat at the Portobello Road Market, had it dry-cleaned and wore it every day for four months straight until the seams began to split.

At that time, Lucy felt that she'd made it. She's there now, four years after finishing her MBA: she's made it. Every item on her list has been ticked off. She is that person. But somehow tonight, she still feels as though she's waiting on the platform in Chadwell Heath, for a train that isn't coming.

Cam pulls the car up to the kerb outside Lucy's childhood home. A small terraced three-bed house with brown stucco coating its exterior. Single-glazed windows and dark thin roof tiles. The windows are opaque black. It's now almost midnight, and her parents are sure to be in bed. In the back seat, Danny moans drowsily. Lucy turns and sees that his eyes are rolling backwards a little.

She gets out of the car and yanks the passenger seat forward to better look at him. Her brother. She now sees that one of his earlobes has been split down the middle, where an earring has been yanked out.

Get out, she says.

Lucy – what the fuck—

And now the lights go on in her parents' bedroom.

You can't do anything right, can you? Danny asks/tells her. And he is suddenly unnervingly sober and looking at her directly in her face for the first time tonight. And she can feel herself shrinking, remembering all the times he has looked at her like that before, and what it has meant when he does. And Cam is at her side, helping her pull Danny out of the car through the folded-forward seat, him groaning as his foot catches on the lip of the door, Cam panting with the effort of it, Lucy holding her breath against the hot moistness of Danny's body, the inside of the car, the drunkenness, not wanting to touch him too much. They get one of Danny's arms over each of their necks and pull him to the front door.

Are you sure about this? Cam asks again.

Just, please, Cam, Lucy snaps, and she registers a look of passive indifference come down over Cam's face like a gathering storm.

And suddenly her dad is at the door, illuminated by the soft light of the hallway, in his dressing gown, faded red and blue stripes, and pint-of-Guinness-shaped slippers, one of them with a hole at the toe. Lucy's dad stoops a bit now, on account of the fourteen-year-old back injury sustained when he fell off a ladder at work and never went to the physio appointments booked for him by his GP because he refused to take the time off. Standing in the doorway, Lucy is struck not for the first time by how much her father has aged since she left home. His face, adorned by unfashionable square-shaped glasses with metal frames, deep lines etched across his forehead like canyons, and a soft yellowing-white moustache the only hair on any part of his head at all besides explosively bushy eyebrows that almost-but-not-quite meet in the middle. Daniel Senior, in this moment, leans against the door frame, propping up his body as he watches Lucy and Cam drag his only son down the garden path.

What's he done now? he asks, resignedly.

I fell down some stairs, Danny slurs at the ground.

I think he got in a fight, Lucy answers.

Let's get him in the kitchen.

They carry him up the front steps and through the house to the kitchen, its terracotta-coloured tiles with sunflowers the same as when Lucy was a child. The house itself is shabby: cluttered with things that Lucy's mother collects, like teapots and old watering cans. Lucy always felt claustrophobic in this house growing up, for the sheer amount of *stuff* that spills off every surface and clutters up every corner and windowsill. It was never a very comfortable place for Lucy to exist in. Her parents never throw anything away, even if it's broken. They abandon objects around the house in a kind of amnesia, as though they are shedding skin as they move from room to room. The walls are lined with photographs of Lucy and Danny in various stages of childhood – formal school portraits, but also the two of them in the garden as kids, at Banbury family birthdays and Christmas parties with Daniel Senior's extended family of four brothers and all their assorted partners and children. The windowsills spill over with Mum's Swarovski crystal figurines: tortoises, owls, spaniels and ballerinas. Lucy cannot fathom how her mother, who is the most image-conscious person Lucy knows, can care so little about the state of the space she exists in.

They set Danny down in a chair at the kitchen table, which is stacked high with opened mail.

Why didn't you take him to hospital? her father asks.

This, Lucy replies quickly, her eyes stinging, gesturing at Danny, who is slumped on the tabletop, a little bit of dribble at the corner of his mouth, is not my responsibility any more.

Her dad looks at her then, and takes off his glasses and cleans them with the sleeve of his dressing gown.

I should probably wake Mum up, he says.

Don't bother on my account. We're just leaving.

I'm Cam, by the way, says Cam, holding his hand out to Lucy's dad.

We're leaving, she says again.

What am I meant to do with him? Lucy's dad asks her, his eyes glassy.

I don't know. I don't care.

She leaves the kitchen, and the house, closing the front door softly behind her once Cam has followed her out, though she feels like slamming it and shattering the fake-stained-glass panel so that it wakes up the whole street.

Chapter Seven

In the car on the way back to Lambeth from Romford, Lucy is reminded of the wedding, the journey home in a taxi after everything happened. The landmarks the same. The tone and quality of light pollution awash across the city sky the same. She registers that Cam is still there – that he's the one driving them home.

Do you want to talk about it? he asks, kindly.

She shakes her head vigorously.

She has tried to bury that night, but it keeps scrambling its way to the surface, desperate for light and air. She is numb from it. She feels nothing. Banburys don't cry.

She remembers meandering through the tables at the reception, dazed, heart hammering.

She remembers dashing to the bathroom, her throat burning, while Uncle Marv shepherded Danny into a taxi. Her mother followed her, calling her name, but she locked herself in a bathroom stall and put her head between her legs, her mind racing, pretending that she didn't exist.

She didn't believe it at first – she couldn't – but as she traced her eyes over the bathroom tiles and tried to stop her hands from shaking, she began to understand. She had always been so different from the rest of her family, in looks and temperament.

She was skinny, pale, ginger and neurotic. Her father was stout and round, and Danny and her mum both had Mediterranean complexions. All of them but her were easy laughers, joke-makers, stiff-upper-lippers who preferred not to talk about feelings. Lucy tried to be that kind of person, too.

She had asked her mother about it once, when she was too young to fully comprehend the significance of these differences; why she looked so different from the rest of them.

Because you're special, Loose, her mum told her. Because an angel brought you to us and made you special.

She took it at face value, maybe even believed it.

When she got older and needed more, her mother pointed her to a great-grandmother who had been a noted redhead in the family.

You must get it from her, she said.

So they hadn't just withheld the truth, really. They had lied to her. It was calculated.

She wondered about calling someone – maybe Nara or Meredith or Anais – but the idea of it made her nauseous. She could never explain any of it to them. She had crafted a certain type of person out of herself for them. She preferred it that way. Meredith whose father was a millionaire, albeit under dubious circumstances; Nara whose family owned a baked goods empire; even Anais who grew up in a detached house, mortgage paid off, both parents with a stable income, her whole life. Lucy didn't think that her friends were so cruel that they would laugh at her parents or her brother. Lucy always knew that the problem lay with her, not her friends. She had constructed this version of herself – this illusion of middle classness – so completely that to introduce her parents, and her upbringing, now to her friends, after all this time, would be to reveal a secret. She code-switched when in the city: the Kentish-Essaxon dialect of her parents with intrusive Rs and glottal stops, stronger when she was back home, masked when at work or around her friends. She realised then that her friends were not her friends, not really; they were accessories who were convenient to this character she had cultivated out of carefully selected fragments of her childhood.

Eventually, while she stared at her hands and counted the spider lines across her palms, she heard the bride, her cousin Hannah on her dad's side, barge her way into the bathroom and call for her.

Are you in here, Loose? she asked. Her voice warbled, pitching up and down; drunk.

Lucy unlocked the door and saw Hannah leaning against the sinks, her veil discarded and stuffed into one of the baskets that had been laid out for guests, filled with tampons and packets of tissues and mini Body Shop moisturisers.

Come here, babe, Hannah said, her eyes brimming with tears, and she dragged Lucy into a reluctant hug. The diamanté stones on the bodice of her wedding dress cut into Lucy's ribs. I'm so sorry, she said, and then she said it again, stroking Lucy's hair.

Did you know? Lucy asked, numbed, pulling away from her.

Hannah and Lucy grew up together, being the closest in age of all of Lucy's cousins, and with Hannah's dad Clive being the closest brother in age to Lucy's dad. They spent their childhood years racing on their bikes up and down the residential road outside Hannah's house in Seven Kings. Hannah was always in love with a new boy, always trying to find a way to be made new through the eyes of someone else. She met Alex – her husband – when he came into the beauticians' where she worked for laser hair removal.

Yeah, I knew, Hannah said, and then seeing the expression

on Lucy's face, she added, Only *recently* though. I overheard Dad talking to Mum about it. I didn't know how to tell you. I thought maybe you might know, too.

I didn't, Lucy replied. I think I'm going to call a cab.

No! Lucy, *don't*. It's my wedding, I want you here. Please. And now Hannah was crying, her perfect make-up, crafted by a professional over two hours this morning, sliding down her face with muddy tears. Lucy saw this and felt nothing.

Lucy, Hannah pleaded.

I'll wait for it outside, Lucy said, pulling up the Uber app on her phone.

And in the cab, closing the door, while her mother, also crying, stared at her from the patio, her dad stoic beside her, neither of them calling her back or following her; Lucy still felt nothing.

And on the journey back to Lambeth, Lucy felt nothing.

And when she got through the flat door, boiled the kettle and filled a hot-water bottle to the brim and wrapped herself up with it in her duvet, she felt nothing.

She still hasn't felt it. Not yet.

She stares out the window at the river that is curling around Canary Wharf like a sleeping snake. She tries to consolidate the feelings churning away inside her.

I had no idea, Cam says, quietly. No idea you had all this going on.

Why would you? she asks him. We don't talk. We're not friends. It's not like we care about each other.

She feels the acidity of the anger as it spews out of her, but as soon as she has said it, she is ashamed. None of this is Cam's fault.

Sorry, she says quickly.

Cam shrugs, his eyes on the road, seemingly unfazed by her outburst.

She circles her wrists with her hands, enveloping herself. The silence settles heavily inside the car.

It doesn't take very much to care about another person, Cam says simply.

And Lucy feels very bad on the inside, like a rotting piece of fruit.

The silence yawns. She opens the glove compartment and flicks through Cam's CD collection, bound in a square leather case with individual sleeves for discs. She comes across a burned one, with 'Anais's road trip mixtape' scribbled across the front in black permanent marker. She can see that Cam has noticed what she's looking at, too.

How are you, anyway? Lucy asks him, awkwardly, attempting a lighter tone.

You mean with that? he asks, pointing at the CD.

Lucy shrugs. Just generally. In whatever way you want to answer.

So you get to know all my secrets, but I can't know yours?

She goes to protest, but she can see that he is grinning in the darkness.

Don't worry, Banbury, he says. They're all safe with me.

They wait at a set of traffic lights, the car idling quietly.

I just thought we were going to be together forever, you know, he says after a while.

And Lucy nods slowly, waiting.

We went to the same secondary school and college together. Anais was always one of those people who can talk to anyone. She's always been a popular girl, even at school. I didn't understand why she ever bothered with me, you know? I was this awkward lanky boy who spent lunchtimes playing Dungeons and Dragons and his weekends watching *Star Trek* re-runs and painting Warhammer figurines with his only two friends. But somehow it worked for us. I always wondered how I could have got so lucky, that she had chosen me.

Lucy doesn't know where to look. With the way the words gush out of him, like water frothing against the walls of his body, trying to escape, Lucy wonders how long he's been waiting to talk to someone about this. She is reminded of how she blurted out her adoption at Nara and Meredith. This is the most Cam has ever said about Anais, a relationship which Lucy has to admit she didn't really understand either. She always thought – she realises now with a flash of shame – that Anais could do better.

We planned out our whole future together, Cam continues. Named our imaginary children, planned our imaginary wedding, decorated our imaginary home. Everything. And then she fucked that Josh bloke, and that was it.

I'm sorry, Cam, Lucy says meekly, keenly aware of how insufficient the apology is even as she says it. She wishes she had the emotional language to comfort him.

He shrugs and laughs shakily. Life goes on, doesn't it?

Yeah. It does.

He sings the Noah and the Whale song softly, L-I-F-E-G-O-E-S-O-N.

I'm sure it will get better, she says, uncertainly.

Lucy has never had a proper, hardcore, meet-the-parents-type boyfriend. She doesn't know, really, what heartbreak feels like. She imagines the way her parents looked when Danny blurted out about Lucy being adopted at the wedding. The way her mum pulled her into her with hands like claws. The look of sympathy and pity mixed with shame on her dad's face, like she was a wounded animal. They seemed to her to be children caught in a lie, awaiting their punishment with grim acceptance. They were not at all sorry for *her*, but themselves. She could tell this by how they looked at each other and not her. How her dad turned away from her so as not to see the expression on her face. She noted when she was leaving how there were pink wine stains unfurling across the tablecloths like spring blossoms, the detritus of the wedding breakfast not yet cleared away. Lucy couldn't feel anything, even in the face of the sick, leaden look of betrayal written across her mum's expression. Lucy couldn't trust the depth of her own feelings. She couldn't excavate them herself for fear that they would drag her down. The idea of being heartbroken is terrifying to her.

Driving back through Southwark, crossing the river, she looks east, out to the estuary, but all she can see is the brown of the night.

Chapter Eight

Lucy arranges to meet Tom, five-eight, non-smoker, in Chiswick after work for a drink. The Sunday before the date, Nara comes over to the flat with a bottle of Kahlua to workshop outfit choices.

What's the nicest thing anyone has ever bought for you? Nara asks her. Lucy knows the answer to this already.

When I was eight, she says, my Uncle Marv bought me the most beautiful doll's house you've ever seen. Expensive. With those Sylvanian Families toys. Remember the ones? The rabbits and that. It was incredible.

Cooool, Nara replies non-committally.

Lucy doesn't tell Nara what happened to the doll's house months after it was given to her for Christmas: that Danny destroyed it by breaking it up into pieces and shoving it into the mud outside the back of their house.

Why do you ask?

This boy I'm seeing, Nara says, he wants to pay for us to go to Paris. It seems a bit much.

Lucy has no reference point for this kind of extravagant gifting.

This is the first date I've been on in over a year, actually, Lucy tells her.

Why so long?

Lucy shrugs. There just never seemed to be an opportunity.

She has to admit, the field has been blasted wide open since she got onto the app, like Meredith told her to. Lucy has been chatting with five different men online, each of them with the potential for drinks in the not-too-distant future. Meeting people in person is hard, especially for Lucy. She tries to come across as wry and witty and astute, rather than frazzled and incapable of normal conversation. She always seems to say the wrong thing. Offends someone in some subtle way she doesn't quite grasp until it's too late – like with Brandon and his club-footed niece. When meeting new people, she has a recurring fantasy that she's going to vomit on them, or otherwise impulsively do something obscene, like strip in public. The last man she dated *properly, in person,* was a 'chef' she met on the train platform at Clapham Junction when she was on her way to the Kube Christmas party. He asked her for her number and, too taken aback to come up with a gentle rejection, she gave him her Instagram handle instead. It turned out he was a fry boy at a Harvester. After a couple of coffee dates, she learned that he still lived with his parents and was five years younger than her. After that she ghosted him.

You're a snob, Nara tells her after she recounts this story.

Lucy is leaning towards a pair of black high-waisted skinny jeans and a pale-pink blouse with oversized tortoiseshell buttons that ties at the belly button. She doesn't know whether to wear black Chelsea boots or a pair of knee-high dark brown riding boots from Boden with the outfit. She has tried both pairs of shoes on three times.

I'm not a snob, Lucy replies, but she doesn't quite believe herself. I just know what I want. There's a difference.

And you want Tom the Tory from Ascot, Nara says, smirking, as she browses his profile on Lucy's phone, using one

French-tipped thumb to swipe through his pictures. Lucy knows that Nara grew up poor, like her, from those French tips. Only poor people who are trying to look rich – trying to fit in – get French tips.

Well, I don't know. I'll find out soon, I suppose.

It's been a week since the incident with Danny, and Lucy hasn't spoken to Cam since that drive home. She bought him a six-pack of Guinness (which she knows he likes because she sees the empty cans in the recycling bin) and left them outside his bedroom door to say thank you. He hasn't acknowledged the gift, but she knows he has drunk them due to the aforementioned recycling waste.

When Cam's not at work, he's in his bedroom, the blue light from his laptop spilling out from underneath the door. The newcomer, Ash, on the other hand, now never seems to stop coming and going; and always at weird hours of the night. They leave for a gig at ten in the evening, guitar case slung across their back, and stumble in the front door as Lucy is getting ready for work or her morning swim, smelling sour with sweat, make-up running down the sheen of their face. When Lucy gets in from work, Ash is waking up, sipping strong-smelling black coffee and wolfing down cereal bars back-to-back, ready to do it all again. Lucy still hasn't ascertained what exactly it is that Ash does for work, except for these gigs that only ever seem to pay them in booze. Lucy has reminded Ash three times that the rent is due next week. It comes out of Lucy's bank account, now that Anais is gone.

It is now that Ash can be heard clambering into the front door. They poke their head into Lucy's bedroom.

Oooh, fashion show, they say. Can I join?

Course, Nara says, before Lucy can answer. I'm Nara, by the way.

Hiyaaa. Oooh, is that an espresso martini? I'll have one, too, please. Nara, what are your pronouns?

Moments later, Ash has brought the majority of their wardrobe into the bedroom: sparkly, bohemian things that Lucy would never choose for herself. Ash dumps all the clothes on Lucy's bed and sifts through them. The way they examine each item reminds Lucy of her mother. There was a time, when Lucy was barely out of nappies, that Erica would dress the two of them in matching outfits: flower-patterned frocks with shiny black Mary Jane shoes and straw hats. Lucy secretly quite liked being a miniature version of her mother. She felt special and important, wearing the clothes Mum had picked out for her, to match. There is photographic evidence of this, framed and mounted on the living room wall in her parents' house. Lucy understands now why it was so important to her mum that they looked alike, especially when objectively they never have.

As Lucy got too old for this type of twinning, her mum still had a significant hand in everything Lucy wore. They shopped together until Lucy was twelve, when her dad had the accident and stopped working and new clothes became a rarity. Hand-me-downs from her older cousins became the norm in the years that followed. Even so, every item in Lucy's wardrobe was personally vetted by her mum.

Her mum always said, If you don't care about the way you look, how do you expect anyone else to care about you?

Once, Lucy went on an unsanctioned shopping trip with a girl from her maths class, Jenny Akinfeo, just to see what it would be like, how it would feel, to choose something for herself. She didn't know what she *liked*, really, because she never had to think about it too deeply. She was fourteen and going through her emo phase, and she was desperate to buy a pair of black-and-white stripey tights from Claire's. She did, clandestinely, because she knew her mother wouldn't approve; selected them from the wall, feeling anxious as she did so, running her thumbs across the cheap shiny nylon. Counted out the coins from her newly acquired paper round. The tights were the most wondrous thing she'd ever owned, she thought. When she came home with them, intending to stuff them in the back of her underwear drawer and work out how she would wear them without her mother noticing, she lost her nerve. She showed them to her mum, heart hammering, who, mortified, binned them.

You're not the kind of girl, her mum said, who wears things like *this*. It's unsophisticated, Lucy.

By looking the way her mother wanted her to look, to behave, to exist in the world as though she were a Banbury, Lucy slowly and organically became a Banbury, without ever realising that she wasn't.

I like this one, Ash says, and Nara agrees. Ash pulls from their pile of clothes a beaded twenties-style flapper dress with a fringed hem. Nara is nodding enthusiastically. She has made more martinis for everyone and is on her third. Lucy is enjoying herself, but feels the nervous frisson underneath the surface of her skin that is ever-present but becoming more pronounced in this moment.

Try it on, Nara says, taking the dress from Ash to examine it before shoving it at Lucy.

No, I don't think it's me, Lucy replies, backing away from the dress.

Oh, don't be a spoilsport.

Lucy eyes the dress. It looks reasonably clean – no visible stains – but it is quite creased. Lucy remembers the bin bags Ash had all of their clothes stuffed into when they moved in. She imagines this dress scrunched up at the bottom of one of those bags, huddled up against the dirty cheap plastic ever since.

Go on, Nara says.

Do it for meeeee, Ash chimes in.

Lucy rolls her eyes, playing the part of the reluctant model, and snatches the dress from Nara. She feels nauseous. She doesn't wear other people's clothes. This is a rule of hers. She pulls the dress over her head, over the top of the blouse and jeans she already has on.

No – take your other clothes off from underneath. We need the full effect, Nara says, and Ash nods enthusiastically.

Look, we'll turn around if you're shy.

I'm not shy, Lucy replies, but they both turn and face the wall, grinning to one another.

Nara has spilled a little bit of espresso martini on Lucy's pillowcase.

She feels as though the room is shrinking. Ash watches the wall expectantly, unlit cigarette hanging from their mouth. They have tried to light it three times in her bedroom, but Lucy has stopped them.

It's fine like this, Lucy says.

Boooooo. Take your clothes off, Nara yells.

Lucy can feel her eyes watering a little. She stares at Nara, hoping to disappear. To pop like a bubble out of existence. Fine, she says, and scrambles the dress off over her head. She unbuttons her blouse and jeans and pulls it back on. She smells the bin-bag smell on the fabric, on her skin. Folds of the textile touch her armpits, the back of her neck, her calves. The sequins scratch at her skin, like tiny flick knives. She shudders into it. You can turn around now, she says, her voice coming out as a squeak.

Wow, Nara says, cheersing her. You look fire.

Tom the Tory will love it, Ash says convincingly, swinging their own glass wildly from side to side.

Nara takes out her phone and snaps an unprompted picture

of Lucy. She flinches as the flash goes off. She can tell that they are teasing her, but it's not clear whether she ought to be in on the joke or not.

It's not me, though, is it, Lucy says, yanking the dress back over her head as quickly as she is able. She can still feel the scratchy fabric on her skin, the plasticky bin-bag smell flooding her nostrils.

Well, I think it's lovely. You don't need to take it off so quickly. It's not diseased.

It smells like bins, Lucy says, red-faced, pulse hammering. And Ash stares at her, martini half-way to their lips. Nara looks away.

Well, fuck you very much, Ash says.

No – no. Not like that. I have sensitive skin, that's all.

Whatever. I'm sort of over this, now, actually. And Ash gathers their dressing-up-box selection from the bed to leave.

No – Ash – don't, Lucy pleads, a little disgusted at the desperation she can hear in her own voice. She is still in her underwear.

Ash turns and looks at her, face impassive, eyebrows raised.

I'm sorry. I'm not good at saying the right thing.

Ash waits a beat, glancing once at Nara, who shrugs, leaning against the wall.

I was thinking something more along the lines of this, Lucy says, re-pulling a black turtleneck from her wardrobe. Nara grins, her eyes a little too wide.

You really are, Ash says, dumping themselves and their clothes back on the bed, a boring old fart.

Lucy meets Tom outside Chiswick train station, her stomach churning with anticipation and possibility. This location is convenient for Tom in particular because he lives in Chiswick, just off the park, and has no need for public transport to meet her.

She steps off the District line train and spots him almost immediately at the entrance to the Underground, leaning against the wall. He looks like his profile picture, which eases her anxiety a little. He's wearing the same thick-rimmed square glasses and a green Barbour jacket with a soft brown collar. He has dark blonde hair and a well-trimmed beard, wide-set eyes and a broad mouth, two features that give him the appearance of a friendly frog from a Disney movie. As she observes this, Lucy finds that she doesn't mind it, his appearance, at all. He seems non-threatening.

She marches towards him, her hands balled into fists, adrenaline making her feel as though she might laugh maniacally at any given moment. She tells herself – as Nara told her – to harness the fear and repurpose it as excited nerves. This too fortifies her. She breezes towards him, a look of practised indifference across her face.

Tom?

He glances up from his phone and smiles broadly. He is slightly shorter than her.

What do we do? Hug? he asks brightly.

They hug – awkwardly – on the kerbside outside the station.

So, where are we going? Lucy asks, using the momentum of the greeting to keep herself talking.

There's a bar on the High Road. It's nice. We can go there for a couple first?

Lucy nods energetically, wondering what he means by 'first'. Has he planned a pub crawl? Lucy's got an 8 a.m. Zoom call with a printer based in Malaysia. She wonders whether she should have postponed. She thought this was a one-and-done sort of thing.

Do you like wine? he asks her as they navigate the throngs of pedestrians on the streets coming in and out of pubs and restaurants. She realises that his polished received pronunciation is masking a Southend accent.

He puts his hand out to stop her from crossing the road into the path of an oncoming car, though she had already stopped. She makes a mental note in the 'pros' column that he is the protective type. She also notes that his shoes, a pair of brown brogues, are real leather.

The bar is more of a pub, with a gastro restaurant-type section with seated dining at the back. Tom chooses a small round table with two bar stools close to the front of the building. He doesn't ask whether Lucy wants to eat, even though it's dinner time. And with her back to the door, every time it opens, she gets a gust of cool air against her spine, making her skin prickle with goosebumps.

Tom opens a tab and orders a bottle of pinot; another good sign. He tells her that this bottle in particular is a pinot *gris* because it comes from France, while pinot *grigio* is from Italy. Lucy gets the sense that this is a fact that he has trotted out many times.

How many of these do you go on? she asks him, gesturing around her at the setting. The pub is slowly filling up with after-work drinkers. Lucy's bar stool is a little bit short on one leg, causing it to bump loudly from one side to the other, making her stomach tip.

These? You mean Hinge dates?

Lucy nods.

Steady on, he says playfully. That's a bit forward of you, isn't it?

Is it?

What would you say if I told you loads and loads?

Lucy shrugs. I wouldn't be surprised.

He clutches his chest in mock heartbreak. You think so little of me?

She laughs and taps her fingernail against the rim of her wine glass. Things seem to be going well. Is this flirting? It feels like flirting to Lucy.

Well, I'll tell you one thing. I'm sick of going out with women who work in finance. Like me, Tom says.

Lucy gets the impression that Tom is very proud of the fact that he works for a big bank. He has tried to explain to her several times, using analogies, what he does for living – moving this many *million* from one box to another – but Lucy can't get past the fact that it very much sounds like money laundering.

What's wrong with women who work in finance?

They've got no personality. They're dry as fuck. We end up just talking about work. It's boring.

Lucy nods slowly, not quite sure what to say. She knows a few men that work at banks, through Meredith, who seems to attract them in droves; but no women. They all seem to be the same type – as though they're related, even – slicked-back pocket-squared latest-iPhone types who drink at private whisky clubs in Mayfair.

That's why I thought I would try a creative type, Tom continues. Like you.

He clearly thinks he is paying her a compliment.

Creative type?

You know. Marketing and all that. Very creative. Don't you work for a scale-up?

Lucy thinks back through her messages, trying to identify what she said that made Tom think of her as a creative type. Her agency gives off the impression of creativity, certainly, at least through its corporate Instagram profile, which is tile upon tile of fluffy affirmations set in mint-green bubble fonts. But her own role – as a senior supplier relations executive and occasional production coordinator on some of the bigger accounts – isn't exactly teeming with creative flair. She tells Tom this and he smiles even wider.

It must be cool, though, he says, to be able to play PS5 in the middle of a workday and call it 'brainstorming'. Madness.

I don't do that, Lucy says, masking her mild offence at the assumption.

He orders a second bottle of pinot *gris* within the hour, and Lucy gulps down half a glass quickly, avoiding looking directly at him. They move on to politics.

Did you vote Leave or Remain? Tom asks Lucy, making her feel uncomfortable. She feels as though she is in one of her re-curring dreams where she is about to enter the examination hall at Imperial for a Business final but has forgotten to prepare for the test.

You tell me first, she says.

Remain, but mainly because of the economic implications of No Deal. How about you?

Same, Lucy replies, trying not to look too visibly relieved. She doesn't attempt to give him her reasoning. He doesn't ask for it. Perhaps he'll assume that she is also fiscally minded. What about in the last election? she asks him.

Tom playfully narrows his eyes at her. What are you getting at? he asks.

Nothing in particular. Just interested.

He takes another sip of wine and considers her, peering at her over the top of his glasses. He has moved his leg so that it is lightly brushing hers under the table, and the touch (which might be accidental) sends a small frisson through her. Lucy can feel the wine fizzing in her fingertips, clouding her frontal lobe in a pleasant, unweighted way that makes her feel floaty and guileless. She can no longer tell whether Tom is deeply mediocre or potentially the great love of her life.

Then he says, I'm a one-nation Conservative.

Nara had been right all along, as she always is with these sorts of things.

So, you believe in . . . trickle-down economics? Lucy asks, perplexed. She's not well versed in the nuances of Conservatism. Is this a David Cameron thing?

Tom enjoys telling her, she can see, about meritocracy and paternalism without state intervention. As he talks about the long arm of government overextending itself to prop up the welfare state, she realises in an acute moment of clarity, through the fog of wine, that she cannot tell him about her dad, who has been on income support and later Universal Credit since he broke two vertebrae. She can't tell Tom about how her dad sometimes needs her mum to help him out of bed in the morning using steaming-hot towels, ibuprofen by the spoonful, very often codeine on top, and packs of Deep Heat to numb him enough to make sitting up straight bearable. She wonders what Tom would think about the fact that she is adopted. *Lucy* doesn't even know what to think about that – not yet. She resolves to answer only vaguely if Tom asks about family, as she does with her friends. But he doesn't.

How about you? he asks, long after she has lost the thread of his speech about Benefits Britain and has resorted to people-watching out the window of the pub.

How about me what?

What's your political affiliation?

Lucy temples her hands underneath her chin. She has had four and a half glasses of wine very quickly, and no dinner. She feels like a normal person, who can hold a normal conversation, and make her opinion known freely and without shame. She watches Tom, who is patiently waiting for her answer.

I voted for Corbyn, she answers. And with Tom's look of

abject horror, she clarifies, He seemed nice!

Tom is shaking his head. Shall I just go now? he says.

No! No, don't be silly.

I was joking.

Unless – you want to go?

Of course not, he replies, smiling, and she feels the relief washing over her.

I didn't know what I was voting for, really, she lies.

She waits for him to fill the void of silence, but he doesn't, continuing to stare at her. She looks around the pub for something to focus on. She can feel a heat rising in her; her pulse beginning to quicken. Excusing herself, she walks up the stairs to the bathrooms, anticipating that someone is waiting at the top of this staircase ready to shove her so that she falls backwards down them. She locks herself in the disabled toilet and crouches on the floor in the corner, letting the walls press into either side of her back. Stares at her shoes and counts the individual stitches on each one until her breathing has slowed. Splashes her face with water and dabs off the moisture gently with a paper towel until her skin seems to have a dewy glow to it, rather than a sheen of sweat. She reapplies a neutral-toned lipstick and returns to their table.

Can't believe I'm out with a socialist, he says, playfully, when she sits back down. This time, she picks up on the teasing note in his voice.

No one's ever called me a socialist, she tells him.

Well – there's a first time for everything.

He grins at her and she smiles weakly back at him. She takes a small sip of wine and feels her nerves smooth out as the liquid slides down her throat.

What are your top three issues?

Issues?

You know – the top three things you based your vote on.

Lucy wishes they had never started talking about politics. She feigns an air of thoughtfulness before saying: Healthcare, education and housing.

That's very sweet of you, but you're forgetting one thing.

What's that?

What really, truly motivates you in the deepest darkest part of yourself, what you care the most about, is money. It is with everyone.

Lucy raises her eyebrows at him, unsure whether they're still being playful or not.

I would contest that, she replies, a little annoyed, drunk.

You can pretend I'm wrong, but I promise you I'm not.

They finally move onto other, less thorny conversational territory, but Lucy is distracted by the memory of being seventeen and circling all the high-paying jobs in the careers brochure. She marvels at how quickly Tom, an abject stranger, has sliced right through to the core of her being. It's not that Lucy wants to be *rich*, it's just that she *never wants to be poor ever again*. Of course, she thinks about – worries about – money constantly.

Tom finally asks her about her family. Lucy answers in as few words as she possibly can, giving very little away. She is well versed, by now, in dodging questions about her family: she's been doing it since her first day at Imperial. She turns the questions around on him, instead, and usefully he doesn't have a problem talking about himself some more. She learns – unsurprisingly – that Tom is an only child. His parents, before his mother died of breast cancer when Tom was twelve, were farmers who founded a property development company and sold it for a small fortune in the late eighties on the tail end of one of the biggest housing booms the country had ever seen. After Tom's mum died, his dad remarried quickly and put Tom into boarding school. The way Tom tells her this story suggests to her that she ought to be impressed, so she pretends that she is.

At ten thirty, she makes a show of needing to leave, aware that they haven't yet moved onto a second venue, and if they did, she would need to stay for at least another forty minutes before making her excuses.

I have an early call, she says.

How early? I have to be in at six tomorrow.

Lucy can tell that he's boasting. That he – like her – trades on his job as social currency. The harder he works, the more responsibility and seniority that he has, the better a person he is on the inside. She insists on asking for the bill anyway, offering to split it but making a show of gratefulness when Tom shoos her and produces a silver American Express card from a leather wallet embossed with his initials.

On the walk to the station, he picks up her hand and slips it into his. Not in the fingers-entwined way which Lucy feels is far more romantic – but in the platonic way a mother might hold a child's hand when crossing the road; the hand perpendicular to its partner. Even so, the same thrill of possibility returns to her, and she reviews him in profile: he has a strong jaw and a barely-there ski-jump bump on his nose, which she likes very much.

At the station, she says goodbye awkwardly, thanking him again for paying for the drinks. He pulls her into a hug and then kisses her – sloppily – on the mouth, his arm still wrapped around the back of her neck. The kiss is very wet and a little frenzied – like a teenager's. Lucy keeps her eyes open. Embarrassingly, she goes to pull away after a few seconds, but his arm, which is still snaked around her neck, locks her head in place.

Finally, when he releases her and they break body contact, she says breathlessly, I'll see you later, in a way she hopes is sexy and mysterious. But the kiss has thrown her, and she might instead be bewildered. There's no way of knowing.

But he stays to wave her off, the same playful smile from earlier on his mouth. She takes care to make her hair swish behind her as she turns away from him, tapping her Oyster and jogging boldly onto the waiting tube. As the doors close, she turns, suddenly exhausted, to see him standing on the platform, watching her go. He's still waving.

Chapter Nine

The following Monday, Lucy has a 10 a.m. with her boss Delilah, who is one of the company's founding executives. Delilah likes to use whiteboards to express herself; wears chunky brightly-coloured earrings made out of polymer clay; and has a very large gap between her two front teeth. Notoriously, Delilah has no time for work team-building events, networking drinks and staff socials. She prefers to get the job done and go to dinner at restaurants with waiting lists with her husband on company time.

Lucy has cultivated a *work persona* for herself – one that is very different to her many other personas. At work, Lucy is someone who exudes quiet confidence. Her outfit choices are immaculate. She takes her lunch between one-thirty and two-thirty, keeping her schedule regular to ensure her colleagues are familiar with her routine. She answers emails efficiently. She uses Post-it notes and a bullet journal to keep track of to-do lists. She is not to be disturbed when she has the global cost tracker spreadsheet open on her monitor. She wears a headset to make phone calls because it's more ergonomic and keeps both of her hands free. When Delilah hired Lucy just under two years ago, she told her that if she could do the job, keep her head down and not rub anyone up the wrong way, they would get on fine. This is exactly what Lucy has done, following Delilah's advice like a religion.

Lucy knocks on the glass-panelled door of the meeting room and lets herself in. Delilah is sitting alone at a large ten-seater table, her ThinkPad open in front of her, horn-rimmed glasses dangling on a chain around her neck.

Lucy, she says warmly, and motions for Lucy to sit down. Good weekend? she asks, and before Lucy can answer, Delilah has moved on. How long have you been working here, now, Lucy?

Almost two years.

Almost two years. You've been with us from almost the beginning, right?

That's right.

What do you like about working at Kube, Lucy?

Delilah has a saucer of chocolate digestives in front of her. She offers one to Lucy. It seems impolite to decline. She takes one and nibbles tentatively at one corner. The crumbs are dry and brittle and claggy in her mouth.

I like the work, Lucy says.

The work?

Supplier relations is very pragmatic. It's often all about problems and solutions. I like being the person to solve problems for others.

Delilah smiles warmly and takes a biscuit for herself.

You like being liked, she says. It doesn't sound like a compliment, the way she says it.

Lucy looks at the sleeve of her blouse, feeling anxious.

Well – who doesn't? she replies.

I'd like to give you a trial for a new position we're opening up in the executive, Delilah says.

Lucy nods, the chocolate biscuit now melting against her thumb and index finger.

It's a lot more responsibility. Longer hours and harder work.

You'll be helping us restructure next year's budget to create cost efficiencies. That means an audit of all our printers, freelancers and distributors. We're haemorrhaging money, Lucy. I'm keenly aware that this is a bend-or-break moment for us. We need to decide whether Kube is going to be able to stay the course or whether we need to cut our losses and sell.

The agency's going bust?

Not quite. But it might do if we don't get a hold on our spending. The first three years are the most challenging for any start-up. Our investors' cash is drying up now, but if we can get through and keep our clients on board, we'll be fine.

Lucy nods again, totally in shock. She's seen lots more red on her P&Ls recently – she had suspicions that there might be a few redundancies – but would never have guessed it could be as bad as this. What would happen if Kube goes bust? There are thirty-odd people working here full-time. And countless freelancers. What would Anais do? What would *she* do?

If you do well on the trial, Delilah says, and Kube stays afloat, we've got a promotion and a pay rise approved for you.

Thank you, Delilah, Lucy says, in her most corporate voice. For thinking of me for this. And for trusting me.

Delilah waves her gratitude away.

And just to let you know, she adds. There are going to be some difficult decisions we'll need to make. Hard ones. So you'll need to get over *being liked*. And you'll be line-managing Anais.

Anais?

Yes. She's a friend of yours, isn't she? She's going to be assisting you on the audit. I'll let her know later today, if you're happy to take on the role.

Yes, absolutely, Lucy gabbles, her stomach turning over. I would love to.

Lucy goes back to her desk, opposite Anais's. Anais is there, an invoice open on her screen. She is WhatsApping someone.

Everything okay? she asks, brightly, perfectly lined eyebrows arching hopefully.

Lucy gives Anais a wobbly smile and wonders how she is going to manage her. She can feel rivulets of sweat driving paths down her back.

Since Anais moved out of the flat and in with the new boyfriend, Josh the personal trainer, things have been *weird* between them at work. Lucy has noticed that Anais now talks to her more often, is more interested in her, and asks her questions – something which she never did when they lived together. When they left the office at the same time and got the tube home together, they did so in silence, with both of them mindlessly scrolling their phones on the Northern line platform despite the lack of reception. Lucy couldn't ever think of a way to start a conversation, and Anais never tried. The last time she saw Anais out of work, at that party in Dulwich. She looked right at Lucy and pretended she hadn't seen her. Now, though, Anais is asking about what Lucy did at the weekend and how the new flatmate is settling in. How is Cam? Is he going out? Who is he going out with? Does he seem sad to you? Has he been reading my texts? This is the kind of information that Lucy doesn't have, because she and Cam never interact, apart from the dinner, which was an abject disaster, and of course the road trip to Lucy's parents with a passed-out Danny in the back of the car.

Lucy is still thinking about Anais when she taps in at the Borough station barriers. Her friendship with Anais, she realises, has always been a necessity borne out of living and working together. Anais and Lucy never had an argument or any friction the whole time they lived in the same flat. But maybe that was because Anais just doesn't care about Lucy, or Lucy's thoughts and feelings and hopes and dreams. The only reason she talks to

Lucy is because she wants to know about Cam. Maybe Anais has secretly always *hated* Lucy. Maybe Cam and Ash hate Lucy too.

Lucy sees this now. Clearer than anything, even with her nose squashed into a banker's armpit on the Northern line. She can smell his antiperspirant, and beneath it the sourness of his body odour. She imagines where exactly in this tube carriage the body odour would be if it were something you could see, like coloured vapour. All over her, no doubt, underneath her clothes and in her ears. She can see now, actually, that this man's crisp white shirt is *yellowing* at the underarms, right in her eyeline. Her cheek basically pressed against this man's sweat. He has nicotine-yellow fingers, with dark thick bristles of hair at the knuckles, and he is loudly chewing gum, with an open mouth so that she can see his fillings.

And there are people everywhere, all squashed into the tube carriage, and very suddenly Lucy feels as though she can't breathe. She tugs her head away from the armpit. But there is no space behind her to move either, because there are more bodies there too, flesh pressed up against the glass and the train wall and each other. Lucy feels very strongly, and with absolute certainty, that she is about to suffocate on this tube, in this man's armpit. There is no space to crawl into, whatsoever. She glances around her and, horrifyingly, in her field of vision everyone's face is melting off, Salvador Dali style, sliding right off their skulls.

Lucy closes her eyes and tries not to cry. She can feel the noise of it travelling up her windpipe. Any moment now, she'll drown in people with melting faces and yellow-stained body parts. Something is happening to her and she doesn't understand what it is. She is certain that she is going to scream at any moment. Or perhaps throw up. She is so full of something foul.

The tube stops at Elephant and Castle station and the doors slide open. She shoves out of the carriage, through the throngs of commuters waiting to board the train, gasping, the slightly cooler air hitting her face. She has a kind of sensation in her belly, one that resembles standing at the edge of a cliff, and thinking fleetingly, What if, *what if* I just threw myself off? Stepped over the edge? What would happen then? What if I jump off the platform, onto the tracks, in front of this train? What if I let it slam into me and crush my body and splinter all my bones into millions of pieces, let my brain tissue get smooshed to goo and splatter all up that Armani fragrance billboard? Who is going to stop me?

Lucy is *crying* crying now, tears hot and stinging and messy, still not able to get enough air into her lungs. The smell of the man on the tube clogging her nostrils and throat. Miraculously, there are no people by the fire-escape stairs and she stands at the corner of them, her breath still coming in ragged gasps, her heart palpitating. She presses her forehead against the tiles on the wall, not caring about the germs. Tears are streaming down her face and collecting as stalactites at her chin. Lucy braces herself against the wall and wills herself to breathe normally. In through the nose and out through the mouth and repeat. Her teeth chatter despite the humid underground air.

She waits for a few more minutes, the time stretching out like it is elastic. She hasn't had a panic attack since she was eighteen. She wonders what could possibly have triggered this one. She feels as though she is six again and her mother is braiding her hair into painfully tight French plaits for school, two matching ones for either side of her head. Over and over and over again, her mum pulls the hair tight like the ribbons of a corset, only to discover some kink or imperfection that means she must start over.

Lucy retouches her mascara and foundation using her make-up compact. Back still against the wall. The traffic of commuters dissipates as rush hour drags on. Lucy waits and waits and waits until her breathing is normal again. Banburys don't cry. She takes out her phone and sees a message from Tom. The message says that he had a nice time the other night and would love to see her again if she were up for it. Despite herself, Lucy grins foolishly. It is so *nice* to feel the interest and validation of another human being. Especially one so clearly well-put-together and mature, like Tom.

Lucy has calmed down now, and she is able to see things a lot clearer. She reminds herself that she is a successful senior supplier relations executive. She has just been offered a very exciting new promotion. She is well on the way to a promising and fruitful career. And now she has a man texting her for a second date. She tells herself that she has many friends and is well-liked among them. She has a busy social calendar and disposable income. Things are looking good, *very* good, really. Things are looking *up*. What an *excellent* day to be Lucy.

And when her breathing is back to normal, and her heart has stopped hammering against her ribcage, she crosses over to the Bakerloo line, buoyant with fresh optimism, and finishes her journey home.

Chapter Ten

On Wednesday morning, Lucy gets up extra early and goes for a long swim at the leisure centre on Tottenham Court Road. The place itself is a little downmarket, with drains leaking the smell of sewage through the place, stained carpets, broken vending machines, and dark mould congregating in the gaps between the greying tiles in the changing rooms. But first thing in the morning, the place is silent, besides one or two pensioners in rubber swimming caps and floral tankinis headed for the heated indoor lanes.

The outdoor pool is one of the only ones in central London, and it seems that hardly anyone knows about it, hidden away as it is behind the wall of a charmless dilapidated office block on the corner of a busy A40 junction in the midst of the Shaftesbury Theatre and the British Museum. It's the last place anyone would ever expect to find a community swimming pool. And at this time in the morning, Lucy practically has it all to herself.

She relishes the cold shock of the water as she slips into it, the smell of chlorine stinging her nostrils, the rich artificial blue hue of the tiles. She conducts an unhurried backstroke in one of the lanes, enjoying the feeling of her muscles using their full range of motion; ball-and-socket joints creaking; the power of her hands, clenched into flat blades, as they propel her through the water; the gasping for breath and the tightness in her lungs as she works the lengths, flinging herself away from the walls of the pool with a practised levering of the knees and ankles when she hits the edge.

She can hear the early-morning traffic of Soho beyond the walls of the leisure centre, despite the roaring of water in her ears: the horns of buses and taxis intermingling with ambulance sirens and the brassy heave of articulated lorries braking at traffic lights. She thinks of her dad, who accompanied her to the pool at Newham Leisure Centre every Saturday morning without fail right up until she moved out – no matter what job he had to be at, and later, after the accident, no matter how much his back protested. He taught her how to slice through the water like a knife. He said it was good for him: the feeling of the exercise. It made him feel stronger; made him forget that his body was failing him in so many different ways. After their swim, her mum would join them at the leisure centre, and they would each eat a cherry bakewell brought along in a Tupperware from the kitchen cupboard, with coffee in a polystyrene cup in the café on the mezzanine level above the pool. An indulgence for all three of them. Lucy wonders whether her father still swims now that she doesn't live at home and he doesn't have someone to go with him. She never thought to ask.

Flat on her back in the water, Lucy watches the sky above her lighten from a cool milky grey to something that resembles spring, as the morning drags on. She feels herself growing stronger.

After the swim and a long, hot, high-pressure shower, Lucy takes the tube into work. Anais is already there at her desk, opposite Lucy's. To be at her desk before Lucy is highly unusual for Anais.

Morning, Lucy says cheerily. She is feeling good today: her

swim has put her in the right frame of mind for work. She feels powerful and cleansed and in control.

Hi, Anais replies, her voice flat.

Anais has been like this since Delilah told her about Lucy's promotion.

Lucy tries to think of something to say to start a conversation with Anais.

I'm getting a coffee, she says eventually. Do you want one?

Anais ignores her.

Lucy opens up her emails and replies to a few, including a couple from Anais herself. She googles *how to resolve workplace conflict*. Tentatively, she asks, Is everything okay, Anais?

Yeah, fine, thanks, Anais says without emotion, and when she looks up to see Lucy watching her, she gives her a smile that looks more like a grimace.

For the rest of the day, Lucy is in and out of meetings with the exec team, including Delilah, learning the ropes of her new role. By the time she's leaving the office, she remembers Anais, but sees that she's already left for the day.

She gets home later than usual, and Ash is up and dressed in the kitchen, their guitar case leaning against the wall. They're smoking a cigarette at the open patio door. The evening is humid with pollution, the sky overcast and murky.

You know, you could literally take two more steps and be smoking in the garden rather than in our living space, Lucy says, trying not to sound sharp but failing.

Ash gives Lucy a look of bemusement and steps onto the patio.

Nice to see you too! they say, their voice sing-songing over the noise of Lambeth Road.

I was also hoping I could get your rent, too, if that's okay, Lucy says, taking a pre-made Greek salad from the fridge. She turns the oven on and shoves in a chicken breast. She hates, in hindsight, that she said *if that's okay*, like paying rent is optional.

I should have it for you after the gig tonight, Ash replies, stubbing their cigarette out on the external wall.

What's the gig? Lucy asks, genuinely curious.

Oh – it's just, you know, a little pub in Brent Cross. Of all places. Honestly, when I got here, I thought I would be getting opening slots at the Electric Ballroom, doing acoustic nights at the Indigo, that sort of thing. So far, all I've had are shitty middle-of-nowhere old-man pubs; either that or 3 a.m. slots at ratty clubs where they want *me* to pay *them* to play. What's that all about?

Doesn't it scare you? Not knowing when your next payday is coming? Lucy asks, trying not to sound too judgemental.

Yeah. Course it does. But it's exciting, isn't it? And it's what I love doing. So, it's worth it in the end.

Lucy nods, now dressing her salad with honey mustard. There is nothing that fills her with dread quite like the prospect of not having a guaranteed job and a steady income. The idea that Kube might be on the brink of collapse is one that she has pushed to the back of her mind and locked in a box to be taken out and examined at a later date, along with the other things that she is actively not thinking about. Like how she still hasn't spoken to her parents about the adoption; how she still hasn't decided how exactly she feels about it. How she's worried that she doesn't feel anything at all.

Ash lights another cigarette contemplatively, staring up at an aeroplane leaving a snail trail of snow-white steam in its wake as it heads towards Gatwick.

The smell from the microwave is back. Lucy opens the door quickly, as though she is hoping to catch the smell in the act of something. Of course, there is nothing there. The stainless steel of the interior gleams. The death-smell lingers.

What about you, Lucy? Ash asks. How's work?

Oh . . . you know. Lucy shrugs. She takes out the bleach spray from the cupboard under the sink and starts spritzing. And then remembers. I got promoted, actually.

No way! Congratulations.

And, surprisingly, Ash pulls her into a warm and genuine hug. That's incredible news, they say.

Thanks. Well. It's just a trial at the moment. To see whether I'm up to it.

Nice. Big pay bump though?

Lucy flushes.

Well – not yet – if they like me, they'll make it official and give me the raise.

What's the raise?

I don't know yet.

And you're already doing the job.

Yes. It's a trial.

Ash taps their bottom lip thoughtfully. So, they say, basically, they're asking you to do the work of a more senior role at the same pay. With no guarantee that you *will* be promoted and get the pay rise? And there's no time limit on the trial period?

They haven't given me any timings yet. But, you know. They're a good company. It's like a family there.

Ash shakes their head, smiling pitifully at Lucy, an expression that makes Lucy want to thump them hard on the shoulder. Corporations can't be your family, Loose, they reply sagely.

Says the one who's getting paid in drinks and can't get a steady pay cheque, Lucy says, snorting, waiting for Ash to laugh too. But Ash isn't laughing. Lucy stills, feeling a coldness settle over her, her stomach tightening.

Do you know, Ash says, flicking the cherry of their cigarette onto the patio, ignoring the ashtray Lucy has pointedly set on the windowsill, you're actually one of the rudest people I've ever met.

Lucy grimaces. I'm sorry, she says. I don't know why I say things like that. It always comes out the wrong way.

Ash laughs humourlessly. It just takes a bit of getting used to, that's all.

I really am sorry.

Do I look bothered? You're funny, Lucy. It's okay to speak your mind, you know. You don't need to bottle it up all the time. One day it's all going to fizz up and explode out of you.

Ash's phone buzzes and they flash Lucy an apologetic look before grabbing their guitar case and bashing their way through the hallway, half-lit cigarette still in hand, and ejecting themself out the front door into a waiting Uber. They give Lucy, who has followed them to the front door, a wave as they bundle themself into the back of the cab.

Good luck with it!

You too, Lucy calls, waving back, but she feels the same suffocating feeling as before crawling up her insides again, like it did on the tube. She is absolutely certain, in this moment, that Ash hates her. She feels the panic attack coming on, building up through her like steam trying to escape. She wonders briefly whether she should alert Cam – ask him for help – as she can see he's in his bedroom, the blue light of his laptop leaking out from under the door. But what could he do, really?

She stands still for a moment – in the open doorway – willing her legs to move. After a moment, they obey her. She locks herself in the bathroom and lies down in the bath, the off-white porcelain cold and soothing against her burning face.

She is reminded of the night of the party at Amber Prescott's house when she was in Year Eleven. It was her first proper party.

She spent an hour dithering between three different outfits. She dyed her hair with Manic Panic to match Hayley Williams in the music video for the *Twilight* song. Lucy knew that if she made the right decision on how she looked tonight, if she did her hair and make-up the right way. If she smiled and laughed in all the right places during people's anecdotes. If she was glittering and carefree and witty and breathless and unbothered. If she got tipsy but not *too drunk* like Danny. Then she'd have done it. It was time all her classmates – the ones who called her weirdo and lanky and freak – understood exactly what Lucy was, *Better than all of you,* and destined for something greater. This was something that Lucy sincerely believed with every fibre of her being; she had to, otherwise what was the point of any of it?

In the living room, Danny sat on the sofa with a fresh beer open, watching some late-afternoon game show on the telly. In one corner of the living room, behind Dad's armchair which was currently occupied by Uncle Marv, was a collection of five or six rusty watering cans stacked up precariously against the wall. On the coffee table, Dad had started the work of disassembling a carriage clock, and had left everything out with the job halfway done.

I need a lift, Lucy told Danny bluntly, trying not to look at the disemboweled carriage clock, spread obscenely across the coffee table like an autopsy.

Hello, Lucy, darling, said Uncle Marv from Dad's armchair, smiling with teeth too small for his mouth. The living room was dark, with only the artificial glow of the television illuminating Marv's face, with all its lines and cracks and its shining dark eyes.

Uncle Marv was not really Danny and Lucy's uncle, but an old friend of Dad's. He babysat Lucy and Danny – almost every day after school – when they were younger, before Dad's accident.

But Lucy was fifteen and Danny was an adult now. There was no need for him to be here so much. Lucy often came in from school to find Uncle Marv sitting at the kitchen table rolling cigarettes, and no one else home.

That's Dad's chair, Lucy said, her voice flat.

Marv looked down as though he'd only just noticed he was sitting on it. Whoops, goodness me, he said, a caricature of himself. He looked at her as though he'd just told a hilarious joke. He feigned dusting down the seat of the armchair and moved to sit on the sofa next to Danny. Danny flinched away from him without taking his eyes off the television.

Yeah, I'll give you a lift, he said eventually.

A corner of fleur-de-lis wallpaper was curling away from the wall behind him.

In the car, Danny said, I don't know why you're wearing that.

He meant the dress she had picked out, agonised over.

I think it looks nice, she replied, her voice small.

You look like an idiot. A try-hard.

This wasn't anything new. Lucy was long used to Danny making sharp, hurtful comments, muttered under the breath, done in such ways that their parents wouldn't notice unless Lucy told on him. And after being scolded by her parents for being a crybaby, for telling fibs, for making up stories, she never did. It had been happening for years. Banburys don't cry. They get on with it. She found that putting up a small resistance was better than saying nothing at all. Silence meant Danny could go on forever. Find all the ways to make her feel inhuman.

He gripped the steering wheel, the whites of his knuckles stark against the dark interior of the car. The sun was setting and the sky was the colour of newly budded azaleas.

You look disgusting, he told her. You're trying too hard. You're pathetic. Everyone will see it.

He always knew the ways to hurt her. The right words to cut through to her bones.

At least I *have* friends, she spat back at him, feeling the humiliation and anger rising up in her, drying out her throat and stinging her eyes. At least I get invited to actual parties. At least people want me around. Who have you got? Uncle Marv? She scoffed theatrically.

Danny brought his hand down hard on the dashboard, slamming it with his fist, making her flinch. Danny had never been violent with her – not yet. But she knew how the violence writhed inside him, just beneath the surface of his skin, barely suppressed.

It was true that Lucy had been invited to a party, but it wasn't necessarily honest that she had friends.

She hung around alone in different corners of Amber Prescott's house, sipping a WKD and waiting for someone to come and talk to her. She sought out Jenny Akinfeo and tried to join her conversation with two other girls from their Maths class. But after a few minutes they drifted away from her, leaving her alone in the hallway. Her nerves prickled at the surface of her skin after what Danny had said in the car. Maybe she *did* look pathetic, a try-hard. Maybe that's why no one wanted to talk to her. Because they could see she thought she was better than them.

She was simply passing him on the stairs when it happened, on her way to the bathroom.

In one moment, there was nothing at all – just the leaden feeling of rejection. And then he – a stranger – was gripping her forearms, pinning them to her sides as though she were an aggressive animal about to strike him. She was trapped by his body, which was bigger and harder and stronger than hers. And then he had his hand on her and in her, the dark blue velvet dress, with sparkly bits that made it twinkle like the night sky, that she had spent an hour selecting in the dim light of her childhood bedroom, hitched up around her waist, exposing her. His hand shoved down the front of her tights, pulling the elastic away. And his eyes were drunk and maybe drugged – at fifteen years old she already knew this look so well from seeing it in Danny – and in the moment she felt nothing – only shock and bewilderment, as though it wasn't really happening to her at all. And then, once it was over, this thick and cloying and unbearable sensation of shame burrowed into the core of her began to grow outwards, radiating, burning through her. It only took a few seconds for it to happen, and he was gone so quickly Lucy could almost convince herself in the days and weeks after that it hadn't. Especially when she told her parents, perched on the edge of the sofa, sweat pooling in her lower back, her hands slick and wringed. And her dad took off his glasses and put his head in his hands and said, You could ruin someone's life with fibs like that, Lucy.

And her mum said, If you're going to be involved with boys at your age, we need to have a chat about a few things.

And Danny said, What's wrong with you? Are you a pathological liar, or something?

But still that feeling of complete humiliation, *loathing*, lingered and threaded through her whole being – and she couldn't fake that. That was no trick that her mind was playing on her.

The worst thing of all of it – the bit that made her sick and ashamed and furious – was that she hadn't said a single thing, hadn't pushed him off, hadn't told him to stop. Struck as she was like a moth pinned to a corkboard. After it happened, the boy (whose name she never found out) rejoined the party and she continued up the stairs and into Amber Prescott's parents' en suite and hyperventilated in the bathtub.

So, now, in a different bathtub, eleven years later, she waits for it to pass. Because it always does.

Chapter Eleven

By Friday, Lucy has ignored three missed calls, two voicemails and six texts from her mother. The WhatsApps from Mum are all variations of the same core belief system that she has propped Lucy up with for twenty-six years: please come home for a visit, we love you very much, we want to look after you. Lucy's feelings about her parents are complicated and unpleasant to think of, so she tries not to think of them at all, if she can help it. She tucks them into the box and shoves them away.

Instead, on Friday night, Lucy texts around to see whether she can fabricate some social plans to get out of going back to Chadwell Heath for a visit this weekend. Nara replies with a voice note to say she is working all weekend on a new product launch (70% *dark chocolate and brandy rocky roads*) which she is hoping to pitch to a buyer at M&S next week. Meredith has gone to a festival in Copenhagen with Helen, Jordan and Angus to take ecstasy and listen to bands that Lucy has never heard of, but pretends that she has. Lucy even thinks about texting Anais for a drink. But the way Anais has been behaving at work recently gives her pause.

She resolves instead to clean the kitchen from top to bottom. This is a grounding and reactualising activity. She scrubs the tile grout with a toothbrush. Delimescales the sink with diluted white wine vinegar and then Harpic. She decides to do the floor too. She squeegees the windows. She takes the grate off the extractor fan and scrapes the thick congealed fat off the stainless steel. She spends half an hour with her head in the microwave again, trying unsuccessfully to get rid of that *smell*. She slams the door shut, defeated, and resolves to try again another day. She tries not to think about how the smell, lingering, is making her want to scratch her own skin off. Exhausted by her brain, she does a David Lloyd home workout video, and drinks half a bottle of wine in the bath.

In her dressing gown and with wet hair wrapped in one of her fluffiest white towels, post-bath, Lucy pads into the living room. Another text from her mum makes her phone vibrate: she ignores it. Cam is in there already, with his friend Paul – also a teacher at the same secondary school in Peckham. Paul has a Tupperware of carrot batons next to him on the coffee table, alongside a half-empty can of lager. He is playing some complex and colourful card game with Cam, who is sitting opposite him on the floor.

The living room is quite bare since Anais left and took all her trinkets and fairy lights: a mid-range flatscreen sits on a white-stained oak IKEA BESTA unit in the corner. The floorboards are sanded down and polished but covered with a Persian-style rug. The two sofas – dark green corded three-seaters, salvaged from Freecycle by their landlady Marcy and draped in fleece throws by Lucy – draw a right angle against the thinly-painted magnolia walls. The furniture belongs to the landlady, not the tenants, and if it were up to Lucy it would all go and she would start from scratch, skirting boards and all.

Paul, who is pale and prematurely married with overlong fingernails, sits cross-legged on the rug, his back against the bottom of the sofa. Lucy has only met Paul once or twice: his appearance is rare at the flat. It always seemed to be Anais's friends from uni saturating the walls with laughter and conversation. Lucy tried to join in with them, when they came to visit for a big night out. She wasn't *invited*, per se, but it's important to ingratiate yourself with your friends' friends. She often found herself shrinking into a corner of the living room, largely ignored by Anais, slicked against the wall with the BESTA, staring at her phone.

Do you mind if I sit in here and read my book? Lucy asks Cam. It's rare these days that she must ask for permission to take up space in the flat: it's usually Cam who is hidden away somewhere, not her.

Cam smiles warmly, Of course.

Lucy settles on the sofa and turns the first pages of *The Body*: a Christmas gift from Nara. The bathtub wine has made her a little fuzzy around the edges, and she soon realises that she has read the same paragraph four times in a row. The words are far too black and stark, the serif font too sharp against the whiteness of the pages, she decides, and this is giving her a headache.

No plans tonight, then? Cam asks when the card game is finished and he and Paul are scooping up their decks from the table.

I know, Lucy says. Embarrassing, isn't it?

Not at all, Cam replies, and he looks confused by her remark.

She returns to her book and Cam goes back to his game. She catches snippets of their conversation, unable to focus on Bill Bryson any longer. The game sounds preposterous.

I'm tapping two mountains to cast Young Pyromancer, Cam says. He places a card on the table directly in front of him, with a picture of what looks like a blacksmith goblin with steampunk goggles and pink hair, encased in tendrils of bright orange fire.

Counter, Paul replies lazily, throwing a blue card on top of the red one Cam has just laid on the table.

Countering your counter with Red Elemental Blast, Cam says, looking triumphant.

Bastard, Paul replies darkly.

And because I cast an Instant, I get a red Elemental creature token.

I don't know why I'm friends with you, Paul says, but he's grinning.

You shouldn't have used Turn to Frog so soon.

Lucy peers over her book. Cam and Paul's cards are on the coffee table, set up in a complex formation, facing one another. From what it looks like, Cam is winning, with far more cards on the table than Paul. Each one of the cards has a fantasy illustration on it: dragons, centaurs, vampires, gold-armoured angels and elven wood nymphs.

What's this game? she asks, folding her page down.

Cam looks up at her warily.

I'm not sure you'll like it, he says. It's not very *cool*.

The comment spears Lucy unexpectedly. Normally, she likes to hear that people think that she's cool. That she doesn't associate with *not very cool* things. Lucy has been striving for cool her whole life. But the way Cam says it – with a bitter inflection – is like it's an insult. She feels as though he's embarrassed of her, in front of his friend Paul, that she'll undoubtedly let him down. Lucy realises, vaguely shocked, that she cares what Cam thinks of her.

Can you teach me? she asks, trying not to frown.

Paul says, Absolutely, at the same time Cam says, I'm not sure we have enough cards.

The table knocks sideways out of seemingly nowhere and Cam winces.

Cam's got a spare deck, haven't you?

Yeah, course, Cam replies.

He sits down next to Lucy on the sofa and talks her through the basic mechanics of how the game works and the different card types: mana, creatures, artifacts and a variety of spells. It *is* extremely uncool, this game. There is extensive fantasy lore around the characters on each card, and each creature has its own illustration to make it look like a background character out of *Lord of the Rings*. Lucy likes the angels and the vampires best, and Cam fishes out a deck made up of black and white-edged cards from a large box of them, all elastic-banded together, and hands it to her.

This is a good starter one, he says. Why don't you play against Paul and I can advise you?

Lucy takes Cam's place at the coffee table and draws her starting hand.

Cam leans over her shoulder, frowning at her hand. She glances over to him. He seems to be concentrating hard on the game. His cheek is very close to hers; she can feel the warmth of his breath on her shoulder. She realises that he is very keen to help her, despite his initial resistance. Cam wants her to win.

I didn't realise you were so competitive, she says, and he turns to grin at her, his face alarmingly close.

Are you joking? Cam's one of the most competitive people I know, Paul says. You should see him on Sports Day at school. There was absolutely some foul play from a certain team last year, as much as this *cheat* refuses to admit it.

It's not my fault, Cam replies, that you haven't got the stamina for the sack race.

Cam coaches Lucy through the game, patiently explaining to her what each card in her hand does, and how the mana system works. She loses her first game to Paul, who is clearly playing to win some sort of proxy victory against Cam, but by the third, she's got the hang of the rules and manages to narrowly beat him, bringing his life counter to zero before he has a chance to force her to sacrifice her angel warrior card: a heavily armoured woman with golden wings and a giant mace. There is unadulterated pride in Cam's expression.

Despite the cringe of it – the nerdiness – Lucy finds that she's enjoying herself. Cam and Paul are unabashedly themselves in their enthusiasm for and total engrossment in a fantasy card game. She relaxes into their company, unravelling her turban towel once her hair has dried to damp curls. They play until well past midnight, when Paul announces that he needs to get the last tube, otherwise his wife Francesca will lose her shit.

Nice to meet you properly, Lucy, Paul says, as he shoves colour-coded deck boxes and an empty Tupperware into his backpack.

As Cam and Paul say goodbye at the door, Lucy collects empty beer cans from the table and floor. She's close enough to the hallway, with the living-room door open, to overhear Paul whisper to Cam, I thought you said she was uptight?

After Paul's gone, Cam returns to the living room, where Lucy is still tidying up, and says, I don't fancy going to bed yet, do you want another drink?

This is the first time Cam has made any such proposal – to hang out with Lucy, besides getting Danny – since the two of them started living together.

Yes, okay, she replies, not meeting his eyes directly.

Lucy is not very good at one-to-one interactions. She prefers to socialise in groups, where she is able to blend into the background, to allow the bigger personalities to do all the work. This way, no one notices how much or how little she contributes to a given conversation. She is effectively able to be a part of something without actively *participating*. Often, Lucy is keenly aware how everyone must think her a fraud: even her closest friends who she has known for many years and feels quite comfortable being alone with. To Lucy, it seems painfully obvious that she is pretending to be at ease when, in reality, she is deeply and excruciatingly uneasy at all times.

Despite this, she has another drink with Cam.

I never asked about how your brother was, Cam says, handing Lucy a gin tin.

Lucy shrugs. He's fine. It was a broken ankle. No serious damage.

You're very calm and collected about the whole thing. If that had happened to my little sister, I would be up the wall.

Lucy smiles. She knows of Cam's sister but can't remember much more than a skinny teenager with features unnervingly like Cam's, who came to stay for a weekend in the box room last August.

It's not the first time Danny has found himself in a situation like that, she says.

Cam smiles sympathetically, and it seems he is making a deliberate punctuation mark in the conversation, emphasising that he will not ask anything further about Danny or Lucy's family, despite the obvious questions that he might choose to ask, hovering in the air between them, low-hanging fruit ripe to be reached for and plucked.

I remember your sister from last year, Lucy says.

Yeah. Bella. She's seventeen. She's going to university next year. I promised she could come and stay for a week or so in the summer holidays and I would take her to look at campuses. God. I wish I was that young again.

Really? Lucy asks, incredulous.

Everything was so much simpler.

I hated it.

Why?

Ugh – you know. Everything. Feeling too big for your skin but too small for the world. Constantly competing with everyone: other kids, your parents, yourself. Feeling as though you're never going to make it. It's like purgatory.

I never really felt like that, Cam says, stretching so that the sleeves of his shirt ride up his forearms. He says: Actually, it was when I left uni and moved to London that I started feeling inadequate.

Moving to London was the best thing I ever did.

He looks at her, one eyebrow raised. She notices that he has a light dusting of freckles across the bridge of his nose, and dark brown eyes that seem to darken further in the dimly lit living room. This is the first time she has noticed these things about Cam.

In the flat above, their neighbours are getting home – from a night out, Lucy supposes – and she hears someone turn on some music. Unexpectedly, 4 Non Blondes diffuses through the ceiling. Cam starts, and looks at her, grinning.

Wasn't expecting that, he says, leaning back on the sofa, balancing his drink on his chest, with one arm flung behind his head, and staring up at the ceiling. After the first few lines of the first verse, he is singing along to 'What's Up?', putting on a terrible nasal falsetto voice to match the singer's. He keeps going, all through the chorus, glancing at Lucy, expecting her to join in, maybe. She can't help but laugh at him.

You've got a promising career ahead, she tells him.

Yep, I'll give Ash a run for their money.

Lucy says, I feel like we've been living in the same flat all this time but I don't know anything about you.

She means that he knows more about her than she does him. She gets the impression from him that now he has these small nuggets of information – her brother, her family, her home – he is intent on clawing more out of her. As soon as she tells him any more about herself, she'll lose the parts that she has meticulously crafted over the years she has been in town; that the real version of Lucy – the one who goes to parties and has friends and is well-adjusted – will start to disintegrate.

She can feel parts of herself peeling away already.

Lucy learns that Cam's parents, Allie and Mike, are both dentists who raised him and his sister in a semi-detached on a cul-de-sac in Datchet. Cam's parents are in the process of separating, and it's getting ugly. His dad has partially moved out, and he's worried about how his sister Bella is coping. He tries to talk to her at least twice a week, but lately she's been avoiding his calls. He went to university at Cardiff and studied History. His favourite period of history is the Russian Revolution. He never really set out to be a teacher; it just happened organically, because he didn't really know what else he wanted to do. The school he works at has a terrible reputation and is on the brink of going into special measures with Ofsted. The teachers try really hard, they go well above and beyond, he says, but the senior leadership just doesn't care. Ever since we became an Academy, it's been a shitshow. They've basically checked out; washed their hands of the kids.

What can you do about it?

Not much, really. Turn up to lessons. Teach the curriculum. Give them as much of a leg-up as we're allowed to for exams. Cross our fingers and hope for the best. Paul is the union rep: he wants us all to strike for new management. But I don't know what that's going to achieve: it's not going to help the kids, that's for sure.

It's almost three in the morning.

I think I might lose my job, Lucy tells him, and immediately she imagines that she is shedding skin, like a snake. She feels some sort of liberation in telling Cam this secret. But she can also feel the rawness of the newly exposed flesh.

Oh? That's a big thing.

The company's about to go out of business, maybe, she continues, quickly, because she doesn't want to stop herself from getting it out. She says, I don't know what I'll do if I lose my job and can't find another.

Are you worrying about it?

Yes. Constantly. I'm worrying about everything, nowadays.

What is there to worry about? Apart from your job, I mean.

Lucy considers this for a moment.

She wonders what she can allow herself to tell him. *I'm worried that everyone hates me: you, Ash, Anais, and everyone. I'm worried that there's something wrong with me because I can't seem to feel anything real.*

She tells him the easier things instead.

I'm worried about Danny, she says. I pretend I don't care, but I know that I do, as much as I try to bury it. I'm worried about my parents . . . I've been having these panic attacks.

The admission falls out of her before she can stop it. Cam straightens on the sofa.

That's really bad, Lucy.

I've had them before and they always pass, after a while. Once work sorts itself out, it'll be okay.

What's going on with your parents? Why are you worried about them?

Lucy looks at him, his face open and honest.

I found out that I was adopted. A couple of months ago. I'm kind of not talking to my family because of it.

Oh. God. That's awful, Lucy. I'm so sorry.

That's why there were such weird vibes when we took Danny to my parents', she says.

And he genuinely looks devastated for her.

We were at this wedding at a golf club – one of my cousins on my dad's side – and my brother Danny was doing the photography. And he was pissed, of course, as per. And I could see my cousin Hannah – the bride – getting more and more upset by it. We were at this putting green, but Danny was all over the place. When Danny gets drunk, he doesn't just do normal drunk-person stuff. You know, make a few inappropriate comments, talk too loudly, fall over and things like that. He's a *nasty* drunk. He was wasted by three in the afternoon. At one point, he squared up to the groom in the middle of the photo call. And so, I just walked quietly over to him. I'm not proud of what I said. It's the most horrible thing I've ever said to anyone. But I was so *tired* of him ruining things, you know? Ruining poor Hannah's wedding. Upsetting our family. Ever since I was a teenager, he's been like this. He hurts people. I said to him in this stern voice that I only ever use on him, I said: If you fuck this up no one in our family will ever speak to you again. You're an embarrassment. You're pathetic. You disgust me. And I must have said it louder than I intended because everyone waiting to have their picture taken stopped and looked at me a little bit horrified. But, anyway, it seemed to do the trick because Danny sorted himself out a bit, stopped trying to start a fight. And when it got to the bride's side of the family – my dad and his brothers and all their kids and whatnot – we all went up onto the putting green to get the picture taken and Danny said, No, not you, Loose. And I said, What do you mean, not me? And he said, Well, you're not really part of the family, are you? Not really? And I just sort of looked at him a bit bewildered, no clue what he was on about, shrugged and laughed it off, thinking he was just being a pisshead. And I went to go up to the putting green, and he grabbed my arm and said – No, no, no. Blood relatives only. And I looked at him again and I could see in his face it wasn't some stupid joke and so I turned around to my parents who were on the putting green already and they had both gone white, their eyes big round dishes in their faces. And so I said, What is he talking about, Mum? And she just sort of shuffled around and looked at my dad, who looked at me. And then Danny said it, loud enough for everyone at the wedding on the golf club patio to hear, You're adopted, Lucy. Didn't you know? It's about time you knew. And then he started laughing at me. Laughing and laughing and laughing until he was gagging and my Uncle Marv had to drag him off to the bathroom. And there on the putting green was my dad, and all my dad's brothers – my uncles – and all their kids. The bride and groom. And I knew just by looking at them. I knew that every single one of them knew. Every single member of my extended family. Except me. Do you think I should forgive them? she asks Cam, surprising herself. As a rule, Lucy tends not to solicit advice from others on the mechanics of her personal life.

She remembers being ten when she and Danny took a trip on the Grand Union Canal in Uncle Marv's boat, before the Olympic Park forced him off the canal and into a leaky flat in Chadwell Heath. How Uncle Marv made them get off at the locks and open the lock gates with big metal keys that looked like crowbars. The gears, stiff at first, clicking satisfyingly as they turned them to open the paddles and let the water into the caisson. And then, when the water pressure was reduced enough, they could heave the gates open, leaning their whole bodies into the wooden balance beams, unsticking the seal. And they watched the canal water pour in, waterfall-like, the power of it roaring into the chamber and swelling the river below.

Now she has said it out loud, she won't be able to stop herself from saying all the things that she ought not to.

I can't tell you what to do, he says. You have to decide for yourself. If these people are important to you – if you want to share your life with them – then you'll find a way to fix it. You will, I promise.

Lucy smiles weakly at him.

She feels now the swelling in herself. The great roaring of it, like the canal water, the smell of it, the taste of it, the way it is grainy between her fingers. She cannot decipher whether she is being emptied out or filled up.

Chapter Twelve

Tom asks to meet Lucy on Sunday afternoon for a coffee date. This second date means that Lucy can text her mother in the middle of the week without guilt to decline her invitation to Sunday roast. When Lucy tells her mum that she can't come home because she has a date, this is satisfactory. Her mum is the kind of parent who will allow her children even the most heinous indiscretions if there were a whiff of a potential partner – which, of course, leads to marriage and grandchildren. Lucy wonders vaguely whether it matters that any children she has won't be technically related to their grandparents. She quickly flushes the thought from her mind, cringing away from the icky way it makes her feel. Mum has already given up hope of ever getting Danny out of the house and settled down with a partner. So the mantle of responsibility is placed squarely upon Lucy. She feels as though she is wading through thick mud these days. She is constantly on edge, her nails – under her new acrylics – bitten down to the quick.

Lucy and Tom make plans to meet in Richmond and go for a walk along the river. Lucy chooses a narrow blue summery maxi dress, ruched at the waist with a square-cut milkmaid neckline and huge billowing elbow-length sleeves. She feels powerful in this dress, which accentuates her décolletage, and makes her copper hair burn red in the sunshine. She feels like a regency heroine out of Austen.

She meets Tom outside the station and they head to a coffee shop on the High Street. As soon as they settle down in a window booth, Lucy becomes aware that she's being tested. Tom asks her things like, where did you grow up? And what do you like about your job? And do you think you'll stay there forever, then? What would you want to do next?

Lucy considers his questions with an affectation of thought-fulness as she sips from her oat milk flat white, taking care not to get any froth on her upper lip. She avoids specifics about her upbringing and family and instead focuses on a hypothetical future.

I think I'd like to run my own business one day, she says. She thinks of Delilah, who is always very busy and very immacu-lately dressed, save for the play-dough-looking earrings. Lucy would like to be that busy – not that she's not busy now. She is: she's been pulling eleven-hour shifts at work just to get the extra budget work done for the exec team. She wants to prove herself in her new almost-promotion. She wants to thrive. She wants to find a way to hide how much Delilah expenses her fancy Michelin-starred restaurant dinners with her husband on the company credit card. She wants the pay rise, most of all.

She still hasn't spoken to Anais properly, and she finds her-self awake at 5 a.m. worrying about that, too. She's been guilty about spending more time with Cam and that seems to make the canyon between Lucy and Anais ever wider. Lucy wasn't intending on picking sides in the break-up, but the fact that she lives with Cam makes it feel like she kind of is. And Anais seems a completely different version of herself, now they don't sleep under the same roof.

Perhaps all of Lucy's friendships are born out of proximity.

She wonders whether Jenny Akinfeo would ever have liked her at all if they hadn't sat next to each other in Maths and Geography for two years and bonded over a very loosely shared love of Guns N' Roses, which Lucy admittedly played up. At one point, when they were sixteen, Jenny told Lucy that she wanted her as maid of honour at her wedding. Jenny now works as a hostess at the Sky Garden, and they haven't spoken since college. Lucy wonders if this scenario will play out again between her and Anais.

On Wednesday, Cam had a spare salmon fillet and texted Lucy to see if she wanted it for tomorrow's lunch and they, along with Ash, who was home and awake at a human time for once, ended up making a stir-fry for dinner together. It was surprisingly pleasant, especially after Lucy had spent most of the day moving numbers around an Excel spreadsheet that seemed to make less and less sense the more she stared at them. She is, for the most part, exhausted. She feels her eyes dragging her whole face down as she travels home on the tube. She feels like it might slide off her head, wholesale. Lucy knows that she can't continue to work at her current output without it having some sort of impact on her mental, emotional and physical well-being. She has a Twitter account: she knows what #SelfCareSunday is. She's aware that her centre of gravity cannot go much lower to prevent her legs from giving out, and flinging her off the tightrope that she has strung out for herself. She doesn't say any of this to Tom. She says, Maybe something in fast-moving consumer goods. Stationery or handbags or something.

Tom smiles warmly. I can see you having your own little boutique out there on the cobbles, he says, pointing out the café window towards Richmond High Street. Lucy nods gamely. She likes the version of herself that he has constructed for them both.

Lucy notices that Tom keeps time with military precision. At three o'clock on the dot, he checks his Apple Watch and says, We'd better drink up, we've still got to go for a walk along the river.

This is the mandated portion of their date.

The timekeeping strikes Lucy as odd, but she reminds herself that she too has strange habits, like with her cleaning and tidying. She wonders what Tom will think of those traits in her, if and when she chooses to reveal them to him.

She imagines her wedding to Tom, which is something she likes to do very early on in seeing someone new. It helps her ascertain whether she is wasting her time. What's the point, she feels, in dating around if the ultimate goal isn't marriage? Lucy is vaguely aware that this approach is the exact opposite of what Meredith advised. But Tom seems nice. It doesn't seem fair on him to treat him as a casual fuck. So, the next logical step, for Lucy, is marriage. She imagines that they will get married on Tom's parents' property in Ascot; from what he has told her, it sounds like they've got a lot of it. She imagines her wedding dress and the table arrangements. Tom is an only child, so there's no need to worry about making a good impression with any of his siblings. His mother is dead, and his dad – from what Tom has told her – likes to keep himself to himself. Lucy thinks their children will be attractive enough: with Lucy's hair and jawline, and Tom's eyes. She imagines him meeting her family for the first time. Her mum, who is prone to hysterics in public; her dad, who chews tobacco incessantly and is never not wearing his fishing jumper. Her brother.

As they walk, Tom slips his hand into hers and fiddles with the ring on her middle finger.

I have to say, he tells her, I'm really pleased to see you in this dress.

Really? Lucy's skin warms, anticipating the compliment.

Yeah. I think it's so weird when women wear trousers.

They walk along in silence for a moment. A family of four on bicycles cycle past them on the towpath, the toddler almost careening into the geese picking lazily at tossed-out bread on the edge of the pavement.

I wore trousers the first time I met you, Lucy remembers aloud, making an effort to keep her voice matter-of-fact.

Oh, well, yeah. But that was just the once. Obviously you wear dresses too. And Tom makes a point of smiling at her dress – her midriff, really – in this sort of condescendingly approving way. It makes Lucy's insides squirm. She resolves to buy more dresses.

At the train station, they say goodbye. Tom is taking the District line and Lucy will take a mainline train back to Waterloo. They hug awkwardly on the bridge separating the platforms, and walk hurriedly in opposite directions. Lucy can feel her fingers trembling.

She can see him, now, on the other side of the station, three platforms away. A train pulls in and she spies him through both sets of windows. She texts him: *I really wanted to kiss you just now, but it felt awkward.* It feels romantic: the right thing to say in this moment. She imagines Tom reading the text and his insides doing a little dance of anticipation.

He takes his phone out of his pocket, on the other side of the station. She makes sure to hold her body in a way that exudes natural confidence and nonchalance, in case he happens to glance up and notice her standing there. The wind from the train tunnel wraps her regency dress around her legs in a way she imagines accentuates her hips. She lets the air thread its way through her hair. She feels rather powerful. On the opposite platform, Tom taps out a reply and returns his iPhone to the pocket of his tweed peacoat; he doesn't look up. She checks her phone; he has replied: *Haha yeah.*

On the train home, she watches her reflection in the window opposite her as it distorts with the curvature of the glass. At one moment, she looks effervescent and pretty in an unusual sort of way; the next, her face warps and she appears deformed. It has started to rain and the roof of the train clatters with the noise of it. Lucy can't tell whether the date was a success or a failure: at times, she felt like she was winning, and at others like he was standing over her ready to bring down the final blow.

She imagines herself now, as she appears to the world around her. To people like Tom. She has worked so hard and come so far to achieve this version of herself. But she can't stop thinking about the box in the back of her brain. The way she doesn't know who she is, truly. Who are her parents? The way the panic attacks keep happening. They are returning in earnest. She is losing control.

She arrives back at Flat 5 and sees that she has another two texts from her mum, and none from Tom. She takes out her ThinkPad and opens up her emails. It's Sunday and she wants, a little bit, to curl up under her duvet and die.

Chapter Thirteen

London is well and truly on its way to summer now, and the heavy fog of the season – a rusty, polluted haze of fast-food fat particles, the traffic fumes of idling buses and dust from the construction workers hammering into concrete with pneumatic drills on Lambeth Road – clogs up the air and settles thickly over everything south of the river, brown as the Bakerloo line. Lucy has taken to walking around the flat wearing earplugs to muffle the sound of the roadworks on the pavement just outside. Cam goes for long walks and Ash wears a pair of noise-cancelling headphones almost twenty-four hours a day. Lucy wonders why they have had to put up with Ash's noodling on their Fender at four in the morning when they could have plugged those fancy headphones into their amp and done everyone a favour. She doesn't raise it though. Ash is still a month behind on rent and Lucy wants to pick her battles.

How easy is it to get someone kicked out of your rental when you're illegally subletting? She texts Meredith who is still acting landlady for her father's HMO in Islington. From what Lucy can ascertain, the purchase of the house was something to do with a tax loophole. Meredith texts back the shrugging emoji.

Lucy works mind-numbing hours at Kube, struggling to

finalise the budget before the fiscal year-end. Anais seems to have checked out completely. Lucy cannot ascertain whether Anais's coldness towards her is because she is now her line manager, or because they don't live together any more and there is no need to maintain their friendship. Lucy instead behaves like her boss, mainly via the medium of passive-aggressive chaser emails and a light touch of micromanagement. Lucy knows Anais doesn't care about the job; that she'll leave as soon as she gets a better offer. But Lucy sees a future for herself at the company. She sees herself as part of the executive board, and likes to visualise herself stepping into her own personal private office at Kube for the first time, rather than the communal open-plan space where she has tried to spruce up her desk with a couple of succulents. She imagines the company rescued, thanks to her cost efficiencies and savvy resource management. She ignores the state of the finances on P&L documents that she is now privy to. She knows the personal private office is what is meant for her. She can feel it.

Any plans this weekend? Anais asks her unexpectedly one Friday afternoon.

Oh – me?

Yeah. What are you up to?

The sudden attention from Anais, after the coldness, is a little bit like whiplash.

Nothing exciting, Lucy says, squinting at her monitor as though she is reading a troubling email. How about you?

Nothing, really. I might pop over, if that's okay?

Lucy glances up at her. To Lambeth Road?

Yeah. Is that a problem?

No. No, of course not. You want to hang out or something?

Maybe, Anais says, distracted. Then she says, Will Cam be home, do you think? And things click into place.

Lucy tries to imagine what it must be like for Anais. To have left her boyfriend and home for a new relationship with Josh the personal trainer, which – if Jenna from Sales is to be believed – is already on the rocks. They've been arguing, Jenna told Kerry in the staff toilets while Lucy was washing her hands. He goes out all night and doesn't come home until the early hours. He's always coked up. He's got a bit of a temper, always getting into fights with other lads. He pulls girls at nightclubs and doesn't understand why Anais gets pissed off about it.

They shouldn't have moved in together so quickly, Kerry responded sagely. And with Anais straight out of a ten-plus-year relationship, too.

She's having second thoughts about it. But she's fucked it, hasn't she, really.

Kerry murmured in agreement and Lucy turned off the tap as quietly as she could.

I don't think Cam will be around, Lucy tells Anais. She is not sure what compels her to say this: truthfully, she has no idea what Cam is doing this weekend.

She has been spending more and more time with him: he invited her to a poker night at Paul and Francesca's, which turned out to be delightful. Meredith – a keen poker player – came too but had to leave early to meet Angus for dinner.

Lucy had never played poker before and it quickly turned out that her beginner's luck was really some serious skill.

Cam joked that she had the ultimate poker face.

Because she's so good at keeping secrets, he said. And then he grinned at her and she knew that she was meant to be in on the joke too. Meredith and Paul were arguing loudly about whose turn it was to deal and paying no attention at all to Cam and Lucy. It felt as though they were on an island, by themselves, and his eyes kept finding hers across the table to share a smirk at how poorly Meredith was masking her horror at the carrot batons nestled in a Tupperware between them – something of a hallmark of Paul's.

At the end of the game, they left and got a drink, just the two of them, at the Three Stags, and talked about nonsense for two hours. Lucy learned that Cam was best man at Paul's wedding and got so nervous about the speech that he couldn't eat anything all day; and then overcompensated afterwards by knocking back too much prosecco and falling asleep on a bench in the car park at 9 p.m. Paul has only recently forgiven him for it, but he was never really angry, anyway. Paul and Cam went to uni together and set up the Board Game Society at Cardiff. Lucy learned – in the brief portion of conversation where they talked about dating – that Anais cheated before, on her gap year to Thailand, and he forgave her. She, in turn, told him about Tom and trickle-down economics. She told him about how much she loves to swim, in the bright early morning before the world has woken up. How it makes her miss her dad. How she used to lifeguard when she was in college, and regrets that she never really kept it up.

Surely you can start again now, though, he questioned her.

What, start a new career as a lifeguard? She laughed. Okay, Cam. Sure.

Well – why not?

She narrowed her eyes at him. I have a job. I *love* my job. I'm on a trajectory at Kube.

She realised, even as she said it, that her words sounded insincere. She felt acutely as though she were a robot. As though she had trained herself to believe it. The thought disquieted her. She wondered what it was exactly that she loved so much about Kube, working for Delilah, supplier relations.

Cam can't swim very well, and therefore doesn't, but promised that he would try it, because Lucy tried Magic: The Gathering and poker.

I think you'll like it, she told him.

Unlikely, he replied, grinning and sipping his Guinness.

It makes you feel powerful.

He looked at her, with a strange expression on his face.

Don't you always feel powerful? he asked her.

She didn't know how to reply, so she looked at her hands and stayed silent.

Now, talking to Anais, she realises with total clarity that if Anais tried hard enough – if she says all the right things – Cam would forgive her, because it's in his nature to do so. Lucy unexpectedly feels a stab of jealousy at this, and it catches her by surprise.

Look, how *is* Cam? Anais asks her. He's not responding to my texts.

Lucy knows this because, at home, she has observed Cam receiving texts from Anais on his iPhone, glancing at the name and swiping to dismiss them without reading. It reminds Lucy of how she deals with her mother.

Cam's fine, I think, Lucy says, trying to keep her tone neutral.

The office is stone quiet, the ticking of the electricity in the warehouse-style light fixtures the only sound.

So – is Saturday or Sunday better? Lucy asks her.

What?

Is Saturday or Sunday better for you to come over?

Oh – actually, sorry, I think I have something on this weekend. Another time?

Lucy forces herself to smile, showing Anais all of her teeth. Absolutely. No problem.

Anais stuffs her phone, headphones and glasses case into her handbag. Her lip liner has bled slightly, giving the impression that she has hundreds of tiny razorblade-like crimson teeth circling her mouth. Lucy waits for her to leave, feigning some last check of paperwork so that they don't have to take the lift down to the ground floor together.

Lucy distracts herself from work, and her parents, and Danny, by spending weekends through July in pub gardens shielding her eyes from the sunshine with Tom, and meeting Meredith and Nara for late-night cocktails on the South Bank. Meredith is having a crisis about whether or not she is in love with Angus.

But he has a girlfriend. He brought her to Helen's party, Nara points out.

So? That doesn't mean I can't be in love with him.

I didn't take you for someone who fell in love. Like, at all.

Meredith shrugs and downs the dregs of her Long Island iced tea.

I'm getting another, she says, and saunters up to the bar.

How are you? Nara asks Lucy, while Meredith is gone.

Oh, I'm fine, thanks, Lucy says.

Really?

Yes, Lucy says, puzzled. Why?

Are we talking about Lucy? Meredith asks, returning to the table with fresh drinks.

Yeah.

Great, she says, slamming a cocktail down in front of Lucy and exhaling deeply. We're worried about you, girl.

What? Worried about *me*?

They are both looking at her intensely, Meredith's eyes narrowed and Nara's sympathetic.

You haven't said anything about – you know – finding out you're adopted, Nara says gently. You just mentioned it once and haven't said anything since.

The box is opening, opening, burning a hole in her head now, lighting a fire that flickers in her peripheral vision.

Have you spoken to your parents yet? Meredith asks.

Lucy brusquely shakes her head.

Maybe you should.

Lucy thinks of her parents, of the looks they gave her back at the wedding as she was getting into the taxi. She feels the dry stinging burn in the back of her throat, threatening tears. She swallows it down.

I don't know what to say to them.

Nara gently places a hand over Lucy's, a tender gesture that makes the crying even harder to deny.

Don't you want to know what happened? Meredith asks. Don't you want to know who your biological parents are? Why they kept it from you for so long?

Lucy looks at her hand underneath Nara's. Of *course* she wants to know the answers to these questions. But she has spent so much time and effort over the past couple of months closing the lid on the box that she doesn't truly know how she feels.

Surely, being numb is better.

Maybe you should talk to them and just see what they're pre-pared to say, Nara suggests. And then decide what you want to hear.

Lucy nods, feeling her eyes sting. Banburys don't cry. They *don't*. Especially not in front of Nara and Meredith.

We're here for you, Meredith says, uncharacteristically quiet-ly. Whatever you decide to do.

It is the look on Meredith's face that does it. She is so full of conviction in the way she says these words to Lucy. The box is open, and it leaks out the same cold metallic sensation of be-trayal from the night of the wedding. The looks on her parents' faces. The way they didn't come after her. This time, she lets it wash over her, lets it envelop her.

I'm angry, she says finally, Nara and Meredith still both staring at her. I'm so angry at them. I'm afraid of how angry I am.

I think that's a normal reaction, probably, Nara says.

I'm so scared of what they're going to tell me. I'm not sure I want to hear it.

Lucy has always thought that she was a certain kind of person: a Banbury. And ever since she left home she has been denying that part of herself: pretending that it – Mum, Dad, Danny – doesn't exist. She doesn't fully understand *why*, but nevertheless that is what she has done. But now. Now she was never a Banbury in the first place. So, what exactly *is* she? What version of herself is this one? What if it's the worst version of all of them?

On an evening in late July, Cam and Paul – via a newly created WhatsApp group for the three of them called GAMES NIGHT – invite her to join their Dungeons and Dragons group and, embarrassed by the prospect of fantasy role play, she says no. Lucy is not in many WhatsApp groups, so being in a new one gratifies her.

She overhears Cam and Paul and a few others playing one evening in the living room, with the windows notched as wide open as they can go, the frames at right angles, the passing traffic and the roadworks sending a breeze that nudges gently at the curtains, and she decides to creep in and watch. She is in a permanent state of trying to defrizz her hair, and the humidity only seems to get worse. She is fascinated by the characters each of Cam's friends role-play – a goblin, a gnome, a (sexy and semi-naked) elf and a human rogue. Cam is a whole other person with these friends, who banter with each other in affected received pronunciation accents and celebrate each other's successful dice rolls, commiserate their failures as though the game had real-life stakes and implications. They hatch elaborate madcap plans to evade the carefully crafted adventure that the gamemaster, Paul, has laid out for them. Lucy can't help but laugh with them.

Didn't you want to join? Cam asks Lucy, after the session is over and the group has left. You were more than welcome. He is washing up while Lucy sits at the kitchen table with her iPad. She is meant to be cleaning up her emails, but she is idly scrolling Instagram instead. She is composing a comment to go under Helen's photo of herself on a sunlounger next to a pool in the Maldives. She is trying not to think too hard about how sloppy Cam is being with the washing up.

No. I couldn't.

Course you could! You'd be brilliant.

As if! Do you know me at all? I'm the least off-the-cuff person ever. I'd never be able to improvise a goblin character or whatever. I'd be too self-conscious.

Cam harrumphs as he scrubs at his hands with a tea towel. Lucy notices that he has some dry skin in between his fingers.

You should get some moisturiser on that, she says, pointing to it.

He glances down. Oh, yeah. I never moisturise. I don't think I even own moisturiser.

Are you joking?

No. Anais was always on at me about it.

Lucy gets up and heads to her bedroom to get her own E45 cream from her bedside table. She returns with the moisturiser and he holds out his hands to her. Confused, she pumps a little into his palm. She glances up at him. He is waiting, a note of sort of *expectation* on his face.

Oh, you want me to do it? Lucy asks awkwardly, and Cam's face immediately flushes.

I thought that's what you were trying to do – sorry, he says, and snatches his hands away, roughly slapping them together and rubbing the moisturiser in. He has turned away from her.

Oh, for god's sake, Lucy says. Give them here.

And she shows him where the dry skin is, and massages the spaces between his knuckles until his hands are warm and smooth. It is, of course, as she anticipated, very strangely intimate. Cam has big, masculine hands. She can't look him in the eye, and she is almost certain that he can't look at her, either.

How long have you been playing Dungeons and Dragons with those friends? she asks, to cut through the tense silence that is beginning to envelop them.

Cam shrugs. Since the beginning of uni. Seven, eight years? It's the same campaign that we started on.

Lucy is shocked by this. I thought you'd only just recently started playing?

No. Why would you think that?

Well – those people, apart from Paul. I've never seen them here before.

That's because we never used to play here. We only played at Paul's and sometimes Aled's.

Aled is the sexy elf.

Lucy doesn't ask the question that she wants to: the question of *why* Cam has only now decided to invite his friends to the flat.

She knows it's because he thought she would judge him. She remembers Paul's whispered words at the front door that first night she hung out with them both. *I thought you said she was uptight.*

She wonders how low Cam's opinion was of her, before all this.

*

On the last day of July, Lucy decides to buy a sunlounger for the scrub of patio at the back of the flat. The concrete is hot with the sun, and the parks are heaving with tourists and weekenders trying to catch some of the unexpected heatwave that has descended upon the city and shows no signs of breaking any time soon. Lucy thinks, Fuck it and adds a paddling pool to her Lakeland shopping trolley, too. And then, Fuck it, again, and buys two extra sunloungers – one for Cam and one for Ash. They arrive in an obscenely large box the following week, the delivery man struggling to ram it through the front door into the narrow hallway of the flat.

Cam is out somewhere, and Ash is still asleep, recovering from last night's gig after which they got back to the flat at six in the morning with a guest and proceeded to have sex to Kate Bush on full blast in the box room. When Cam gets through the door, Lucy has already assembled the three loungers – yellow for her, green for Cam and purple for Ash – in the garden. She has swept away the cigarette butts and dust and detritus from the paving slabs, and mended the broken fence panel – something she is particularly proud of, having discovered an old toolbox behind the fridge – that allows the whole of Lambeth Road to peek into the garden. She has opened the window as wide as it will go. She has pumped up the paddling pool and filled it with cold water from the hose tap.

What's this? Cam asks, stepping out onto the patio, squinting at the newly assembled furniture.

Well, I thought it would be nice to be able to sit out here from time to time, Lucy says. Seeing as the weather's so nice and the parks are packed out.

He looks at what she's done, his eyes narrowed. Lucy realises that perhaps she has overstepped. This is a bit much. She always does this: misjudges a social scenario and either goes massively over the top or does nowhere near enough. It's Ash's welcome dinner all over again. *It's like she's desperate for us to like her.* Maybe Cam and Ash don't want to spend more time with her. Maybe it was silly to assume that they would.

It's brilliant, Cam says, grinning. He holds his hand up for a high five, which Lucy slaps limply. The sound is unsatisfying.

Let's tell Ash, Cam says.

He wakes them up and drags them out of their pit, bleary-eyed and nest-haired, into the garden.

I am hanging, Ash says miserably, out of my asshole.

Look what Lucy did, Cam tells them.

Ash looks at the newly renovated garden. It's the bare minimum: there are no plants or hanging baskets. The wood varnish is peeling away and the bins are overflowing. But Ash squeals with excitement.

LUCY! they shout. THIS IS AMAZING!

And they throw their arms around Lucy, unexpectedly. Ash smells like stale cigarettes and stale bedsheets. Lucy accepts the hug anyway, feeling slightly emotional.

The purple one's for you, she says, pointing it out.

Ash's eyes widen. Look, this is really lovely, but you know I can't give you any money towards it, right? I know I'm late on rent – don't worry, I'm on it – but I'm pretty much skint.

Lucy waves a hand at them. Of course I'm not expecting money for it.

And Ash beams again at her.

Let's call it a present to the flat. A welcome present, maybe.

This has made my day.

You only woke up five minutes ago, Cam says wryly. Is the bar that low?

I got misgendered four times last night. I felt like dogshit. But *this.* It's *exactly* what I wanted to do when I moved to London.

This is what you wanted to do? Cam asks them, incredulous.

Yeah! It's rad.

It *is* pretty rad, Cam agrees.

I want to do something to say thank you, though.

You can cook me dinner, if you like, Lucy replies. Vegetarian, of course. Sorry you got misgendered, though. She tentatively slips her arm through Ash's.

Ash shrugs, resigned. It's bound to happen when I'm this fucking fabulous, isn't it?

You're the most fucking fabulous person I know.

Agreed, Cam says.

And Ash queues up Fleetwood Mac's *Rumours* on Spotify and plays it out of a Bose speaker that they retrieve from their bedroom and balance on the kitchen windowsill, and Cam drags the paddling pool into the middle of the patio, and they set up their sunloungers so they can each dangle their feet into the pool, thrusting out from the centre of it, reclined, like a three-pronged star. And over the sound of Stevie Nicks, they can hear the pneumatic drill pummelling the concrete pavement out front. But it doesn't really matter. It is the perfect evening.

Chapter Fourteen

Lucy dreams that it's Christmas and she is back in Essex with her brother Danny and her father, decorating someone's house. The house is huge – a mansion, almost, something off *The Real Housewives* – with ceilings so high that Lucy can't reach them. She takes a ladder from the top of her father's van and leans it against the wall, but even with both feet on the top rung, legs wobbling, tense elastic bands stretched to snapping, she can't reach the ceiling to glide a paint-slicked roller across its surface.

For the children to accompany Daniel Senior to work over the holidays was a long-held tradition in the Banbury household. Her mum used to joke that Daniel Senior would have Lucy and Danny's future children out painting houses in the freezing dead of winter, fingers rigid around paintbrush handles and breath coming out in puffs of steam, while they were still in nappies. Daniel Senior would tell his children that to accompany him on jobs would teach them the value of hard work and an earned wage. This was before his injury, of course. Danny called it child labour, and he wasn't wrong. It always made for an awkward, not-quite-fully-jovial dig across the table at Christmas dinner. Remember when you pimped us out for painting and decorating, Dad? I wouldn't call it pimped, Danny. It was an important life lesson you needed to learn. Yeah, it felt like it when I took the top of my finger off with the sander and you sellotaped a bit of kitchen roll to it instead of taking me to the walk-in.

Despite the guff about learning about the world of work and the value of money, Lucy knows that the real reason that she and Danny were forced out on her dad's jobs was because the Christmas tips were extra generous if you had two pale, skinny dots in tow, holding paint cans as big as their heads and shivering on the doorstep of some footballer's mansion in Brentwood.

In the dream, Lucy still can't reach the ceiling on that top rung of the ladder, though she realises now that she's not a child in this dream but a grown woman. She looks to the base of the ladder and sees her father watching her.

Let me do it, he says, his face sagging with age.

No, your back, she replies.

Then let Danny do it. He's taller than you.

He can't, Dad. He's drunk.

And Danny is drunk and throwing screwdrivers at the wall in the bathroom – a giant ornate gold-plated monstrosity with a tub the size of a swimming pool. There's someone in the bathroom, there with Danny, but she can't work out who it is. It's just a shadow, really, cloaked in the corner of the room, or maybe lurking behind the door, ready to shut it with a soft click as soon as she looks away. She can feel the presence of it. The someone.

You're going to get us into trouble, Lucy tells Danny, and she feels as though she is maybe a child after all.

I don't care.

Danny.

Nothing worse, he says, than the trouble I'm already in. And the door to the bathroom slams, the loudest and most devastating of noises, and before it does, Danny is staring at her, this look of horror and desperation and despair on his face. She realises now that his mouth has disappeared, and in its place is a smooth stretch of pale skin.

And there is another noise, like screaming and metal on metal, that almost overlaps with the slam of the door, and now she sees her father at the bottom of the ladder, his torso bent, sickeningly misshapen, his eyes milky and glazed over.

Lucy wakes up panting, her neck slick with sweat and her hair pasted across her face. She realises that she's been crying in her sleep. She can still hear the voices from her dream, she thinks, but then she realises there are voices in the flat. Momentarily, she feels her heart drop out of her chest. The voices are coming from the hallway. She checks her phone, wondering whether to call the police or not, before recognising Cam's idiosyncratic inflection in the deeper voice. It's almost four in the morning and she'll need to be getting up for her swim before work in a couple of hours' time. Lucy wonders whether something has happened to wake up Cam and Ash. Then she realises that the other voice belongs to Anais, not Ash.

She speculates briefly about going into the hall to see what's going on. Or listening at her bedroom door, at the very least. But both of these actions seem far too invasive. She has a curious feeling in her belly, like she is falling.

Cam's voice, as it always is, is level and even-handed. Anais's voice rising, becoming more volatile. Lucy can tell by the tone that she is crying, or just about to cry, or has just stopped. Lucy rolls over and takes her earplugs from the bedside drawer. She texts Cam, her throat burning: *Can you two keep it down please?* And she returns to a fitful and unpleasant sleep.

She swims, in any case, despite the undersleeping, because she knows that it will clear her head and help her think rationally, but she cannot dispel the noise of metal upon metal, the ladder clattering to the floor. As she propels herself through the water on Tottenham Court Road, the sounds roar in her ears, louder than the water and the traffic and the city. She thinks of how her father used to swim with her, before she left home. How he loved to.

She steps onto the busy street outside the leisure centre and finds her dad's name in her phone, her bones aching, the memory of the dream, the noise of the ladder, thick in her mind. Her lungs feel as though they have too much air in them.

Loose? Her dad picks up on the second ring. It's only just gone seven in the morning, but he is an early riser: the longer he is stationary, the worse his back suffers, so he tries to sleep as little as possible.

Dad?

How are you, darling?

I've just been for a swim. Do you remember when we used to go together?

Every Saturday morning at the leisure centre.

And Mum used to meet us in the café afterwards for a cherry bakewell and a cup of tea.

Lucy can hear her father smiling down the phone. This was one of the small indulgences of her childhood.

Do you still go swimming, Dad? At the leisure centre?

No, no, chicken. Not any more. My back.

Lucy remembers the dream again. The metal screaming sound of the ladder as it happened.

Do you remember when you had your accident?

There is a pause down the phone as her dad considers this. Lucy waits, watching a cyclist pull up to the traffic lights and unclip his shoes from his pedals.

Yes, course I do.

Was it my fault?

What are you on about?

Was it my fault, that you fell off the ladder?

Lucy – what—

I just remember that I was meant to be spotting you. Support-ing you, putting my weight on the bottom rung, or something. And I got distracted by something Danny was doing and looked away, and took my weight off, and that's what made the ladder fall over.

Lucy can feel herself beginning to cry.

I'm so sorry, Dad. I didn't mean to do it.

Darling. Darling. What's all this? Stop crying. It wasn't your fault. It wasn't Danny's either.

Lucy stops, feels the grooves of her iPhone against the pads of her fingers.

Are you sure?

Never been more sure of anything. I was taking a short cut. Standing on the top rung to reach something when I should have extended it. It was my own bastard fault.

Lucy leans against the wall, her damp hair curling around her neck.

I could've sworn it was my fault, she tells him. She remem-bers, too, the things Danny whispered to her on the ambulance ride to the hospital, their dad the colour of ash, strapped to a board while a medic tried to steady him. The way Danny looked at her, hands locked around her wrists, while they were waiting for their mother to arrive at A&E. She came eventually, her hair whipped across her face as though she had been slashed with a knife.

Lucy hears her father sigh on the other end of the line. You've always had an overactive imagination, chicken, he says, firmly. When she doesn't say anything in response he asks, Will you come and see us?

She nods again, feels her mouth stretching into a silent grimace, the emotion trying to get out of her, but she won't let it. She can't.

I want to know about the adoption, she chokes out, her voice wonky. I want to know what happened.

We'll tell you all about it. We will. I'll talk to Mum.

Do you promise?

Yes. I promise. And, Lucy. No more of this nonsense about things that happened years ago. All right? There's no need to drag it all up.

Lucy feels as though she is going to die in this moment.

OK, Dad.

I love you.

I love you, too.

See you soon.

The line goes dead. And Lucy slides down the wall to the floor. Her fingers are trembling so violently that she drops her phone, face down on the pavement. She picks it up and sees that the screen has smashed into a spider's web of cracks, each of them meandering their own diversions across the glass.

At the office, she reapplies make-up in the bathroom. She monitors her breathing, her panic levels, as she does. She feels once again in control of herself and her emotions. Work will do that for her; that's why it's so important to have a good job that she enjoys.

At ten thirty, Anais exits the lift into the office, her hair a little dishevelled, her clothes creased. Upon closer inspection, Lucy sees that her eyes are red-raw and puffy and her make-up is at least twelve hours old. Anais throws herself into her desk chair, unceremoniously dropping her bag on the floor.

Is everything okay? Lucy asks, tentative, remembering the voices in the hallway last night.

Sorry I'm late, Anais replies.

That's not what I meant.

Anais shrugs, her expression defiant. She is daring Lucy to exercise some sort of authority over her. She knows, just as well as Lucy does, that Lucy really *has* no authority, even though she is now Anais's line manager. The waters of Lucy's role at Kube are now so muddied by the meta-promotion that she is becoming increasingly unsure of herself. One thing she *is* sure of is that everyone at Kube has noticed it. This uncertainty in the way she holds herself and speaks. When she delivers tasks in meetings, Jenna makes faces across the room at Kerry. Perhaps it was always there but has just become more pronounced as Lucy is now required to exercise power and control. She understands now that she is a target for people like Anais. Anais is daring Lucy to reprimand her. She knows that Lucy can't, and won't, do it. She has no power; she has no control. She never has. It's not in her nature.

Just let me know if I can help, okay?

You can tell me what the fuck's going on with Cam, for starters, Anais mutters, her tone bitter.

I meant more along the lines of work.

Anais rolls her eyes dramatically and fires up her laptop. Let's just get this day over with, she says.

That evening, Ash bounces into the kitchen, holding their Mac-Book in one hand in a manner that makes Lucy itch to snatch it from them and place it gently on the kitchen table, the lid softly closed. Ash is gleeful. They open the door into the garden and let out a jubilant screech into the sky.

What happened? Lucy asks as she adds bean sprouts to a hot wok.

I got a gig.

Oh. Really? That's great. Lucy arranges a smile on her face.

I mean, I got a *paid* gig.

Oh! Amazing!

Ash lets out another joyous scream and spins around the kitchen, their fringed blue kaftan billowing out behind them like a mermaid's hair.

I can't believe it, they say.

Where is it?

Camden Assembly. Will you come? *Please* say you'll come.

At this moment, Cam can be heard in the hallway returning from a training day at school. He pads into the kitchen in his socks.

What's going on? he asks at the exact same moment Ash says, Cam, I got a gig.

He gives them an incredulous look.

A gig?

A *paid* gig.

Oh! Well, shit. Congratulations! That's fantastic news. Where is it?

Camden Assembly.

Niiiiice, he says, nodding approvingly.

Ash grins. You have no idea what the Camden Assembly is, do you?

Cam shrugs and laughs.

Will you come and watch me? Ash asks Cam.

Lucy stares at her bean sprouts, the moisture leaking and bubbling out of them and mixing with the sesame oil sizzling at the bottom of the pan.

Yeah, sure. I don't see why not. You coming, Lucy?

Lucy looks up, not expecting to be called upon.

When did you say it was?

Friday. And then, reluctantly, Ash says, I'm not on until mid-night, but you know. We can get drinks before or something. You could bring some friends if you like. Lucy, you could invite Tom.

Lucy almost laughs aloud at the thought of Tom in his tweed and his chinos and loafers at Ash's gig. She and Tom have been keeping to a timetable of dates over the past month or so, almost religiously. Tom invites her for a drink every Tuesday after work and they sometimes end up going back to his flat to watch a film together. Normally something about the war: Tom's choice. She has learned that he is very into Airfix modelling. They haven't had sex yet, but she thinks they probably will soon. It's not that Lucy doesn't want to; it's just that Tom seems to be waiting for something, but she's not sure what. On Sundays, they normally go for dinner in the early afternoon, followed by a long walk. She likes that he is interested in her; that he texts to ask her how her day has been. Twice he has sent flowers to her office, to her public delight. His blatant affection for her warms her bones. Lucy has never been involved with anyone who is so obviously mature, emotionally healthy and put-together. It makes a nice change for her. With Tom, she can imagine herself as the version of herself that she is meant to be.

Yeah, maybe I'll invite him, she says.

Maybe I'll invite Anais, Cam says, staring out the window absent-mindedly.

Anais? Ash says, incredulously.

He looks at Lucy rather than Ash as he answers. Yeah. Why not?

I thought you dumped her.

Well. She's having a hard time at the moment. She needs a friend.

It's settled, then, Ash says brightly. I'll be fifth-wheeling you at my own gig. I love it. It's perfect. I'm going to wear my big stompy boots.

They let out another yelp and sprint into their bedroom, a thousand pounds' worth of laptop still thrust aloft like the torch of Lady Liberty; moments later, Lucy hears them on the phone with their nan, sharing the good news.

Sounds like fun, Cam says to Lucy's back.

She feels him looking at her. Feels the sleeve of his sweatshirt brushing against her as he moves past her to get to the fridge. She lets the bean sprouts fry long past their due, prodding at them with a wooden spoon. She notices that Cam is waiting for her to reply. For some reason, she is afraid to turn and meet his eyes.

Yes, I'm sure it will be, she says eventually.

Lucy texts Tom about the gig and is surprised when he accepts enthusiastically. They meet for dinner at Ichibuns, an oriental-American fusion place in Soho's Chinatown that serves cheeseburger spring rolls. But the Friday-night bustle of the place, heaving with tourists and after-work city revellers and tipsy girl gangs, means it's almost impossible to maintain a conversation.

Tom has come straight from work and is wearing a dark navy Hugo Boss suit, with a pink shirt underneath with a matching silk pocket square. Lucy appreciates the attention to detail with the pocket square and the fact that Tom is wearing brown distressed-leather shoes which offset the formality of his work clothes. The suit is tailored to make him look slim and tall with broad shoulders. Lucy is wearing a black ballerina skirt of gathered tulle and a buttoned cream-coloured ribbed vest with spaghetti straps, her hair – freshly oxblood-tinted – scrunched into a low bun at the base of her neck and a pair of gold-plated chandelier earrings with marine-blue Greek evil eyes set into them.

Are you looking forward to it? Tom shouts as they are waiting to be seated.

What. Ash's gig? she shouts back.

Yeah.

Yeah. I am. Are you?

Yeah, I've never been to a gig before.

Lucy raises her eyebrows at him and he nods, confirming.

Why?

I just don't like live music that much. I don't like any music, really.

Oh.

How about you?

Lucy shrugs non-committally as they sit down.

When things were really truly awful at home, with Danny, when she was sixteen, seventeen, she saved up all her money from her lifeguarding and escaped to West London. She spent her nights hovering alone at the backs of places like the Astoria (demolished for Crossrail), the Hammersmith Palais (demolished for luxury student accommodation) and Earls Court (demolished for a new 'urban'(?) housing development), her arms ringed with plastic fluorescent shag bands, black nail polish chipping, waiting for Hayley Williams or Mark Hoppus or Brendon Urie to come onstage and rearrange her worldview. She spent hours scouring YouTube for new music to obsess over. It's been a while since Lucy spent a week trailing some obscure American midwestern emo band around pubs in Kingston. Lucy knows how to dress for a gig, especially in the summer, and this is not it. If it were up to her, she'd be in a pair of jeans. But, of course, Tom has already expressed his feelings on women in trousers. And Lucy is a different kind of person now.

She learns some other things about Tom: that he wants to have three to four children and to live on a farm, somewhere that is rural enough but also within a commutable distance of London. Maybe on the outskirts of Guildford, he thinks. Or maybe Redhill, which is a straight train ride to Monument station where he disembarks for work. Here is the life that he has so clearly mapped out for himself. It's surprising how easy it is for Lucy to imagine herself fitting into that life. She wonders whether she could push herself to have children, though it's something she has never previously been interested in. Lucy feels that the sacrifice required by women to enjoy the maternal burden is too great: that she'd rather disappoint her parents and live a moneyed and cosmopolitan life as a high-powered executive. It seems almost impossible to her that one could ever do both: she can't think of a single woman in her own life who has done it successfully, except maybe Delilah who has generational wealth. Lucy doesn't have generational wealth; Tom, whose father is nouveau-riche, will have an inheritance earmarked already. Being with someone like Tom suddenly makes the whole world seem a little more accessible to Lucy. Tom has such clear goals and aspirations. If he wanted to move to Dubai tomorrow, he could. She wonders what her mum would say about all this, and then immediately feels the stab of guilt and shame at the thought of her. She wouldn't know what Erica thought, because she doesn't know about Tom. She doesn't know much about anything going on with Lucy at the moment, because Lucy has made certain that this is the case. She remembers her dad's words on the phone to her, asking her to come home. Maybe it's time, she thinks. Maybe it's time to sort this out. Maybe it's time to open the box.

Are you okay? Tom asks her, biting into his third cheeseburger spring roll. He has a little bit of melted cheese stuck in the corner of his mouth, clinging to a wiry strand of his beard. Lucy has ordered a bowl of teriyaki chicken udon. The decor of the restaurant, she notices, is a mishmash of American and Japanese cultural references. A plastic mould of a Cadillac is fused convulsively to the wall, manipulated to fit inside the mock interior of a minka.

I'm fine, thanks, Lucy says, taking a small sip of her sake. She feels as though she could gulp it down in one mouthful. But caning booze in front of Tom is not part of the version of herself that she has been cultivating for him.

They sit quietly for a little longer, finishing their food. Lucy is somewhat relieved that they can't really talk over the swelling noise: she's not sure, she realises, how long she could maintain a conversation with him.

After the meal, they walk to Snog and Tom buys them each a miniature tub of frozen yoghurt. This is difficult for Lucy and something of a push for her, because she tends to avoid eating food standing up or on the street. Tom chooses salted caramel for himself and Lucy goes for the matcha tea, which she immediately regrets because the first scoopful that melts on her tongue confirms that it tastes disgusting.

Is yours nice? Tom asks.

She wrinkles her nose at him and shakes her head.

Can I try some of yours?

He widens his eyes at her, horrified, and then laughs awkwardly. Lucy laughs too, not quite sure what the joke is. He doesn't offer and she doesn't ask again.

It's only ten o'clock, but Lucy begins to worry that they are going to run out of things to do soon, and things to talk about.

Why don't we head over to the bar now? Lucy asks. We can watch some of the acts that are on before Ash.

Tom shrugs his agreement and they descend to the Northern

line. The tube is very busy and Lucy doesn't have to look at Tom or interact with him here. She is pressed against the window and she feels claustrophobia settling over her and compressing her chest. But the doors to Camden Town open just before the scream that is bubbling away in her throat can escape from her lips. She follows Tom up the escalator and out onto the busy Friday night high street.

Chapter Fifteen

The Camden Assembly's upstairs room is only half-full by the time they arrive. They queue on the stairs for their tickets, Tom below and behind Lucy. She stares straight ahead, feeling her nerves prickling at her skin like needlepoints. Tom is saying something to her but she cannot hear him. Eventually, he leans up and shouts in her ear.

You could turn around and look at me while I'm talking to you, you know.

Lucy, heart hammering, pastes on an apologetic smile. She turns around and sees the stairs, steep and narrow, falling away into darkness.

She says, Why don't we swap places, then?

This is easier than explaining.

They each collect a stamp for their hands from a girl on the box office with neon-green hair styled into four-inch spikes. Tom smiles politely at her and then at Lucy.

Ready? Lucy asks.

They head into the venue portion of the pub: a low stage with a PVC banner for a three-months-out-of-date noughties indie club night slung up against the back wall. The space itself is small: probably fitting no more than two hundred people. The bar is tucked into the corner, with one harried-looking bartender fielding a throng of fifteen or twenty punters all crowded around him, the sticky skin of their bare arms touching. The place, Lucy remembers from the last time she was here to watch an Australian all-girl emo band, is grubby and loud and haphazard. Everyone seems to be vaping despite the distinct NO VAPING signage dotted around. There is no one onstage at the moment, with tech guys assembling the instruments ready for the next act.

Do you want a beer? Tom asks Lucy, a wary expression on his face as he eyes a group of five girls aged no more than nineteen or twenty, with e-girl stripes in their hair, nose rings and flared trousers in a variety of pastel hues sitting cross-legged in a circle on the floor.

Lucy nods enthusiastically, forcing a smile, and he disappears into the crowd at the bar, his monogrammed leather wallet retrieved from inside his jacket, glasses gently steaming.

And then, near the front of the room, leaning against the wall with two red cups in his hands, Lucy spots Cam, all six-plus-feet of him clearly visible above the heads and shoulders of the other people dawdling near the stage. She waves enthusiastically at him, and after a moment spent trying to catch his attention, he notices, grins and waves back at her. She makes to move through the crowd to join him at the edge of the room, but he is also moving towards her, so they end up in the middle of the throng of people, squished against each other. Cam holds his two drinks aloft so that they aren't jostled by the crowd.

GOOD TO SEE YOU, he shouts at Lucy.

YOU TOO, she says.

WHERE'S TOM?

HE'S GETTING DRINKS. WHERE'S ANAIS?

SHE'S GONE FOR A CIGARETTE.

AH, OKAY.

They stare at one another awkwardly for a moment, the gawky

smile on Cam's face surely mirrored in Lucy's own, she thinks.

SHALL WE GET OUT OF THIS CROWD? he suggests after a moment and they elbow their way out of the throng of people to the opposite wall.

Lucy perches on the windowsill. She looks back to the crowd and realises how big, how suffocating, the wash of bodies looks from the outside.

Coming to places like this reminds me how close to thirty I am, Cam tells her mock-despairingly.

I don't know. Most of these teenagers are dressing how I used to dress in my emo phase, Lucy replies.

You had an emo phase? Cam is delighted, his face breaking into a conspiratorial grin, his eyes glittering.

Don't laugh.

Not at all. This is thrilling news. He playfully elbows her in the ribs and she laughs, noting how 'not at all' is something of a catchphrase of his, an idiosyncrasy, and tucking that piece of information away in her brain, some sort of personal secret triumph of her very own.

I would have loved to meet baby emo Lucy, Cam says.

Trust me. You wouldn't. I was miserable and socially awkward.

No different from now, then, he says.

I don't know whether or not to take offence at that, she says, feeling her smile waver a little.

Trust me, Cam tells her. It's a compliment. A cactus is the best kind of person.

Prickly, you mean.

Yep. But resilient. And, you know ... something about flowers. The metaphor ends there, I think, he says, frowning comically.

Lucy wonders whether Cam is flirting with her. She suddenly feels deeply self-conscious, feels a blush creeping up her neck.

She has lost the levity of her demeanour and now she can't think how to continue the banter.

So, how's it going? she asks instead, struggling to keep her tone as light as before.

Yeah, good, thanks. How about you? He takes a small sip of lager from one of the cups.

Yeah. Good. We went to Ichibuns for dinner. Have you been? Cam shakes his head.

It's like Japanese-American fusion dining. So delicious.

Wow. Sounds good. Me and Anais had a Nando's.

A Nando's? That doesn't sound like Anais.

Yeah – well – I'm on a teacher's wage. So if she insists on me paying, she's going to have to forgo the Japanese-American fusion dining.

Lucy feels her face flooding with colour again, inexplicably. But he's smiling, the corners of his eyes crinkling.

I'm just teasing you, Banbury, he says.

Now who's the cactus? she replies, her hands trembling a little.

They watch the crowd without talking, and she feels her pulse return to a normal rate. Lucy's mind is racing to think of something else to say to Cam, ever desperate to fill the silence. She must remind herself that Cam is a naturally quiet person. It's okay to be quiet sometimes. It's quite nice, actually. She notices Anais pushing her way past the bouncer, flashing her hand stamp in his face. Anais marches over to Cam and Lucy where they are standing.

Hey, she says, smiling broadly. Somewhat disconcertingly, since Anais is still ignoring Lucy at work. The only time Anais speaks to Lucy these days is to ask what's going on with Cam.

Hi, Anais, how's it going?

Anais smiles swiftly and wanders over to Cam, snaking an arm through his. She plucks the second beer from his hand.

Where's your boyfriend, Lucy? Cam said he was coming.

Tom. He's not really a *boyfriend*. He's just at the bar getting drinks.

I just think it's so cool you've met someone.

Oh . . . really?

Anais is still smiling at her, showing all of her teeth, her whole body angled into Cam. Yeah. After such a long time, right? It must get so lonely being single. You poor thing. I don't know how you do it.

I wonder what Ash's set is going to be like, Cam says quickly, extracting his arm from Anais's, as though he has only just noticed that they are linked.

Ash bounces over to them, then, and pulls each of them individually into big enveloping hugs, including Anais.

Nice to meet you, they tell her enthusiastically, I've heard so much about you.

It takes Lucy a second to realise that they've taken something. They have an overstimulated, skittish look about them, in the same way that Meredith does after she's done one too many bumps of mandy in the Clapham Infernos toilets.

Anais wiggles her eyebrows at Ash, All good things, I hope, she laughs.

Nah, not really, Ash says, a genuine beaming smile still stretched across their face.

Anais stiffens a little before laughing again, her eyes nervously darting to Cam's face. He seems to be watching the next band doing a hasty soundcheck and hasn't heard what Ash said. Lucy takes out her phone and pretends to see an important text, and taps out a rapid, non-existent reply.

Moments later, Tom sidles up next to her, with two more red cups.

Hi, he says, smiling a little too brightly.

Oh. Guys, this is Tom. Tom, this is Ash, Anais, Cam.

Nice to meet you, Tom says, flicking out his hand to dispel the spilled beer and holding it out to shake. It seems awfully formal after Ash's bear hugs, but each of them oblige him with a handshake.

Lucy realises now how completely removed this scenario is from a normal Friday night for Tom, at his whisky club or dining in one of the late-night gastros around Liverpool Street. It occurs to her that he looks incredibly out of place amidst the clientele of the club – even among their small group, all of whom, besides him, have dressed casually, with Cam in jeans and a fitted black T-shirt that shows off (to Lucy's surprise) built triceps and smooth elbows, and Anais in a pair of pleather leggings, an oversized Led Zeppelin shirt and her trademark perfectly drawn cat-eye eyeliner. Ash is the exception to the rule in their usual bohemian mess – tonight wearing the fringed gold flapper dress they tried to put Lucy in for her first date with Tom, with a silky green kaftan artfully draped over their shoulders, scuffed Doc Martens and at least two chunky gold rings shoved on each finger. Their thick dark curls are knotted up with a golden lamé bandana, strands exploding out of them and exploding outwards. They look manic and beautiful. From afar, Lucy realises, their little group probably looks quite odd.

So, you're the girl whose gig we're watching, is it? Tom asks Ash conversationally.

It takes Lucy a fraction of a second to realise that Ash has stiffened next to her. Ash points sheepishly to their they/them pin, which is fastened, glittering, to the hem of their kaftan.

Oh, Ash isn't a girl, Cam says quickly, offhandedly, though Lucy can see that his jaw has tensed, as though he is speaking through gritted teeth.

It's no problem, Ash says, laughing uneasily, as they turn away to shout something at one of the techies on the stage.

Lucy explained Ash's pronouns and gender identity to Tom on the walk over from the station, but he seems to have forgotten already.

Ash has now run off to tune their guitar – or whatever it is they need to do before they're on. Cam engages Tom in a conversation about work and listens with increasing detachment as Tom explains in great detail the benefits of the Lifetime ISA versus the Help to Buy ISA and, if Cam wanted to get on the property ladder, which one he should go for. Cam catches Lucy's eye and shoots her a knowing smile – a smile that says, *Really, this guy?* And Lucy can't help but grin back at him. She immediately feels a stab of guilt about it: she and Cam are making a joke at Tom's expense. Tom is actually a very nice, very stable and generous sort of person. He is driven and motivated. These are indisputable facts.

Lucy avoids making further eye contact with Cam and instead stands next to Anais, her eyes fixed intently on the stage.

So . . . what's new with you? Lucy asks Anais, feeling incredibly awkward.

Anais glances at her. Not much.

Lucy nods in what she hopes is a thoughtful way.

Things are going good with Cam, actually, Anais comments.

Really? That's great.

Anais turns to Lucy and smiles now, squeezes her elbow lightly.

I think we might get back together.

Aren't you still with Josh, though? Josh the personal trainer? Lucy can't help but ask, ignoring the way her throat is burning.

Well. Yeah. But that's not the point, really.

It's not?

What me and Cam have, it's *so* much bigger than this little thing with Josh. It's like . . . life-altering, you know? We were going to get married.

Yeah. He told me.

Cam told you that? Anais looks at her again, her eyes narrowing.

Before Lucy can answer, the compère has emerged from the side of the stage and introduced Ash Marsh. A half-hearted round of clapping precedes Ash themself floating onto the stage, clutching in one spindly hand, wrists jangling with bangles up to the elbow, the neck of an electro-acoustic guitar that seems far too big for them. They plug it in and settle on a bar stool in front of the mic. They don't say anything at all. They carefully and methodically remove their bangles and the rings on their fingers (what was the point of them, then? Lucy wonders) and strums out the opening chords to the song, tentatively as though they are a newborn foal standing up on its own for the first time. Seemingly satisfied, Ash launches immediately into an energetic and throaty version of Fleetwood Mac's 'Second Hand News'. It seems bizarre at first – Ash in their hippie garb, the unaccompanied guitar, and their smoky voice against this upbeat song and their tiny frame draped in all the colours of the rainbow. But after Lucy's ears get used to the noise, the way Ash's voice juxtaposes against the melodic guitar strings, she begins to enjoy it. The rest of the crowd seem to be enjoying it too, several of them clapping along and some of them stomping their feet.

When Ash finishes, there is an uproarious round of applause, with whooping, screaming and cheering, before they immediately continue with the set, with barely a moment's pause, diving head first into a cover of Jefferson Airplane's 'Somebody to Love'. Soon, the whole floor seems to be vibrating with the collected enthusiasm of the crowd: Lucy and Anais merge into the wash of people – nearer the back – and dance together, screaming at Ash as they do. The unpleasantness between them is forgotten in this moment.

And then there's a slower one – an Ash original – about second-chance love. The lyrics are moving and heartfelt, and Lucy finds herself swaying with the rest of the crowd. She hasn't noticed that Tom has finished telling Cam about stocks and shares investments and has meandered through the crowd to slip into the gap next to her.

Are you having a good time? Lucy asks him, trying not to shout too loud so as not to disturb the quietness of Ash's love ballad.

Yeah, great, Tom replies, and then says, You look beautiful tonight.

Lucy smiles at him, trying to accept the compliment gracefully, but the way Tom says it seems insincere. The smile does not reach his eyes. It seems suddenly very obvious to her, in a moment of clarity, that Tom is pretending too – just as much as she is. Even more so, when he slips his hand down her back and rests it tentatively on her right bum cheek. As soon as the song is finished, he smiles at her again – that same smile that doesn't go all the way to his eyes – and kisses her on the cheek. She notices that he keeps glancing over to Cam, who is still leaning against the wall in the same spot, transfixed by Ash's performance, oblivious to them both.

She excuses herself to the bathroom and stands in one of the hot cubicles, the walls scrawled with love notes between girls. She counts to ten, flushes the toilet and washes her hands, running some cold water across the back of her neck and her wrists for good measure. When she returns, she stands on the right-hand side of Anais so that Tom can't get to her.

Ash finishes their set to a jubilant uproar from the crowd.

They leave the stage with a grin that splits their face in half, and are immediately mobbed by a group of excitable girls while the next band sets up their equipment on the stage. Lucy can feel her heart swelling on behalf of Ash and this glorious moment.

Anais pulls out her phone and slinks out for a cigarette. Tom offers to get a round in and disappears back into the crush of the bar queue.

So that's what they've been doing in their bedroom this whole time, Cam says, sidling up to Lucy and nudging her in the ribs. What did you think?

I'm in shock, to be honest, Lucy replies.

I can't believe they've been playing gigs for free.

They watch as Ash extricates themself from the gang of squealing girls before being stopped by a couple who talk at them animatedly while they stare, beaming, and a little dazed.

I'm so happy for them, Lucy says without prompting.

Me too, Cam says.

Tom returns with drinks and tries to talk to Cam about hunting. Lucy has noticed that he talks a little bit too loudly, that his laughs are slightly forced.

I'm not really into hunting and shooting and that, Cam tells Tom.

Tom scoffs, the noise exaggerated again. That's what they all say, he replies.

Who do you mean, 'they'?

Oh, you know.

Cam turns his whole body to Tom, an expression of annoyance on his face.

No, Cam replies, I want to know what you meant. Own it.

Oh, I don't know . . . people from Slough, let's say, Tom replies with another forced laugh, shrugging.

That's not what you were saying, though, was it?

Cam's voice is level and calm and even friendly, but hostility radiates from him like heat, and Lucy can see that Tom is turning away from him, his smile faltering, looking at Lucy for help. She herself can't speak. She has never seen either of them behave like this before.

Anais returns from the smoking area and immediately starts complaining about the bouncer who was checking her out.

What do *you* think of hunting, Anais? Tom asks unexpectedly, cutting into her speech as soon as she pauses for breath, and Lucy feels herself going rigid. She sees Cam's exasperated expression.

Hunting? Anais asks, quirking one eyebrow.

Yes. You know. Pheasants, foxes, that sort of thing.

Oh, God. It's awful. You don't *hunt*, do you, Tom? I only eat white meat, you know.

Tom glances at Lucy again, nervously. I only do it on my dad's land, he says, uncertain, once he's realised that Lucy isn't going to help him out. It's pest control, really.

Pest control, my arse, Anais replies, waving a hand in dismissal. It's sad men with tiny willies desperately trying to overcompensate.

Lucy snorts despite herself and, seeing the look on Tom's face, immediately regrets it. She realises that Anais is a bit drunk, actually. She's a bit drunk, too. She suddenly wishes that Tom weren't here at all.

Ash returns to the group and tells them that they're going to stay and watch the rest of the bands. It's bad manners to leave after your set.

I think we're calling it a night, Tom tells them, answering for Lucy too. Cam makes pointed eye contact with her, eyebrows raised quizzically.

What do you want to do? Cam asks Anais.

Maybe we could go on somewhere else? Anais replies, and

at Cam's confused expression, she stands up on tiptoes to say something into Cam's ear. But because she's drunk, and he's so tall and she's less than five-two, she doesn't quite reach his ear and has to shout over the music anyway. Everyone can hear what she says: Let's go somewhere quiet to talk.

Cam sort of shrugs and nods at her and they each say goodbye, and Ash does another round of bone-crushing hugs, earrings pressed against cheeks, still hyperactive from the high of the performance and, Lucy guesses, a controlled substance or two.

Lucy and Tom, and Cam and Anais, say goodbye outside the venue and head off in different directions. Tom insists on accompanying Lucy home before catching the night tube back to Chiswick. On the almost-empty Bakerloo line tube, he sits opposite her, a stony unreadable expression on his face. He says nothing as they walk from Lambeth North tube station to Flat 5. It occurs to Lucy that Tom hasn't seen where she lives before and she feels suddenly self-conscious.

Do you want to come in? she asks Tom at the door, wondering why she's even bothering. She doesn't know if she even fancies him any more after tonight. She is wondering, actually, if she ever liked him at all.

I don't know, Tom says.

Is everything okay? she asks him, feigning ignorance.

Yes, fine, thanks. I'll come in for a bit.

She pours him a neat gin and they end up having underwhelming, saliva-heavy sex – their first time together – on the living-room sofa. This is not Lucy's first choice, but Tom seems really into it, so she lets him. She will need to hot-wash the blankets tomorrow, now. Afterwards, he lies heavy on top of her for a little too long for comfort, until she starts shivering beneath him and insists they go to the bedroom.

As soon as they're under the duvet, Lucy lets out a big fake yawn.

You really embarrassed me tonight, Tom tells her quietly, taking off his glasses and setting them on the bedside table.

What do you mean?

You didn't stick up for me. With the whole hunting thing. You kept flinching away from me when I tried to touch you. I don't know what's going on with you.

I'm sorry, Lucy says. I didn't realise I was doing that.

We're meant to be together, aren't we?

Are we?

I thought we were.

Oh. Okay. Well, I suppose we are, then.

When you're in a partnership, you need to have each other's backs.

Lucy says nothing, the word *partnership* dancing spasmically around her head, and she stares up at the black ceiling, hoping that he has ended the conversation, and he will now go to sleep. Her heart is fluttering in a way that makes her feel unsafe, as though she will not be able to breathe once she has fallen asleep.

Tom rolls over to spoon her from behind, locking her into place with his arms. She can feel his flaccid dick, cold and damp, against the back of her hamstring and it takes all her energy to stop herself from flinching away from it.

Don't ever do that to me again, Tom says quietly.

Chapter Sixteen

The next morning, Lucy wakes before Tom and stares up at the ceiling, heart hammering, her torso locked to the bed under his forearm. She is trapped beneath him. She can hear a pneumatic drill from the roadworks outside. There is a tea-coloured stain that has appeared on the spot on the ceiling directly above her head. Tom's clothes are crumpled in the corner of the bedroom. She forgot to close the curtains last night, and she can see through her window the silhouette of a bedraggled cherry tree against the lush blue of the morning sky. The last of the blossoms, brown and dehydrated, cling to the twigs that fringe the branches. There is a tree exactly like this one outside her childhood bedroom window, back home.

She thinks about the last summer at home with her parents and Danny. The blossoms bloomed late that year, too. She was seventeen years old, almost ready to go to university. She already had her conditional place confirmed at Imperial and had spent most of the summer selling her old, most juvenile things on eBay, and deciding what needed to be taken when she moved into her flatshare in September. Lucy had done it: she was going to live in London. She was getting out of this house.

The prospect of university was always deeply appealing to Lucy: a new place, somewhere that no one knew her, where she would reinvent herself completely from the ground up. She was *tired* of being the lanky ginger girl who didn't talk, with the alkie brother. She felt as though she had marionette strings tied around her wrists and ankles and neck and she was being dragged into the ground. She felt that she had become the smallest possible version of herself. She was ready to be someone else: someone better.

Danny spent most of his time outside, building the shed in the garden that would one day become his studio, his sweatshirt off and slung over the edge of the fence, and cans of cider lined up neatly along the flower bed. The work was difficult. Uncle Marv sometimes helped Danny measure and cut wood, pour concrete into foundations or whatever it was that they needed to do. They listened to Absolute Radio on the DAB propped against the patio, and Lucy heard it through her open bedroom window; she spent most of her time making lists, sticking colour-coordinated Post-it notes to her lilac wallpaper. She separated the possessions she hadn't already sold into things she wanted, things she needed, things she could throw away and things of sentimental value that were ultimately useless to her.

She tried not to talk to Danny, whenever she could avoid it. Even though she was seventeen and he was in his twenties, he treated her like they were both still children. If she passed him too close in the kitchen, he reached out and pinched the skin above her elbow, hard, bruising her. It had been a long time since Lucy made any attempt to stop this sort of behaviour. She realised that the crying and screaming she did when she was younger – *Danny is hurting me* – was interpreted by her parents as the behaviour of someone who was soft, and the Banburys were not soft. Lucy found it easier to put up with it than to tell on Danny and risk the poor opinion of her parents who didn't believe her. Perhaps she was a liar: perhaps she had imagined all of it. But she felt his presence, the malicious energy rolling off him in waves, when he yanked a small clump of her hair while she washed her father's dishes at the sink. She knew that when she got into university, got away, she'd never have to think of him again. This was the moment, in the very near future, that she could truly become herself.

Lucy extracts herself from the vice-like grip of Tom's arms, that have been locked around her all night, making her sweat and ache and her pulse flutter nervously. She throws on a T-shirt and pads into the living room to get the blankets on the sofa washed. Her head is pounding with too much beer and not enough water before bed. She opens the coffee table drawer and dry-swallows two ibuprofen, the chemical film of the tablets coating her tongue and making her teeth chalky. It is then that she notices Cam lying on an airbed behind the sofa, sandwiched between it and the wall, a sleeping bag twisted awkwardly around him and bunching at his ankles. He is staring at his phone, which he holds directly above his face, his arms straight vertical lines. He hasn't noticed Lucy yet.

Hi, she says, and he drops his phone on his face.

Morning.

You didn't sleep on this couch last night, did you?

No way. The floor's more comfortable than that thing. Why?

No reason. And Lucy collects up the blankets that cover the cushions. I'm just going to give these a wash.

Lucy Banbury, Cam says, a sort of repulsed yet triumphant smile spreading further across his face, you dirty dog.

I don't want to talk about it.

Whatever you say, pal.

Why are you in here, anyway?

Anais was a bit too drunk to go home last night, so I thought I'd throw her in my bedroom instead of trying to get her back to

Josh the personal trainer all the way in Walthamstow.

Cam's voice is light as he says this.

How're you feeling about all that? Lucy asks, feeling brave, as she stuffs the blankets into the laundry basket.

Cam shrugs.

Where did you end up last night? Must have been a heavy one.

Only at the Three Stags, but she ordered shots. I told her I want to be friends. She's a bit of a mess at the moment. I'm worried about her.

I think she had the impression you were getting back together, Lucy says, feeling guilty for gossiping, but nevertheless compelled to tell Cam.

I think I've been unintentionally sending some mixed signals, Cam replies, sheepishly.

You care about her.

A statement, not a question. Cam nods.

We'll just see what happens now, he says.

Lucy busies herself in the kitchen. As she boils the kettle, she scrolls through her unanswered WhatsApp messages: two from Meredith inviting Lucy to a warehouse rave last night; one from Nara that reads simply *Have you spoken to your mum yet?*; and the most recent one from Anais earlier this morning. It is a picture of her, a selfie taken in Cam's bed, the light streaming through the curtains behind her. She is twisted around, half her face burrowed into the pillow, a coquettish expression on it. She looks beautiful – even in old make-up and bird's-nest hair and with a burgeoning whitehead and the sheen of a hangover sweat across her face.

Lucy can see, in the picture, the back of Cam's head on the pillow next to Anais's. The background of the photograph, of course, is the walls and window of Cam's bedroom.

So Cam slept in bed with Anais last night; at least for some of it, anyway. These must be the mixed signals that Cam is talking about. Lucy wonders why he bothered lying to her about it, what made him get out of bed in the night and blow up the airbed in the living room. Why Anais thought she ought to send the evidence to Lucy, who now texts her *Congratulations* because she can't think of anything else to say.

She showers and picks out an outfit. Tom is still KO'd in her bed as she rubs moisturiser into her face before applying make-up. Spitefully, glancing at Tom's sleeping form as though he might wake up and catch her in the act, she selects a pair of mom jeans from her wardrobe, rolled up at the cuffs, to wear with a lilac sleeveless blouse and a pair of black platform-soled Vans.

She sits on the edge of the bed and watches Tom, wondering whether to wake him up or not. It's gone ten-thirty. He is snoring. The idea of waiting around in this room, this flat, for him to wake up, seems a little unbearable. She looks at her phone again. *Have you spoken to your mum yet?*

She thinks of the promise she made to her father.

She prods Tom gently with one finger and his snores deepen. She spritzes herself with some Daisy by Marc Jacobs and closes the door softly behind her.

Cam has moved from the airbed to the kitchen, his dark chestnut-coloured hair stuck up in all directions from sleep.

Tom is in there, she tells him, gesturing with her head to her bedroom door. If he wakes up, can you, like, entertain him or something? I'll text him, too, to tell him I'm going out.

You want me to *entertain* him? Cam asks, incredulous, a slice of beans on toast paused halfway to his mouth. He looks cute, Lucy realises, catching herself smiling fondly at him.

Sorry, Lucy says, flatly, I know it's a bit weird. I just need to get out—

And there must be something that looks like desperation in her face, or perhaps Cam can detect the feeling of sinking dread that is turning her stomach cold, because he waves his toast at her. Of course. Absolutely. Do what you need to do. I'll sort him out.

She gives him a grateful look and rushes to the door. As soon as she's out on Lambeth Road, she feels her breathing ease, and she inhales the summer air, lets it wash through her lungs and cleanse her. She already feels the hangover, the ugly feelings she has to do with Tom that she can't quite articulate to herself yet, dissipating, as she walks toward the station.

She buys a takeaway coffee from the hole in the wall by the Sainsbury's and idles on the pavement. She pops in her AirPods and finds herself tapping herself into Lambeth North and wandering into the lifts down to the tube platform. She is boarding a tube to Oxford Circus and switching onto the Central line, sweat pooling in the small of her lower back as the hot stale air drags itself through the vents of the carriage, to Liverpool Street. The route is muscle memory, almost, although she hasn't travelled it in what seems like a lifetime. There is a woman opposite her on the tube who has no teeth.

Soon – in no time at all, really – Lucy is walking up the stairs to the station exit at Chadwell Heath, gripping the barrier a little too tightly because it feels as though she might topple backwards down them, not quite remembering how she got there, not realising that this is where she was going until this very moment. She wanders down the railway bridge, past the vape shop and the off-licence, past the builders' merchants and the Chinese dried noodle packing factory, and towards her parents' house – her family home, really, although it feels a little alien to her nowadays.

In the warm summer daylight, the house looks worn out. It

is a little squat in shape, with a scrubby patch of grass in the front, squared off by a low brick wall. It has something called subsidence, which Lucy doesn't really understand, but it leaves her father in a constant state of panic. There's nothing special about the house: it looks exactly like the seventy other houses lined up like dominoes along this residential road. But Lucy can see the faint chalk-like marks of 'Lucy and Danny's house' scribbled above the front door. She must have been less than six years old when Danny convinced her to scratch the letters into the brickwork, balancing her on his shoulders while she reached up with a piece of flinty slate from the shingle in the back garden. Mum lost it when she saw it, and Lucy took the fall for the both of them – something that seemed to happen a lot in their childhoods – and spent a Sunday digging out grout and black mould from between the tiles in the bathroom with a toothbrush as punishment. Mum made her wash the graffiti away too, but the damage had already been done, the wonky letters carved into the soft brick to leave a permanent imprint. When their dad came home from work and saw Lucy's handi-work, he burst out laughing.

Now that she's here, staring up at the marker above the door, she's wondering what for. What she could ever hope to achieve from a conversation with her parents. Whether it will make her feel better, or worse. She has a suspicion, she realises with mild dread, that it will be the latter. She remembers what Nara told her. See what they're prepared to say. Decide what you want to hear.

Lucy feels an eerie sense of calm settle over her as she walks up the garden path and rings the doorbell. It's her dad who an-swers the door, holding a potted basil plant.

Oh, Loose. Hello, he says. He adjusts his glasses and pulls Lucy into a one-armed hug, his other hand preoccupied with the basil. He holds onto her too tight, a little too long. His flannel work shirt is soft, and he smells of soil and mown grass and the sun and cigarillos, and underneath is the scent of laundry detergent and his shaving cream and she feels such a potent stab of homesickness that for a moment she worries that she might cry. There is nothing she wants more than to let her dad look after her, curl her up on the sofa with a blanket and a hot chocolate, and listen while she tells him all about Tom and Cam and Anais, and how the panic attacks are back, and how she feels as though she is a fraudulent version of herself, and everyone hates her because she is simply unlikeable, how she feels like she is losing control of herself.

She knows that she could never tell him those things, though. Especially not now.

Come and sit in the garden with me, Dad tells her when he releases her. This is something that Lucy enjoys about her father. Daniel Senior is someone who says what needs to be said and nothing more. He is someone very comfortable in his own company. Mum compensates by speaking enough for the pair of them, and then some.

Where's Mum? Lucy asks as she follows him through the house, past the framed school photos lining the staircase walls; past the weird brass cat statue that functions as a doorstop to keep the kitchen door open; past the ugly terracotta-coloured tiles and the weird half-dead cactus collection on the windowsill, and into the garden. The garden is Daniel Senior's retirement project, because he can't be idle. Having undertaken back-breaking (literally, in his case) manual labour his whole life, Dad always tells Lucy, if he slows down or stops now, all his brittle bones with their worn-through cartilage will seize up and he'll turn to stone.

She'll be home soon, Dad replies. She's just popped out for bread.

He leans against the door frame as she settles down at the garden table.

Garden looks amazing, Dad.

Thanks, chicken. I'm doing the herbs today, and he points out the freshly composted flower bed against the eastern fence where a rosemary bush seems to be taking over. Basil next – and then all the others. Thyme, mint, coriander. The whole shebang.

It looks good. Did you do it all yourself?

You know me, Loose.

She watches him from the patio as he goes over to the flower bed, the basil still in its plastic pot in his hands. He has a square mat that he is using to kneel on, protecting his knees from the hard earth, but Lucy can see how his face contorts in pain as he lowers himself, his cheeks flushing with the effort of it.

For God's sakes, Dad, she says quietly. He pretends not to hear her.

Dad had always had a plan to franchise out some of his business with regular clients. Subcontract some of the people he had worked with over decades – roofers and plumbers and bricklayers and plasterers – and start a bit of a supply-and-demand firm. Local and trusted tradesmen. That way, he could still be involved in the work and make money through commissions without the manual labour, without having to put himself through excruciating pain by demanding more than his body was capable of. Once he was up and running and making a good living, he thought maybe he might go to the local community college and do a course in business management. He'd talked about it for years, even before he fell off the ladder. Take an early retirement, maybe. Move them out to the coast. He was sick of the pollution and the traffic and the noise.

But then the markets crashed. Lucy didn't understand it, fully, although later, at university, she would learn all about the housing crisis in the States, sub-prime mortgages and banks taking greater and greater lending risks until the whole thing came tumbling down. At fifteen, she heard words like 'credit crunch' on the news and could only conjure the image of a cartoon cereal box monster with dollar signs instead of eyes. All too quickly, the work dried up for Dad. Many of his best, most of his well-paying clients were Canary Wharf commuters living on the Jubilee line. No one wanted conservatories, kitchen refits, or their exterior walls repainted when they couldn't afford to feed their kids. But Daniel Senior couldn't afford to feed his kids either. So he took the early retirement without any of the perks, and signed on instead.

Eventually he makes it into a kneeling position on the ground and digs a small channel in the soil and eases the basil plant into it.

Perfect time for it, he calls over to Lucy. We'll be in the mid twenties by next week.

Once done, he begins the gargantuan effort of standing, using the handle of an iron shovel wedged into the ground to support himself. He looks unstable as he hauls himself up, and Lucy knows he is trying to keep his expression clear of pain for her sake. She realises, perhaps for the first time, that her dad is going to die one day. And that his back is only ever going to get worse, more painful, a millstone ever-increasing in size and weight around her father's neck, and the necks of her mother, and Danny too.

Where's Danny, Dad?

Gone out somewhere. God knows. Do you want some lunch, chicken? When Mum gets back, we'll have sandwiches.

Inside, Lucy sits at the kitchen table and watches as her dad busies himself with the kettle and teabags. He hums along to the radio, seemingly contented, but she can tell that there is a nervousness to his movements. He is waiting, she thinks, for her to say something.

She has a text from Tom from an hour ago – *Where the fuck are you?* – and realises with a flash of guilt that she forgot to text him to let him know she was going out. She imagines him waking up in her bed, bewildered and smelly and hung-over, and being greeted by Cam in the kitchen instead of her. She wonders what he will wear today – he slept naked and the only clothes he has with him are the over-formal suit and shoes. She pictures him emerging from her bedroom in his underwear, and then again in his suit. Both seem equally ridiculous.

She texts back a quick *Sorry* and considers typing out an explanation – the claustrophobia of the flat; the feeling of being exposed that comes with sharing a bed with someone, having sex with them, even though she has showered and is ostensibly clean, the smell of him on her lingers and makes her feel vulnerable and dirty; the need to get some fresh air, watching Cam eat beans on toast and feeling suddenly desperate to see her own mother. Tom completely slipped her mind. But the idea of explaining all of this to him is exhausting to her. She leaves it at *Sorry* and returns her attention to her dad, who sets a cup of tea in front of her – strong, with no sugar and a dab of milk– and they sit quietly and listen to Lynyrd Skynyrd. They talk about very little, which is how they both like it.

Lucy remembers the familiar sensation of feeling at ease in the company of her father, especially in silence, which is rare for her; something she hasn't felt since Hannah's wedding. In fact, she realises, her whole body and mind has been tensed for this moment, for this visit that she didn't know she needed to undertake until she was getting off the train. Now that she's here, she can feel herself uncoiling, her mind unwinding, as she remembers the easiness of being Erica and Daniel's daughter, in spite of everything, both of whom, on the whole, are very loving and nurturing people. And then she remembers – again – *why* she's here, and more importantly, why she's angry with them.

I need to talk to you and Mum, Lucy tells him.

Yes, Daniel replies, taking off his glasses and rubbing at the lenses with the hem of his flannel shirt.

Will she be back soon?

As she asks the question, they can hear keys turning in the front door, and a moment later, Lucy's mother is hauling Aldi bags for life into the hallway, knocking over a novelty duck-shaped boot stand in the process.

Hellooooo, she calls, singing. And just like the moment she saw her father, Lucy is struck by a curious and painful nostalgia that is a dull bruise in her gut, at hearing her mother call through the house, announcing her arrival. The way she always has, for as long as Lucy can remember.

We're in here, Daniel calls back.

Lucy goes to help her mother with the shopping. When Erica sees her, she stills, sets the bags down at her feet. She has wrapped her hair in a faux-silk paisley handkerchief, though Lucy can see at the edges the chocolate-brown is threaded with more silver than ever. Erica looks like Helen McCrory: utterly glamorous, with a full face of make-up daily. A scarlet lip and 1950s-winged eyeliner for the Saturday morning shop. Her dark eyes are swimming with water. Her fingernails are long red spikes, only stick-ons from Boots, but nevertheless impressive.

Hi, Mum, she says.

Her mother pulls her into a tight, shuddering hug and kisses her on the cheek. She smells, comfortingly, of cigarettes and white musk.

Where've you been, you silly goose? she asks, and Lucy has to blink to stop any tears spilling over her eyes and betraying her.

I just needed some time, she says.

Chapter Seventeen

They put the shopping away together, the three of them. Mum talks about everything – work at the launderette, her friends from bingo, her encounter with an overexcited cocker spaniel up the high street last week. Dad hums in agreement and cuts slices of cheese with a serrated knife. No one can cut the perfect thickness of a slice of cheese, in Lucy's opinion, besides her dad. This is what it has always been like here at home: Mum fills silence with anecdotes and chit-chat, the quiet of the house seemingly unbearable to her. Lucy, and Dad, and Danny when he's at home, and even Uncle Marv who is here more often than Lucy is, listen and daydream and make the appropriate noises of agreement or outrage or interest in the appropriate places. No one talks about anything more emotionally difficult than bingo or the football or the sister of the brother-in-law of a friend of a cousin getting hit by a bus in Romford high street. Everything is surface level and there's no point dragging up ancient history, and Banburys don't cry. Lucy wonders how she is going to get them to tell her what happened to her. How she came to live in this house, how these people came to be her parents, how she became a Banbury. What happened before and after. Who her biological parents are. The circumstances of her birth. Where to even begin? The thought of it all is overwhelming. Lucy examines the grain of wood on the table while Erica talks, half-paying attention to her mother.

Everything all right, love? Mum asks, pausing halfway through her detailed recounting of Miriam next door's hip surgery. Lucy looks up at her mother and sees that same expression on her face from before – the expression from the wedding. One of pity and guilt and concern. The lines on her forehead like canyons etched out with rivers over thousands of years. Dad chops carrots and says nothing, his head bowed. Lucy is thinking of being five and having her hair plaited by her mother. The matching shoes. The bonnets. The way Mum twisted her hair up until it felt like it was being ripped from her skull. If Lucy had inherited Erica Banbury's genetic material, what would she look like? What kind of person would she be? She wonders whether her real mother would have been so preoccupied with how she looked. Maybe it wouldn't matter so much because surely they look alike. Her and the mother she has never met, out in the universe somewhere, tethered to her by an invisible thread. Erica, as though she has heard what Lucy is thinking, screws her eyes shut.

What's that face for? Lucy asks.

What face?

This one – the one like you're feeling sorry for me.

I don't feel sorry for you, Erica says, her voice pitching up. What a stupid thing to say.

Lucy inhales and then exhales very slowly, allowing her eyes to trace the edges of the window frame.

I want to talk about my adoption, please, she says very quietly, pressing her fingers against the table.

Her parents glance at one another: fleeting, fearful glances. She feels suddenly monstrous. Should it really be so important to her? To know what happened, to put her parents through the telling of it?

At this moment, the front door slams shut and Danny arrives in the kitchen, dressed in a scrubby grey T-shirt and jeans. The tension visibly leaves her mother's shoulders at his arrival, a distraction from the conversation at hand. Lucy feels every muscle in her own body tighten with apprehension. She has not seen or spoken to Danny since that night in Stratford. He has a medical boot on his left foot and a crutch to support his weight.

The prodigal daughter returns, he says upon seeing Lucy sitting at the kitchen table, pausing to rest on the crutch. Danny registers her presence without any hint of surprise or pleasure.

In the daylight, Lucy can see more of what the drink is doing to him. This is a test she has for him, one that she's conducted for as long as she can remember. How fucked-up does Danny look today? How many drinks has he had? Looking at him now, she can see the bloated pinkness of his face, the round belly that looks almost pregnant, despite the fact that his clothes hang off his skinny frame – collarbone protruding sickeningly at his shoulders. His voice wavering a little as he speaks, his hands shaking involuntarily. The blood vessels in his eyes are swollen and stark against the yellowing whites. She can smell him, too: the alcohol being dispelled from him as his liver does its work: it comes off him in his breath and sweat, sickly-sweet, putrid.

He opens the fridge and takes out a can of Budweiser.

Hello, love, Erica says, and lights a cigarette.

Lucy watches as Danny takes the beer – and two more tucked into each of his back pockets – to the shed at the end of the garden. He does not say anything more; he doesn't acknowledge the last time they saw one another, on a housing estate in Stratford. Lucy wasn't expecting him to. She realises that she has been grinding her teeth. The sun beats down on the shed as Danny unlocks the door and slips inside.

You're letting him drink at home? she asks her mother, unable to help herself.

Mum picks at her fingernails, cigarette hanging out the corner of her mouth. Lucy notices that her thick foundation is cracking around the lines on her face.

I'd rather he drinks here than out there, she replies defensively, gesturing to the front door, the world outside. We have *friends* all over the place. Your father's brothers. The girls at the launderette.

The last time I saw Danny sober, Lucy says, was, what, two years ago? Three?

My sixtieth birthday, Dad replies.

Lucy stares at him and sees the lines on his face, the whiteness of his moustache, the way his glasses sit slightly wonky on his face because they need to be adjusted.

You're enabling him, Lucy says. You're hiding him away because it's easier than getting him help and having to admit to everyone your son is an alkie. Because you don't want to be embarrassed.

Dad has put together three cheese sandwiches with all the trimmings: pickle, mayo, tomato, et cetera. His face is unreadable. The kitchen is suddenly too bright.

It's not like people don't know, Lucy continues. Everyone knows. You think it's not obvious? Look at Hannah's wedding.

Daniel Senior stills. Mum snatches up her car keys from the table and goes into the hall. For one awful moment, Lucy thinks that she might be leaving – abandoning the conversation, and her – but she hangs them up on the coat hook by the front door and returns to the kitchen.

You need to understand how we see it, she tells her. When Danny was little, he didn't get much attention from us. We were so focused on work, and on looking after you, that he was just sort of left to his own devices. We weren't there for him. We weren't good parents to him. We let him down.

That's what you really think? You think all this is down to you? she asks them.

Well, not all of it, Mum replies, but definitely a helluva lot of it.

I just don't understand, Lucy says, feeling her temper flare, why you've got *beers* in the *fridge*, for crying out loud.

This is the most that any of them have ever talked about Danny's drinking. It is the only time Lucy has confronted them about it. Danny and his alcoholism has always been something that they have collectively and subliminally agreed to pretend isn't happening. But today is about Lucy, about her getting answers. And Danny has ruined it all over again. She cannot stop the agitation from thrumming through her.

Nice for you, it must be, Dad says, with your fancy job and flat and your salary and your social life up town. You're not living with him, Loose. You're not seeing the day-to-day. How about you live here, hey? Come home and live with us and see what it's like. *Then* you can have a say in how we deal with him.

Dad boils the kettle, signalling the end of the conversation. It is unlike him to say something so pointed. Mum looks nervously from him to Lucy, fiddling with her rings.

Who stocked that fridge, Mum? Who put the beers in there? Lucy asks, turning her attention to her mother, who once again looks supremely guilty.

Well, it wasn't me, Mum lies, her voice shrill.

It's not like he cares whether they're cold. It's not like he wouldn't drink water out the toilet if it had an ABV percentage.

Leave it, Dad says forcefully, through his teeth, slamming the kettle hard onto the counter, making the plates clatter and all three of them jump.

Lucy stares at him, all of the warmth of earlier, the homesickness she felt as he hugged her on the doorstep, now gone. She feels the rage, simmering unbearably beneath her skin, bubble out of her like lava.

She realises that she is standing up, her chair shoved roughly away from her, across the floor, her hands balled up and her fingernails cutting rivulets into her palms.

I shouldn't have come, she says.

No, darling, don't say that, Mum responds, her voice now wobbling. Please just sit back down.

I want to know the truth.

What truth?

The truth of what happened. To me. How come I ended up being adopted.

Mum pinches the bridge of her nose. She stands and goes to the kitchen drawer. She opens it and removes a thick, overstuffed manila folder.

She sits back down at the table; the sandwiches her father made are still there, the crusts turning stale.

We always wanted a little girl, her mother says, after taking a long and pronounced drag on her cigarette. We wanted one of each. The full set. We were trying, obviously, but not getting pregnant. Danny was getting older, and so were we, and we wanted a baby who could play with her big brother. We wanted to still be young when we watched our little girl grow up. And I was getting these headaches, Mum continues, touching her forehead lightly. And the doctors didn't know what they were. We did all the tests. I had CT scans. And they couldn't find the cause of them. They thought maybe it was the extra hormones I was taking to try to get pregnant. They took me off of them. So we just put up with it and thought, maybe, there wasn't a chance for us. After a couple of years, we signed up with an adoption agency. It took months and months and months. Assessments, meetings, endless forms. Every aspect of our lives under a microscope. We were still waiting for final approval when you came along.

Lucy grips the edges of the table, her whole body suddenly heavy. As though if she lets go she will sink down into the centre of the universe. She has never heard any of this before.

It was Dad's cousin Wendy. You remember Wendy, don't you? She's a maternity nurse. With the hair? Well. Wendy worked at the Medway Hospital, in the maternity unit, up until 1995 and someone left a little baby on the steps of the maternity ward. Little tiny thing, premature, umbilical cord still attached. Squawking and wheezing for England. Little fists punching at the air. That was you.

Lucy's parents are looking at one another, not her. Her father has come to stand behind her mother and rests both hands gently on her shoulders.

Lucy feels as though she has left her body completely, as though someone else is hearing these things, not her.

Her mother continues, And they couldn't find whoever it was who left you there. Checked the CCTV and everything, but nothing lined up. There was a county-wide police search. A television appeal. It was in all the newspapers and everything. They thought even if the mum didn't want to come forward, maybe another family member would. The idea was that it was a teenage mum, who maybe didn't know she had been pregnant, so the police were asking for the parents of teenage daughters to check on them for signs of a recent labour. But no one answered; no one came forward for you. It was like you'd appeared out of thin air: one moment there was nothing and then there was you.

As her mother talks, Lucy imagines it happening, as though it is a dream. Not her own secret history. Not her own origin story, her own life.

She pictures the entrance to the Medway maternity unit. A hospital that she knows well. The squat, square, brown-bricked building. A woman – a girl, really, if she truly had been a teenager – with an alien in her arms, terrified, alone, with nowhere else to go.

She must have been so scared, Lucy says quietly, and her mother nods, flicking her eyes up to meet Lucy's, her own despairing expression a mirror.

So they got you inside, on the ventilator and all the rest of it. And things weren't so strict back then as they are now. There was a social worker involved almost immediately, yes, but there were no available foster parents, there was a shortage, and we had almost completed the approval with the agency to adopt. While you were still in your little incubator at hospital. And when you were strong enough, they let us take you home. And we just knew straight away. That you were the one for us. You were *our* little girl. The one we had been trying for. It would only be more perfect if a stork landed on the doorstep and dropped you off in a straw basket.

We had to have you, Dad says. We just had to.

I can't tell you how many assessments we had to do; how many therapists, social workers, home visits, psychiatrists and all the rest of it, to make sure we were suitable. It took a long time, but, yes, eventually you were ours, her mum concludes.

And that's it, Dad says, with finality.

It happened so quickly. But it seemed to take forever, too. Once we had you, it made complete sense. You were what we had been waiting for, Loose, all that time.

Lucy stares at both of them, unsure what to process and how to process it.

It was really just that? she asks them. That's how it happened? Yes. It really was.

Mum picks up the thick manila folder filled with papers. Here's everything, she tells Lucy, handing it to her. Birth certificate. Health visitor records. All of our different examinations. The newspaper clippings. Everything.

Lucy opens the file and pulls out an envelope. Inside is a tiny wristband – a baby's hospital bracelet – on it, in faded biro block capitals, it says: BABY LUCY DOORSTEP. She stares at it. Then she puts it back into the folder and closes the flap.

She tries again to picture her mother – her biological one – on the steps of the Medway. Perhaps a little blood on the concrete, a crying baby, nothing more.

What time of day was it, she asks them, when they found me outside the hospital?

It was around lunchtime, her mother answers, from memory. October the fourteenth. Your birthday, obviously. It was a beautiful, crisp day. Blue skies.

Lucy imagines it: the sun glazing the scene – perhaps alighting upon a redhead, perhaps setting fire to hair the colour of apricots.

She digs her fingernails into the soft grained wood of the kitchen table, holding on.

And you knew nothing about her, Lucy confirms. Her name, where she came from. Who she was. She feels the weight of this knowledge bearing down on her, hopeless.

Dad is pointedly looking at Mum.

Well, not at first, she says, registering his look.

She takes out an old envelope, from the same drawer, yellowing, with faded spidery handwriting across the front.

When you were nine or ten, she says, the hospital got this letter. It's from your birth mother.

She slides it across the table to Lucy. Lucy stares at it, afraid to touch it, as though it might burst into flame.

We've never read it – neither of us – we promise you.

Were you *ever* going to tell me? she asks them, feeling the dull flair of her temper.

Mum says, miserably, I knew that eventually you would need to know the truth. I was saving this for you. For that day when we told you. It's just that, the older you got, the harder it became to let go of you. That's how we felt: we thought that once we told you, we would lose you a little bit. That you wouldn't be our baby any more. But I think, in a way, by not telling you the truth, we were halfway to losing you anyway.

Her dad squeezes Lucy's elbow gently. She stares down at the letter.

I don't know what to do, she says, struggling to keep the emotion out of her voice. I don't know whether I want to open it.

You don't have to decide today, her dad says. You can put it away for now, if you like. Or we can hold onto it for you.

Lucy picks up the letter, feels the grain of the paper underneath the pads of her thumbs. It is a sacred object. She slides it into the folder, along with all the other documents. Her own personal history is laid out before her, now, but she is afraid to touch it. Afraid of what it might tell her about herself; what it might do to her.

She looks out to Danny's studio shed, windows dark.

We made him promise not to tell you, her mum says, registering where her gaze has been drawn.

He had to keep it a secret until we were ready, Dad says. Of course, that was a huge mistake. We didn't realise we would never be ready.

Did he know the whole time?

Yes, he was six years old: old enough to piece together what was going on.

Lucy is thinking of Danny as a child again, her big brother. Despite everything, she feels her heart drop for him. A little boy with the biggest secret any of them could ever imagine, surely. He must have felt the weight of it every day. The way her mother doted on her, and how Dad was never around because of work, leaving Danny palmed off on Uncle Marv most of the time. She thinks of how, as a child, her parents threw her these birthday parties beyond what they ever could afford. Danny never had a big birthday party. How Lucy always got new clothes from the shops in town, while Danny had charity shops and hand-me-downs from cousins.

Lucy picks up the folder of documents – the letter – and hugs it to her chest. She can feel it burning against her skin.

I need to go, she tells them.

Why?

I don't know.

She can feel her chest tightening. The documents burning.

When will you come back? Mum asks.

I don't know.

Will you come back, at all?

I don't know. I'm sorry.

She looks at the pair of them. They are nervously glancing at one another, just like they do with Danny when he is too drunk at a family function, just like at the wedding. As though Lucy might at any moment throw something across the room or set a fire unexpectedly. They are a little bit afraid of her. And she is afraid, too. Afraid of what comes next. Afraid of all of the secrets that have been exposed. How they might fester and warp and evolve in the daylight.

She pictures the Medway, again, her whole body burning and leaden and exhausted.

How did she leave me? she asks her parents. When she left me on the steps?

They cast confused looks at one another.

What do you mean, chicken?

She cannot stop herself from asking the question, from completing the picture in her mind's eye, even though it makes her throat tighten. How *was* I, when they found me? Did she wrap me in a blanket? Was there a crib? A car seat?

Her mother stares at her with sad, resigned eyes, the lines around them more pronounced than ever underneath her make-up.

It was a box, she says. When they found you. You were in a cardboard box.

Chapter Eighteen

When Lucy arrives home, she finds an empty Rituals gift box under her bed and places the documents carefully inside, without looking at them too closely. She tries not to think about anything too deeply. She can feel the nervousness, the screaming abyssal panic clawing at the fringes of her consciousness. She is afraid that if she lets herself feel it – the secret of her own history, the version of herself built out of this new knowledge – she is going to fall down down down into some dark void. She is afraid of what will happen if she does. She is afraid of the person that she always was, without knowing.

The most sensible thing to do is to put her new knowledge into the other box, in the back of her mind, and shove it somewhere dark and out of sight, too.

This is the best thing to do.

She texts Tom and apologises the next day, realising that she never responded to him, explaining that she had an emergency with Nara, who is a friend Tom has never met, so there is no risk of him trying to verify the story and realising that Lucy has lied.

Lucy continues to feel nervous whenever she speaks to Tom. Sometimes when she receives a WhatsApp notification and sees that it's from him, it is as though a concrete block has been dropped into the centre of her body and has shattered her ribcage and flattened her lungs. She interprets these feelings as excited nerves: the prospect of a future with Tom.

She agrees to meet him for dinner after work on Tuesday, at a quiet, dimly lit Portuguese restaurant in Bloomsbury. He is waiting for her at the table.

You're late, he says.

I thought you said seven thirty?

I said seven.

I'm sure you didn't.

Gratifyingly, a waitress comes to take their drinks orders. Lucy is never late. She makes a point of being early, actually. She is certain that she has the time right.

Tom digs a corner of the menu under his thumbnail.

The thing about being late, he says, is that you're telling me your time is more important than mine.

I'm sorry, Tom.

They sit in a protracted silence that seems to flood the whole restaurant, despite the tinny piano jazz cover playing through the overhead speaker.

How was the rest of your weekend? she asks him.

He shrugs non-committally.

I saw on Twitter something about the interest rate dropping, she goes on, nervously. Is that good for you at work?

Maybe if you didn't get your news from Twitter, he replies, you would know.

Their meals arrive. Lucy smiles sheepishly, her pulse quickening, as she spears a piece of chicken thigh with her fork.

It dawns on her, in this moment, that perhaps he is punishing her for leaving the flat without him the other day.

She pretends that she hasn't noticed his disposition.

I'm just wondering, Tom says after some time.

Lucy's head snaps up from her main course. Yes?

I was wondering whether you wanted to meet my dad.

Lucy notices that the chicken she has been eating is under-cooked. Ever so slightly pink on the inside. She pushes the plate away from her quickly, acutely aware of the bacteria multiplying in her gut.

Well?

Tom is looking at her, waiting for an answer.

She wonders whether, if she meets Tom's dad, he'll expect to meet her parents. Expect to meet Danny.

I'm not really sure, she tells him, feeling her insides squirm with the undercooked meat.

Really?

She hesitates. It's quite a big step, she says.

He stands up abruptly, startling her.

I don't get it.

Get what?

Get you. You're all over the place.

He flings his napkin to the table, venomous. It flutters harm-lessly through the air.

You think you're so much better than everyone else, don't you?

She hears him say it and she remembers the same words coming out of Danny's mouth. Lucy was seventeen-almost-eighteen, in the midst of her A-Levels. Back-to-back exams, five or six a week. Danny was building the shed with Uncle Marv in the back garden while Lucy revised in her bedroom, trying to keep him away from her. Or herself away from him. Sometimes he let himself into her bedroom when she was out and stole money from the shoebox that she kept under her bed, with all of her savings from her paper round and her lifeguarding job. The London fund, she called it in her head.

He was in there now, staring at all of the Post-it notes on her walls, when she opened the door. The Post-it notes were colour-coded, and perfectly perpendicular. Her mother was at work. Her dad was in bed with Deep Heat strapped to his back. Uncle Marv in the garden painting the shed. On each Post-it was a list of bullet-pointed revision notes in Lucy's careful cursive hand.

What are you doing? she asked him, feeling her fingers flicker nervously across her textbooks. She set them down on her bed, waiting.

You're just so good at this stuff, aren't you? he told her.

I'm just trying, she said and he laughed hollowly.

Just *trying*. What, and I'm not?

You know that's not what I meant, Dan.

You think you're so much better than everyone else, don't you?

No, I don't.

I'm sick of it.

He swiped a hand across the wall, tearing the Post-it notes from their positions, the glue unsticking. They fluttered to the floor, each of them, like dead birds dropping from the sky. Lucy couldn't stop herself from letting out a furious shriek.

Fuck off out of my room! she shouted, childish, grabbing him by the shoulders. She felt the fury building up inside of her. That deep and illustrious hatred for him that was always festering away just at the corners of her consciousness. She hated him, she hated him, she hated him more than ever in this moment.

He stumbled a little under the force of her grip, because he was drunk and his balance was tenuous.

Think you're so much better than everyone else, he said again, panting, as she wrestled him out of her bedroom.

You think you're so much better than everyone else, don't you?

They were at the top of the stairs, now, and he shoved her hard, on instinct, to get her away from him, she thought. She saw it in his eyes, though, that there was some small part of him that meant to do it.

And with his push, she went backwards down the stairs, rolling down them like a rag doll. Each carpeted step, the corner of it, hitting her somewhere in the ribs or the waist or the abdomen.

And at the bottom, she lay there for a moment, dumbfounded. She looked up at him watching her, panting. Neither of them could quite believe, she thought, that he had finally done it. The overt act of violence, out in the open for both of them to see and name.

And then: the pain. First in her right forearm and then burning a searing-hot path up to her shoulder. A throbbing, dense pain that made her cry out.

Danny rushed down to meet her, a sudden look of panic in his eyes. Loose?

She couldn't answer. The pain was everything. She wailed instead.

Get up, Danny said, his voice urgent. Stop messing about.

And then: a key turning in the front door lock. Mum, coming into the house, back from her shift.

Helloooooooo, she called.

She opened the door and stood on the threshold, staring at them both, eyes narrowed.

What's going on? she asked them. Lucy, are you all right?

But all Lucy could do was roll away, through heaving dry sobs, and pull herself up with her good arm to lean against the wall, the wind knocked out of her, nauseous from the pain.

She fell down the stairs, Danny said quickly, nervously.

Lucy gnashed her teeth at him.

Oh, Lucy, her mum said, dropping her handbag on the shoe rack. You need to look where you're going, chicken.

The pain was sickening.

Later, at the hospital, a doctor relocated the bones of her forearm back into her elbow joints. The splint they gave her only lasted a day: she wrote the rest of her exams hissing through the pain, determined that there would be no retakes. She didn't let herself cry. There was no point. She would be out of the house by September.

And she was.

You think you're so much better than everyone else, don't you?

Now, Lucy stares at Tom, feeling the bile rising inside her. She feels the ghost of the dislocation in her right elbow; rubs it subconsciously.

I don't know what you're talking about, she says to him, her throat burning.

Chapter Nineteen

Dump him, Meredith tells her the following lunchtime, when she relays what happened with Tom. They have met in Borough Market to get falafel wraps and green super-smoothies before returning to their respective offices. Meredith is doing some consultation work at a car rental app company nearby and is in the midst of rewriting all four hundred pages of FAQs on their website with SEO-friendly keywords. She is being paid an extortionate amount of money to do so, even after her agency has skimmed its cut off the top.

I have never, *ever* been so bored in my life, Meredith complains, I've half a mind to quit.

And do what? Lucy asks, paying for her falafel wrap and stashing the food in her handbag, wrapped in foil and napkins. She will eat it properly – with a knife and fork on a plate in the break room at Kube – later. Talking to Meredith helps Lucy to keep everything tucked away in the box. Meredith doesn't ask the kinds of questions that Nara does: the kinds of questions that penetrate Lucy to the centre of her soul and expose all the ugliness that she has been trying to hide. Meredith helps Lucy not to think about the letter. The documents. The way her mind spirals when she is awake in the middle of the night, tries to conjure up the face of an imagined biological mother. Where is she? How old? Alive? Dead? She has latched onto the idea of her mother being a teenager. Let's say she was sixteen or seventeen when she gave birth. That would put her in her early forties, now. Still young, still with so much life ahead of her. Would she and Lucy be friends if they ever met? The questions, once they are out of the box, press down hot on her chest until she struggles to breathe.

Erica keeps leaving her voicemails, but Lucy won't listen to them, not trusting herself to. She rejects the calls as they come in. She dismisses text notifications without reading them.

It is far simpler and easier to talk to Meredith about work and dating and search engine optimisation.

I don't know what I'll do, Meredith shrugs. Maybe just work for my dad for a bit? Maybe take a year off.

Lucy says nothing. The idea of having no monthly income makes her feel sick, but she is not Meredith, who grew up in a Georgian townhouse two roads away from the Natural History Museum, and had a twenty-four-hour au pair stroke nanny stroke maid until the age of twenty-one, like a real-life Blair Waldorf. Meredith, like Blair, is also prone to *popping to Paris*.

I think you need to drop Tom the Tory, Meredith says through a mouthful of floured tortilla.

Why? I like him.

God – don't sound so certain, hey, Loose?

Lucy shrugs, unsure how to respond.

The whole point of getting you on the market was to help you feel less uptight. And, congratulations, I think you have possibly found the most uptight person in the country.

I don't feel uptight.

Really, because you're giving it off in *waves*, hun. And Tom is fucking red-flag central. He threw a tantrum in the middle of dinner because you didn't immediately agree to meeting his family.

You make it sound a lot worse than it actually was, Lucy replies. He was just frustrated, that's all.

Meredith continues: This is the first guy you've dated in, what, over a year? If you get serious with the *first* – literally, the *first* – guy who shows the slightest bit of interest, you're not proving anything to anyone. You're not changing. You're not growing.

I've got nothing to prove, Meredith.

Don't you want to try new things? New experiences? Don't you want to play the field for a bit and learn something about yourself? You're twenty-six, for chrissakes.

I'm learning lots of things about myself all the time, Lucy says, taking a sip of her kale smoothie. I don't need to do that through the prism of the male gaze.

Oh, bullshit, Meredith splutters, but in a good-humoured sort of way, and they both start laughing. This is what Lucy likes about Meredith: she is blunt and cruel, sometimes, but she's also hilarious and honest, and doesn't spare feelings. Lucy wishes she could be more like her.

The sun is turning the concrete warm as they say goodbye and return to work. Lucy feels buoyant as she takes the lift up to the Kube floor. In the break room, she unwraps her lunch and chews thoughtfully, daydreaming. She has ignored more of her mother's texts and phone calls, and thrown herself into a busy calendar of summer brunches, picnics in Regent's Park, nights out in Soho and pub garden roasts. She has avoided thinking about the argument with her parents – the way she stormed out, which she is ashamed of – all together. She has been avoiding Cam, too, because she doesn't understand why he lied to her about staying in his bed with Anais, or why Anais felt the need to text Lucy the evidence, and it feels weird and uncomfortable to her. A few times, they have crossed paths in the kitchen and Cam has struck up a conversation: an anecdote about one of his kids at school, or some chat about Magic: The Gathering. But Lucy always replies in one- or two-word answers until he abandons the conversation, deflated and confused.

The other night, he texted her from his bedroom to tell her his sister was coming to stay for a few nights, instead of knocking on her door and having the conversation. She has repelled him. Lucy doesn't understand why this makes her feel so awful, doesn't want to acknowledge or examine these feelings too closely.

Anais hasn't been back to the flat since the night of Ash's gig, as far as Lucy can tell. She has been at work every day and a little friendlier with Lucy. She is in the break room now, pouring herself a green tea from the hot water machine. Once her tea is poured, Anais hesitates before taking a seat at the same table as Lucy.

How's it going? she asks, delicately steeping her teabag.

Good, Lucy says, covering her mouth self-consciously. How about you?

Yeah. Good. And she smiles broadly, like she has a secret that she wants to tell Lucy.

What?

I think he wants to get back together, you know, Anais says, the words gushing out of her fountain-like.

Oh. Really?

He wants to go for a drink tonight. Anais is beaming.

Is that what you want?

Duh!

Well. Congratulations. That's amazing. Lucy is hyper-aware that her voice is flat. She can't seem to make it match the enthusiasm of her words.

D'you know, it's so stupid of me, but I actually thought there was something going on between the two of you there, for a hot sec.

Lucy chokes on a piece of chickpea and coughs loudly. She sees the little crumbs of falafel hit the table as she coughs. Disgusting. She is mortified, recoiling from the germs she has expelled from her own body. She rushes quickly to the cupboard for antibac and kitchen roll.

I wonder if I can move back in. Will it be a crowd if there's four in the flat, do you think? Can we kick Ash out?

Lucy scrubs at the table, eyes focused on the mess.

Maybe one step at a time? she says quietly and Anais nods enthusiastically, her eyes shining. Have you told Josh the personal trainer? Lucy asks.

Oh – yeah . . .

Aren't you still living with him?

Well, you know, he's around a lot. But things are . . . not great – I think I need to get rid.

Yes – maybe do that before you move back in with Cam? Lucy suggests, trying not to sound too patronising, too defensive, too furious on Cam's behalf. Does Cam know that he's around a lot? she asks as she washes her hands. There are no tea towels on which to dry them.

What is this, Loose, the Spanish Fucking Inquisition?

Just. If it was me, I'd want to know.

Well, it's not you, is it? It's not you.

Lucy grimaces at Anais, unsure what to say.

Anais mumbles an excuse about a meeting and leaves her there, hands dripping with soapy water, cold falafel congealing on her plate.

Ash has another gig tonight, and Lucy hates the thought of being alone in Flat 5 while Cam is out with Anais, undoubtedly falling back in love with her. Anais snaps her laptop shut at five-thirty on the dot and heads to the toilets to reapply make-up and change clothes. She emerges in a mist of Gucci Guilty and an impossibly flattering sunshine-coloured dress. Lucy can't help but stare a little bit. She realises after a moment that it's the same dress she tried on in Zara a few weeks ago but abandoned because it looked terrible on her.

You look amazing, she says, aware that her mouth is open.

Thanks! Anais grins at her, her face shining with highlighter and naked hope, the friction between them from earlier forgotten. Are you here much longer?

I just need to get some month-end reporting done, Lucy replies, but Anais has stopped listening.

Okay! See you later! And she waves breezily as she calls the lift, her hair flung back and billowing down past her shoulders.

Lucy bristles at the *later*, wondering if Anais means later as in at work tomorrow, or later as in tonight, when she comes home with Cam.

She stares at Excel, pretending to add numbers to spreadsheets until the office has cleared out. Delilah stops by her desk, today wearing earrings in the shape of giant pink Lego bricks.

Lucy, she says, I just wanted to say what a stellar job you've been doing with the costings. Greg is really pleased. She smiles condescendingly, one hand resting on Lucy's shoulder. Lucy resists the urge to shrug it off.

I'm happy to help, she says, robotically.

I can really see a bright future for you here, Delilah says, earrings wobbling in a jolly sort of way. Keep up this work ethic and you'll be running the place! She laughs hollowly and Lucy laughs along with her, unsure exactly what the joke is. Lucy has seen the books, now that she has the new role, and even with their relentless cost-slashing, there is nothing that looks bright about Kube's future. The exec team are filing personal expense claims up the wazoo. The company is oversaturated, with too many employees on the payroll, and not enough clients to justify them. Kube needs to pick up new business fast, or start making redundancies. Lucy's pay rise is seeming more and more like a pipe dream. She has spent the past two years establishing her reputation at Kube, making herself indispensable to Delilah: a valuable asset. But the prospect of having to find a new job is becoming more real by the day. The thought of starting over – of change, of giving up all that she has worked for – is so terrifying that she only lets it linger for a moment before pushing it away.

She says goodbye to Delilah, who has a reservation at the Ivy with her husband, and wonders what the hell she's still doing here.

After hours of scrolling Twitter and watching a YouTube video about TERFs, the fluorescent lights in the office go onto their motion-sensor programme and the floor is flooded with darkness. It's nine o'clock. She decides it's time to go home.

Lucy takes the tube – thankfully quiet – to Lambeth North and exits. She wonders whether Cam has returned from his date with Anais yet – whether Anais is with him. Lucy instead walks down the road towards Elephant and Castle. It's still a little light out, the throes of the height of summer now upon the city, the sky a deepening indigo colour, saturated with the artificial hues of the street lamps and headlights and traffic lights and police lights. The air is warm but not humid: a gentle breeze trailing around Lucy's ankles as she wanders through Imperial Dog Park, past the War Museum and the giant slate-coloured double cannon in front of it, resplendent in floodlights. Despite the pleasantness of the evening, the park itself is relatively quiet, with only a handful of walkers – some of them with dogs – trailing through the winding tanned pebble-dashed pathways and weaving through the sparse trees. Ahead of her, she can see the tower blocks that demarcate Elephant and Castle roundabout. Why does she even care what's going on with Cam and Anais? They were together, living with her, in the flat, for a year before and it never made the slightest impression on her. So what has changed?

Lucy tamps down the rising panic in her, sitting on a bench near the entrance to the museum, watching as a sandy-coloured dog – off its lead, which isn't allowed – noses around in the bushes before cocking its leg and relieving itself up a piece of the Berlin Wall set in the concrete. Lucy counts her breaths – a technique she learned from Instagram. She can feel her heartbeat slowing as she regulates her breathing. The open air and stillness and picturesque majesty of the museum all help.

The dog is still here, rustling around quietly in the bushes so as not to disturb her. It keeps sort of glancing at her, like it's waiting for her to say something.

Her breathing exercises abandoned, Lucy holds her hand out to the dog, like she has seen others do when they come across one. Lucy has never been a dog owner herself: her parents were too busy with work to be able to look after one, though she always thought she might quite like having one. University accommodation, student flats and rented house-shares never allowed for pets. Her first-year flatmate had a contraband guinea pig that escaped from its cage one night and was found a week later hibernating in the bran flakes, fat and happy.

The dog approaches Lucy's outstretched hand and immediately shoves a wet brown nose into her palm. She squeals involuntarily and jumps back. Whose dog is this? God knows where that nose has been.

The dog is still staring at her retracted hand, though, and she

sees now that it has big, shining brown eyes like melting chocolate buttons. It looks like the Andrex puppy, except older and
much fluffier. Maybe a golden retriever, although Lucy doesn't
know the first thing about breeds.

A man with a whippet is coming round the corner of the
museum.

Excuse me, Lucy calls to him. Is this your dog?

The man, in a polo shirt and chinos, shakes his head at her
and continues.

Lucy checks her bag and finds a Nature Valley bar from
breakfast that she forgot to eat. She unwraps the bar and breaks
it up into several small pieces. The dog watches her do this with
heightened interest. It stays very still as she handles the food.
She holds a small piece of granola bar out to the dog and it
snaps it up greedily, pointed canines grazing the edges of Lucy's
fingers but not hurting her.

She sees now in the dim light, as the dog eats, that it has
patches of fur missing on its chest and back, with hard raw cal-
loused pink skin exposed underneath. It is about as tall as Lucy's
mid-hamstring – big, really – with a huge barrel-like chest and
a thick neck. It has no collar.

It wags its tail vigorously as it chews on the granola bar. Once
it's finished, it looks expectantly at Lucy.

Those eyes might be the saddest ones in the whole world, she
thinks.

She gives the dog another piece of granola bar. And the rest.
By the last couple of bites, the dog has got the hang of taking
the food gently from her hand without snatching or accidentally
nipping her fingers, causing her to yelp and jerk her hand back
quickly, which frightens it.

It has been half an hour, now, and no owner has arrived to
claim their missing dog.

Where's your mum? Lucy asks the dog, half expecting an answer.

It looks at her, sad. She can feel her heart swelling.

She brushes the crumbs of the granola bar from her dress and checks her handbag for hand sanitiser, but no dice.

Well, bye then, she says to the dog. It looks at her.

She turns to leave the park, towards the brick-walled exit to St George's Road. At the mouth of the wall, where the park turns into the pavement, she looks back. The dog is standing at the bench, where she left it, staring after her. She can see the dog's ribs from here, now better illuminated by the lamplight from a distance. Its ears – floppy and silky-golden – are too big for its face.

You can't come with me, Lucy tells it, and the dog takes this as some sort of confirmation, because it trots over to her, its tail – swishing behind it like a golden palm frond – pitched high. It joins her at the exit. No, you can't, Lucy says.

The dog is smiling at her, big black mouth open wide to show its long white canines and a lolling pink tongue. It pants enthusiastically.

You *can't*, she tells it.

She turns one last time and marches out of the park, this time forcing herself not to look back. She only makes it twenty paces down the street before she turns around. The dog is standing at the park entrance, still staring after her.

Lucy is suddenly thinking of the Medway maternity unit, the baby in the cardboard box. A crisp sunny October morning almost twenty-seven years ago.

She swears under her breath.

Come on, then, she calls to it, jerking her head in a motion that indicates it should follow.

The dog trots happily along to meet her.

*

Back at Flat 5, Lucy doesn't know what to do with the dog. What do dogs eat? Where do they sleep? What do they need? She does some googling while the dog splays itself out like a starfish on the kitchen floor. There are strange smells coming from it – not just the standard dog smell, but smells that denote infection and rot. In the light of the flat, she can see that the dog's skin is much worse than she originally thought. The fur is almost gone entirely in some places, and on the back of the dog's legs are thick, black, tough calluses that look like the pads of its paws, but creeping up almost to the base of its tail. Lucy has not tried to stroke the dog yet; she is worried about what might be buried under what fur it has left, and what exactly is causing the bizarre skin condition.

Instead, she boils some rice on the hob and cooks a chicken breast from frozen in the oven. Once this is done, she lets it cool before presenting it to the dog to eat – which it does, greedily, making snuffling grunting noises as it wolfs down the food, skidding Lucy's pasta bowl across the floor with its snout as it licks the edges clean with that enormous pink tongue. She tries not to track the saliva and snot streaked across the bowl as the dog eats. She resolves to throw the bowl out as soon as the dog is gone.

The sky is black and the road outside uncharacteristically quiet. She watches the dog for what seems like years, there in the dim kitchen, listening to the soft whirring of the fridge. She can smell the microwave again: the odour is now somehow stronger than before.

She fills a second bowl with water and refills it after the dog slurps half of it up and dashes the rest from heavy jowls across the lino. She watches closely, itching to clean up, unsure what to do next.

Just after midnight, she hears a key in the front door and voices fill the hallway. It's Cam and Ash, coming in together after meeting up on the road on their respective journeys home. They are in a very involved conversation about which *Iron Man* movie is the best. She hears Ash say, Ugh, why does it smell like dog in here? And then they emerge into the kitchen and Ash goes, It proper stinks of d— Oh my God.

Cam follows and stops behind her, keys hanging from one index finger loosely at his side. Lucy is a little surprised to see that Anais is not with him.

Where did *that* come from? Ash asks.

I found it at the Imperial War Museum.

What the fuck were you doing at the Imperial War Museum?

Is he hurt? Cam asks.

I don't think so, Lucy replies. Just hungry. *He?*

Cam points at the now glaringly obvious pair of enormous testicles between the dog's back legs.

He approaches the dog tentatively, holding out the back of his hand. The dog lifts his head and sniffs cautiously before withdrawing.

Can I say hi? Cam asks it.

Ash stares, mouth agape, an expression of abject horror on their face.

I don't really do dogs, they say.

Lucy grimaces apologetically at them. I couldn't leave it – him – there, she says. I think he's a stray.

They each sit quietly at the kitchen table and watch him as he sniffs around the kitchen before curling up by the back door and promptly falling asleep. Cam gets a blanket from his bedroom and lays it out on the lino. Lucy boils more rice and refills her pasta bowl.

What are we going to do with him? Ash asks. No one answers.

They sit in the quiet closeness of the kitchen and watch the dog. After a while, Ash rolls their eyes and goes to their bedroom to noodle around on their guitar with their headphones plugged in.

Are you okay? Cam whispers to Lucy as they keep vigil.

Yes, she whispers back. Are you?

Yeah.

As they watch, the dog's breathing becomes slower and heavier until he is snoring very softly, his wet-black nose wriggling and twitching, the giant pads of his paws convulsing as he dreams. Lucy can see the imprint of his heartbeat through the side of his big barrel-shaped ribcage. The kitchen is warm and peaceful, cocooning the three of them in its dim glow.

Chapter Twenty

The next day, Lucy calls in sick to work. Cam is on summer holidays. They have both barely slept, each of them taking it in turns to sit with the dog in the kitchen, while the other naps on the sofa. At 2 a.m., the dog retched up the entire contents of his stomach, undigested chicken and all, which caused some commotion and brought Ash out of their bedroom, only to throw up their arms in exasperation and announce that they were going for a walk. Today, in the early bright of the morning, Cam makes an appointment at a local vet.

We'll need to check if he's microchipped, Cam says. The owner might be out there looking for him, after all. And we'll need to get him jabbed up with vaccinations. The vet will know what to do about the skin, too. It looks like mange to me, but I'm not sure. There's probably fleas, as well. He'll need deworming.

Cam has taken out his phone and is typing out a list.

How do you know so much about dogs? Lucy asks, stirring milk into two mugs of tea. She is still in yesterday's clothes, her make-up smeared down her face. She had almost forgotten about it – the urgency of the dog now eclipsing all other aspects of her life. She hasn't opened the three texts sitting in her notifications.

I come from a dog family, Cam replies, not looking up from his phone. We've had German shepherds, mostly. Not retrievers.

My sister worked at a rescue centre and was always bringing strays home. Some things are universal with dogs.

Your sister? Isn't she only a kid?

Oh – no – my other sister.

Lucy goes to ask more, but he has quickly turned back to his phone, his body angled away from her, and is typing out a text.

Thanks so much for helping, she says uselessly instead, setting down his tea in front of him.

Not at all. And he glances up at her, smiling warmly. We need to get this guy sorted, don't we? He is now speaking not to Lucy but the dog, who is in the back garden scratching his left ear with his back leg, with a kind of impressively studious dedication. After he is done scratching, the dog paces the garden in small circles, laps up some water from the paddling pool with a giant tongue, and sniffs the air, his ears pitched back.

He is quite sweet, really, isn't he, Lucy says, blowing on her tea.

God knows what's happened to him. He's a state.

Their eyes meet for a moment, Lucy and Cam's, and they are just as sad and resigned as each other. The dog comes indoors and lays himself down on the kitchen floor, heaving a sigh to match the mood.

There is some debate about whether they should try to get a lead on the dog to get him to the vets. Of course, there is no lead to be used, but Cam wonders whether he should run to Pets at Home and buy one.

I think he will follow us, Lucy says. That's what he did when I brought him home. If he's a stray, he'll have good street sense.

So, they tentatively open the front door and, as predicted, the dog follows them patiently along the road, never straying into the traffic, into the underground car park, trotting happily at Lucy's heels. He seems mainly bemused with them.

The car is another issue: the dog doesn't know how to get into it, staring at the open boot, pacing agitatedly as Lucy and Cam make soft coaxing noises to get him in.

I don't know if he'll let us lift him, Cam says, and Lucy agrees.

They compromise by putting more crumbled-up granola bar in the boot of Cam's car, and the dog eventually gets the gist and launches himself into the boot, his hind legs springing with impressive power.

The vet is called Max, a man in his late thirties with a kind bearded face.

Cam is nervous, fiddling with the zip on his hoodie.

Max checks the dog's teeth and paws and estimates that he is about three years old. He uses a handheld device to scan the dog for a microchip. There isn't one.

What do we do, then? Lucy asks.

Well. You can leave him here with me if you like. And I'll arrange for kennels for him.

What will happen to him?

They'll get him cleaned up and vaccinated, and do some behavioural testing and try to get him adopted.

Lucy watches the dog. He is smiling broadly, panting and accepting the treats Max offers him from the palm of his hand. Long trails of dribble extend like string from the dog's mouth. The skin on his back is a ferocious pink colour, blotchy and infected-looking.

No one is going to want to adopt this dog, she tells Cam, and Cam nods grimly.

What if no one wants him? he asks Max.

Well, they'll try to keep him happy in the kennels. He'll live there for as long as they can keep him. Sometimes, though, dogs who can't find homes get put down.

The dog is still grinning broadly. He is now trying to lick Max's beard.

Lucy feels as though her heart is about to fall out of her.

The other option, of course, is that you take him yourself.

This is how Lucy and Cam leave the vet's practice, four hundred pounds poorer between them, with the dog, now vaccinated, dewormed, de-flead and rubbed raw with a concoction of anti-septic and steroid creams, fresh phone-box-red collar strapped around his neck, and matching lead attached to Cam's hand. Lucy has a range of tablets, eardrops, a brush, dog shampoo, poo bags and nail clippers in her handbag, and is carrying a large bag of fibre-rich dry food. The dog – leadless all his life up to this moment, it seems – is dragging Cam towards the car with a ferocious determination, wheezing as he strains against the lead, his legs skidding out from under him.

Back at the flat, at lunchtime, Ash is emerging from their bedroom rubbing gunk out of their eyes. Cam has been to Pets at Home, while Lucy keeps watch over the dog. The dog now has a red soft-covered bed by the kitchen door, a set of bowls, two stuffed toys and a pig's ear, which he now chews on contentedly, leaving drool in a pool at his paws.

Oh, no fucking way, Ash says, eyeing him warily.

Lucy is ready for this conversation.

Ash, she says. You are two months behind on the rent.

Ash stares at her, eyes narrowed. Lucy stares right back.

Marcy won't have it, Ash says, seemingly be trying to convince themself rather than anyone else.

What Marcy doesn't know won't hurt her. Besides, if we tell Marcy about the dog, we'll have to tell Marcy about you.

Ash stares a moment longer, from Cam to Lucy to the dog.

I want nothing to do with it, they say.

Cam says, fair enough.

I'm not walking it. I'm not feeding it. I'm not picking up its shit from the garden. I'm not making eye contact with it. Okay?

Fine.

What are you calling it, then?

Cam and Lucy look at each other. We haven't thought about it, Lucy says.

Probably needs a name, though.

What about . . . Winston? Cam says, grinning.

Winston? Ash says, incredulous. *Really?*

You found him at the Imperial War Museum, didn't you?

Seems a bit Empire to me.

Lucy thinks then of the tiny hospital wristband in the manila folder in the box under her bed, a wretched feeling suddenly coming over her. BABY LUCY DOORSTEP, it said. So her parents were not the ones to name her, then, she realises. The hospital staff must have given her the name Lucy. Or perhaps a social worker. The realisation hits her very hard and very suddenly, like a freight train. She feels as though she cannot breathe for a moment.

She wonders what the name her real mother gave her might be.

Whether she thought of a name for her at all.

Perhaps the letter will tell her.

She can feel it watching her, burning a hole in the back of her head, tucked away in the box under her bed.

She stares down at the linoleum, her whole body suddenly rigid and thrumming with a strange adrenaline, wonders whether she should read the texts from her mother that she has been ignoring, and feels very acutely that she is about to die.

And then she looks at Winston, who is watching her inquisitively, his head tilted ever so slightly to one side.

He trots over to her and nuzzles a wet nose into the palm of her hand. After a moment, she runs her fingers through the fur behind his ears, which he seems to like.

Yeah, Winston will do, I suppose, she says quietly.

We'll need to get his bollocks chopped off at some point, too, Cam says matter-of-factly.

Ash dramatically throws their head back. For the love of *God*, they say.

They spend the weekend getting Winston used to his new surroundings and training him to walk to heel on the lead, taking him out to Greenwich Park. Cam – truly a dog person, Lucy has discovered – knows how to train Winston with treats and positive reinforcement. Winston is a true Londoner, they decide, because he has excellent tube and bus manners. He even waits for the disembarking passengers to get off before dragging them on, falling just short of yanking the shoulder out of the socket of whomever is holding his lead. Cam and Lucy bathe him in the paddling pool in the garden, turning the water a putrid greybrown colour. Despite the repulsion she feels at the sight of the dirty water, Lucy kicks off her shoes and steps into the paddling pool to better lather the special antifungal shampoo the vet gave them into what little fur Winston has left. She tries her best to ignore the invisible centipedes that are crawling all over her. The bacteria off Winston's skin colonising at the bottom of the pool. After they are done, she disinfects it with bleach as Cam watches on, puzzled. Winston seems to enjoy being bathed, tipping his head back, his mouth stretched wide revealing that ginormous pink tongue.

What if he dies? she asks Cam, as she rinses Winston clean with the hose. Now that the dust and muck of the city is gone, his fur gleams like threads of spun gold in the warm sunshine.

She finds that she is warming to him even more so now that he doesn't smell like her dad's fishing maggots. The dog, not Cam.

You can't go through life, Cam tells her, thinking that the ones you love are going to die at any moment.

She sprays him with the hose. Cam, not the dog.

They learn that Winston likes to have things in his mouth. Not food, or human hands, but soft things, like cushions and teddies. Lucy gathers up the soft toys of her childhood and presents them to him. Cam finds an unused loofah and an old pillow under his bed. Winston takes those too. He collects his toys into the corner of the living room and wanders the flat with a plush Bugs Bunny hanging out of his mouth. Ash mutters, For fuck's sakes under their breath when they see this, but says no more.

Lucy can't call in sick to work forever, so she takes herself into the office on Monday to give the appearance of being engaged in her work – but, also, she does have budget meetings that she needs to attend. Anais is hyperactive: she chatters about *Love Island* and the news and her weekend.

Don't you want to ask me how it went with Cam? Anais asks her at lunchtime. There is a note in her voice that Lucy doesn't understand.

Oh, yeah, Lucy says, her voice flat. How did it go?

Amazing. We're working things out. Slowly. He doesn't realise what a good thing we had. It's going to take some time to bring him around, I think. But I know there's still something there.

Anais seems to watch her very closely when she talks about Cam, which makes these conversations especially exhausting for Lucy to arrange her face into a convincingly neutral expression. She wonders why Cam didn't bring Anais home the night she found Winston, if their date went so well. She doesn't dare ask about Josh the personal trainer again, whom she is almost certain Anais is still seeing.

Delilah hovers at their desks and takes Lucy off for private, hushed chats to discuss departmental budget cuts.

You're doing a wonderful job, Delilah tells her as she sips iced coffee through a disintegrating paper straw. Stellar work all round, she says. Also, we need all of the key account managers to give us back the iPads we got them last year.

No problem, Lucy says flatly. She can feel the acid in her stomach curdling like bad milk. She notices that bits of the paper have got stuck to Delilah's plum-coloured lipstick. She does not point this out to Delilah.

When Lucy arrives home from work, she is greeted by Winston and Bugs Bunny hanging from his mouth by the head. Winston accepts her pats graciously. She realises that she is enjoying the sort of unconditional and all-encompassing affection that the dog has for her.

In the kitchen, Cam sits at the table with a girl who is vaguely familiar to Lucy: tall, with dark eyes and dark hair, young-looking, a teenager even, wrapped in a jumper and a giant knitted cardigan despite the weather. From her earlobes dangle giant hoop earrings.

Hi, the girl says. Lucy, isn't it?

Yes, Lucy replies, puzzled, as she flicks the switch on the kettle. She glances at Cam who is grinning.

This is my sister, Bella, Cam tells her. She's going to stay for a few days while we do some university tours.

The resemblance clicks, now, and Lucy sees that Bella has the same high cheekbones, the same smiling eyes as Cam. She remembers catching a glimpse of this girl when she came to stay in the box room for a weekend last summer.

You're not the one who works in a rescue centre, are you?

Bella and Cam exchange a strange look, one that Lucy cannot decipher. The mood between them changes, almost imperceptibly, the air suddenly fraught with tension.

No, that's the older one, Cam says. Naomi.

Gosh, I love your hair so much, Bella tells her.

Oh, thank you. It's oxblood.

Bella smiles politely.

I like your earrings. They really suit you.

Thanks! She grins at Lucy stupidly, and Lucy finds herself grinning back.

Lucy busies herself with her green tea while Cam and Bella fuss over Winston, and talk about their own family dogs: two elderly German shepherds called Milo and Sasha. How they speak about the dogs, as though they are younger siblings and members of the family, makes Lucy feel warm. From the way Bella handles Winston – letting him sniff her hands and wrists extensively before attempting to scratch him behind the ears; the way she doesn't flinch when he makes a sudden movement or barks loudly at the pigeons in the garden – Lucy knows that she is just as comfortable with dogs as Cam is. She wishes that she, too, were a natural when it came to Winston. She tells them this, joining them at the kitchen table.

Not at all, Bella says, in a way that makes Lucy suppress a smile because she is so like Cam in how she says it. Look at him. He loves you.

At this moment, Winston has got his chin rested in Lucy's lap, his eyes closed and a look of complete bliss on his face as Lucy rubs the space between his eyes with her thumb. They are in the kitchen. She can smell the microwave but cannot try to scrub at it with Winston blocking her way.

They take Winston for a walk on Tuesday evening – the three of them – around Burgess Park, and Lucy listens as Cam and Bella talk about her university choices. Bella is visiting because Cam has promised to take her around UCL, UEL, UAL, SOAS, King's and Imperial. Upon hearing that Lucy studied at Imperial, Bella launches into a thousand and one questions about what it was like.

It was hard. But I loved it, Lucy says. It was the first time I felt like I had total freedom. She thinks of Danny, her parents. She tells Bella about the faculty buildings; the staff; her finance degree; the library; the nightlife; the people.

With every question, Bella gets even more excited, her face stretching into a broad grin that is so like Cam's that Lucy has to stop herself from pointing it out.

Bella tells Lucy that she wants to go to Warwick, but Cam wonders whether somewhere closer to home is better.

I don't like the idea of you being all alone somewhere, hours away from me or Mum, he says.

That's the whole point, Bella says. She launches Winston's ball across the park. Obligingly, he sprints away after it, his tongue trailing behind him. He can't quite slow himself enough in time to collect the ball, so he skids comically across the grass and ends up roly-polying to a stop.

Back at the flat, Lucy cooks for the three of them: salmon fillet and broccoli. She dresses the fish with lemon juice and pepper, wraps it in tin foil and fires up the grill. But she isn't paying too much attention to the cooking because she's listening to Bella's stories of Cam's embarrassing teenage haircuts.

Remember when you grew a mullet? she asks him, laughing.

I thought I told you to never speak of that.

Nevertheless, Bella already has her phone out, giggling, and is showing Lucy the pictures.

Look at the state of you, Lucy says good-naturedly.

Hey. I looked cool, for the time.

Yeah, if the *time* was the eighties.

He throws a bread roll at her and she catches it deftly before launching it back at him.

The food turns out fine: they eat companionably, as Bella and Lucy talk about their mutual favourite bands.

After dinner, Bella tells them that she's going to call her boyfriend in Cam's bedroom.

Have you got a boyfriend, Lucy? Bella asks her as she's clearing the plates from the table.

Well. Kind of, Lucy replies. She can't help but glance at Cam, who is smirking, pretending to check his phone.

Tom the Tory, he says amusedly, under his breath.

Hey!

He shrugs, a look of faux innocence painted on his face.

What's he like? Bella asks.

Oh . . . He's . . . You know. He works in finance.

Coooool, Bella replies flatly.

Nice to meet you, Lucy tells her as she bids everyone goodnight, and Bella – surprisingly – hugs her deeply.

Lucy takes two beers out of the fridge and hands one to Cam. He accepts it gratefully, and sips silently as she washes the dishes in the sink.

I don't understand why everyone keeps shitting on Tom, she says, letting hot water run over her fingers and soak the plates.

Cam says nothing for a beat, his demeanour suddenly changed.

Come off it, Lucy, he mutters.

What do you mean, come off it?

She cannot bear to turn around and look him in the face, but she still hears him let out an exaggerated sigh.

I don't know why I have to be the one to tell you this. But he's not right for you. He seems kind of terrible, in fact. I don't understand why you're settling for him.

It's interesting that you think I'm *settling* for him, she says, biting back her irritation. I always felt like he was out of my league. Look at his job. His upbringing. He's exactly what I need. Lucy can hear herself saying these things – registers how ridiculous she sounds – but she can't stop the words from tumbling out of her mouth. She feels her face turning hot.

Cam snorts dismissively. Do you really think so little of yourself, Lucy? Look at you. Why are you interested in *money* and *breeding*?

Lucy swallows the lump in her throat. She is reminded of something Tom said to her on their first date in Chiswick: *What really, truly motivates you in the deepest darkest part of yourself, what you care the most about, is money.*

Maybe Tom has been right about her all along.

It is now that she turns to look at Cam.

I don't expect *you* to understand.

What's that supposed to mean?

She cannot answer him. She knows that he is thinking what she is: that Cam has a reasonably wealthy family, that he gives off all the cues of middle classness, that if his life fell apart tomorrow, his parents could transfer a grand into his bank account, no questions asked, no skin off anyone's teeth. Like Ash's grandparents do for them. Cam knows as well as Lucy does that she doesn't have that safety net. Perhaps he doesn't realise that every decision Lucy has ever made has been about constructing one for herself.

He stares at her, his eyes blazing with an emotion she doesn't quite understand. It is as though he is daring her to say it out loud, his jaw tensed.

Finally, after what seems like an age, he says, You're an intelligent and sensitive and beautiful person.

She lets out a scoff. Oh, *please.*

Stop it. You are. And I don't understand why you're changing yourself to suit him. You're pretending to be someone you're not. To please someone else? It makes no sense to me.

Lucy can feel the colour rising in her cheeks. *Intelligent and sensitive and beautiful.* She tries to think of a time anyone has called her any of those adjectives before, and she can't. The bar is on the floor, really.

She thinks instead of what Danny told her, and what Tom repeated: *You think you're so much better than everyone else, don't you?*

She can feel her breath quickening as she thinks of it. She grips the edge of the sink, bracing herself against it.

You okay? Cam asks, his voice coloured with concern.

Lucy nods her head vigorously, not trusting herself to speak.

Are you breathing?

She shakes her head. She can feel the tears coming, squeezing themselves angrily from her ducts, her throat hot and tight.

He comes to stand next to her at the sink.

I'm not pretending to be someone else, she lies, through gritted teeth, trying to keep the anger from her voice.

I think you are, he says gently.

The problem is, she realises, that she doesn't know what part of her is pretending any more. And what part is really who she is, deep down in her bones. The part that she was born with. The part that she has inherited from strangers who abandoned her at the hospital doors.

You don't know anything about me, she says. And she throws

the last dish onto the drying rack, forcefully, relishing the overloud clattering sound it makes as it slams against the other crockery.

She leaves him there, his mouth a little bit agape, a look on his face that she doesn't fully understand.

Chapter Twenty-One

Lucy wakes up the next morning with a horrible taste in her mouth. Her phone is ringing. It's Tom.

She answers it, feeling her fingers curl up.

Hi, he says softly.

Hi.

I wanted to apologise for the other night. I was acting like a moron.

It's okay, Lucy says. Her whole body feels malleable, like soft warm clay.

I just wanted you to be excited about meeting my family.

I know. I am excited. It's just—

I think my dad would like you.

Would he?

What about Saturday? We can go and visit for the weekend.

Erm. Okay.

You're really important to me, Lucy.

And at those words, she feels herself relax. It is nice, as always, to hear how she matters to someone else. Maybe she and Tom are meant for each other.

You're important to me, too, she replies. She can hear his smile down the phone.

*

She heads into the kitchen, feeling quite pleased with herself about Tom and how lovely he is to her, most of the time, how she was right about him. Nevertheless, she cannot face the office today, and she is anxious about leaving Winston. So she flings an email out to Delilah to say that she will work on the budget re-forecast from home, choosing to make the statement rather than ask the question. A bold move for her. Flicking the switch on the kettle, she notices the plate that she threw onto the draining board last night, wedged at an awkward angle amongst the other crockery from how it landed. She wonders whether she can pretend her argument with Cam never happened; whether he will do the same. Bella is fast asleep on the airbed in the living room. She makes herself a coffee, and then, after a moment's hesitation, makes another for Cam. Cam takes his coffee white with one sugar, she remembers, surprised that she knows this. He drinks coffee in the morning and tea after lunchtime. She takes both mugs to his bedroom and knocks lightly.

Cam is sitting up in bed, Winston asleep on the floor. His laptop is open on his knees. Upon seeing her at the door, he closes it softly.

You okay? he asks her.

Peace offering? She holds up the mug and he smiles.

Come on, then.

She perches nervously on the edge of his bed as he gulps the coffee down. Lucy has never been in Cam's bedroom before. She has certainly never been on Cam's bed. She looks around. Cam's bookshelves are packed with classics and thick fantasy hardbacks: *Catch 22* and *A Game of Thrones* and Tolkien and Angela Carter and Douglas Adams and Terry Pratchett and Margaret Atwood and Ursula K. Le Guin, all jumbled up together. On the other shelves mounted to the walls are deck boxes of Magic: The Gathering cards, and Warhammer figurines. There is an *Empire Strikes Back* art print on the wall behind the headboard. She wonders how much of Cam's stuff was out and on display like this when Anais still lived here. Winston heaves himself up onto the bed too and promptly falls asleep once again, his ribcage rising and falling slowly as his breathing deepens, his body warm against Lucy's legs. She closes her eyes momentarily and breathes in, one big deep gulp of air.

I just wanted to apologise, she says. For snapping at you last night.

You don't need to apologise to me.

Lucy picks at her fingernails, suddenly uncomfortable with the intimacy of this interaction. She is wearing her pyjamas. Cam is not wearing a shirt and she can see the broad plane of his chest, which is smooth, the sinews in his shoulders.

It's none of my business what goes on between you and Tom, Cam says tentatively. If you like him, and he makes you happy, that's all that matters.

He wants me to meet his dad, she says out loud.

Oh, wow, Cam says, his smile strained. That's . . . good?

I don't know. I don't know if I'm ready to.

Okay. I mean, that's fine too, if you're not ready.

I'm not feeling very good about the person I am at the moment, she tells him, feeling the bad taste in her mouth worsening as she says this. She runs her tongue across her teeth.

Do you want to talk about it?

Lucy hesitates before going to her bedroom and taking out the box from under her bed. It feels hot as she lifts it. She comes back to Cam and hands it over to him.

What's this?

All of the documents to do with my adoption.

Have you looked at them?

Not yet. I don't know whether I want to or not.

Can I?

Yeah.

Cam gently slides the lid off the box.

He leafs through the pages gently, his glasses sliding to the end of his nose, not really looking or reading. Lucy watches him, feeling a strange sense of calm settle over her, the notion that the box is no longer her secret alone. She buries her fingers into the fur on the back of Winston's neck and he stirs and nudges at her hand with his nose.

There's a letter, Lucy tells him, from my birth mother. She is looking the other way: she doesn't want to see something – some scrap of upside-down writing or a photocopy – that will give her knowledge she's not sure that she wants yet.

Cam places the lid back on the box, handling it as though it is a newborn baby.

When did you get all this stuff? he asks her.

The day after Ash's gig. I went to my parents'.

Cam pinches his chin thoughtfully. How did it go with them?

Lucy feels it again, settling over her, though muted in this context – in the bright early morning of Cam's bedroom, the sunlight diffusing through the curtains and turning Winston into spun gold. The way the secrets are open wounds, inviting infection, now that the scabs have been ripped away. How they might make her feel, and how this unknown terrifies her.

I'm not sure, to be honest, she says.

What you do next is up to you, he tells her.

But I don't know what to do next. I don't feel very in control of what's happening.

That's okay. These papers aren't going anywhere. You can wait years if you want to.

She threads her hands together and runs her fingers across her knuckles. She feels as though she can trust Cam in this moment. That all of her secrets are safe with him.

I love my parents, so much, she says. But I think they've done bad things. Not maliciously. Just by the nature of circumstance. They've made some bad decisions, and it's made things difficult for me. Difficult for Danny.

Like what?

She shakes her head, screwing up her face.

She is thinking of the secret they made Danny keep when he was only a child. Never believing either of them, never being around, so that Lucy and Danny constructed their own little world with its own set of warped rules – their own dysfunctional family – just the two of them.

Not for the first time, Lucy wonders what kind of person she might be if she'd had different parents: if she had stayed with her biological parents, rather than been adopted. If Mum is right, it might not have been such a good life. A too-young single mother, maybe. It's easy to imagine the rest of the story. Maybe drugs. Maybe homelessness. Poverty. Or maybe something entirely different. Maybe a young mother forced to give up her baby by a controlling family, motivated by shame. Maybe parents who have been trying to find her ever since.

She won't know unless she reads the letter.

Even *thinking* about it feels like a betrayal to Erica and Daniel.

But then, by keeping the secret all these years, surely it's them who have betrayed her.

Is there something intrinsically more sacred, more special and life-affirming, about being among your own blood?

She asks Cam this question.

Surely one isn't better than the other, he muses, frowning. It's just different.

Just different.

Parents are just people, Cam says. Like everyone else. Families are messy whether they're functional or otherwise. They're fallible.

Are your parents going to get divorced? she asks him, remembering that he said they might.

It looks like it.

I'm sorry.

He shrugs. It's long overdue, to be honest. I think what's more important, he continues, are the people you choose to have in your life. Rather than the ones you must have, by virtue of your birth.

She puts her face to Winston's neck and inhales.

God, that dog loves you, Cam says, and her heart is swollen.

Do you forgive me? For being so awful yesterday?

He waves his hand at her. You weren't being awful. But it's forgotten. Let's never speak of it again.

She smiles.

Friends? he asks her, and she nods, ignoring the way the word slices through her, making her bones thrum with a strange energy.

Do you want a hug?

She hesitates a moment, before sidling up to the pillow end of his bed, and he pulls her into a warm and generous hug. Winston joins them, laying his whole body across Cam's shins. It is nice and uncomplicated and pure.

In the late afternoon, Cam finds her in the garden, listening to a true crime podcast, splayed out on the yellow sunlounger.

Shall we go somewhere? he asks.

What, us? Lucy squints up at him, her fingers fluttering nervously.

Yes, us, Banbury.

They decide to take Winston for a picnic. After some protracted debate about where they ought to go, and some googling,
they decide on Leyton Flats in Epping Forest. Cam insists
that he should drive. They load Winston, and a picnic blanket
and ham sandwiches and crisps and Fanta into the back of the
Micra. Lucy feels a strange excitement thrilling through her as
she reads the postcode out to Cam and he keys it into his phone.
The anticipation of an adventure. It's been so long since she felt
it. She is reminded of going to visit Uncle Marv on the canal
as a child. The greenness of the marshland. Not little pocket
squares of it, like how it is in the London Borough of Lambeth:
but the untouched kind that stretches to the horizon. She props
her feet onto the dashboard and lets the sun warm her shins as
Cam drives. They listen to a playlist of Cam's choosing: Boston
and Toto and Led Zeppelin and T-Rex. Stuff that reminds Lucy
of her parents.

She grins at him as he sings along to each song, word-perfect,
putting on a silly falsetto voice to sing 'Hold the Line', glancing
at her to check whether or not she's laughing. She is: she can't
help it. The way Cam takes on the small joys of his existence
wholeheartedly, and unapologetically, is infectious. The windows are all the way down and Winston in the back seat has got
his own face hanging out of one, his tongue a streak of pink to
the wind on the North Circular. She pushes Cam's sunglasses
further up his nose for him on the Redbridge Roundabout.

Leyton Flats itself is not so flat – not the vast yellow-straw-
grassed planes of Lucy's imagination – but rather lush dense
forest crammed in around the edges of the glass-surfaced boating
lakes. They walk the shaded paved brown footpath that borders
Hollow Ponds, the sun periodically breaking through the trees
to bear down on the backs of their necks. They let Winston off

his lead so he can explore the foliage, running in and out of the bushes, inquisitive, nosing at the dry loose earth at the roots of the silver birches and oak trees. On the lake, couples and families are lazy in old-fashioned white rowboats with pinewood oars.

Shall we see if we can get Winston in one? Cam asks as they settle on a dry sandy patch on the edge of the lake. Winston has already waded armpit-high into the lake, his face beaming with pure bliss. The water laps up to the shoreline like a tide.

Lucy shakes her head no.

The water is dirty, she tells him. Look.

She points out the oil-slick of goose waste on the surface near where they have spread the blanket. The birds' feathers trapped in the foliage at the edge of the water. The sludge at the roots of the trees. The birds are everywhere, actually. She can smell them. She suddenly becomes conscious of what their food is and is not touching. Whether it is covered over and protected from the horseflies that dot the air. She can feel herself becoming fidgety, looking at the food on the blanket. She feels herself itching to take it all away, spoiled as it is, and throw it into the lake.

It's all right, Cam tells her. He has been watching her expression with some curiosity. Relax.

Lucy stares at him. How do you do that?

Do what?

How do you know what I'm thinking? Before even I do, sometimes.

Cam shrugs. Intuition? I don't know.

You're very good at it.

At school, we have to watch out for the quiet ones.

And I'm a quiet one? I don't know how to feel about that. *You're* a quiet one.

He laughs and leans back on the blanket, his arms bent behind his head, the picture of ease.

That's why we've got to stick together, he says. She finds herself staring at him, for a little longer than is considered polite. But he is staring back at her too, holding her gaze. They are locked in this strange, charged moment with one another.

And then Winston is trotting out of the lake, splashing loudly, and the moment is broken, all his goldenness illuminated by the sunshine, seemingly fascinated by the pleasing slapping noises the water makes as each of his feet hit it.

What's Bella doing today? Lucy asks, to change the subject.

She's doing some sightseeing with some of her Twitter friends. And tomorrow we're going on a couple of campus tours. SOAS and UCL, I think.

Is she staying for long?

A week or so, I think. Sorry – she'll be out of your hair soon.

No – no – I didn't mean it like that. I think she's wonderful.

He smiles.

And your other sister, Naomi, do you get to see much of her?

Naomi?

Yes. She's the one who works in kennels, right?

Yes, she did.

Do you not get on or something?

Lucy sensed a strange tension between Bella and Cam when Naomi's name was mentioned. She waits for him to answer, watching Winston, and when after a stretch of time he hasn't said anything, she turns to see him staring blankly at the lake, his jaw tensed.

Cam . . .?

Naomi is – was – our older sister. She died.

Oh . . . god. I'm sorry. I had no idea.

Not your fault, is it?

Lucy waits for him to say more, her hands useless. She wipes them absent-mindedly on her shorts. She suddenly feels awful for never asking. She remembers how she felt when she met Bella. Mainly, an overwhelming jealousy at how seemingly perfect a relationship the two of them had. How her and Danny would never have anything close to what they do.

We don't have to talk about it, if you don't want to, she says quietly.

It's just . . . it was two years ago. It still feels like it happened last week. It's still . . . hard.

Of course.

She had leukaemia, Cam says. So, it wasn't a surprise. She first got sick when she was a baby, I don't really remember her ever being healthy. She'd been in remission twice, and then it came back and she went downhill quickly. I've spent a lot of time assessing the temperature in my family, you know? Keeping things level. Being this, like, emotional neutraliser. Trying to make everyone happy, all the time. My parents constantly argued, even before Naomi died. Bella disappeared into herself, wouldn't talk to anyone about anything. So, a lot of the time, I was this thread holding everyone – everything – together. And now I'm not there and Bella is kind of losing it.

She's not coping at all. And now my parents are separating. I just think, he says, if I can keep her in London. Or closer to home, at least. I can keep an eye on her. Make sure she's all right.

Cam, Lucy says, not sure what else there is to say.

He drags his hands across his eyes, and looks at her.

Sometimes, he says. I feel like I'm not in my own body. Ever since Naomi died. Like, I'm watching someone else live my life and I'm just kind of stuck in this weird void where things happen to me but I can't really feel them. I've never told anyone that before. I'm scared that I'm sort of losing a bit of myself.

She goes to him and pulls him to her, his head on her shoulder, his hands loose across her back, and she lets him cry very very quietly into her shirt. Lets her fingers weave into his hair in a manner that she hopes is soothing.

I don't know what to do, he says. I don't know how to stop feeling like this.

I'm here, she replies.

They sit on the edge of the lake and talk about other things. What Cam was like growing up; his mum and dad. Bella. Naomi. As they talk, Lucy feels the air lighten around them. It is so easy to talk to Cam about anything. He tells her about his short-lived career as a children's magician when he was at university.

Possibly the nerdiest thing I've heard about you yet, Lucy tells him, laughing.

Cam shrugs, Hey. That job paid for my first car. *And* it made me want to teach. I got a lot out of it. Anyway, he continues. What about you and your emo phase? I'm desperate to know more about this.

Lucy rolls her eyes at him, smiling. She tells him about her mother and the matching outfits.

It was extremely uncool, she says. Looking back on it. When I was a kid, though, I loved dressing like my mum. I thought she was the most glamorous person in the world. We looked so unlike one another in terms of our biology. I think it made me feel closer to her.

So . . . what happened?

Lucy shrugs, looking away. She remembers what happened, but she can't tell Cam, she doesn't think. Her dad's accident when she was twelve. Suddenly, there wasn't any money for new clothes, or much of anything. With Dad needing round-the-clock care in the first couple of years, there wasn't much time for

Mum to spend hours planning her wardrobe with Lucy, or to help her do her hair.

I acted out. Went through my teenager phase. Got desperate for someone to pay attention to me, she says. All the typical bullshit.

And then . . . what, you changed your mind again?

He is referring to what she's wearing now. A dark blue halter-neck and a pair of dusty pink paper bag shorts. She learned about Kibbe in her early twenties and she has been dressing herself as a soft classic religiously ever since.

Lucy looks down at herself, and tries to visualise herself as she imagines Cam must see her. She can't quite manage it. She doesn't know what version of herself he is looking at.

She says, thinking of her mother, The way other people look at you is one of the few things in the world that you can control.

She thinks, too, of her first undergraduate seminars; her first job at Doughnuts when she left uni. The way she so quickly assimilated to how the other, wealthier, more popular and aspirational people around her were dressing. Even so, she has always had a deeply embedded suspicion that no matter how nice she dresses, no matter how much she spends on expensive haircuts and perfume and make-up, no matter how much she creates this version of herself, everyone can *tell*. They will look at her or smell her or listen to her speak and there will be something about the way she looks or smells or sounds that she can't get rid of, that she can't wash off. They will know where she came from, and they will know that she doesn't belong.

She has been glancing up periodically to check that Winston is nearby, but when she does this time, she can't see him immediately.

Where's Winston? she asks Cam, immediately tense.

He stands up and calls his name. She does too – peering into the dense trees, around the bushes at the edge of the lake, she feels the slow ebb of panic in her fingertips. She looks out to the water and sees him there – a little golden head bobbing next to a buoy.

He's over there, she calls to Cam, and then calls out to Winston again. He must be a hundred yards from the shore. She can see his black, shining eyes and his mouth, wide open and smiling. She calls him again. He doesn't move away from the buoy. What's he playing at? she asks Cam, and then she realises. He's stuck, isn't he. He's caught himself on the buoy. He must have got his collar hooked to it or something.

A cold and grave sensation of dread falls over her immediately. She feels her breath beginning to quicken.

How can he have got stuck? Cam asks, incredulous, a note of panic in his own voice. He can't be.

But he's not coming back. What are we going to do?

We're going to have to go out and get him, Cam says.

Lucy stares out to Winston. He grins back at her, none the wiser to their shared alarm on the shore.

We need to go now, Lucy says. Her mind races with the life-guarding protocols from the NPLQ training she took when she was sixteen, drummed into her so thoroughly that she can recite them like the Lord's Prayer. She kicks off her trainers, yanks her socks off too, and pulls her phone from her back pocket, throwing it onto the ground. She jogs up to the water, stares down at the sludge. The tiny creatures crawling in it. The bacteria. She can already feel it on her skin. Her heart is hammering. Winston is going to drown. Winston is going to die.

I'll go, Cam says quickly.

No. You're not a strong swimmer. And he's a long way out. I need to do it.

Shall I see if we can get a boat?

There isn't any time. *Fuck.*

Lucy feels as though she is going to cry. She tries to force herself to step into the water. Her body won't let her. She can feel her whole self grimacing, cringing away from it. She is turned to stone.

Come on, she tells herself quietly. Get in the water, moron. *Get in.*

She steps into the water and recoils immediately as it touches her foot. The peat swills up around her toes. Tiny black particles of dirt. She breathes out slowly. Winston lets out a strained yelp and her heart drops like a stone.

Lucy, Cam says.

Yes, I'm going. I'm going.

She braces herself and wades further in. Feels the lake water drift up to her knees, her thighs, soak her shorts, waist-deep now. Winston is still out there by the buoy. She shivers. She is accustomed to swimming in heated, chlorinated, clean swimming pools. The breeze sends it lapping at her stomach. And then the ground beneath her is no longer there, and she is swimming. She propels herself through the dark water, thinking only of Winston. Not of the pond skaters and the flies and ducks and what they have left on the surface of the lake. The reeds that snake around her ankles as she forces her body into a swift front crawl.

She is there next to the dog in moments – no time at all really – and as she slows herself to come level with him, he licks at her face, treading water. His fur is soaked through and matted, clinging to her as she grabs hold of him around the chest. As she suspected, his collar is snagged on the metal wire that suspends the buoy in place. She unclips it easily and Winston is immediately on his way back to the shoreline. His own front crawl as strong as hers, if not stronger. She follows him with a laboured breaststroke, until they are both back at the edge of the lake. Cam is waiting with towels for both of them. He hurls one at Lucy and captures Winston in a second one, fiercely rubbing his fur.

Winston, Winston, he says. You pillock. What were you doing out there?

Lucy drags herself out of the water, her clothes saturated and leaden. She wraps a towel around herself, shivering, her heart hammering.

His collar got caught on the buoy, she tells Cam, her teeth chattering. She feels the dirt of the lake sliding down her back, her legs. The muck clinging to her skin. She feels disgusting.

Cam checks Winston's neck for wounds.

He looks fine, he says, and Lucy lets out a sigh of relief.

Winston seems totally oblivious to the fright he has given them, his tongue lolling happily, panting heavily. He shakes his whole body and sends a fresh spray of water over them.

Are you okay? Cam asks. It is not clear whether he is talking to Winston or Lucy.

I thought he was going to die, Lucy says, the filth of the water forgotten.

He didn't though, Cam says, the relief etched across his face. You got him.

You got him.

Chapter Twenty-Two

It doesn't take long for the freezing lake water to get into Lucy's bones. They drive back to Lambeth, Lucy and Winston soaking wet and leaking onto the tired upholstery in the faded interior of Cam's car. Lucy, conscious of the bacteria crawling all over her, is too agitated to make conversation, and Cam seems to understand this and doesn't prod at her. It's more important to get Winston clean and dry first, so they bathe him in the garden, rinsing the dark silt-like particles from his fur with the hosepipe, lathering his special prescription shampoo through his coat. It's not until hours later that Lucy gets to take off her own damp, ruined clothes and get under a hot, high-pressure shower. She scrubs herself all over twice. Even then, she feels dirty. She feels the grime in the folds of her skin: behind her ears, between her fingers, on the backs of her knees. She tries not to think about it. She wraps herself in white towels and meditates. In the moment, nothing had been more important than getting Winston safely out of the water. But now, left alone with her own thoughts and the stink of the lake clinging to her, she can't stop thinking about it.

You look like an angel, Bella tells her when she sees her, remarking on her white turban towel and dressing gown.

Lucy tries very hard not to cry, her throat burning. She feels as though there are bugs from the water crawling all over her skin. She lets Winston sleep on her bed with her. Breathes in his biscuity dog-smell. Listens to his slow, sleeping breath.

On Thursday, Lucy works and Cam takes Bella to see different universities around the city. She still seems, to Lucy, to be delighted to be spending time with her brother, to be treated like an adult by Lucy and Ash, who she engages in conversations about their work and lives, in which she seems genuinely interested to hear their answers. She is totally fascinated by Ash's gender identity, and Ash is very obliging in answering her borderline invasive questions. Lucy spends a very long time explaining to her what she does for a living.

It sounds pretty boring, to be honest, Bella says after Lucy has clarified profit and loss for the third time.

I love it, Lucy tells her, and as she says this, she notices how robotic she sounds. She wonders what exactly it is she likes about supplier relations and Kube. She likes the stability of it, yes. And the routine. But now both of these things have been disrupted she is not so sure what there is left to enjoy. She doesn't like suppliers; she doesn't like relations – or rather, relating to other people. The work is exhausting and repetitive. She doesn't like being micromanaged by the overzealous Delilah.

It sounds like you hate it, Bella argues, shrugging. You should be a teacher. Like Cam.

I'm *definitely* not cut out to be a teacher.

Why not?

I don't know how to talk to people.

Well, you're talking to me fine. Cam's great at it, Bella tells her.

Do *you* want to be a teacher?

No. I don't know what I want to do. I don't even know what I want to study at uni.

Whatever you do, Lucy tells her, I bet you'll be amazing.

She has no evidence to back this up, but Bella seems to take the compliment at face value and beams at her, delighted.

That night, Bella decides that she wants to go to a karaoke bar.

I've never been to one, she whines to Cam. When's the next time I'm going to get to do *karaoke* in *London*? I bet they don't have Lucky Voice in Warwick.

We don't know if you're going to Warwick yet.

I'm going to Warwick, and there won't be *any* karaoke, and it'll be *all your fault*.

It's so transparent to Lucy that Bella is working Cam. She can see him wavering, Bella needling him until he gives in.

This is going to cost a fucking fortune, he says under his breath as he googles Lucky Voice on his laptop. Bella has conveniently decided to go and call her boyfriend as soon as talk of booking fees has come up.

You're a pushover, Lucy says, from the opposite sofa, grinning.

What are *you* up to tomorrow night? Cam asks her.

Me?

Yes. You.

I was meant to meet Meredith and Nara for drinks after work.

Lucy doesn't mention that she is also meant to be travelling to Ascot with Tom on Saturday morning to visit his dad for the weekend. A big step for her and Tom. A step in the right direction, she thinks. A natural progression. She hasn't spoken to Tom in a few days, actually. She's been so preoccupied with everything going on with Winston and her parents that she has forgotten to reply to his texts.

Why don't you come? Bring them, too, if you like. I'll invite Ash. And maybe Paul and Francesca.

Really? That's a lot of people for karaoke.

The more the merrier, hey? Let's all make fools of ourselves.

She raises her eyebrows. Lucy is not the type of person to wilfully make a fool of herself. The idea that she might have to, if she accepts Cam's invitation, wars with the warmth she feels at being invited along in the first place.

Also, it's cheaper to group book, he adds, and she snorts into her coffee.

She taps out a quick text to the group chat. *Anyone fancy karaoke tomorrow instead of All Bar One?*

Nara replies five minutes later. *Erm. YES. I love karaoke.*

Meredith concurs.

Lucy has already texted Tom to cancel Ascot. She barely registers her annoyance at his reply: *Wow. I don't know why I'm even surprised.*

The following night, they squeeze into the tiny purple-uplit room in Soho: Lucy, Cam, Bella, Ash, Meredith, Nara, Paul and Francesca, who seems to Lucy to be painfully shy. Ash and Lucy have kitted Bella out in Lucy's high heels and make-up, and she has been smuggled into the building in the centre of a group huddle on the basis that she is still about four months shy of the legal drinking age. Once inside, they order finger food and each pore over the song book, squished up on uncomfortable sofas. Meredith orders mojitos for everyone – including Bella – and demands to go first. She belts out a Whitney Houston number in what is categorically the most tone-deaf rendition anyone in the room has ever heard. Lucy worries that Meredith will be embarrassed and want to leave. As the person who invited her and Nara, she feels responsible for them, wants them to have a nice time and enjoy the company of the rest of the group. But once the song is over, and Nara makes a very loud, very immature fart noise, both thumbs down, Meredith bursts into laughter, her face relaxed.

Bella does a Paramore song, and when it becomes clear that Lucy is the only other person who knows the words, drags her up to the front of the room to duet into the microphone. Lucy can feel her palms slickening with sweat as everyone else watches them politely, unable to sing along. She reminds herself that she is doing a nice thing for Bella and this is not about her. She imagines Danny arranging a night of karaoke for her at seventeen before sending her off to university. It's impossible: so far removed from her reality that it seems absurd. She wonders whether she is about to have a panic attack, but before she can examine her stress levels, the song is over and she sprints back to her corner of sofa, clapping politely at Bella when she realises that everyone else is.

Ash chooses Stevie Nicks and, unsurprisingly, nails it.

Fuck off, you're not meant to be actually *good*, Paul yells at them as they finish the song and bow with an exaggerated flourish.

Paul is next and Ash boos him loudly when the opening bars of an Ed Sheeran song start playing. Then Nara sings a hammed-up version of 'He Had it Coming' from *Chicago*, forming a chorus line with Meredith and Bella.

Then it's Cam's turn.

What song are you going for? Nara asks. It seems as though everyone is shouting now, a little hyperactive from mojitos and the hilarity of everyone's bad singing.

The rubber seating is unpleasant against Lucy's skin. In her head, she is thinking through all the ways she can get out of singing when it comes to her turn. Despite this, she is finding herself enjoying the evening: settling into her presence here.

Her phone buzzes with a text from Tom and she locks the screen without checking it, looking back up to Cam as he makes his selection on the karaoke machine.

The music starts, and the rest of them exchange confused looks as they try to work out what the song is.

This one goes out, Cam says dramatically into the microphone, to Miss Lucy Banbury.

And he points at her to delighted whoops from the others.

And he starts singing.

Of course. Lucy can't help but burst out laughing.

The song is 'What's Up?' by 4 Non Blondes.

Cam belts out the whole song, which he is objectively very bad at, the tips of his ears red as he locks eyes with her in what seems to be a very deliberate way.

And Lucy can't look away from him, can't help the grin that is stretched across her face, making her jaw ache and her cheeks strain. She cannot help but laugh, as he makes a show of himself, totally carefree in his ridiculousness, so at ease with himself, his hair all mussed up and his arms flailing around theatrically as he belts out the song. Inexplicably, she feels a little emotional, as though her heart is going to burst, as though she's going to cry.

By the first chorus, everyone is screaming along with Cam, and he has broken away from looking at her to conduct them, his voice straining to hit the high notes. By the end of it, Paul has slid off the sofa and is wheezing on the floor silently, his shoulders juddering up and down, tears streaming down his face. Nara gets on her knees, with an expression of pure joy, and mimes worshipping Cam.

Stunning, Meredith screams, waving her arms in the air. Sublime. One of a kind. Outstanding.

Cam shrugs, masking his own laughter, and walks over to Lucy pointedly, takes her hand and kisses it in a show of mock chivalry.

It seems as though the booth has suddenly gone very quiet before Bella and Ash start up the whooping again.

Lucy feels her whole face flood with colour, hot and prickly. She is unsure where to look. She rubs at her hand, the skin where he kissed it burning pleasantly with sensation.

It doesn't escape her notice that Nara and Meredith are sharing a very pointed look with one another. When it's almost her turn to choose a song, she feigns needing fresh air and accompanies Meredith to the smoking area. Bella clatters out after them, unsteady in Lucy's heels, which are a size too big.

Are you having a nice time? Lucy asks her, relishing the cool breeze on her shoulders.

Oh my god, it's the fucking *greatest*, Bella screeches, yanking Lucy and Meredith into a hug, each of her arms wrapped around their necks.

Okay, no more mojitos for this one, Meredith says.

Can I come and hang out with you again?

Of course. Any time.

I'm so glad Cam and Anais broke up, Bella says abruptly, her face a little hazy from tipsiness. He's so much more fun now.

Oh. Okay, Lucy replies. I thought they were getting back together?

I think he's in love with you, you know.

Oh, *please*, Lucy replies before she can stop herself, feeling her face once again turn warm, suddenly very aware of her own pulse and the small guilty curl of satisfaction in her belly that she tries to ignore. Meredith chokes on her cigarette.

On Saturday, Lucy and Bella nurse hangovers and watch movies together while Cam locks himself in his bedroom to lesson-plan before driving Bella back home to their parents' house. Tom texts Lucy a picture of a peacock that lives in his father's garden. He has gone to visit without her. Lucy can't bring herself to care all that much, but she replies with a heart-eyes emoji. She and Bella say a heartfelt goodbye and exchange numbers before Bella leaves. Bella seems to like Lucy, which is unexpected. Ten minutes after she has left in Cam's car, she is already texting Lucy with a list of gigs she wants to go to in the coming months. Lucy realises objectively that it is not the greatest triumph to have a seventeen-year-old think that you're cool. But she feels warmed by it nonetheless, and she genuinely likes Bella.

When Cam gets back, they take Winston for a walk along the South Bank. He has bought a clicker on Amazon. Every time Winston walks to heel, they are to click the clicker and give Winston a small treat. Winston has already filled out a little, his ribs less prominent and his exposed skin less raw-looking. He has learned to take treats gently from the palm of the hand, using only his crooked front teeth rather than the scary pointed fangs. His ears flop about in whatever direction the wind takes them. He is overwhelmingly inquisitive, stopping to sniff every lamp post, every piece of rubbish skidding its way across the pavement, every person's feet and shopping bags.

It's the first time Cam and Lucy have been alone together since karaoke on Friday night. The way he looked at her. The strangely charged atmosphere between them that seems to grow stronger the more time they spend together. The way he kissed her hand – which must have been a joke. Of course it was a joke; he was just messing around, playing a part.

As they queue for the ice-cream van, Cam's phone rings and he pulls it from his pocket, handing Winston's lead to Lucy. She can see the caller ID: it's Anais. Cam rejects the call.

Shouldn't you talk to her? Lucy asks, feeling very much like she is overstepping but asking anyway.

Cam looks at her with an incredulous expression. His hair is messy but in an okay sort of way. He has dark pits beneath his eyes and an angular jaw which is now tensed.

You're getting back together, after all, Lucy says, shrugging and turning away. Her bones are turning leaden. The way he can't give her an answer. Of course it was a joke on Friday. Stop being so ridiculous.

What are you on about? Cam says, eyebrows shooting up. The ice-cream man is asking for their order, so he turns away from her to deliver it.

Lucy admonishes herself for saying the wrong thing again, feels her gut plummeting. She buries her hands into the healthy patch of fur on the back of Winston's neck, and strokes him softly.

You like the blueberry, right? Cam asks.

She takes an ice cream graciously from him, smiling up. She pretends that she is not feeling a deep and tangible relief that he doesn't seem angry at her.

They sit on a bench outside the Tate.

Look – Lucy – about Anais, Cam begins, but she holds the ice cream up, motioning him to stop.

It's none of my business, she says, I shouldn't have asked.

But – it's not what—

Let's just forget it, okay? I don't want to know. It's nothing to do with me.

She's not my girlfriend, he says firmly, before she can protest any more.

What?

She's not. We're not getting back together.

Lucy frowns, thinking of the picture that Anais sent to her – the one of them in bed together. What Anais said to her at work about how things were going well.

I don't know whether Anais knows that, Cam.

Cam leans back on the bench, stretching his long arms out wide, and splaying all of his fingers to the sky. He looks tired.

It's not over between you two, is it?

He looks at her sincerely. Honestly? No. It's not. I would like it to be. But we were together for ten years, or thereabouts. It will take some time, I think. But there's no coming back from this. Not for me, anyway.

Cam looks as though he wants to say something else, but he stops himself, and instead there's a look on his face that she doesn't understand.

They walk home in a comfortable quietness, and the sun is glorious above them, and Lucy eats the ice cream as they walk and forgets to feel uncomfortable about eating while standing up. She has a strong urge to take Cam's hand in her own, but she tamps it down and pretends to be busy watching the river, which is casting off reflective shards of light in the most beautiful and unnerving manner.

Chapter Twenty-Three

On Sunday morning, someone is banging at the door of Flat 5. Lucy listens, half-awake, as Cam pads down the hallway to open it. And then hushed, irritated voices. Moments later, there is a knock at her bedroom door. She drags herself out of bed and opens the door a fraction. Cam stands there, his face directly level with her. It is a shock to have him so close, so early in the morning.

Is everything okay? she asks him.

There are some people here to see you. Your parents.

My *parents*?

What do you want me to do? he asks her, sincerely, and she realises that if she told Cam, right now, that she couldn't face them, he would get rid of them, no questions asked, and do it in a polite and respectful way so that no one's feelings got hurt.

She looks down at her fingernails. Lucy's parents haven't come into town for a casual visit before, not ever. The last time they were here with her was when she graduated.

I need to talk to them, don't I?

Cam gives her a small smile. It's up to you. But my professional opinion is that you probably should.

She nods, resigned. I'll get dressed. Can you . . . ?

Yeah, the kettle's on. Take your time.

When Lucy enters the kitchen, Cam is chatting easily with her mum, who is dressed in what Lucy knows to be her very best clothes – her nicest black jeans and a floral off-the-shoulder top – with her hair washed and straightened, and her wrists jangling with beaded bracelets. Daniel Senior is in the same thing he always wears – a half-zip fishing jumper and an ancient pair of khakis. Cam has served them both tea and is introducing them, now, to Winston, who is happily accepting treats from Lucy's dad, his tail wagging at lightning speed.

You didn't tell us you got a dog, chicken, her mum says, turning to Lucy. You always wanted one, didn't you?

She kisses her on both cheeks, which seems strange and formal and not like her mum. Lucy sees now that the smile – coated in lipstick that doesn't quite conceal the dry cracks in her lips – is faltering at the edges. Her eyes are too wide.

What's going on? Lucy asks.

I just had to pay six pounds to park outside your flat for an hour, is what, Lucy's dad says, unhelpfully.

We've got a visitor's permit, you should have said, Lucy replies.

Cam makes himself busy with teabags.

So, what are you doing here?

She sees now how delicately both of them are holding themselves, as though they aren't sitting fully, with all the weight, on the chairs that Cam has offered them at the kitchen table. That her mother is tapping her teaspoon nervously against the lip of the Snoopy mug Cam has given her. She is aware that the last time she saw them was when they gave her the manila folder, which is now once again tucked away safely in the box under her bed.

I've been trying to get hold of you, Erica says. I think your phone's broken.

My phone's not broken, Mum. I'm just ignoring you.

Even as Lucy says it, she cannot stop the venom in her voice. She wants to take it back – immediately – but she can't. She sees her mother's face drop marginally. Her teaspoon makes a tiny crack in the Snoopy mug – a piece of ceramic chipping off and pinging across the room. Lucy watches it skitter across the floor into the corner of the kitchen by Winston's water bowl.

We have to stop this, Lucy, her dad says.

Cam has crept out of the kitchen, barely seen, his back pressed against the wall, crab-walking. Through the open door, Ash has come out of their bedroom and is peering into the kitchen, curious and bleary-eyed. Cam takes them by the shoulders and steers them away. Despite the gratification of this small gift of privacy, Lucy can feel the tension rising in her.

Her mother takes a deep, shuddering breath.

Your Uncle Marvin passed away, she says. That's why we're here. Because you won't answer the sodding phone or reply to a text. The funeral's next weekend, and I think he would have liked it if you were there.

Lucy sits down at the table, she feels the rage leaking out of her, like water through a sieve.

Uncle Marv died? What of?

Heart attack, we think. Danny's the one who found him. In his flat. He'd been gone for two days. Danny's in a bit of a state about it.

Lucy puts her forehead to the table, letting her arms form a cradle for her head.

Mum has lit a cigarette.

You need to do that outside, Lucy says.

Her mum ignores her.

Uncle Marv, Lucy says, to no one in particular.

And Danny, finding him.

Lucy feels her throat burning.

Is he drinking? she asks.

He's four days tomorrow, Daniel Senior says. Hasn't had a drink since he found Marvin. I don't know how long that's going to last, though.

They were close, Lucy says, meaning Marv and Danny.

Will you come to the funeral, at least? he asks her. Uncle Marv deserves that.

Lucy doesn't feel very strongly, she realises, about the death of Uncle Marv. Uncle Marv does not represent a significant presence in her life. If Lucy was really honest with herself, she never did really like him: he always seemed just to be *hanging around*, taking up space in their home, like the stale cigarette smoke embedded in all the upholstery.

Death is inevitable. She knows that. Uncle Marv has died, and one day her mother and father will die, too. One day Danny will die. Cam and Ash and Winston will die. One day she will die. One day her biological parents will die. Perhaps they're already dead, even.

She tucks that thought away to be examined another time.

She is ashamed to find herself relieved that it was Uncle Marv, and not someone else.

Yes, of course I'll come.

Good. And Dad stands up, not quite sure what to do with himself.

I'm sorry, Lucy says. He was your best friend, wasn't he?

Known each other since school, he says, over fifty years. And he takes his glasses off to clean them with his sleeve. Lucy stands up and wraps her arms around him, breathing in his familiar comforting dad smell. She turns and hugs her mum, too.

Have you decided what you're going to do with all of those papers we gave you, chicken? her mum asks nervously, her chin resting on her shoulder as they hug.

Lucy stiffens. She feels it more acutely, then. Feels the box under her bed watching her through the wall, from the other room. Burning a hole into the back of her head.

No, I haven't. Not yet.

Well, will you tell us when you do know?

Lucy nods as they separate, not trusting herself to speak.

The thoughts are overwhelming – the secret history is claustrophobic, bearing down heavy on her chest. It makes her feel hot and breathless. Her throat stings.

She imagines her parents dying now, tomorrow, having never resolved this fraughtness between them. The questions they haven't yet answered. It's unbearable.

I was just wondering . . . she begins, and then falters.

What's that, Loose?

I was wondering . . . where I got my name. The name Lucy. Who gave it to me? Was it the hospital? It just occurred to me that . . . that . . .

She tries to tell them about the little hospital bracelet, impossibly small for a human being. LUCY DOORSTEP BABY. Tries to explain how she came to realise she had the name before she ever became a Banbury.

But she can't get the words out.

She says instead, I'm not feeling like myself at the moment, Mum.

And she feels herself beginning to cry. Quietly at first, stopping the sound coming out of her so instead it heaves her shoulders, takes control of her body, up and down, up and down, the sobs racking through her like waves crashing against the seawall. And she tries to stop herself, tries to make her body rigid and impenetrable, teeth clenched, because she's a Banbury. And Banburys don't cry. But her mother pulls her close and strokes her hair and says, All right, it's okay. And lets her cry all into her best top, tears and snot leaking all over it. And her dad comes over, too, stooping slightly because of his back, and he pulls the pair of them into his own hug. And they don't say a thing to her, they just let her cry and cry until she is completely spent.

The box is still there, under her bed. Still watching her. Still waiting. She is thinking of it as she wakes up the next day and heads to the leisure centre before work. She swims fast, feels powerful as she propels her body though the water; the chlorine stings her nose and eyes and fills her mouth. She pounds at the water, length after length after length, and after a while she starts to feel a little bit better. A bit more in control, like her life isn't falling apart around her. In the changing rooms, she takes time over her make-up and hair and clothes. She wants to look normal, but there's something off. Her hair won't dry the right way: her parting looks strange and off-centre even though it's in the same place that she always has it. Her blouse for work has become crumpled in her gym bag and she can't flatten out the creases. She can feel the panic building in her at the sight of these small imperfections in her appearance.

She stops for coffee on Tooley Street on the way into work. She has already had too much, having downed one in the kitchen before leaving the flat this morning, is already over-caffeinated, her fingers jittering as she rides the lift up to Kube, her shoulders trembling with adrenaline. Almost as soon as she's in the office, Delilah is at her desk.

Quick chat? she asks.

Lucy nods enthusiastically. She follows Delilah into a meeting room which – in typical Kube style – has two egg chairs suspended from the ceiling with chains, rather than regular conference chairs. Delilah hops into one of the egg chairs, kicking off her

Crocs and folding her bare feet underneath her, utterly at ease. She indicates that Lucy does the same. But Lucy is wearing a pencil skirt and heels. She perches precariously on the edge of her egg chair, trying unsuccessfully to stop it from swinging too wildly by digging the spikes of her shoes into the carpet tiles.

Lucy, Delilah says, making a bridge with her fingers and peering at Lucy over the tops of the half-moon glasses she wears but doesn't really need.

Delilah, Lucy responds, nervously.

I've spoken to the exec and they're absolutely thrilled with the work you've been doing on the efficiencies.

Thank you.

Really, just stellar work. I knew you were the right person for the task. I'm incredibly proud of everything you've done.

Lucy smiles, a little wobbly, still riding a caffeine high. With the momentum of the chair, which is still swinging back and forth, she can't focus on Delilah's face properly. She wonders whether Delilah is about to officially offer her the promotion.

Delilah continues. So, with the data you've pulled for us we've identified two or three additional areas where we can make some savings and really protect the bottom line.

Okay.

One of the areas is supplier relations.

Delilah pauses, waiting for Lucy's reaction. Lucy's egg chair continues to swing gently from side to side. Supplier relations is Lucy's department. There are only three employees in the department: Lucy is one of them. Delilah is one. Anais is the other.

We think the department is oversaturated, Delilah continues, businesslike, when Lucy doesn't respond. So, we're looking at redundancy packages. We think that supplier relations is a one-person job. What do you think, Lucy?

Lucy stares. She doesn't understand what Delilah is trying to say.

Sorry, Lucy says, trying to keep her tone level, is my job safe?

Oh, god! Of course it is, darling. Of course it is, for now. But unfortunately we are looking at the possibility of removing the junior role from the department and fold those responsibilities into one more senior position.

So you mean . . . Anais.

Yes, Anais. I've spoken to the exec and they've signed off on a redundancy for Anais's role.

Lucy doesn't know what to say.

This must be difficult. I know she's your friend.

Yes.

But the good news, Delilah says, rapidly brightening her tone, is that once we have streamlined our teams we will be able to look at promoting from within some of those teams. You've done some incredible work for us, and it hasn't gone unnoticed.

Delilah leans over and squeezes Lucy's arm, making her flinch.

We're drawing up some paperwork for Anais right now, but we'll need to let her know by the end of next week.

Who's going to tell her? Lucy asks, feeling completely deflated.

Well. She's *your* direct report, Lucy. So . . . you'll be telling her. I'm sorry about that. But it's completely necessary.

Lucy stops trying to steady her egg chair, her feet drifting away from the floor, and the chair swings wildly like a pendulum.

Greg is really envisioning you as a future leader within the company, Delilah continues, not waiting for Lucy to respond. There are lots of eyes on you. I'm hoping you can step up.

Absolutely, Lucy says, completely numb. Of course. You can rely on me.

That's what I thought, Delilah says brightly, squeezing Lucy's arm again. She claps once suddenly and jumps up, retrieving her Crocs. So, can I leave it with you, then? I'll get the paperwork sorted by Thursday latest. Thanks so much, Lucy, I knew I could count on you for this.

She gives Lucy one more sympathetic smile and slips out the door.

Lucy wanders to her desk. Anais has now arrived. She grins at Lucy as she approaches.

Guess what, she says.

What? Lucy asks, thinking to herself *I am going to fire you next week*, and she feels sick.

I've decided. I'm going to end it with Josh. I feel so good about it, Lucy. I feel like I'm about to start a new chapter in my life. I'm buzzing!

Lucy smiles as best as she can.

I'm really proud of myself, Anais says, her eyes shining, her toothy smile splitting her face in half. This is a fresh start for me and Cam.

I'm proud of you, too, Lucy replies. And then she excuses herself and vomits quietly in the bathroom.

Lucy doesn't want to be in the office any longer than she needs to: watching Anais humming under her breath and smiling her big beautiful smile at every passer-by seems tainted. Lucy is a traitor: she is going to commit the ultimate betrayal. There is no question that she will do as Delilah asks, because that's the kind of person that she is. Cheaper than the real thing and nothing on the inside. Uptight. Thinks she's better than everyone else.

At home, she tries to work on emails curled up on the sofa with tea, but she can't concentrate. Only Winston's sleeping stirs her: he gives out little yelps – his paws twitching as though he is running – as he dreams.

He's like Ash, Cam says. He's nocturnal.

What? Ash asks. They are hung-over and grumpy, wrapped up underneath a duvet on the opposite sofa watching *Come Dine With Me*.

Lucy gives up on work and instead watches a YouTube video on her iPad, headphones in, on how to groom a golden retriever at home.

Hey, she says to Cam. Watch this. And she scrunches up next to him on the sofa, and hands him an earbud so that he can watch the video too.

They learn that all the extra wispy bits of fur are called *furnishings*. And the glorious pale gold beard of fur on Winston's neck is a *bib*.

They look up the dog jet-wash device that the professional groomer in the YouTube video is using on her dog.

Cam snorts at the price. Who spends that much on cleaning a dog? he asks her bewildered. Lucy quickly closes the tab.

As Winston's fur has started to grow back in – in thick, luscious golden ringlets – his coat is becoming more and more unmanageable with the brush. The whole flat is coated in a layer of thin white strands of dog hair. They find clumps of it in corners and wrapped around table legs. Even Lucy's bed and clothes. It doesn't bother her as much as she thought it would. She is even getting used to Winston's dog smell, which is distinctively *dog* but also *clean*.

She tells Cam this.

He smells like digestive biscuits, Cam says, grinning.

That is exactly right, she replies.

She has, more than once, buried her face in the dog's neck and inhaled. The smell of him is fast becoming a comfort for Lucy. He is big and warm and soothing, and demands affection constantly from the humans around him, when he's not asleep.

Her phone pings: it's a WhatsApp from Tom. *How about Sunday to meet my dad? We can go for dinner?*

She quickly responds. *Sorry, I've got a funeral on Sunday.*

She hopes that he doesn't ask more questions, though she has told Ash and Cam all about Uncle Marv. But then, she is a little puzzled when he doesn't.

How about Richmond on Saturday, then?

Lucy wonders at how often they meet in places that are convenient for Tom but deeply inconvenient for Lucy. She taps back a quick reply in the affirmative, ignoring the squiggly feeling in her belly, before realising that she hasn't told Tom about Winston.

She notices that Cam has been surreptitiously reading the text over her shoulder. She glances up at him and they lock eyes for a moment.

Sorry, he mutters, brow furrowing. I wasn't spying.

Do you mind if I take Winston to Richmond Park with Tom?

His eyes narrow temporarily – so quickly that she almost doesn't notice before his expression flattens once again. The smile he had on earlier has quickly disappeared.

Do what you want, Cam says, an edge to his voice that Lucy doesn't understand, he's your dog.

He's *our* dog, Lucy replies.

Cam shrugs and looks away.

Unless you don't want to look after him? Sorry, I thought—

No! No, of course I want to, Cam replies quickly, looking at Lucy directly now, his face apologetic. I just didn't want to assume.

Lucy grins at him and he grins back.

Can you both just fuck, please, Ash says from beneath the duvet, so we can get rid of the weird vibes going on in this house? I can't stand the tension.

269

There is a beat, unbearable, where no one says anything at all. The shock of what Ash has said settles coldly over the room. On *Come Dine With Me* a contestant's Eton mess has not set overnight in the fridge. He lifts the mould and the liquid white gooey mess spills out thickly from underneath it, completely ruined.

What? Lucy says, feeling the blush creeping up her neck.

Ash doesn't respond, suddenly engrossed in the programme, a faux-innocent look on their face, their lips quivering.

Lucy mutters something about dinner and edges herself out of the room. But not before she sees Cam snap his head to stare at Ash, a *shut the fuck up* look on his face.

Ash shrugs at him, now looking rather satisfied with themself, pulls the duvet up to their chin, and promptly falls asleep. A moment later, Winston helps himself up onto the couch, uninvited, and curls up into a neat doughnut at their feet, his giant paws tucked underneath him.

Chapter Twenty-Four

Lucy meets Tom outside Richmond station, brimming with a curious sense of déjà vu. She has brought Winston along. She feels that it's very important that Tom likes Winston. She feels as though the future of their relationship depends upon it. She wonders whether she ought to start calling Tom her boyfriend. She suspects that he wouldn't like it: that he would prefer *partner* instead. She spots him across the road, coming out of an independent coffee shop with paper cups. He waves at her, and the squiggly feeling in her belly disappears.

Of course Tom is right for her. He's a gentleman. He knows what he wants. He *likes her.* The way he is sometimes rude to her is because he is hurt by her inattention, which is *undeniable proof* that he cares about her. The feeling of being liked, being wanted, being valued, is the best in the world. And that's what Tom gives Lucy. But when he lifts his arm and she notices that he has a dark ring of sweat coming through his shirt, she feels slightly repulsed for unclear reasons.

Everybody sweats, she tells herself, except Prince Andrew. Everybody sweats. Don't be ridiculous.

None of this is important: what's most important is that Tom likes her and wants to spend time with her.

Tom skips through the traffic to meet Lucy where she stands

with Winston. Lucy is wearing a pair of shorts. Tom never explicitly mentioned whether shorts are off the table in the same way trousers are, so Lucy is taking a risk. She is also finding that she doesn't much care about whether or not Tom prefers skirts. Since finding Winston, Lucy is prioritising the practicalities of walking a dog – especially one that doesn't know how to walk to heel and tends to go apeshit at the sight of a squirrel – none of which involve maxi dresses and sandals. As a result, she has made some adjustments to her wardrobe. Her high-waisted denim shorts come to her mid-thigh and have little scraps of floral embroidery around the cuffs. She is wearing a cream-coloured Bardot-neckline bodysuit underneath and a wide-brimmed straw hat which she is still not sure about but trying out in any case. On her feet are sturdy walking shoes. She's going to get weird tan lines. But it can't be helped.

Tom draws level with her and gives her an awkward hug – the dog and coffees preventing them from committing to it – and kisses her on both cheeks.

This is him, then? he asks, handing Lucy her flat white.

This is him, she says.

Tom bends down and musses Winston's head. Hello, Winston, he says, affecting a baby-talk voice that makes Lucy's innards curl up like old satsuma peel. Winston seems unbothered by the fuss.

They walk to Richmond Park and wander up the hill on the cycleways, avoiding the bikes as they dart past. The sky is a glorious open stretch of blue. Lucy can feel her skin warming up as they walk. Tom takes her hand and puts it in his, which is nice. All of the ugliness of the last few weeks between them – the night he stayed over, the way she ran out the next day, and the awkwardness since – falls away in his presence. Lucy wonders whether she is afraid that Tom is her soulmate. That must be why she can't stand the thought of being in his presence. The situation is deeply overwhelming. But now, walking through the park with Winston acting as a buffer, she looks down at their interlinked hands and smiles. Everything seems manageable.

She risks letting Winston off the lead to give her knees a break. Since Winston arrived and she put a lead on him, the force of him pulling along has been sending shockwaves through her knees, and they are now constantly aching. She tells Tom about this.

He needs to learn to walk to heel, Tom says.

I know that.

Tom tells Lucy about the clicker technique and how to teach dogs to walk to heel. Lucy already knows all of this, but she doesn't want to embarrass him by cutting him off, so she lets him carry on. She prefers to let Tom talk so that she doesn't have to think of something interesting to say, which can be exhausting.

After the walk, at the train station, Lucy invites Tom back to Flat 5. She can tell he's reluctant.

You know how much I hate going central on the weekends, he tells her.

Lucy knows that if he doesn't come back to hers, she'll have to go back to his box room off Chiswick High Road and his little shelf of political biographies, and his weird quiet flatmates who are much older than him and make Lucy feel uncomfortable. She doesn't want Winston in that cramped flat, either. He'll be desperate for some space to roam around.

It will be nice. We can watch a film, she says, struggling to keep the quiver out of her voice. This is the first time that Lucy has outwardly pushed back on Tom. She is not totally sure what has made her do it.

Tom checks his watch and then his phone. He is waiting for Lucy to change her mind about this and go back to Chiswick with him. He glances up at her with this look of sort of conde-scending expectation. She makes an effort to hold his gaze. She *does* feel powerful. She deserves to get what she wants.

Fine, he says, sighing dramatically, I'll come back to yours.

We can just chill out, Lucy says.

Will your flatmates be there?

Lucy shrugs. Maybe.

Tom rolls his eyes.

They take the train and Winston is very well-behaved, curling up at Lucy's feet, only snapping his head to attention when the doors hiss open at each stop. Tom sits opposite her and she busies herself fussing over Winston so she doesn't have to talk to him. She is finding that the dog is a good filter for social interaction and consequently feels calmer than she has for a very long time, in public. She buries her hands into the gold-spun fur on the back of Winston's neck and practises breathing.

At the flat, in the living room, Ash has a share-size bag of Wotsits and they are trying to score a goal in Cam's mouth with the cheese puffs, flicking them from one couch to the other. Wotsits are scattered across the rug and underneath the coffee table. Winston darts around the living room and snaps each of them up with surprising delicacy. Lucy can see Tom's nose wrinkling.

What are you two up to tonight? Cam asks after they have all greeted one another. He is not making eye contact with Lucy. She remembers their conversation the other night, when Cam told her that she could do better than Tom. Feels a little triumphant, even, to have Tom standing here with her, so well-dressed, so put together, proving Cam wrong again. She imagines that Cam and Ash are impressed by Tom, by their relationship, which is so very mature and well-adjusted.

We thought maybe a film, Tom replies.

Nice, Cam says, and turns back to Ash, ready for another Wotsit to be pinged into his open mouth. Lucy and Tom stand awkwardly in the doorway, .

Why don't we go out for dinner? Tom says forcefully, gripping her elbow and steering her away from Cam and Ash. She had hoped they would stay in and maybe hang out with Cam and Ash a bit more, but she nods anyway, feigning enthusiasm.

Tom waits for her in the kitchen while she changes into a lighter pair of cotton shorts and a vest..

Why didn't you go and sit with Ash and Cam while you were waiting? Lucy asks, when she emerges from her bedroom.

Tom shrugs and sips at a black coffee he has made for himself. They can hear Cam and Ash laughing in the next room.

They go to a gastro place under a railway arch in Waterloo and nurse pints while they wait for their meals. Lucy has ordered a chicken Caesar salad; Tom has ordered fish and chips. The pub is heaving with bodies, and the food takes forty-five minutes to arrive.

Are you pissed off at me? Lucy asks Tom, irritated but unsure why. Tom has been nothing but pleasant to her all day, but there's a sort of edge to him that she hasn't noticed before now. He seems annoyed to be with her, but she can't exactly explain to herself why. Something about the way he impatiently taps the table, picks up the salt and pepper shakers and examines them before slamming them back onto the table, apparently dissatisfied with them. At Lucy's question, he looks up at her.

No! he says too quickly. Of course not.

They eat in silence, when the food eventually arrives, the leaves in Lucy's salad wilting and miserable. Tom's chips are cold.

This is unacceptable, Tom says.

It's fine.

Let's get the manager out here.

No – really – don't.

Excuse me, Tom says, snapping his fingers at a passing wait-ress, who has a large ketchup stain on the front of her shirt and already looks as though she's about to cry. On one arm, she has balanced six or seven dirtied dinner plates.

How can I help you? she says, her eyes wide, already prepared for the onslaught. She must know, as Lucy does, by the look of Tom, that he's going to be an arsehole about this.

Our food is cold. Look at her salad, he says, jabbing a fork into Lucy's plate and lifting a leaf to better show its wiltedness.

I'm so sorry about that, the waitress responds, a horrible fake smile carved across her face. Her shoulders are quivering.

It really is okay, Lucy says. We can see you're busy. Maybe we can just settle up for the drinks and we can go somewhere else.

No, Tom says forcefully. I want to see the manager.

The manager's not here, the girl replies, he's at one of his other restaurants.

And this one is clearly going to shit in the interim, Tom says.

Tom, Lucy says, mortified.

Look, who's the highest-ranking person here? Tom asks, ignoring her.

The girl looks around expectantly, as though someone might emerge from underneath one of the benches in the beer garden and save her.

Well, it's me, she replies.

You?

Yes. Me. I'm the supervisor on this shift.

For fuck's sake, Tom says, throwing his cutlery onto the table. Lucy flinches at the noisy clatter.

Let's just go, Lucy says again, tentatively placing her hand on Tom's arm.

The service here is disgusting, Tom says sneeringly at the girl, whose eyes are now big puddles threatening to spill over.

I'm so sorry, Lucy tells her. As Tom storms towards the pub, she slides cash out of her purse and puts it down on the table to pay for the food. Her stomach growls angrily as she follows Tom back through the heaving bar and out the front entrance onto the busy A-road.

What an absolute joke, Tom says, kind of laughing to mask the rage in his voice.

Lucy says nothing.

Why didn't you back me up in there? Tom asks her.

She has never seen him like this – nostrils flaring with anger.

What do you mean, *back you up*? Lucy asks. And then, bravely, because she is also angry and humiliated, You were acting like a troll.

This is just like how it was with your flatmate.

My flatmate?

You know. What's-her-name. When we went to her gig.

It's Ash. And it's *their* gig, Lucy corrects him, her stomach boiling.

You don't back me up.

They stand in the street and stare at one another.

Let's go back to yours and order something in, Tom says, his voice now low and apologetic.

Lucy looks at his face and feels a wash of pity for him.

Okay.

They travel back to Flat 5 in silence. Lucy can feel her insides congealing.

By the time they're home, Ash has gone out and Cam is in his bedroom with the door open, laying on his bed typing on his laptop while Winston snores softly at his feet. He calls out hello to them as they pass. Lucy waves back, but Tom ignores him. The growing sense of unease that Lucy has about this evening is swelling up inside her, flooding her cheeks with blood. She wants to ask Tom to leave, but she doesn't know how.

They order Thai food. Lucy suggests that they invite Cam to join them and Tom shoots her an incredulous look and she doesn't mention it again. They eat at the kitchen table in silence. Lucy opens a bottle of whisky that she got sent by one of Kube's clients and pours them both a measure into mugs with cubes of ice cracking as the warm liquid hits them. Tom gulps his drink down.

I don't know what's going on with you, Tom tells Lucy as they eat, with that dog.

Lucy's heart drops, because she thought for a moment Tom was going to say *with Cam*. She is acutely aware that Cam's bedroom door is open and he can probably hear everything Tom says. Tom has the kind of loud voice that disregards the comfort or nearness of other people who might not want to hear him.

What do you mean? she asks.

You literally found it in the street, and now you've, like, adopted it, or something. And it's all over your furniture and your clothes. I can smell it on you.

Tom shovels another forkful of noodles into his mouth. One of the noodles snakes down his chin, leaving droplets of sauce in his beard.

She waits for her throat to stop wobbling as Tom eats. She digs slim crescents into her palms with her fingernails.

Well. I don't know, she says, trying her best to stay composed, I like the dog. I thought you liked dogs, too?

Tom gives her a look.

It said on your profile.

My *profile*?

Yes. Your dating profile.

He snorts. Do you really think anything anyone puts on their profile is true?

Well. Everything I put on mine was true, she replies, and Tom laughs. I don't get what's funny.

Just eat your dinner, he says, still smirking at her.

I'm not hungry any more, she says, setting her fork down on her plate. I've had enough.

Tom rolls his eyes, exasperated, his mouth full of food.

He says, There's no need to be so dramatic.

She doesn't answer him. She has already decided that after this evening she is ending it with Tom.

They watch a film, *The Wolf of Wall Street* – Tom's choice – and Lucy idly scrolls Instagram while it plays. She is going to text him tomorrow morning, she decides, and tell him she doesn't think it's going to work. There is something about Tom tonight that feels volatile. He has had two more whiskies and is getting visibly drunk. He laughs too loudly at all the wrong bits in the film. He drags Lucy over to him on the sofa and locks her under his arm, like he did that time he stayed over after Ash's gig. Lucy realises that he is thinking he will stay over tonight, reeking of whisky and sweating out alcohol as he sleeps.

I think I want to get an early night, Lucy says, I've got that funeral tomorrow, remember? She realises that she is taking the coward's way out, by not telling him face to face that it's over. But there is something about him that makes her afraid to do it in person. With Danny, Lucy taught herself all the ways to avoid a confrontation, to placate him when he was in a rage. She finds herself running through all the same tactics now, with Tom.

She makes a show of yawning, which Tom doesn't seem to notice. The credits on the film roll and it's almost midnight. He makes no move to leave the sofa. They sit in silence. Tom stares at the wall. Lucy can feel herself beginning to shiver.

I'm going to bed, Lucy says, standing up.

Fine, Tom replies, still not looking at her.

You should probably get going too, she says, for the last tube.

Tom heaves himself up from the sofa, wobbling a bit because of the whisky.

You're really going to throw me out? he asks.

I'm not *throwing you out*, Lucy says, affronted. I'm just telling you . . . I'm going to bed, and I want a good night's sleep before the funeral.

She hovers at the doorway, waiting for him to follow her. Despite the tension that is thick in the air between them, Lucy is feeling more like her true self than she ever has before in Tom's presence. All of the feelings of frustration and anxiety she has been masking for him, pretending to be another person entirely, are beginning to froth angrily to the surface. And it feels good.

He does finally start to move, slowly and reluctantly. He wears the expression of a child that has been told he can't have a milkshake. In the hallway, she lets him kiss her goodnight, suppressing the urge to push him away. But she herself pulls away too quickly, before he's finished, and he pushes her, hard, against the wall. Not in a violent way, she thinks. More of a passionate way. Tom is in the throes of desire, she thinks, as he kisses her sloppily.

He moves his hand down her waist and up inside the hem of her dress. She can feel his fingers hovering at the waistband of her underwear, and that night at Amber Prescott's from when she was fifteen is suddenly right there in the frontal lobe, and she is hyperventilating rapidly, pushing her forearms into him.

He doesn't understand what she's doing. Perhaps he thinks she's changed her mind. That her sudden movement is a display of passion and desire, too, and he kisses her harder, his fumbling becoming more urgent.

There's an apple stuck in her oesophagus. She cannot move.

She is acutely aware of the familiarity of this sensation. She remembers it from before.

She feels her whole body go limp, like it did that time. But when it happened back then, it was so quick that it was over before she had even realised what was happening. This time, it's different. It's like everything is going in slow motion. She can feel all of it more acutely, with more clarity, like all of her nerve endings are standing to attention.

And she hates it; hates him. The smell of booze on his breath, the warmth and weight of his body, the fumbling of his fingers the same feeling as before, inside tights, except now there are no tights. Lucy has never liked the feeling of the breeze on her bare skin. She is trying to be better at this. The hairs on his forearms. Tom's body is blocking hers against the wall, suffocating it.

She imagines the shards of her body, shattered, stabbing into him.

He is still there.

No – he's being romantic. He's trying to be romantic.

You have to tell him to stop. *You have to tell him to stop.*

She grits her teeth and, with all of the strength she has, shoves him hard.

Tom, she manages to pant out when he pauses for breath.

He goes in to kiss her again, his mouth wet and cold.

Tom, she says.

What?

Get the fuck off me.

She practically shouts it, her face and eyes streaming like she was underwater for just a couple of seconds too long. She pushes him off of her, gasping for breath, the elastic of her shorts snapping back against her skin, stinging, as he lets go. And for a moment it's not Tom looking back at her. It's the boy with no name. And she's fifteen years old.

But then he says, What the fuck, Lucy? too loudly, and he is Tom again.

Just – get – away – from – me – she gasps out, leaning over her knees, her breath coming in ragged pants like Winston. She waves a hand at him, indicating to give her space.

He turns away and slams a fist quick and hard and loud into the wall.

Cam comes out of his bedroom.

Is everything okay? he asks. Winston is at his heels.

Fine, thanks, Tom replies loudly, falsely cheery.

Just go, Lucy tells him, still gasping for air.

Lucy, what's going on? Cam asks.

Get out, she shouts, louder than she intended, and Tom, a little scared-looking, who was about to approach her, relents and lets himself out the front door.

I'll text you, he says, and then slams the door, his silhouette diminishing slowly from the frosted glass panel. And suddenly the flat is very quiet, despite Lucy's ragged breathing and the TV still rolling the credits of *The Wolf of Wall Street*, and Winston panting.

Lucy is at the other end of the hallway, as far away as she could get from him, unsure how she got there. She still cannot breathe properly. Her lungs have sealed themselves shut, screaming fire-hot in her chest. Hot tears stream from her eyes. Snot bubbles at her nose. Her heart thunders in her chest. Her whole body aches with the effort. She feels as though she's drowning.

Put your head between your legs, Cam says gently, and she does. He doesn't approach her, still leaning in the doorway of his bedroom. Now breathe with me, he says. Are you ready? Nice, big, deep breaths. In for three and out for three, okay? Nice and slow. We'll do it together. Ready? In, one two three. And now out, one two three.

Lucy breathes, counting in her own head, too.

That's it. Much better, Cam says.

They breathe together, Cam counting the numbers in an even tone, soft and quiet. After what seems like hours, once Lucy has regained her breath, once her lungs have stopped screaming, she slides onto the floor and sees that Cam has done the same, his back against the door frame. Winston has lain down next to him and he rests one hand gently on the dog's head as he watches her. At her movement, though, Winston jumps up and trots over to her. He licks her damp face and she can't help but laugh, despite the horrible murky despair she is feeling in all of her bones.

Can I get you anything? Cam asks. Water?

No, I'm fine, thank you, Lucy replies, ruffling Winston's ears.

Do we need to call the police? Cam asks her, deadly serious, surprising her.

Oh – God – no. It wasn't that bad.

It sort of looked that bad, Lucy. Do you want to talk about it?

She looks up at him, aware that her face is streaked with sweat and tears and snot.

No, not really, she replies.

Okay.

I just . . . she starts, and Cam waits. I just don't want to see him ever again, that's all, she says.

Cam nods. Okay.

There is the sound of a key sliding into the lock in the front door and for an irrational moment Lucy thinks it's Tom coming back. But it's Ash, of course, filling the hallway with the refracted purple light of their sequinned bomber jacket.

Oh . . . no, they say simply, as they encounter Lucy and Cam and Winston on the floor, and then Lucy's face, her body still heaving with the aftershocks of what has happened, her face red-raw.

Ash immediately crosses the dim narrow corridor to where Lucy is on the floor and pulls her into a ginormous, enveloping hug. They smell of peppermint and tequila and Aussie Mega Shampoo. Lucy lets them hold her there, totally exhausted. She feels as though she cannot hold herself upright any more. She has lost control of her body. She can feel the tears pooling once again in her eyes. She tries not to sob. Ash shushes her and rocks her gently, and the four of them stay like that in the hall with its ugly off-white wallpaper, peeling at the corners, in the dark, for what seems like forever.

Chapter Twenty-Five

Lucy wakes up early to three missed calls and fourteen texts from Tom, all of them having arrived between 1 a.m. and 5 a.m. She swipes them all away with her thumb without looking.

In the kitchen, Cam is spooning bran flakes and texting at the table. He glances up as Lucy walks in and flicks the switch on the kettle.

Hey, he says, through a mouthful of cereal, how're you feeling?

Good, thanks, how are you? Lucy says brightly, forcing herself to smile at him. Her cheery tone is at odds with everything that happened last night, she knows, but she can't stand the thought of having a debrief with Cam in the kitchen at the crack of dawn. She feels as though all of her insides have been pulled out of her and exposed to the stinging air. She cannot think of last night – of Tom – without feeling nauseous. And there's the box under her bed, too, still watching her as she moves quietly through the flat, through the world, prickling at the skin on the back of her neck as it does. She is spent.

Through the open back door, only the dimmest, first signs of traffic can be heard on Lambeth Road. The sun is barely up; the sky a swirl of pinks and lilacs, the street lights still on, illuminating the concrete blue. Despite this, the warmth of summer is palpable: they are heading into a heatwave.

Lucy pours herself a coffee and turns away from Cam, trying to stop her mind from recalling what happened: the feeling of Tom's body on hers, his hands on her skin; it felt violent. It *was* violent.

Just let me know if you want to talk, Cam tells her, and the look of pity on his face is etched into every pore. She can't stand that look.

You don't need to look after me, you know, she says, resigned.

I know, Cam says, shrugging, to her relief understanding the intention of her words: that she is not trying to be cruel. But you're my friend. I care about you. I want to make sure you're okay. Ash does, too.

It is the day of the funeral. She has no time to think of the details of what happened between her and Tom. Her thoughts turn instead to Danny: Uncle Marv was Danny's only friend. He is hanging onto his sobriety by a single brittle thread. She steels herself, imagining the inevitable encounter she will have with him later today. He won't be drinking – she hopes. She can feel her pulse beginning to quicken. She closes her eyes and starts counting. Cam watches her and says nothing.

She takes the tube, and then a train, and then an Uber to the crematorium in Ilford. She is early and no one else is here yet. It is common for Lucy to be the first to arrive. She is used to it. She buys herself a coffee in the café across the road and people-watches, until she sees her parents' old Honda Civic pull into the gates of the crem. She finishes her coffee and wanders back over to them. It is almost the end of August, now, and the heat of the morning bears down on her, cooking her in her dark blazer and slicking the back of her neck with sweat, setting her hair on fire. Out of her parents' car come her mother and father and Danny, in a suit too short for him at the wrists and ankles. Mum has opted for an elaborate coal-black fascinator. Daniel Senior has managed to get away with a half-zip under his suit jacket. Lucy approaches them and briefly hugs each of her parents.

All right, Danny, she says to her brother.

Loose, he replies, in a tone of voice that suggests he doesn't have the energy to say any more.

She can see that he is sober: he is a sickly pale white, the yellows of his fingernails and teeth and eyes ever more pronounced because of it. He is shaking: trying his best to stop his teeth from chattering. Even his voice has an arrhythmic wobble to it as he discusses the logistics of the funeral procession with Dad: who will carry the coffin, and so on.

There aren't many people coming, Dad says. We'll need to get some help from the driver and that.

When the hearse arrives, shortly after, it is clear to Lucy that this funeral will be small: only a smattering of others have come, most of them men her dad's age or older. Old drinking buddies and school friends. Her father greets each of them warmly. Danny leans against the wall, chain smoking, eyeing the coffin in the back of the hearse with an expression Lucy puts closest to contempt.

It is soon very clear that between the men assembled, they will not be able to carry the coffin themselves. The driver and the other men from the funeral directors are recruited and then a couple more from the crematorium's back office. Between them, they manage to get the coffin – a spare light-wood varnished box without flowers – into the chapel.

Are you ready, Dan? Lucy asks him.

He throws his cigarette away and nods at her, his expression a mask.

Let's get this over with, he says.

And there is something in the way he looks at her in that

287

moment, that Lucy remembers very clearly the sound of a bath-room door slamming – loudly – in their home, and perhaps in another home. That was the year Uncle Marv bought her the doll's house, she realises. The year of the bathroom door slam-ming, and Danny crying somewhere in the house, alone. There was something about the doll's house that always put her off of it. Something about the bathroom was not quite right. She drew all over it, in the end, with felt-tip pens, and she had no pocket money for a month for being so ungrateful and spoiling such a nice thing.

Do you remember that doll's house he got me? The Sylvanian Families one? Lucy asks Danny.

Yeah, course, he says, grimacing. How could I forget?

Not long after she drew all over it, Danny took the doll's house, and all the little rabbits and mice and whatnot from the Sylvanian Families sets, and smashed it all up, and threw everything into the ditch beyond the fence at the back of the garden. Lucy wasn't much bothered about the house itself, but her little families were so very precious to her.

They are the last into the chapel, and only the front two rows are filled. They take their seats and, rather than pay attention to the service, Lucy pays attention to Danny. He holds a lighter and tobacco pouch between his fingers, which are vibrating, sometimes minimally and sometimes violently, forming great arcs in the air around him.

The minister talks about Uncle Marv's life: his love of horses, and his drinking and gambling, which are framed as harmless vices in the eulogy, rather than the things that brought Uncle Marv down, and everyone in his orbit down with him. The congregation mumbles through a non-denominational hymn. Nobody cries.

After the service, Uncle Marv's mourners mill around the

remembrance garden. A few of them lay flowers by a little indicator with Marv's name on it. No one knows what to do now. There is no wake: Uncle Marv had no family and the funeral itself was cobbled together at the barest minimum expense between Dad and the landlord at The Partridge, which was Marv's local. Uncle Marv's old canal boat, moored in a dry dock in Dagenham since he moved into his flat, is being sold to pay off some of his debts, and Mum and Dad are now talking about how they need to find a way to take it up to an auction in Stoke, as they are the executors of Marv's estate. Danny stands near the exit to the car park, shivering. Mum becomes involved in a long and animated conversation about loft extensions with one of Dad's friends' wife. Soon, the minister comes out and asks them to move along because the next funeral will be arriving soon. Sure enough, out front there are a dozen mourners glaring at Uncle Marv's party as they make their way to the cars.

You're coming back to ours, aren't you, chicken? Mum asks Lucy – the first thing she has said to her directly since the beginning of the funeral.

Lucy nods and jumps in the back of the car.

On the short journey to the Banbury house, the four Banburys are silent, the air only punctuated by Dad's talk radio. The commentators are discussing whether or not the death penalty should be reinstated for terrorists. Lucy watches out the window as they pass the bookies, the vape shop, the Chinese dried noodles packing factory with the strange smell and the post office distribution centre. They pull up outside the house. It is not even lunchtime, and Lucy feels disoriented: the early start this morning and the protracted nature of the funeral makes her feel as though it is much later in the day.

Shall I do a lunch? Daniel Senior asks. His answer to everything.

I might need to lie down for a bit, Erica says, kicking off her shoes at the front door and starting up the stairs.

The house is dark and cool inside, converse to the baking bright heat of the garden. Lucy lets herself out onto the patio and drags out some garden furniture, taking off her own heels and rolling up the cuffs of her trousers. Danny has already let himself into the shed at the end of the garden, leaving the door ajar, and has thrown open the tinny single-glazed windows on its side. Lucy can see a broad white backdrop has been set up inside against the wall. Danny's lighting equipment is meticulously labelled and hanging from special hooks installed in the roof.

It looks good, Dan, she calls to him.

He turns to look at her but doesn't answer, his face a ghost through the window. Moments later, he slams the door shut.

Something about the sound of the door slamming makes her flinch, as though startled from a bad dream.

Lucy closes her eyes and lets the sun warm her. She tries not to think about anything at all. There is so much not to think about, she doesn't know where to begin. Danny has turned on the radio in the shed and it is soft and soothing, muffled by the birds who land on Dad's feeders attempting to extract seeds from them. It is not long before she has fallen asleep on the patio, her legs propped up on a second chair; the noise from the road minimal compared to that on Lambeth Road back home.

When Lucy wakes up, the sun has moved across a significant portion of the sky, but the heat hasn't let up at all. She realises that she has been dribbling slightly from the corner of her mouth while she slept.

She wanders into the kitchen, where her dad is sitting at the table reading the paper.

Lunch for you, darling, he says, indicating the sandwiches and tortilla chips he has laid out buffet-style.

Lucy picks up a cheese sandwich and takes a generous bite.

Thanks, Dad, she says.

That's all right, love.

Love you.

Love you, too.

She helps him water the garden with the hosepipe and a watering can for the baskets, while Danny fusses around in the shed. Her mum must still be asleep.

Shouldn't we check that he's not drinking? she asks her dad, indicating Danny's figure through the window.

Dad shrugs. He says, if he's going to drink, he's going to drink. Us popping our heads through the door won't stop him.

Lucy nods, understanding.

He needs to want to stop. And he needs to do it on his own.

Sorry I haven't been here much, Dad.

I don't blame you, chicken. But I need to ask you a favour.

What's that?

When we go to Stoke, to sell Marv's boat, will you keep an eye on him? Just drop in on him once or twice. We'll be gone for a few days. I know I said us being here won't make a difference. And it won't. I'm just a bit worried about leaving him by himself.

Lucy wants to say no. But looking at her father now, she can't.

Course I will.

She thinks again of Danny slamming the door to the shed shut, and there's something about that noise. She can feel something waiting behind the door. Something waiting to be let out.

Chapter Twenty-Six

Work the following day is a blur: Lucy feels as though she is sleepwalking through it, still dazed from the events of the weekend. Anais sits opposite her, cheery and upbeat, none the wiser about her impending doom. Lucy has to stop herself from blurting it out – *I'm going to sack you on Friday* – every time Anais speaks to her.

Guess what, Anais whispers to her at lunchtime.

What?

Me and Cam are back on.

Lucy stares at her, momentarily stunned.

You are?

Yesssss. We sorted it all out last night. We went for a drink and talked it through. Well, we're almost there with it, you know? Cam wants to take it slow. I just need to get rid of Josh the personal trainer and I can move back in.

Seriously?

God! Yeah. Why do you look like that?

He said he wants to take it slow?

Anais looks uncomfortable. Yeah, well, not in as many words. But that was the general gist of it.

Lucy feels very strongly as though her heart is falling out of her.

Loose – what's wrong? Aren't you happy for me?

Yeah. I'm really happy, Lucy tells her. Really happy for you.

She takes the tube through rush hour, trying not to scream at the bodies pressing into her from every angle, the limbs that jostle her as she tries to exit onto the platform. She can feel this creeping sense of dread that has been bearing down on her, and now it is leaking through her, cold and metallic, all through her bones and the sinews of her muscles and her blood vessels and everything. The earworm sound of a door slamming playing over and over and over in her head. Her heart is constantly fluttering in her chest like the wings of a hummingbird. Even walking from the station to the flat, she feels the cars and sirens jolting her, making her flinch away from the road. She doesn't understand what's happening to her.

She turns her key in the lock of Flat 5's front door but realises with some confusion that the door is already open. Lucy lets herself in, noting now that there is loud music emanating from the kitchen.

She wanders through the hallway, following the noise. Ash is in the kitchen entertaining three friends, one of whom stands out because he is a man in his forties with long, stringy silver hair and a black leather strip tied at his collar instead of a tie. He looks like a character in a Wild West film. Ash stares at him with big, shining bright eyes, a beatific smile stretched across their face, sipping gingerly from a glass of red wine.

What's going on? Lucy asks, setting her keys on the table. She looks around for Winston: he is curled up in the corner of the kitchen, seemingly unbothered by the strangers.

Didn't I tell you? I'm having a few friends over tonight. A sort of networking event. Oh, god, Lucy, I'm so sorry. I thought I'd put it in the group chat.

Ash, it's Monday night?

Ash's eyes are wide as dinner plates. I did ask, Loose.

Lucy takes out her phone and opens her WhatsApp – complete with now over fifty unread texts from an assortment of people: Meredith, Nara, Tom, her mum. Sure enough, in the Flat 5 group chat she sees that Ash sent a message last week asking to have some friends round – a gathering – and Cam replied with two thumbs up emojis.

I'm sorry, Lucy says, I'm not on top of things at the moment.

Ash pulls Lucy into a hug. Thanks for being so cool about it.

Lucy doesn't respond. She is watching someone put out a cigarette on the kitchen floor.

Ash is now passing around sambuca shots and Lucy takes one gratefully, knocking it back and letting the aniseed burn down her throat and dispel the anxious nerves brewing inside her like a snowstorm.

Is Cam home?

Yes.

I'll just take Winston into his bedroom, I think.

You like him, Ash says matter-of-factly.

Who? Lucy asks, eyeing the silver-haired man dubiously.

Cam, duh, Ash replies, turning away from her conversation to join theirs. They are, each of them, partially shouting to be heard over the music. The light bulb in the kitchen is dim and casts an orange glow across everything.

What is this, secondary school?

Oh, I invited Nara and Meredith, by the way. I hope you don't mind.

Lucy stares at Ash, dumbfounded. She remembers that Ash met Nara and Meredith at karaoke. She doesn't know whether to laugh or not. She is a little angry that Ash has befriended her own friends so quickly: friendships that Lucy has spent years cultivating into the easy relationships that they are today.

I'm taking Winston now, she says, and Ash waves her off.

Lucy leaves Ash in the kitchen with their friends, and wanders to Cam's bedroom door, with Winston following her dutifully. 'Return of the Mack' is now shaking the walls of the flat. She knocks gently on Cam's door. She can see the light spilling from the crack at the bottom, meaning he's inside.

He calls out, Yeah? And she opens the door an inch.

Hi, she says.

Hi, he replies. He is laying on his bed, almost horizontal, reading a Philip K. Dick book.

Can I come in?

Of course.

She sets herself down on his bed.

Are you struggling with all of that? Cam asks, pointing at the wall, on the other side of which is the kitchen and the bodies. The doorbell rings and more people are heard entering. Ash's excited voice pierces the walls.

No – I'm not struggling, Lucy answers, prickling at that comment. I didn't realise it was happening. I didn't check my messages.

I thought so. How the tables have turned, hey? Well, you can hang here if you want.

I don't, thanks.

Lucy can feel herself becoming defensive, and is unsure why. She's suddenly very annoyed at Cam. Perhaps Cam is trying to sew her back together in the same way he is trying to with his own family, with Anais. Perhaps she is a burden to him.

I can look after myself, she tells him.

I know you can, he says. He sets the book down on the night-stand and sits up a little straighter on the bed. Do you want to talk about what happened? He asks. With Tom? The funeral?

She thinks of Danny, how skinny and shaky he was at the

funeral. The look on Tom's face as he slammed the front door, as though he were going to eat her. The door slamming again and again in her head, on a permanent loop. The leaden feeling in her bones. She feels as though her veins might explode. She wants to throw something across the room.

No. I don't want to talk about it.

Okay . . .

I have to sack Anais on Friday, Lucy says.

Oh. Shit.

I just thought you might want to know.

Cam raises his eyebrows. Does *she* know?

No. I can't face telling her. I don't know what I'm going to do.

They sit quietly. The frantic staccato of blue police lights momentarily illuminate Cam's bedroom via the window.

Anais and I are finished, Cam says. Really and truly. I'm not messing you about. We're not getting back together.

Lucy looks at him, and then quickly away. He is all rumpled up, in a dark grey T-shirt that is creased but clean, his hair sticking out left and right. His is clean-shaven normally but she notices now that he has a little two-day stubble. She can smell the scent of his laundry detergent coming off him. He looks tired: lilac crescents underneath his eyes, his face drawn. Despite this, she notices other things, now, too. The way his hands bridge together when he's trying to make a point. The vein that comes out on his neck when he's irritated. His mouth is closed, but despite this she knows that inside there are strangely pointy canines, like a vampire's, only seen when he laughs genuinely, tipping his head back, his eyes dancing with mischief. His ears, which are small, the tips turning red when he gets shy. His physicality: he is a narrow, unassuming sort of person but secretly strong: with lean muscle working underneath the skin. It is only now that Lucy is noticing these things about him.

It's not really any of my business.

Well, yeah—

She told me that you were getting back together. Literally today, at work. She said you decided to get back together last night.

We went for drinks. But it was to tell her I wanted to be friends. That we were done.

He takes a deep breath.

The thing about Anais, he says, is that if she decides she wants something, she will engineer things in a way that ensures that she gets what she wants. She's *very* good at it. She likes to have ownership of things. She likes to have ownership of *me*. I'm only realising that now, I think.

Lucy says nothing, feels her throat burning, wants desperately to reach out and touch him on the arm or elbow, to calm the stormy look shadowing his face. But she can't. It doesn't feel right.

I think she was manipulating me, Cam continues. And I'm only now really fully understanding how much.

She sent me a picture of the two of you in bed together, Lucy says, not able to help herself, taking out her phone. She quickly navigates to WhatsApp, to the shot of the back of Cam's head the night after Ash's gig.

Cam looks at it, frowning. I don't know when this picture's from, but it's not new.

He points with one long finger at the pom-pom fairy lights draped around the window frame in the background.

She took those fairy lights with her when she moved out. This couldn't possibly have been taken recently.

Oh.

Also, I slept in the living room that night, he says meaning-fully, looking at her directly in the face, his own face urgent, and she feels uncomfortable that he's staring at her so intensely.

Why would she lie about it? Lucy asks, speaking more to herself than to Cam. Well, she didn't lie. Not really. She just kind of manipulated the facts in a way that made it seem as though one thing was happening when it was completely the opposite.

I think, Cam says, that this is about Anais wanting to be in charge. Wanting to engineer things to suit her. So that she gets what she wants.

But why is she getting *me* involved?

Banbury, Cam says simply.

She looks up at him and his eyes are burning into hers with such a dark intensity that she is momentarily breathless. It is the same look from the night at the karaoke bar. A look that sends a frisson through her, a sense of unbridled relief, as though she has just come up for air after swimming underwater for a long, long time.

They sit quietly for a moment, listening to the raucousness of the party increasing in volume.

Banbury, Cam says again, I need to tell you something.

What's the matter? she asks, quietly.

He doesn't answer her, only continuing to watch her, his lips forming words but no noise escaping his mouth.

I—

At that moment, Lucy's phone rings. It's Tom. She stares at it for a moment, dumbfounded, her heart suddenly hammering.

Don't answer it, Cam says, quietly.

Lucy holds the phone in her hand and can feel herself trembling. She watches Tom's name on the caller ID screen.

Cam leans over and gently takes the phone from her hands. He rejects the call.

Then, the sound of a glass smashing and a chorus of 'wahey's. She feels herself stiffen.

I should go and see what that was, Lucy says, edging her gaze away from his.

Yeah, okay.

She closes his bedroom door with a soft click, the way he looked at her still smouldering in the front of her mind.

In the kitchen, Lucy pours herself another shot and throws it back. She has decided to enjoy Ash's party. Even though it's Monday night. Even though there are cigarette butts stamped into the floor. She deserves to have fun.

Nara and Meredith have arrived and greet her, each of them cheering as they spot her. She is mildly stunned at their enthusiasm for her presence.

Lucyyyyyyyyyy, Meredith sings. You're *here*.

I literally live here, she replies.

Where have you been, actually? Nara asks her, one immaculate eyebrow raised, as she sips her gin and tonic.

Lucy is trying to decide what to tell her, but before she can say anything, Ash is back and introducing them to a girl dressed like a pirate, and the silver-haired man, whose names are Petra and Sylvie. Petra is already very, very drunk.

Petra's pronouns are she/her and she works at the Duke of Cambridge, Ash says, as if this is enough of an explanation as to how they know her. And Sylvie is he/him. He's a manager. Have you heard of Tori Hansen? He manages her.

Lucy hasn't heard of Tori Hansen, but Sylvie's reason for being here at the party is now apparent. She tries hard to look impressed.

You work in music, Lucy says, that's cool. She can't think of anything else to say to him and he doesn't seem interested in having a conversation with her, so she stands awkwardly in the group while the others speak. Her mind is still spinning from the conversation with Cam. She has another shot for good measure. Nara is telling some story about a house party she went to recently where everyone ended up taking their clothes off.

It was mortifying, she says. I couldn't get out the front door because there was a naked man leaning against it, passed out.

Meredith is screaming with laughter.

How the hell, she says, do you get yourself into these situations?

I try to avoid them, Nara says. They just seem to come and find me.

Lucy is in the living room an hour later dancing in what she hopes is a wistful and interesting way to some melodic drum and bass mix that has been loaded up on the Spotify app on the TV. She notices that someone has spilled a drink on the coffee table. She tries to ignore it, but after ten minutes or so she gives in, and finds a cloth to clean it up. Nara is still in the kitchen, in a deep-and-meaningful with a girl with a shaved head. Meredith, Ash and Sylvie have all disappeared. She sees them later coming out of the bathroom. She suddenly feels incredibly drunk, the sambuca kicking rhythmically around her brain until it feels too big for her skull, so she goes into her bedroom and sits down on the edge of the bed, her hands clasped together.

The room is quiet and dark, her bed made neatly, with each of the four corners of the duvet tucked underneath the mattress. She assesses her panic levels, and is surprised to discover that they are low. The alcohol has made her stop caring about how the people at this party – Ash's friends – perceive her. She thinks that maybe she can be fun and interesting and sociable and normal, now.

She finds Nara and drags her into the living room to dance. She dances and dances and dances, feeling free and hopeful and joyous, and after a while Nara is gone, and Ash is there, euphoric, saying, Lucy, look at how fit I look today. Don't I look amazing, and they do, like an angel maybe, and Lucy says, You look so amazing. You look so, so amazing. Ash says, Look at my boots. Look at them, aren't they the best fucking boots you've ever seen. They are the best fucking boots I've ever seen, Lucy replies. And now two men are in the kitchen having some sort of argument. One of them has smashed a glass on the kitchen countertop. Lucy goes into the cupboard under the sink for the dustpan. One of the men is bleeding, but she doesn't know which.

I think you need to leave, Lucy says quietly, but she can't be heard over the music.

Nara is behind her and hears her.

Oi, pricks, she says. Take it outside.

They are ignoring her. Their voices getting louder and louder. One of them pushes the other. Lucy can't properly focus on either of them, her head foggy.

The only other people in the kitchen are Nara and Lucy. Ash is now in the garden smoking with Meredith, and everyone else is in the living room playing beer pong. Light spills out from underneath Cam's bedroom door.

One of the men now throws a punch.

Hey, hey, hey, Nara shouts, and she grabs him from behind and tries to pull him backwards. Lucy copies her, grabbing the other man who is standing nearest to the back door, wearing a chain on baggy jeans and a vest like a nineties grunger, and tries to drag him out onto the patio. She now sees that Petra, Ash's friend who is dressed like a pirate, is draped over one of the sunloungers, completely wasted, her eyes rolling backwards into her head. Lucy swears loudly.

She has managed to drag the grunger into the garden, but he trips backwards down the steps and falls on top of Lucy, taking her to the ground with him.

She sees now that Cam is at the back door. He walks forward quickly, long strides, and Winston is there too, barking. Cam yanks the man off of Lucy, pulling him roughly to his feet, his expression unreadable in the dark.

That's it, Lucy shouts, get the fuck out.

That's you too, dickhead, Nara shouts to the other man.

Let's go, pal, Cam says quietly, pushing the man back into the kitchen.

Between them, they drag the two men to the front door and shove them out onto the street. One of them has dripped blood all through the hallway and it seeps into the carpet, the splotches turning brown.

Nara holds up her hand for a high five. Cam accepts it wearily.

Are you all right? he asks Lucy. She is brushing grit off her clothes from the patio. He brushes a little off her bare shoulder that she has missed.

She nods, not meeting his eyes with her own, trying to ignore the way her skin is tingling where he made contact, the way he is looking at her as though he felt it too: the almost-imperceptible electrical current that passed between them when he touched her.

I think we might need to wrap this up soon, he says, checking his watch.

Nah, not even, Nara says. It was just those two dickheads. Everyone else is fine.

Cam looks to Lucy, his eyebrows raised, questioning. It's only just past midnight. Lucy doesn't want to be the square who stops everyone's fun and starts throwing people out. She doesn't want Cam to be either. She is feeling a strange kind of adrenaline coursing through her – a sort of abandon that she hasn't felt before. Is this what it feels like not to care?

Cam is ushering Winston back into his bedroom and closing the door. There is broken glass twinkling in the carpet.

Fine, he says.

I might need someone's help with Ash's friend Petra, though, Lucy says, remembering her semi-comatose state on the sunlounger in the garden.

Cam and Lucy drag Petra up from the sunlounger in the garden and take her into the bathroom. Someone has left a thin, perfectly cut line of powder on the top of the porcelain cistern. Cam brushes it away into dust.

Petra, you need to throw up, Cam tells her, matter-of-factly.

She rolls her head and makes a small moaning sound.

Oh my god, what's wrong with her? Nara asks, poking her head around the door frame.

She took something, Lucy says.

Now, Ash has arrived in the doorway beside Nara, cigarette in hand, swaying to Modest Mouse.

Ash, what did she take? Cam says.

No idea, mate, Ash replies, grimacing.

Petra says, I need to be sick.

Yes, we know, Cam says. Can you try to make yourself sick?

Lucy looks to Cam, a feeling of sheer panic in her veins.

I can help, Ash says, elbowing their way into the bathroom. Petra is draped across the toilet bowl, pirate hat abandoned somewhere in the flat, a look of despair on her face. I'm going to stick my fingers down her throat, Ash says, yanking off their rings.

Are you sure you're okay to . . .? Cam asks.

This is not my first rodeo, kids.

Lucy walks out of the bathroom and waits by the door. She cannot bear the thought of watching someone else be sick.

Can you hold her head up for me? Ash asks Cam.

It doesn't take long. Lucy goes to find bread and water and towels. When she comes back, she sees that Petra has vomited all over Ash's hand, over the toilet seat, onto the floor, over herself. Everywhere except the actual toilet bowl. She hands the supplies to Ash, who is stroking Petra's face. Petra is now looking a little less lethargic. She has started crying.

I'm so fucked, she says.

I know, Ash says. But we're going to sort you out, all right?

Ash and Cam get Petra into the bathtub and hose her down. Then they hose the floor for good measure, and spray it with bleach, and scoop up the watery-bleachy vomit with the towels. The smell is overwhelming. Once Petra is thoroughly soaking wet, Cam and Lucy lift her out of the bath and take her into Ash's bedroom. Sylvie is already in there though, passed out on top of a pile of coats.

Who the fuck is this guy? Cam asks.

That's Sylvie.

Meredith is in the hallway as they drag Petra back out, one arm draped around each of their shoulders.

Hun, Meredith says to Lucy, enthusiastically. Thanks for the invite, but I need to bounce. Helen is at Tiger Tiger and Rita Ora is there. Has anyone got any ket?

It's *Monday night*.

Oh, fuck off.

Meredith lets herself out the front door with air kisses for Lucy and Cam. Petra is starting to cry again.

Let's put her in my room, Cam says.

They lay her on top of the duvet.

Lucy gently undresses her out of her sopping pirate clothes while Cam waits outside and Ash gets pyjamas. Ash hands Lucy the fresh clothes around the door. A pair of shorts and a T-shirt that says 'Rude of you to assume I'm cis' on it. Lucy helps Petra, who is now semi-conscious, into the pyjamas. Ash has disappeared again.

You can come in now, Lucy says to Cam, and he does.

Petra is lying on the bed in the foetal position.

Guys, she says, on the brink of tears again. Guys, I'm so sorry, I got too wasted.

Shhh, Lucy says. It's fine. Go to sleep now. I'll get the washing-up bowl. If you wake up and want to be sick, be sick in there, okay?

Petra nods miserably, tears leaking out of the corners of her eyes.

Time to move people on? Cam asks Lucy, and she nods.

Lucy gets the washing-up bowl and attempts again to brush the broken glass up from the floor. Winston watches her. The temptation to make things orderly.

She heads to her bedroom, hoping to sit quietly for a moment and do some breathing exercises, away from all the people, who are being rounded up slowly and methodically by Cam. When she opens the door, she sees Ash starfished across her bed, boots still on and dead asleep. Lucy slips their boots off.

Come on, Winston, she tells him, after she has returned to the hallway and collected the glass. He follows her back into her bedroom and jumps up onto her bed, curling up next to Ash, who is now snoring loudly.

Cam has turned off the music. Lucy opens the front door and ushers people out, nudging those whose conversations linger on the doorstep over the threshold. She is in disbelief that this many people fit in their tiny little flat. When the last person has exited, she slams the door and deadbolts it. Cam is standing in the living room, staring at the wreckage of the party. Empty cans and cups everywhere; crisps and booze and cigarette butts splattered across the floor and the surfaces.

Jesus, Lucy says.

The rest is just as bad, Cam replies. Let's just go to bed and sort this out in the morning.

Lucy nods, but now everyone is gone, and she can see the full extent, she can feel the panic rising again. Cam has disappeared, so she grabs a bin bag and starts cleaning the living room: she'll have to sleep on the couch tonight, seeing as Ash has commandeered her bed. The thought of being in here with all the rubbish and the sickly-sweet smell of curdling alcohol makes her want to scream. She gets out a pair of magnolias, trashes everything and bleaches all the surfaces she can get to.

It's a while before she notices that Cam is in the doorway watching her.

I was going to sleep in Ash's bed, he says, locking eyes with her. But that Sylvie bloke is still in there.

Ash is in mine, Lucy replies.

He helps her finish the cleaning and, pleasingly, she sees that he is in fact a diligent cleaner, buffing out rings on the coffee table and emptying half-full cans into the sink in the kitchen before adding them to the recycling, which he has separated out from the rubbish using a different bin bag.

I'm sorry I didn't help that much with that pirate girl, she says while they clean.

What are you talking about? he replies. You were a huge help.

You might have noticed, I'm not very good with mess. And dirt. And anything unhygienic.

Cam is quiet as he collects empty cans from behind the sofa. I had noticed that, he says. Why is it?

I don't know. I think it's . . .

Cam sits down and waits, his expression inquisitive.

I think it's about being in control, Lucy says, after some thought.

You don't like not being in control.

Lucy nods and turns away from him, finding herself unable to face his understanding. The way he is so ready to see her as the best version of herself. It's more than she deserves.

I spent so much of my life, before I moved to London, feeling out of control. Feeling as though I couldn't be in charge of my own *fate*, I suppose.

And do you feel in control now?

Lucy ponders it. Does she feel in control? Does she feel powerful? She thinks of the box under her bed, all of the secrets it contains. She thinks of Danny. The door slamming.

I feel like . . . I'm spiralling, she tells him.

She imagines the secrets, black and rotten, are spilling out of her, through her nose and her windpipe, choking her. She is drowning in them.

But for a moment, in the dark hum of the living room, Ash's snoring across the hall audible through the wall, as they clean in companionable silence until the worst of the detritus is gone, it feels manageable.

Let's never do this again, Cam says, grinning at her, and she bursts out laughing.

I think I'm too old for house parties, she says, and he nods sagely.

Where are we going to sleep?

Chapter Twenty-Seven

They decide, eventually, after the living room is as clean as it will ever be tonight, to drag all the sofa cushions onto the floor and make a pillow fort, using blankets and pillows to pad it out. Lucy changes into a T-shirt and shorts – her sleeping clothes – and suddenly feels very awkward.

What side do you want? Cam asks, standing stiffly by the door. He has changed too, into an old *Star Wars* T-shirt and a pair of flannel sweatpants. She is deeply relieved that he has decided to stay fully clothed for this. His fingers are interlocked and his hair is sticking up.

I don't mind, Lucy says. She is drunk enough not to care very strongly about how unusual this is, how uncomfortable it ought to be. But still, she is suddenly filled up to the brim with nervous energy. It starts in the pit of her stomach and rises up through her – sternum, chest, throat – until she feels taut as a coiled spring. She shakes her arms, involuntarily, like someone has walked over her grave. She climbs in under the blankets and Cam turns off the light. Moments later, she feels him disturb the blankets and lay down next to her, the heat of his body radiating underneath the covers and warming the space between them. She is very careful not to touch his body with any part of hers. She thrashes around until she has carved a dent in the cushions to lie comfortably in, and rolls onto her back, her arms flush against her body. This is not a natural sleeping position for her, but it's the only way she can be sure she won't touch Cam.

This is a bit weird, isn't it, Cam says, stating the fact of it rather than asking the question.

Lucy giggles, trying to mask the nervous flutterings her synapses are firing off in little flurries.

It's fine, she says uselessly, words failing her.

How are you feeling now? he asks. It's not clear what he's referring to. It could be the chaos of the party, the fact that she must sack Anais, the thing that happened with Tom yesterday. Even Danny and her family and the whole business of her being adopted.

I feel okay, she answers.

Okay, he says. Goodnight, then.

How are *you* feeling? she asks. And she sees his mouth grinning in the dark, his eyes closed and his teeth glittering.

I feel good, he says.

That's good.

Yes.

'Night then.

'Night.

She lies in the dark and stares up at the ceiling, listening to the cars and buses thunder past outside. The flat, on the inside, is oppressively quiet.

Do you realise you know more about me than anyone else? Lucy asks him quietly, as the thought is occurring to her. You know almost all of my secrets, she whispers.

But Cam's breathing has deepened and he is snoring, softly and inoffensively. He doesn't answer her.

*

It's sometime in the very early morning – Lucy knows that it's morning because even though through the window she can see that the street lights are still on, the sky is lightening to a dark slate grey, no longer the polluted brown-black of the dead of night, and there are the first hints of birdsong – that she wakes up. It must be no later than four. She has woken because she has become aware that her body is sort of wrapped around Cam's. She is sleeping on her front, her face smooshed into the pillow, and one arm and one leg on her right side are flung across him. Curled around him, really. She is aware first of the heat of his body on hers, making the small domain of their bed almost un-bearably warm. The temperature outside – August city summer morning heat – must already be in the low twenties. She is suddenly very aware of every part of her body, feels adrenaline coursing through her like an electrical current. How has this happened? And, more importantly, has Cam noticed? She can feel the contours of his body where her own is touching it: the hard plane of his chest, her forearm gently rising and falling with it, and the sinews of his quadriceps. He smells of tooth-paste and Radox and human. She is suddenly aware that one of his own arms is beneath her head on the pillow, and she has been sleeping in the crook of his elbow. She wonders how she can extricate herself from him without his noticing. She watches as a blackbird lands on the window ledge and cleans its feathers, its early-morning call audible through the glass. She sets about removing herself from Cam with as little disturbance as possible, gently lifting her arm away from his chest and trying to untuck her hair from beneath his pillow.

She glances at him as she does, and the ever-brighter morning light illuminates his face, pale and soft. She sees that the corner of his mouth is quirked up ever so slightly and recognises the expression.

You're awake, aren't you, she says.

He smiles broadly.

Yes, he whispers back, eyes still closed.

Why didn't you wake me up and tell me to move?

You looked so peaceful, I didn't want to ruin it, he replies.

She frowns, not sure where to go from here.

Sorry about that, she says.

Not at all. It was quite nice, actually.

He has half-opened his eyes and he is looking up at her, sleepy and bedraggled, his hair like black ink spilled on the pillow; his jaw square and shadowed. He is smiling at her crookedly; this smile that feels so familiar to her now. The way he saves it just for her, like he is sharing a secret with her. There is something so simple about the way she feels about him, she realises. Even with the mess of their respective relationships, it feels so very easy to be around him. There is something pure and uncompromising in their friendship.

She leans back into him, relishing the warmth of his body. He snakes an arm around her and, gratifyingly, pulls her a little closer into him. She can feel more of his frame, the solidness of his body, the unexpected strength in those arms. He smells familiar, the scent of his shampoo like an old friend. Before she can think too hard about what she's doing and stop herself, Lucy burrows her face into his neck, and he stops breathing. She instantly regrets the show of affection, feels her stomach turn to lead.

Sorry, she says.

Not at all.

I didn't mean to do that. I don't know what I was thinking.

Banbury?

Yes?

Stop talking.

Okay . . . Do you mind if I . . .?

What?

He leans his head up a little bit, to look at her better. She had meant to readjust his arm underneath her to make it more comfortable, but now she finds herself face-to-face with him, her nose millimetres from his. And up close she can see things about him that she has never noticed before: like there are little flecks of dark green in his brown eyes, and he has a tiny, almost invisible scar in the curve of his nose on the left-hand side. And one eyebrow is slightly longer than the other. And he has the tiniest chip in his front tooth. And he is looking at her with a new expression, unfamiliar, one she has never seen before. His eyes glittering in this darkness.

And very suddenly – she doesn't quite know how it happens – she is kissing him. The transition from staring to kissing is so seamless it is as though it never happened. And he is kissing her back, softly at first, tentatively, unsure, waiting for her to pull away, to realise her mistake and run from the room. Lucy expects this of herself, too, and she imagines it happening, objectively, as she kisses him. It is as though the person Lucy knows that she is – cautious, meticulous, rational – is gone, and this new version of herself is the one kissing Cam. And she *likes* kissing him.

He pulls away momentarily, only to mutter, Is this okay? into the corner of her mouth, and she is saying into his, Yes, it's okay. And his mouth crushes against hers once again, and she feels herself press her body against his as he sits up to better pull her into him. And their breathing is synchronous, ragged and desperate, their hands twins in the ways they run across one another's bodies, above blankets and *Star Wars* T-shirts, across shoulder blades and backs and hips and waists. He is careful not to go too far, she notices, not to stray across the most secret parts of her. Her body is tingling with the adrenaline of it, of

Cam. The way he looks at her and speaks to her, as though he is truly seeing her, is the way that he kisses her. She feels, in this moment, as though he is drinking her up, that this is *right* and perfect and exactly what they are meant to be doing, and she wants to do the same to him, with the ways his hands dance across her and send shivers of longing through her and—

And, just as suddenly as it began, it has stopped. Cam pulls away from her, rapidly, jarringly. His hands find her shoulders. The abruptness of the movement from the frantic way they were kissing to this stillness of him now, as he looks at her, is sharp, like a cold knife slipped between the ribs. She stares up at him, determined not to look away this time, and wonders if the expression on his face – breathless, tender, but fierce – mirrors her own.

We should stop, he says.

She doesn't understand why – what exactly it is that has given him pause – but she nods in agreement.

Yes, that was a terrible idea, she lies. She can feel herself crashing back down to earth, the temporary euphoria of the kiss quickly dissipated, leaving a fog of rejection settling around her, her body leaden.

Lucy, I need to tell you how much—

You don't need to, Lucy says, cutting off the platitudes before they can spill from his mouth and make her want to cry. You're right. This is a mistake.

Lucy, he says again, a look of total anguish settling across his face.

You don't need to say anything, Lucy replies, using every muscle in her body to keep her voice level and emotionless. Let's pretend it didn't happen, okay? I've had a lot to drink.

She sees the naked emotion in his expression replaced, slowly but absolutely, with a mask of indifference.

Yeah, of course, he says. That's probably for the best.

She lies back down, taking care to leave a canyon of space between them now, her heart racing so fast she is sure that he can hear it hammering against her ribcage.

I think . . . I'm going to take Winston out. It's almost time for his walk, Cam says quietly.

It's, like, four in the morning.

Yeah, but still.

And he stands up awkwardly, unwrapping himself from the blankets that were moments ago tangled around them, cocooning them in their frantic embrace. Lucy says nothing as he leaves the room, his feet padding softly against the floorboards.

Minutes later, she hears the jangle of the lead being clipped to Winston's collar, Winston's claws clicking against the lino and, as though it never happened at all, Cam snaps the front door shut softly, and Lucy lies alone in the dim light of morning, her body like dead weight, flush against the floor, wondering at what she has just done.

Chapter Twenty-Eight

Lucy tries to go back to sleep in the pillow fort, her mind racing. But the kiss and the whiplash of Cam leaving has left her wide awake and humming with energy. She waits for Cam's side of the bed to go cold before she gets up. It is so early that she has time for a long and punishing swim before work, despite the little sleep she's had. The thought of seeing Anais puts the fear of God in her. Will Anais take one look at her and know what she's done? How will she ever forgive her? The fact that Anais and Cam are broken up, and Anais effectively lied about it, and Lucy is slowly realising that Anais is not really a very good person, and never has been as long as Lucy has known her, is inconsequential; Lucy has done a terrible and unforgivable thing. Not to mention, she's about to make Anais redundant too. It occurs to her on the tube into Borough, mortifyingly, that it might be *Cam* who has lied, not Anais, and they are in fact back together. The thought makes Lucy, whole body pressed against the doors by the bulk of a Canary Wharf middle manager, feel even more sick. She is hot and uncomfortable, and despite the extended high-pressure shower she had after swimming, hoping to scrub all evidence of last night off of her body, she can feel the alcohol leaking out of her pores, coating her in a sheen of high-glucose sweat in the humidity of the tube carriage, trickling down her back, and it's only eight in the morning. Even with a light sleeveless summer blouse and thin cotton maxi skirt, by the time she's at her desk, her hair will be a ball of frizz and half her make-up will already have sweated off.

In a rare show of punctuality, Anais is already at her desk when the lift delivers Lucy to the Kube offices.

Morning, Anais says, breezily.

Morning.

Late night last night? Anais asks, and Lucy feels herself tense.

Yeah, a little bit.

Well, I'm getting green tea. I'll grab you one, too.

Thanks.

Of course.

They work in silence for most of the morning. Anais seems to be in a good mood – her phone calls with clients particularly chatty, her smile broader. Unlike Lucy, she looks like she's had a proper night's sleep.

At lunchtime, she sits down with an avocado salad at her desk and continues to tap at emails, humming to herself. She catches Lucy staring at her.

She grins. Leans over Lucy's keyboard to whisper.

Me and Josh are done, she says. You know, Josh the personal trainer?

Yeah. I know.

Well. Last night, I told him it was over. Blocked him on everything. I feel so *good*, Loose! I can't believe how toxic that whole thing was.

I'm really happy for you.

You don't realise how fucked-up something can be until you are on the outside of it, Anais says.

I know what you mean, Lucy replies, stomach curdling, thinking of what Cam told her last night, thinking of Tom,

316

whose texts have now tapered off, and shuddering.

So, the lease on my flat is up in November, so I'm just waiting to see what the vibe is with Cam, whether I can move back in. You know? Or maybe I might spend some time at my parents'. I can commute in for a bit while I work out my next move.

Wow. Anais.

This feels like the start of a new chapter, you know?

Can we talk in private for a second?

Anais pauses and frowns at Lucy.

What, now?

Yes, now. Please.

Anais shrugs and puts the plastic lid back on her salad. She follows Lucy into one of the glass-panelled meeting rooms.

Lucy breathes deeply, counting.

What's going on, then? Anais asks.

I need to tell you something. Because it sounds like you're about to make some really big life decisions and I think you should know the facts.

Lucy, you're scaring me.

I just think you need to know this.

Fine. Just tell me quickly. Because I'm freaking out, now.

Lucy sits down, and feels her fingers trembling.

Okay. Well, first of all. Kube is going to make you redundant on Friday.

Anais stares at her, her jaw dropped open, her face stricken with shock. Oh my god. You're sure?

Yes. I'm really sorry, Anais.

Those fuckers.

You just might need to think about jobs before you make any living arrangements, you know?

I'm going to kill Delilah.

Anais, sit down for a second, please.

Lucy can feel the tears at the corners of her eyes already.

There's something else I need to ask you.

Okaaaaaay.

Are . . . are you and Cam really getting back together?

What the fuck is that supposed to mean?

It's just . . . there's been some things Cam told me, and then things you told me, and it just sort of doesn't add up . . . and I *know* it's none of my business but—

What did Cam tell you?

Lucy hesitates.

I just don't understand what's going on. And . . . I need to tell you something, Anais. This is really hard, but I think you have a right to know.

Anais's face turns poisonous.

I fucking knew it.

Anais . . .

Just fucking tell me, Loose. Get it over with.

Okay. I'll tell you. Last night, we had a bit of a party at Flat 5. A few of Ash's friends and stuff. Lots to drink. It got quite rowdy.

Yeah. And?

Lucy swallows, stares at her hands, not sure how to proceed.

Anais says, quietly, Something happened, didn't it?

Lucy nods, her throat burning.

Something between you and Cam?

Lucy looks up at Anais and nods again, and she sees Anais's face change from a look of fury to one of complete devastation.

I'm so sorry, Anais. It was so stupid. A mistake. We both agreed.

What exactly happened?

Lucy takes a deep breath. We kissed, she says.

Anais closes her eyes and breathes in deeply through her nose, bringing her hands to her forehead in prayer.

I knew it, she says. I knew there was something going on with you and him.

There's *nothing* there, Anais, I prom—

After that gig, I knew something had changed.

Anais . . .

It would almost be better if you *did* fuck, Anais says, eyes still closed.

And Lucy nods in agreement. There's something about the kiss, and the fact that that's all they did – the intimacy of it – that makes it so much worse. Lucy feels nauseous.

It's my own fault, Anais says, her eyes flying open and staring directly at Lucy, tears brimming. Lucy reaches out to touch her shoulder, but she flinches away. It's my own fault. I'm the one who cheated, not him. He's totally within his rights. I'm glad you told me, anyway.

I couldn't not. You *must* know it was a horrible mistake. It won't happen again.

Anais continues. If I'd just had a bit more time, a little bit longer, I know he would've changed his mind. I *know* it.

Anais looks up at her, assessing Lucy's expression, her pleading tone, her body language.

Me and Cam are meant to be together, she says, red-faced. We're made for each other.

The way she says it is like she is trying to convince herself, as well as Lucy.

Lucy is suddenly aware that, through the glass panelling of the meeting room, several of their colleagues have been watching their exchange, Jenna from accounting brazenly staring, her mouth hanging open.

I can't work with you, Anais says. Not now. I'll write my notice this afternoon.

No, Lucy says quickly. Don't do that. Wait for the redundancy package.

Anais's eyes widen. What's the redundancy package?

Check your contract. It's three months of paid garden leave, and a bonus for every year at the company.

Anais nods vigorously, her eyes narrowed. Lucy notices that Delilah has stopped next to Jenna and is now also staring, unabashedly, at Lucy and Anais's exchange.

We have to go out there, Anais says, and pretend that nothing has happened.

Lucy nods slowly.

Anais says very quietly and very sincerely, I want you to know you're dead to me.

Lucy ignores the way that stings and says, Yeah, I know. We just need to stick it out until Friday, okay?

Fine.

And they leave the room, Anais first, and then Lucy, making eye contact with no one. They return to their desks and Lucy sees that she has three new missed calls from her mother, and she wants to throw herself through one of those repurposed upcycled industrial factory windows and splat herself onto the concrete, and never have to live in her own body with her own thoughts and feelings ever again.

They work the rest of the day in a stony silence, attracting worried glances from their colleagues in other parts of the office. Delilah walks by twice and asks Everything okay here, girls? In a falsely cheery voice. They both nod and smile at her over-enthusiastically. As soon as Delilah is gone, they return to their work in silence. As Delilah meanders through the office and has loud performative conversations with colleagues, Lucy realises that she is faking it. She is pretending to be another version of herself. Lucy suddenly cannot believe she ever imagined herself as Delilah: having Delilah's job, Delilah's life.

Lucy lets Anais leave first, at five thirty on the dot, grabbing her handbag before her laptop has fully powered down and legging it for the lifts. She makes herself wait five minutes before she makes a move to leave herself. Once again, the thought of going home, having to speak to Cam, tell him what she's done, and reckon with the fact of what happened last night, makes her want to get on a tube and go in the opposite direction. But Winston is at home, too, and he needs her. And she has made a commitment to him. So, she takes the Bakerloo line, the heat of the Underground doing nothing to dispel the cold apprehensive fear that has embedded itself into her bones like limescale.

She walks slowly back to the flat, and as her keys turn in the door, she is gratified by Winston bouncing up to her, Bugs Bunny hanging from his mouth, tail wagging so fast that it is a golden blur. He barrels his full weight into her and leans against her legs, accepting her pats, black lips stretched wide into a grin. She buries her fingers into the thick fur around his neck and breathes in his dog smell.

Hello, my gorgeous boy, she tells him.

Hello, human, he seems to say back.

She lets him lead her into the kitchen and places her keys down on the table before pouring out some kibble for Winston's dinner, and refilling his water bowl. The flat has been cleaned, spotlessly, which is a relief to her. She wonders whether it's Ash or Cam who has done the work. She checks Ash's bedroom and sees that they are asleep – Sylvie the mysterious silver man gone from their bed – and then checks her own to see that her bed has been made. She listens briefly at Cam's door, notes that no light is coming from the gap beneath, and briefly leans against the frame, feeling herself sinking, the weight of Cam and Anais and

Tom and Danny dragging at her until she is sitting cross-legged on the floor .

The key turns in the lock and Cam is standing there, in the front doorway, on his face a grim look of resignation. Even now, she feels her fingertips fizz at the sight of him: her heart fluttering inconceivably, in spite of everything. He sees her immediately, down here on the floor, and he sort of smiles at her in a sad way.

You okay? he asks.

Yeah. Fine.

Don't lie, Lucy.

She says nothing.

Do you want to talk about what happened?

His face is so hopeful, she realises. And her heart swells for him. She wants nothing more than to go to him and let him pull her into a hug and smell his unique Cam-smell, Radox and toothpaste and human, and forget about everything. But she remembers last night, remembers the force with which he pushed her away, disengaged from her. Remembers the conversation with Anais in the office today. And she can't.

No. I don't want to talk about it.

Okay.

He passes her into the kitchen, fussing Winston as he goes.

Lucy heaves herself off the floor and follows him.

I want you to know that I told Anais about what happened, she says to his back as he opens the fridge and checks its contents, his backpack slung onto the table next to her keys.

Why did you do that? he asks, without turning around.

It was the right thing to do. I told her about the redundancy, too.

She waits for him to answer.

Anais has nothing to do with it, Cam says finally, turning around to look at her properly. He looks tired. Devastated, even.

Maybe not. But she still deserves to be told the truth.

In the garden, the lawn chairs and the paddling pool are in a state of disarray, one of them tipped to its side and the paddling pool shoved awkwardly into a corner. Lucy unlocks the back door and steps onto the patio.

I hate the secrets, Lucy says, eventually, as she rearranges the furniture. I hate that I don't know what's going in my life, that I'm so out of control of it. How I'm meant to be feeling at any given time. It's horrible. Anais deserves better than that.

Through the open door, Cam nods, resigned, and looks at the sink.

I have to tell you something, Cam says, and Lucy's heart leaps into her throat.

What is it?

I need to go home, I think. For a bit. To help my mum out. I tried to tell you last night, in my bedroom, but . . . Tom called you . . . and after that . . .

What happened?

My parents are getting divorced. Officially.

God. Cam. I'm so sorry.

It's fine – you know – it's not a surprise. It's been coming on for a long time. Ever since Naomi . . . passed away. But Bella isn't handling it very well. I think I need to go home and be there for my mum. Be there for Bella.

Cam shrugs. He is trying, it seems, not to cry himself. He looks down at Winston instead of at Lucy. She digs her nails into the grooves of the wood on the table.

It's probably better if I move out, he tells her.

Her whole body has turned to lead.

The lease is up in September. I'll pay until then, of course. And then it's up to you and Ash if you want to renew it or not.

But I'm going to go home in a couple of weeks, I think. As soon as I can.

Can I do anything?

He shakes his head vigorously. I don't think there's anything anyone can do. It's just a fact, isn't it? I don't know how to help her, he says, and Lucy recognises that feeling of helplessness, of total abandonment in him: she feels it herself, all the time. She feels it now as she looks at him.

So this is it, then, she says.

This is it, he replies.

Chapter Twenty-Nine

Cam retreats to his bedroom, and Lucy to hers. She feels that something terrible has happened. Something fundamental has been broken. And it's her own fault. The kiss. The way she has treated Anais. Lucy knows, deeply and truly, that the reason Cam is leaving – the real reason – is that he can't stand her. He must find her disgusting. The same way everyone else does. She is a terrible person.

She sits on her bed and stares at the ceiling. She feels that same leaden, unbearable sensation of loneliness – rejection – crashing over her again and again. She wonders if she ought to call someone – Meredith, Nara – but it feels as though it might be too much effort; that they won't want to hear from her. She feels as though she has been spending the last few months peeling back all of the layers of her skin and now, all that she is is the exposed tissue: muscles and sinew and bone and ball-and-socket joints, and if she touches anything, it will sting, and if she speaks to anyone or sees another person, they will think her ghoulish and monstrous.

She wants to be in someone's company, but she knows that nobody truly likes her. There is another part of herself, further inside her, that knows that this is deeply irrational. But she can't help herself. The feeling of repulsion with her own self swells up and spills out of her, frothing over the edges of her and taking up all the oxygen in the room. The simplest things seem to her to be a monumental effort. She wonders if there is something broken inside of her, from the fact of her adoption, or what Danny did, that is now rearing its ugly head, ready to consume her from the inside out. She reasons that it can't be about any of those things. No. There is something wrong with her. Something she was born with, to make her this unpleasant and deceitful person, a caricature of herself. This is the reason her own mother didn't want her: that she was left on the steps of the Medway in a cardboard box. The person she has become, slowly, gradually, without her realising that it was truly happening, each new building block carefully selected and stacked into the type of human she is now, is all her own doing. It's all her own fault.

She walks into the kitchen, searching for keys. Winston is there. He skitters away at the sound of her shoes on the linoleum. She can't find her keys, *she can't find her keys,* and the microwave is making that same smell again, the smell that makes her itch. That smell will never go away, she knows now. It doesn't matter how much she scrubs and bleaches and disinfects. The scent has permeated the very essence of the microwave.

She takes out the toolbox from behind the fridge and spends some time finding the right screwdriver that will fit the tiny screws that keep the stainless-steel casing secured to the rest of it.

She unscrews the top panel of the microwave and, with some effort, lifts the panel away.

The smell is getting stronger.

And underneath it, buried amid the venting holes, burrowing into the circuitry: a nest of writhing maggots.

She shrieks, launching the screwdriver at the wall in reflex, and backs away from it quickly, her heart hammering.

All this time, she has been living with this filth.

She edges closer to the microwave, peering over the top of it to observe the maggots. There are hundreds of them, pink and brown and beige. All of them frenziedly alive.

She can feel herself trembling, her breathing coming in short gasps.

She tentatively places the panel back onto the machine and screws it back into place. She unplugs the microwave, the smell of the maggots flooding her nostrils. She tries very hard not to gag, and heads for the door, carrying the microwave in her arms like a baby.

Before she is out of the front door, she hesitates, then sets the microwave on the doormat. She runs into her bedroom, scrambles underneath her bed. Extracts the box. *The box*. She yanks the door of the microwave open and shoves the box in.

She calls a lift by the emergency stairwell takes it up to the top floor of the building. The doors of each flat are red, exterior doors, with brass numbers drilled into their faces. They look out onto the walkway, into the open air, a brown brick wall lining it. It is the sixth floor. A soft breeze and the golden hour. She feels it on her skin. Below, there is a paved brown courtyard, deserted due to its entrance being blocked off by the roadworks. The microwave is balanced on her hip. It is heavier than she expected. She drags it onto the ledge that separates the walkway from the nothingness, panting.

And she tips the microwave over the edge.

And she watches as it falls down down down through the air, gathering momentum, until it hits the concrete below, the door levering off and launching itself away from the carcass in a spectacular fashion, the safety glass exploding in a crescendo of glittering shards. The box inside explodes too, the papers billowing across the courtyard like strange white flightless birds. They land in the cracks in the paving slabs. Burrow into the corners of the walls. The sound is louder than she expected, and a car alarm activates nearby.

A man in the flat opposite opens his window and eyes the microwave, and her, suspiciously. He is shouting something at her, his face a mask of anger, but she can't hear him.

She imagines how the collision of metal and concrete has vibrated through the maggots, imagines that they have been shocked to death upon impact. She relishes the sensation of her chest expanding as her lungs fill up with air. The box is not hot any more. It is not staring at her from down there, prickling at her skin. The documents are running away from her, burning up like paper lanterns. Turning to ash.

And then, inexplicably, Cam is down there, having scrambled over the roadworks cordon to the north of the courtyard. He is staring up at her, shielding his eyes against the bright low sunlight. He is wearing a scruffy grey T-shirt and jeans and no shoes. His shoulders heaving up and down.

She cannot hear him either, over the roaring in her own ears. But she can see what he is shouting at her.

Lucy. Lucy. Lucy.

But Cam's going to be gone soon, she remembers. Cam is leaving.

She retreats from the ledge and thrusts her body at the fire-escape door leading to the stairwell. And she's in the stairwell and she's running down the stairs two at a time, not quite sure where she is planning on going but knowing it can't be back in Flat 5. Not now.

And behind her, back at the top of the stairs, the fire-exit door slams shut.

And there it is again. The door slamming – closed or open, she is never quite sure. The deadbolt clicking it shut, or the handle ricocheting off the wall behind.

She stops on the stairwell and leans against the wall.

She is a child again. Maybe eight or nine or ten, she's not so sure. And she's in a house that is unfamiliar to her. Maybe one of her father's decorating jobs. Maybe Uncle Marv's new flat in Chadwell Heath. Maybe somewhere else. And she sees them in the bathroom. Danny. Uncle Marv. And Uncle Marv watches her watching him. Watching them. She doesn't understand what she's looking at. She doesn't understand any of it. But Danny is crying. And it makes her cry too. Makes her scream. Banburys don't cry. They get on with it.

And later, back in their own home. The chalk-lined LUCY AND DANNY'S HOUSE above the front door, barely there. You wouldn't notice unless you knew where to look. She is sprinting up the stairs, three at a time, and she's in her bedroom. She slams the door shut. The door ricochets, again and again and again. The door is the sound that has been spiralling in her head. Danny is nowhere, her parents are working, but Uncle Marv is here, on the other side of the door. Pleading with her. Please don't tell anyone, Lucy. Please forget it. Be a good girl. You didn't see anything at all, did you?

It's almost Christmas. The next day, Uncle Marv arrives at the house with a brand-new doll's house for her. The most special thing she has ever owned. She loves it more than she has loved anything in her life, ever.

Have you forgotten? Uncle Marv asks her.

She hasn't, but she tells him yes.

You didn't see anything, did you?

No.

You didn't see what you thought you saw.

And she believes him: she is only a little girl. How could

Uncle Marv, who is so generous and kind, who looks after her and Danny, do something so bad? He couldn't. Look at this beautiful doll's house. The perfect kind. The kind Lucy wants to live in, one day.

She saw nothing, she tells herself, she tells him.

Good girl.

And over time, over days and months and years, she tells herself that she didn't see what she thought she saw, over and over again. And eventually, in the midst of everything else, she forgets.

Until now.

She pictures the bedroom door slamming, again and again. Danny behind a different door with a stranger. It has always been a stranger in all of her imaginings, but deep down she has known that it was never a stranger. That this is not a dream but a memory.

And the thing behind the door is finally ready to be let out. It's Danny. Of course it is. The rot of it blasted across the concrete. She feels her body sinking to the ground with the realisation of it; must cling onto the wall with her fingernails to hold herself up.

She takes out her phone and thumbs through her contacts to Danny's number. Her hands shake violently as the call rings off. She tries again, and again, and again. No answer. She tries the house phone and gets her parents' corny answering machine message. She remembers that her parents are in Stoke selling Uncle Marv's canal boat. Remembers the promise she made to her father to check in on Danny. Danny is alone. She feels herself beginning to panic. A strange, strangled, alien wail comes out of her mouth. Her phone clatters out of her shaking hands and bounces down one, two, three concrete steps before landing face-down on the floor. She crawls down the stairs to pick it up. The screen, dark and now even more splintered than before, beyond repair, is dead.

Before she is fully aware of what she's doing, she is out of the stairwell, sprinting down Lambeth Road and hailing a bus. The microwave forgotten, the papers forgotten. Nothing else in this moment matters except Danny. Danny who is alone somewhere, with Uncle Marv dead, trying to stay sober or maybe not at all sober any more, maybe drinking himself to death. Lucy feels the panic rising as she climbs up to the top deck of the bus. She must find Danny.

The river curls and tightens with each turn of the bus like a rope around the ankles; the buses red cells carrying protein molecules through blood vessels to organs. The concrete below. The grime and dust and dirt.

She sits at the front of the top deck like a king. Like a mermaid nailed to the bow. She feels the rhythm of the traffic inside her, the sky awash with darkness, the microwave on the ground, the water of the lake on her skin, seeping through into her bones, rotting her from the outside in.

Danny.

And after what seems like a lifetime, buses and tubes and the run from the station, she is outside her childhood home in Chadwell Heath. The cracks that run down the sides of the walls like dark canyons. The subsidence that means the house is sinking and will one day be nothing more than a hole in the ground. Perhaps the hole will go straight to Australia. Perhaps it will go straight to hell. She sits on the wall for a moment as the sun sets, her heart pounding, breathless, feels the cloying dampness of her own sweat. There is an old green tricycle – Danny's from a lifetime ago – buried into the fence, grown in with the weeds. She can't remember what happened last night. She can't remember a single moment of her life, up until now. She knows that something terrible has happened. And it was in this house. And it was her fault.

She slams her fist against the front door, again and again and again, calling Danny's name.

The house is dark and there is no answer.

Danny, she shouts – screams – Danny. Where are you? Open up.

She pictures Danny in the house, in the darkness. Passed out in some corner. A low tolerance after a stint of sobriety. Choking on his own sick. She feels the tears leaking from the corners of her eyes as she calls his name, but the house stays dark.

She takes a loose brick from the front garden wall, dusty and disintegrating in her palm, and launches it at the house. It falls uselessly into the middle of the lawn. She picks up the brick again. And she walks to the living-room window and slams the brick against the glass, again and again and again. The brick against the window is the door in her imagination slamming, over and over and over again. The door is slamming itself closed and open at exactly the same time. And at first, there's nothing – the tiniest of scratches, the colour and texture of dry ice – and then a splinter, a chip. The dull thunk of the brick against the glass methodical and rhythmic. Another, and another, and then a spider's web of cracks, spiralling out across the pane of glass. She sees her own face in it, illuminated by the setting sun that sits orange and pink beyond the house, distorted by the shards. Hair flaming, eyes streaming black, witch-like, soulless-like.

She heaves the brick once more and it penetrates the house, glances off the windowsill in a perfect curvature, and lands harmlessly, once more a brick, on the rug in the living room. The house is a desert, the warmth of it palpable through the window. Stillness and darkness and nothingness, despite all the things that clutter it up. And then there's Danny – behind her – come from the back garden, trembling, teeth chattering, eyes wide and yellow, so pale he might be a ghost.

Loose, what the fuck are you doing here? Did you *smash the window?*

You weren't answering the door, she explains uselessly.

I was in the shed. What the fuck are you doing here? he repeats.

I don't know, she replies simply, sitting down on the grass. I don't know. I wanted to make sure you were okay.

She feels her skin peeling away, the last of the layers gone, and now her heart is falling out of her chest.

Will you tell them? she asks Danny.

Tell them what?

Tell them what Uncle Marv did to you.

She lets the truth of it settle between them like the fine morning mist.

Danny sits down on the floor next to Lucy. His whole body is vibrating uncontrollably. He is still very, very ill, Lucy realises. But he is not drunk. The sobriety is attacking him. He has taught his body over the past almost-twenty-years to depend upon one thing, and now he has taken that one thing away, and it is rioting against him.

She lets the relief that he's not dead yet wash over her, and begins to sob.

Let's go into the house, he tells her, an incomprehensible look on his face.

I don't think I can, she says.

She follows him instead to his photography studio at the back of the garden. She has never been inside before. The shed – to her surprise – is exceedingly clean, with all of the different bits of tripod and lenses and light fixtures in their proper places:

333

with colour-coded cubbyholes mounted on the walls and notice-boards with different negatives pinned up neatly. The cleanness and neatness and precision of how things are put away reminds Lucy of herself.

Danny goes to his desk and picks up a camera. He takes a screwdriver and tries to unscrew a compartment on the casing. He cannot get the screwdriver to do what he wants it to do because he is shaking so violently.

Can I help? she asks him, pressing the heels of her hands into her eyes. She feels herself calming under the fluorescent lighting, the realisation that Danny is alive, that he's okay, quieting her.

He eyes her suspiciously and then ushers her over.

See, I need to get this screw out so I can get this compartment open, he says, showing her. There's a roll of film lodged in there and I can't get it out.

Lucy takes the screwdriver, ignoring the wavering in Danny's voice that makes her heart leap, and inserts it into the tiny screw.

I wanted to ask you something, she says, as she twists the compartment on the camera open, for a moment irrationally terrified that maggots will spill from the chamber. She notices now that Danny is skinny – even skinnier than he was before.

Yeah? he says gruffly.

Are you eating? That's not what I wanted to ask. But are you?

Danny shrugs. I've got no appetite, he says. I'm detoxing.

Do you remember why Uncle Marv got me that doll's house that one Christmas?

Danny stiffens next to her.

It was over the top, she says. Mum and Dad never bought us anything close to that expensive. He got you a BMX the same year, didn't he? Why did he do that?

He had a lucky streak at the bookies. He didn't have kids, so he spent it on us instead.

Yeah, maybe, but it's something else.

Lucy has slipped the compartment open, now, and rather than maggots, a tangled roll of film spills out. Danny collects it up and quickly shoves it into a small box he has taken from a drawer. He crosses the floor of the studio, to the other side, away from Lucy.

We need to keep it in the dark, he says, otherwise it will be ruined.

It was to do with a promise, Lucy says, persisting, ignoring the frightened look on Danny's face. She realises that she's not afraid of him any more. Because I saw something I shouldn't have, she continues, a question in her voice.

He hurt you, didn't he, Lucy says, a statement rather than a fact. The thing that has been dancing around the fringes of her consciousness now illuminated, as though directly under one of the huge LEDs in the studio.

Danny says nothing.

And I saw it happen. And he made me promise not to tell. He told me to forget it. And he bought me that doll's house so that I would.

Danny says, I thought it would be over when you found us. But then you never told. You never told anyone.

I don't think I ever really understood what it was that I'd found. I'm so sorry, Danny.

He stands before her, his shoulders sagging, a look of unique devastation on his face. He looks as though he is deflating before her.

He was so deep into my life. Into every part of it, Danny says. He helped me to build this, for fuck's sakes. He throws his arms up, indicating the studio. I don't know what to do now. I don't know how to wash him off me.

Lucy says nothing, feels herself shudder with the weight of

the grief she feels for her brother. She wants to go to him and hug him, but there's too much space between them now. He is all the way over there.

He's dead, anyway, Danny says, his eyes wide and wild and haunted. It doesn't even matter.

He walks out of the shed, and she follows him.

You could tell them. What happened, Lucy says. Now that he's gone.

They are now in the garden. Danny sits, and leans back into the dew-soaked grass and watches the pigeons in the gutter on the roof of the house as they clean their feathers.

They would never believe me, he says simply. They never believed you, did they?

She feels herself deflating with the truth of it.

We have to make them believe you. We can do it together. We'll tell them together, if you like.

No, he replies quickly, his jaw set. I need to do it myself.

That's why you hurt me, Lucy says, isn't it? Because he was hurting you and I didn't help you.

Danny turns away from her.

You were just a kid, he tells her, shaking. It wasn't your fault.

But so were you, she replies.

Chapter Thirty

Danny convinces Lucy to stay for the night.

I don't know if I can stay here, she says. Too many bad memories.

You can't go home like this. You're a state.

He's right. She cannot stop herself from shaking, just like him.

She sleeps restlessly in her old childhood bedroom, exhausted, and in the early morning, he calls her a cab from his phone, seeing as her own is smashed, still lying in the corner of the fire-escape stairs, and walks her to the pavement outside the front of the house to wait for it. They stand in silence, watching the beginnings of morning commuter traffic trundle by. She feels a sharp clarity in the morning air, inhales it and lets it fill the gaps in her brain, clearing the fogginess of the evening.

What am I going to do about that? she asks Danny, pointing at the smashed living room window.

Don't worry. I'll sort it.

You will?

Yeah.

What are you going to do now? she asks him.

I don't know.

Promise me you won't start drinking again. That this is the last time.

I can't make a promise I don't know I'll keep, Loose.

The cab seems to take an age to arrive and another to carry Lucy home to Flat 5. She watches the city from the window, early-morning dusty pink, reminded of the same journey she took with Cam at the beginning of the summer. She turns the key in the lock and Winston skitters round the corner of the kitchen and bounds up to her, Bugs Bunny in his mouth. She notices that Bugs Bunny is down to one ear as she musses Winston's fur. She feels marginally better that he's so excited at her presence. Then, she registers that there are voices murmuring from the living room, then frantic footsteps, and Ash in the hallway, phone in hand, mouth agape.

She's here, Ash shouts. She's back.

What?

Out of the living room and into the hallway come Cam, followed by Meredith and Nara.

Don't ever, Ash says, *ever* do that again.

What are you talking about?

You didn't come home, Cam says, his face haggard. Do you realise that it's eight in the morning?

We were worried *sick*, Loose, Ash adds, furious.

They pull Lucy into an angry, frantic hug.

Your phone was off. We thought something terrible had happened. We thought you were having an episode. Cam says you threw the microwave off the roof.

Meredith now comes over and assesses her.

You look an absolute mess, hun, she says diplomatically. What the fuck happened?

Ash is now on the phone again, saying, Yes, yes, she's home

now, she's just walked in. Thank you so much. Thanks for all your help.

Why are you two here? Lucy asks, totally bewildered, looking to Meredith and Nara.

We didn't know who else to call, Cam says. I don't have your parents' details. Or your brother's. I thought I should drive over, maybe. But then I couldn't find your parents' address in my phone history. I thought maybe Tom . . . he trails off, before gathering himself. But I don't know where he lives, either. The only other people I could think of who might know something was these two.

They all go into the living room and sit down on the raggedy couch. Nara makes tea for everyone and they sit silently, sipping. Meredith is clutching her mug to her chest as though it's a weapon.

No one could get hold of you, Nara says, close to tears. We wanted to check you weren't dead. That you hadn't been abducted or something.

Nara wanted to check you weren't dead, Meredith clarifies. *I* wanted to go for breakfast at Frederick's, but now I've been dragged south of the river.

It's just not like you, to be out all night, Ash says, and Lucy is not unaware of the irony of this, coming from Ash. But she says nothing, feels her frantic pulse, smells her own sweat on her clothes. Feels ghoulish. Feels as though she is about to cry.

You can't disappear like that, Nara says sternly. There are nutters everywhere. You need to make yourself available so we can check in with each other.

I dropped my phone. I'm sorry.

The same goes for the rest of you, Nara says, nodding at Meredith and Ash and Cam.

Hey. Why am I involved in this? Ash asks.

339

I'm just saying; we've got to look out for each other.

Lucy lets Ash lean their head on the crook of her shoulder and feels suddenly very soothed by the comfort of human touch.

I really am sorry, Lucy says again. She wants to crawl into bed and sleep for a year. I didn't realise you would be worried.

She looks to Cam, who stares back at her with sad eyes.

Of *course* we're going to be worried, stupid, Nara tells her. You're our friend. We care about you. We want to make sure you're safe.

Lucy looks at each of them in turn and sees it in their faces. The naked affection they have for her.

Are you going to tell us what happened? Where you were?

So, she tells them.

She tells them everything, from the very beginning, although it comes out all garbled and in the wrong order. She tells them about the adoption, how the revelation of the adoption happened, at the wedding, with Danny. How Danny always wanted to hurt her and she never quite understood why. Her parents, how they never believed her. Uncle Marv. How it's all useless now because Marv is dead and Danny is ruined, and Lucy wonders whether she is too. Whether she'll ever get the stink of shame off her, the feeling that she has been carrying around with her like a weapon she can use against herself since she was fifteen, and maybe even younger if she thinks about it properly. Maybe when she was eight and Danny started hurting her – probably because that's when Uncle Marv started hurting him; maybe when she was twelve and her dad broke his back. She didn't realise until now that she thought she might have deserved all the bad things Danny said to her. She deserved everything that came her way. That she was truly, fundamentally, at the very core of herself, rotten from the inside out, and undeserving of love.

I always thought there was something wrong with me, she says. I've been having this sort of low-key feeling that everyone hates me.

She can feel her eyes leaking tears as she talks, her body shuddering with the power of unspent sobbing. She cannot let herself cry in front of these people. It feels as though she has split open her ribcage and bared her heart to them.

There isn't anything wrong with you, Nara tells her.

Bad things have happened to you, Meredith says softly. That doesn't make you a bad person.

Cam tells her, It's okay if you want to cry.

So she does, and they surround her like warm air, gather her up gently and carry her.

Chapter Thirty-One

Meredith and Nara leave after breakfast, making Lucy promise to get a new phone and never turn it off while ushering one another out of the door. The three of them that remain, exhausted from different kinds of sleepless nights, go to bed in the bright early-morning light. Lucy wakes up at three o'clock in the afternoon, sandwiched between Ash and Winston who have squeezed into bed with her. She realises, with a sharp stab, that it's Wednesday. She is meant to be at work right now. She doesn't even have a phone to call Delilah with some concocted excuse. Ash is sucking their thumb, with one arm flung behind their head, hair spilling across the duvet. She watches their chest rise and fall with their breathing, mirroring Winston's own. Despite the panic that she has flaked on work – so unlike her, so very like a bad dream – there is something about the three of them together in her bed that makes Lucy feel safe. She wants to stay there forever.

The sun beats down through the pale thin curtains, heating her skin, so she delicately extracts herself from the duvet, careful not to wake Ash, and ushers Winston out of the bedroom. In the living room, Cam is asleep on the sofa, snoring softly. Winston immediately trots over to him, nuzzles at his face, and he stirs.

Want to go for a walk? she whispers, and he smiles up at her.

A tired, resigned, sad smile. But a smile nonetheless. And once again she feels her heart swell for him.

They take Winston to Archbishop's Park near the river, and they sit on a bench and people-watch, saying very little to one another. She lets Winston up onto the bench with her and he rests his head on her lap while she scratches behind his ears. His fur is almost completely grown back now, and he has a thick luscious gold-spun coat.

Love you, mate, Lucy tells him.

Love you too, he seems to say back to her.

She and Cam and Winston wander along the South Bank and watch the skateboarders under the overpass, and the street vendors selling sweet roasted chestnuts along the riverbank. It is a beautiful day and the sky is big and bright. Blackfriars Bridge is heaving with tourists and screaming kids and street performers; the noise of steel drums and trains on the bridge and the music coming out of a bar, the roar of the river and the ferries crossing almost deafening. It all feels like a dream, after last night. Lucy feels jet-lagged. She can tell that Cam feels the same: the way he rubs his eyes with the heels of his hands.

Do you want to talk about it? she asks him.

Which bit? he replies, turning to look at her, smiling ruefully. Even under the tiredness, the shadow across his jaw, the way his hair sticks up straight, the rumpled T-shirt that he fell asleep in, he looks at her with that same intensity, that indecipherable expression, that makes her skin hot and prickly. Even now, in this moment, she wants to pull him into her.

All of it, she says.

I collected up your papers, he says abruptly. The ones you threw off the balcony, and the box too. I put them back under your bed. I hope that's okay.

343

She stares at him and lets out a breath she didn't realise she was holding. Didn't realise how much it meant to her, the box. It's no longer burning, now – just a quiet simmer.

Thank you, she says.

I thought you might regret it.

I did.

I haven't told Ash that I'm moving out.

Let's tell them today, Lucy says.

I feel like once they know, it's real. Does that make sense?

Lucy nods.

I don't want to go, he says, quickly, as though he's been desperate to say it and now it's a relief that he finally has. I don't want to go home.

Why not? You never liked living in town. You said so yourself.

He glances at her sideways while they wander, with Winston, through the busiest sections of the promenade, across warm brown-bricked pavements, and find a quiet spot by the Oxo Tower. They sit down on a bench and stare out to the north of the river: St Paul's Cathedral, Bank, the Tower of London.

I don't like London, he agrees, finally, after an extended silence. But I feel like ... there's a lot that I'm leaving behind, now.

Anais?

He laughs humourlessly. For Christ's sake, Banbury. It's you. I'm talking about you.

She ignores the twisting of her stomach and forces herself to look at him squarely.

The other night. You said that we should stop.

Yes, I did.

I thought you'd changed your mind.

I didn't want something to happen like that. After that party and after what happened . . . with Tom. I thought that you would regret that, too.

She stiffens. That's not your decision to make.

I know. I can see that now.

That's one thing I don't regret. I promise. I only said that it was a bad idea because I thought you'd changed your mind. But I didn't change mine. I was just scared of . . . being out of control. Being hurt.

He sighs. And now I'm going away.

You need to be there for your family, for Bella, she tells him.

I know.

I feel like I miss you, she says. Even though you're not gone yet.

Me too.

I just wish, Lucy says, and then is unsure how to end the sentence. What does she wish?

Me too, he says again.

It's not our time, yet, is it?

No, not yet, I don't think.

The sun comes in long, dusty, lazy shafts through the trees and casts complex mottled shadows across their faces.

They walk back to Flat 5 together, and Lucy slips her hand into his, and it feels very right to be doing that with him. Not tense or awkward or fraught with meaning: just nice, and simple, and with the sensation of crawling into fresh bed sheets after a very long and difficult day.

They tell Ash, and Ash bursts into tears.

What am I going to do? they wail.

Well, you can still live here. We just need to find a new flat-mate, Lucy says, matter-of-factly. It's not that big of a deal.

Wow, thanks, Cam says, grinning, and Lucy rolls her eyes at

him as she wraps an arm around Ash, who is sobbing dramatically into their hands.

Can Sylvie come and live here?

Absolutely not. Never.

They go into the back garden and Cam rearranges the garden loungers that Lucy bought for them. Lucy clears all the leaves out of the paddling pool and fills it up with water from the hosepipe. They sit in a circle, feet dangling in the water.

I've been thinking, Ash says.

Yeah?

I've been thinking that maybe London isn't for me. Maybe with Cam leaving it's a good time for me to go, too. I need to go back to Poole.

Really? Lucy feels a flutter of panic at the fringes of her consciousness. Where has this come from?

I've been here *ages*. Ages, yeah? Months. And I did some maths the other day to work out how much I've earned from gigging. It's less than a grand. In all this time. Like, eight hundred and fifty quid. Not even two months' rent.

I don't understand how you're living, Cam says, leaning back on his sunlounger and shielding his eyes from the bright sky.

My grandparents keep sending me top-up money. But it's not fair on them. They're dropping their life savings on me, to help me to pursue a career that isn't going to happen.

So, what, you're giving up? Cam asks, incredulous, and Ash shrugs solemnly. No. No way. You can't do that. You can't give up on your dream. Cam sits up straight and stares at them, serious. Nothing is an instant win, Ash. It takes hard work and dedication and—

Lots of money. Which I don't have.

It's your *dream* to be a musician.

Well, I can't afford my dream, Ash says dramatically.

346

Cam looks at Lucy, eyebrows raised like *say something to them, back me up,* but Lucy grimaces. She doesn't blame Ash for giving up, not really.

Sometimes it's the most we can do to just stay alive, she tells them both.

Yeah, exactly, Ash replies.

They stay in the garden sunbathing until the sun dips below the buildings beyond the fence. They order a curry because it feels like a momentous occasion.

There's so much to do, Lucy says, over dinner, taking a sip of wine from a mug at the kitchen table.

You know that even if we both move out, we're here for you, right? Ash tells her.

Yeah, of course I know that.

I don't think you do.

Lucy smiles grimly at Ash.

You have a wonderful life, Cam says gently. You have lots of friends. You're well-liked by everyone. You have an incredible job that you love.

It strikes her in that moment how much Cam sounds like her, when she is trying to convince herself of these things.

That's what I tell myself, she says. But I don't. I hate my job.

You're very loved, Cam says.

Yeah, we love you, Ash replies, shoving a Bombay potato into their mouth. Don't we, Cam?

And Cam says, Yes, of course, genuinely and without hesitation. Even if you're a prickly cactus sometimes. He grins at her, his eyes sparkling.

It feels like you've been hiding. You don't need to hide from us.

I'm trying not to, Lucy says.

And she knows that she has already decided that this is the

truth of it. She knows that in this moment, crammed into the kitchen with Cam and Ash, everything seems okay. She knows in the deep pit of her soul that they love her and she loves them, each of them with their idiosyncrasies and abrasiveness and the ways they say things but their meaning gets mixed up and inherited in a way they never intended. And it doesn't matter if they both disappear and she's alone again, this will not change. She knows that they are the kinds of friends who she'll see in a year's time and it will be like no time has passed at all and that this is a rare and precious thing that should be cherished.

She also knows that tonight, in the dark of her bedroom, while she tries to sleep and the flat is dead silent, she'll tell herself the opposite. That she'll remember all of the hideous things she's done in her life; all the ways she has withheld herself from the people who love her and call her their friend by pretending to be someone else, for fear of . . . of what, exactly? It is not entirely clear to her any more, who or what she is hiding from. She wonders at how she has created this impossible prison for herself, by pretending to be someone who is fundamentally not herself. And as much as she tries to be the truest version of herself, the weight of it will bear down on her, and she'll find it hard to breathe and she'll feel so very lonely and alone. And it will seem like there is no way at all that she can climb out of this pit. And when they're gone, it will get worse; it will feel like starting again from the beginning, building herself piece by piece from the ground up, all over again. And it will *hurt* – the kind of intangible, deeply embedded pain that can't be soothed quickly or easily. But she must remember what it's like in this moment. To bask in the glow of friendship that is unconditional and uncompromising and at times messy but at other times glorious. She must capture it and bottle it and store it away to be examined and reimagined and relived at a later date. Because that is the way that she must learn to be alive.

Chapter Thirty-Two

On Friday, Lucy takes Winston into work. She feels the deep and fortifying comfort of him whenever he is close to her. She has not cleared Winston's visit with Delilah or anyone else. She has not made any explanation for her absence yesterday or the day before. She braces herself for the inevitable bollocking. She feels a little as though she doesn't really care.

Today is the day that she has to officially tell Anais to leave. Anais will be gone, and then next week Cam will be gone and, not long after, Ash will go back to Poole, too. It feels a little bit like they have all failed in some way or another. But there is also a tender and tenuous sense of liberation Lucy feels, and she knows is shared by Cam and Ash, as she takes the lift up to the Kube offices, with Winston splayed out on the floor of the elevator like a pancake. He smiles up at her and says, It's okay, you've got this. And Lucy says, I know.

Anais is already at her desk when Lucy enters the office floor, Winston trotting along behind her obediently. There are looks from Jenna and Kerry and the others. Delilah actually stands up at her desk and takes her glasses off to get a better look at the dog.

Lucy drops her bag on her desk.

Hey, she says to Anais.

Hey, Anais replies, not looking at her.

Shall we go and have a chat?

This is it, isn't it?

Yeah. This is it. Are you okay?

Yes. I'm great, actually.

Anais follows her into one of the glass conference rooms. Winston comes too, sniffing the corners of the skirting boards with interest.

Anais perches on the edge of the table, arms folded across her chest, so Lucy stands, because to sit feels somehow inappropriate.

So, what's the vibe? Anais asks. Have you got a speech prepared?

She doesn't say this spitefully, Lucy notices. She is more a little amused by the whole thing.

Are you going to be okay? she asks Anais.

Oh, yeah, I'm going to be fine.

She seems to be sincere, her perfectly lined eyes creasing into a knowing smile. Anais looks beautiful, as ever.

I think you've done me a big favour, Loose. I don't know how long I would have spent trying to get back to Cam. All the time I would have wasted on him.

Really?

Yeah. Really. I've already booked a flight to Thailand.

Lucy inhales deeply and can feel her hands shaking as she slips out a sheaf of papers from the manila folder Delilah gave her earlier in the week.

Anais, you've been working here at Kube for just over a year . . .

There is no crying or tantrum throwing or stropping. Anais sits quietly as Lucy goes through the logistics of the redundancy with her.

I'm really sorry to have to deliver this news, Lucy says, when she's finished. She feels strangely calm: nothing like she thought she would. It helps that Anais seems to have already processed the news.

It's not your fault, is it? Anais says. It had to be one of us. And it was probably going to be the one who constantly pulled sickies and turned up late most days and threw up on Greg at the Christmas Party.

Lucy grimaces, unsure how to respond.

Is that everything, then? Anais asks.

I think so.

Thanks for . . . you know. Giving me a heads-up. Thanks for looking after me.

You're welcome.

I still hate you, though.

Yes, I know.

I hope you make him happy.

Anais doesn't need to clarify who she is talking about.

Lucy holds the door to the meeting room open for Anais and lets her out into the office. Of course, everyone is staring, craning their necks over the tops of their monitors to get a better look at what has been going on.

Lucy stands awkwardly while Anais clears her belongings out of her desk: old chapsticks, notebooks, bubble-gum-pink pencil case, a gag Secret Santa gift that is a framed photograph of Gemma Collins.

Delilah wanders over in a pair of yellow Crocs, oval-shaped shell earrings rattling like castanets.

Anais, darling, she says, pulling her into an unexpected hug.

Anais shoots a look of pure panic at Lucy.

Delilah, she says tonelessly once she is released.

I just want to say what an absolute joy it's been to have you working with us.

Anais shrugs. Okay, thanks.

You're always going to be part of our family, aren't you?

Anais rolls her eyes. Yes, absolutely.

We look after our family, Delilah continues, turning to Lucy, a curious expression on her face. And where have you been, young lady? she asks, her jolliness masking the strange violence in her voice.

I'm sorry, Lucy tells her, having already rehearsed the excuse. I had a family emergency. I lost my phone so I couldn't notify you.

Even as she's saying it, she recognises how weak the apology is. But she can't muster up the wherewithal to care, now. After everything that's happened, Kube seems so small – so ridiculous, in the grand scheme of Lucy's life. She tries to remember why she ever thought she loved this job. She can't.

But Delilah just shrugs, Lucy's absence seemingly already forgotten, as she turns back to Anais. There is a sickening wretchedness that has settled over Lucy. Winston is edging closer and closer to Delilah's Crocs, transfixed by them.

Anais has now packed all her things into a bin bag that Delilah has helpfully retrieved from the kitchen for her. The whole office – all thirty of them – continue to stare.

Well. This is it, then, Anais says, and now she seems to well up a little as she looks at Lucy and shrugs, resigned.

Delilah air-kisses her dramatically on both cheeks.

Anais moves from desk to desk and bids each colleague farewell, bin bag swinging loosely from her wrist, pendulum-like. There are hugs and tears: Anais is a popular member of the workforce. She stops for long and sincere conversations.

I must say, though, Delilah says, her voice abruptly clipped, that was very well handled. She is still standing next to Lucy as they watch Anais on her circuit of the office.

Really? Lucy says, raising her eyebrows at Delilah.

She actually seems *happy* to be leaving. How did you do it?

Well, I don't think she's really happy. I think she's putting on a show.

Either way – what a performance. Standing ovations from all of the exec.

Lucy stares at her.

At that moment, her new phone, picked up yesterday afternoon pings in her pocket. She only transferred a handful of contacts over – the important ones – which feels somehow cleaner. She sees that she has a WhatsApp from Danny. Danny, who never texts her, ever.

The text says, *I told Mum and Dad everything.*

A second, an afterthought, which pings through rapidly after the first, is simply an *X*.

The third is a GIF of a dancing Jeremy Corbyn, captioned with 'Here we . . . here we . . . here we fucking go!!!'.

Lucy can't help but grin at the text, her eyes stinging. She doesn't know whether to laugh or cry. She feels her throat burn for Danny.

Delilah is still talking.

We'll of course, she whispers conspiratorially with a sly smile, be discussing your progression in the company very soon. And I must say, it's looking *very* positive. Now that you've shown what you're capable of. Of course, we can't have any more unexplained absences. But, I think, in light of this, we can overlook it this time. We're all *very* impressed.

Lucy feels *very* sick and has to dig her fingernails into the palms of her hands to stop herself from excusing herself to the toilet. She stares back at Delilah, trying not to look complete-ly horrified. This is no family, she realises. Anais knew that already.

She feels a curious sense of calm fall over her as she watches Delilah's earrings; her cracked plum-coloured lipstick. Winston is now sniffing one Croced foot. Delilah lifts her foot and shoves his face away with it. Winston jumps backwards, his hackles at pinpoints, his lip curled up in a warning.

Lucy calls him to her, alarmed, and he winds himself around her legs.

I hate this job, she tells Delilah, realising the absolute truth of it as it comes out of her mouth. I hate it. I hate my job.

Delilah blinks at her, her smile sliding off her face like melted ice cream. What? she says.

Lucy marches to the kitchen, Winston at her heels, and takes out a bin bag from underneath the sink. Anais – who is halfway round the office – looks at her quizzically.

I'm coming with you, Lucy says, as she passes her on her way back to her desk, where Delilah is still standing, befuddled. I'm handing in my notice, Lucy tells her, and now that she has said it, she feels all the venom that she has been pushing deep deep down in her belly rising up, seeping out of her. She hates her job. She hates supplier fucking relations. She hates Delilah and her stupid fucking earrings.

Excuse me? Delilah says, a small drop of spittle flying from her mouth.

I'm leaving, Delilah. Today. It was a pleasure working with you.

You can't do this. There's a notice period. You're contractually obliged—

I'll work my notice if you want me to, Lucy tells her. But I'll be collecting my holiday entitlement in my last pay cheque.

Delilah's mouth has fallen open.

Is there anything else? Lucy asks her.

I don't understand, Delilah says, taking her glasses off and letting them hang loose from her neck on the beaded chain attached to them.

Lucy pauses to think about it.

I just don't like the person I'm becoming here, she says. It's not me. It never has been. I was just pretending that it was.

Lucy is emptying the contents of her desk drawers from her pedestal without pausing to sort through it.

Are you really sure about this? Delilah asks her, sitting down on a swivel chair.

Delilah, Lucy tells her. Kube is going down. I know it. You know it. I've seen the books. I've seen the P&Ls. It doesn't matter how many redundancies you make; how many cost efficiencies. It's still not going to cover that financial black hole the exec has dug this company into. This makes total sense to me. I'm getting out while there's still cash flow to pay my final salary.

As Lucy speaks, Delilah's face turns into a mask.

You're a silly little girl, she says quietly. Think you know what goes into making a company work? How to run a business? You don't know the first thing. Thinks she's a fucking business guru because she's got an MBA and two years of account management? *Please.*

Lucy laughs, wonders why she is not shrinking from Delilah. If Delilah had said these things to her three months ago, she would have had a nervous breakdown and gone into hibernation. Lucy realises that the feeling of not caring any more is a freeing one.

Even with my little old MBA, I can see dozens of mistakes on your books, Lucy tells her. Who's paying for your 'client dinners', hey? Is there a reason your husband hasn't bought any direct marketing business from us, yet? How many lunches at The Ledbury is it going to take? Can't wait for that one to come up in the audit. Does Greg know?

Delilah says nothing, her lips pressed into a thin line so that all Lucy can see is a plum-hued slit sliced across her face.

Bye, Delilah, she says. It's been a pleasure working with you.

Anais has finished her circuit of the floor. You ready? she asks as she approaches Lucy.

Delilah is silent, staring directly past them, statuesque on the swivel chair.

They exit the floor into the lift lobby, bin bags and handbags and Winston in tow.

Didn't think you had it in you, Anais says quietly as they call a lift. Lucy feels jittery with adrenaline, her pulse bouncing around her like a ping-pong ball.

Neither did I, she says.

Greenwich Park at sundown is gold-drenched, the light reflecting off the river and making the people – the grass, the observatory, the museum, even the concrete – seem a little bit more magical.

Lucy and Winston climb the hill, taking long, hamstring-clenching strides on the path up to the Observatory, which resembles a sandstone temple against a sky the colour of cornflowers. Once they reach the top, Lucy, wheezing and defeated, collapses into the long grass and looks out to the city: the Roman palatial structures of the Queen's House and the National Maritime Museum immediately at the bottom of the hill, creamy-white, and behind them, the hazy-shaped Lego blocks of Canary Wharf, and further west, the Walkie Talkie, the Gherkin, the Shard.

Winston burrows into the grass, elongating, tongue lolling and canines poking over his lips, which are stretched into a broad sloppy smile. He leans his whole weight against Lucy as she pets him, his fur ever richer where it has grown back in.

They sit and watch together as the sun sinks into the city, turning the trees different shades of green as it makes its slow progress across the sky.

As the sky pinkens, Lucy wonders at what she has done.

The euphoria of her dramatic exit from Kube earlier is dissipating quickly. And in its place – as much as she tries to tamp it down and ignore it – is a cold and unmistakable dread.

She has left her job. She has no other job lined up. She has no income. She has rent due on a flat of which very soon she will be the only tenant.

What now, hey, Winston? she asks him.

He sneezes loudly, his whole head spasming with the force of it, and snaps at a dragonfly.

She takes out her new phone and instinctively checks the balance of her savings account.

Next, she opens the notes app.

She titles a list 'Things I am good at'.

She writes: numbers, organisation, cooking, swimming, listening, looking after Winston, Microsoft Excel.

Next, she writes: 'Things that I care about'.

This time she lists: Winston, Mum, Dad, Danny, Cam, Meredith, Nara, Ash, living in town, being independent, doing a job that I love. Then, reluctantly, she writes: money.

She thinks about it some more, and adds: birth parents, feeling her lungs squeeze.

She opens a third new note and types: 'Things that I want'.

She stares at the screen, her thumbs poised over the keyboard.

She types, earnestly, Sort things out with Mum and Dad.

And then, Find out about my birth parents.

After that, she is at a loss.

What is it, exactly, that Lucy wants?

She looks down at Winston again.
He licks his nose, panting, dark eyes shining.
Sorry, pal, he seems to say, this one's all on you.

Chapter Thirty-Three

On the following weekend, Lucy steels herself and calls her father, inviting him to come swimming with her. The flat is unbearable: Lucy hates watching Ash and Cam both slowly dismantle their lives there, packing their things into boxes and taking their cutlery and crockery out of the kitchen drawers to be wrapped in newspaper. She knows that soon she will open the door to Flat 5 to find all of Cam's things boxed up and ready to go, and Ash halfway through packing, and soon after that, they will both be gone, and she will feel the cold and dense loneliness settle over her again like a dark and heavy fog.

She meets Dad at Newham Leisure Centre at seven in the morning on a Saturday and they power through fifty lengths together, each in their own lane, parallel to one another, yet synchronised. Her dad's body more broken than ever before but strong in its attack on the water. He matches her pace easily. She enjoys the sensation of the chlorine stinging her nostrils. Enjoys the echo of the swimming pool, the steamed windows and the roaring of the water in her ears. She remembers why she loved to swim with her dad so much: the simplicity of this shared task.

They get coffee in the café on the mezzanine above the pool afterwards. Soon, Mum has arrived with cherry bakewells stacked in a Tupperware. Their old tradition from years ago. She settles on the third seat at their rickety café table and smoothes her hair back. She looks tired. They both do. Lucy gives her a tentative hug, feels her hands resting gently on her back.

She tells them that she quit her job. And sees them both glance at one another, panicked expressions muted. Banburys don't quit their jobs. Especially without something else lined up. There's nothing more important than having a steady income.

She explains what happened at Kube. Her dad listens quietly, his fingertips pressed to his lips.

After she has finished the story, he tells her, I'm proud of you, Loose.

She smiles sadly at him. Thanks, Dad.

You can always come home if you need to, Mum says.

She can tell from their faces that they already know her answer.

I can't come home.

I know, chicken.

I want to live by myself. Find a smaller flat, maybe a bit closer to home. But there's too much that's . . . happened.

I know.

And Danny . . .

Daniel Senior takes his glasses off and wipes away the condensation with the corner of his flannel shirt. She notes how when he's back on dry land, he hunches over, like his whole body is folding in upon itself.

How is Danny? she asks.

Still not drinking, Mum answers, smiling forlornly.

Lucy lets out a breath that she didn't realise she was holding. That's good news.

He told us everything that happened, Dad says.

She waits for him to say more. Her mother holds her face in

her hands. Dad is struggling to let the words out of his mouth. His face screwed up in distaste.

Eventually he says: What happened to him. What Marv did to him.

Lucy can feel her bones sinking into the ground, her wet hair stuck to the sides of her face. The fluorescent light overhead sputtering.

And what he did to you.

Mum says, We never knew, with Danny. We weren't paying attention. Spent too much time working.

You were trying to give us all a better life.

And when you tried to tell us . . . we never believed you.

It's all ancient history. There's no point dragging it up now.

All those times you tried to tell us what was going on. And we ignored you. We failed you both.

And now, to her horror, she sees tears sliding down her father's face. His shoulders shuddering. She is aware of the bizarreness, mostly of the situation. The pink plastic chairs. The café table with one leg shorter than the rest so that it wobbles a little bit. Her father, who she has never seen cry in her twenty-six years, now crying before her. Banburys don't cry. Banburys get on with it.

Can you ever forgive us? he asks her quietly.

Dad, she says without hesitation. Of course. Of course I can.

She means it with her whole body.

And she puts her hand over his and feels the weathered, papery skin on his hands, hands of a man who worked himself to injury to prop them all up, to keep their heads above the water.

You don't need to ask, she tells him.

They go home together and sit in the kitchen of Lucy's childhood home, and talk and cry and remember things about before:

the good parts of Lucy and Danny's childhood. And there *were* good parts, Lucy knows that. She needs to be reminded of them, of the times before it all went wrong. And she feels a little bit of peace, with the secret history of their shared past on the table before them.

She says to her mum, I've decided that I want to find out about my birth parents. I want to try to get in touch with them.

She offers them this information as though it is on fire, as though they might have something with which to put it out.

The box: back under her bed at Flat 5, the papers collected up from the courtyard by Cam and carefully stacked and sorted.

I just wanted to check, she continues, that you were both okay with it.

If that's what you want, Mum says, reaching for her across the kitchen table, we'll help you as much as we can. We're here for you.

And deeper into the day, she remembers she was meant to be meeting Meredith for lunch. In the mess of her parents, she had forgotten.

She hesitates before texting her the address. Half an hour later, Meredith is calling her.

I'm outside your house, she says. I can*not* believe you dragged me to *Essex*. Where exactly are we going to eat?

Do you want to come in?

And she goes to the front door and opens it, with a thudding heart, and in comes Meredith, wearing an Alexander McQueen trench coat. And Lucy is nervous for this collision of two worlds: feels slightly dislocated at the sight of Meredith in the hallway of her subsiding childhood home, kissing her father on both cheeks and complimenting him on his fishing jumper. She worries how Meredith observes her parents and her family home, and how her parents will interpret her friend. But they all exchange hugs and handshakes and have cups of tea all squished up into the tiny kitchen, filling the space with their chatter and laughter. And Dad makes cheese sandwiches for everyone. And the air is warm and smells of something good.

Epilogue

It is October. Lucy is almost twenty-seven years old. Ash is in Poole, and Cam is home in Berkshire with his sister and mum. She is renting a studio flat in Lewisham. Not what she ever imagined for herself, but all she can afford for now. A ground floor with a scrub of patio. The landlord is pro-dogs, so Winston is here too. She remembers her younger self, imagining her life in London. A new-build flat with a balcony and hanging baskets, views of the city, east of central. For a little while, it felt like she had made it. But then it didn't.

She applies for a whole bunch of different jobs, part-time, minimum wage. Ash, who has made a living on casual work and zero-hours contracts, helps her with the job applications and the psychometric tests.

What is it exactly that you want to do? Ash asks her one evening on a video call as they tackle a job application together. Ash dictates answers – the ones they know will get Lucy past the algorithm that screens the thousands of applicants, to the human beings reading the CVs – as Lucy types them in.

I don't know, Lucy says, and she has never been surer about anything in her life. I'm going to take whatever I can get, she tells Ash. And work out what I like.

Who are you and what have you done with Lucy Banbury?

Lucy grins and shrugs.

She has never been less in control of her own life.

She is learning how to live with it.

She speaks to Cam on the phone very often. Upon his advice, she books an assessment with an NHS Talking Therapies service. The wait time is five months. She can wait.

She plans a dinner party for everyone. A flat-warming, of sorts. Starts a new group chat. Ash, Cam, Meredith. Nara. Even Paul and Francesca. She sets a date. She cleans the flat inside and out. She has managed to find two jobs: one as a lifeguard on Tottenham Court Road (with the added perk of a free swimming membership) and a second at a newly opened dog shelter off Lewisham High Street. She spends far too much of her first pay cheque on food and nice new plates. She only has two of everything of her own. Two dinner plates. Two knives. Two forks. Two spoons. And so on. She idles a Saturday afternoon slow-cooking a joint of pork in a crock pot: marinated in onions, garlic, cinnamon, sugar and chilli. She has done two practice mushroom wellingtons, and the third one – on the evening of – is for Ash. She picks out a dress. One her mother would like. She curates a playlist. She polishes the coffee table again. Realigns the salt and pepper shakers.

As she waits, seated on the edge of the sofa in her little studio flat picking at her fingernails, she imagines that none of them will come. That they will all play a horrible trick on her and leave her here alone with this pork shoulder and miles of puff pastry stretched across the countertops. They will instead go out for dinner without her. She lets Winston wind himself around her legs, buries her fingers in his fur. His eyes are shining. He knows something special is going to happen.

And then the intercom rings. She stands too quickly, startling

Winston, and forces herself not to sprint to answer it. It is Ash, with a rolling suitcase and a bouquet of crushed and wilting dahlias.

Sorry, they say, thrusting them at Lucy. Someone sat on these on the train. And then, promptly, they shriek very loudly.

Winston, confused, starts howling, as he does when the fire alarm goes off in the Tesco Express across the road.

I missed you *so much*, Ash shouts, yanking Lucy into a tangled hug, flowers once again squished between them. And then they sit on the floor and drag Winston willingly onto their lap.

And not long after come Paul and Francesca, with a home-made potato salad proffered forth in a Tupperware.

Then Nara and then Meredith, who has brought Angus along, and insists upon stroking his earlobe at all times.

They are all now crammed into the tiny square of Lucy's new flat, with one exception, the patio doors flung open to let the air in, not enough seats for all of them, so they sit on the floor and the countertops instead.

As Lucy pours wine, Meredith asks her, Is he coming, then? quietly, conspiratorially.

Lucy pretends she didn't hear her, that her stomach didn't do a backflip at the insinuation of him.

She hasn't seen him in two months – not counting Facetimes. She isn't sure, entirely, where they stand, what exactly they are to one another, now that the dust has settled. She invited him tonight, but he'd said that it might be a push to make it. He has a new job – Head of History at a sixth form near his parents' house – and he's been working late most Fridays. Lucy is trying very hard not to listen out for the intercom, just in case. Trying hard not to imagine him, now, on the DLR, drawing ever closer to her.

Ash is telling the rest of them about their new job as a kayaking instructor – which is, in fact, their old job – back home in Poole. Meredith is thinking of taking a trip to Dubai and dropping hints that Angus should come with her. Paul and Francesca are wondering about moving out to Redhill. They are laughing at something Paul has said. And Lucy is here, too, in the centre of this vortex.

And then, a little later, just as they are about to sit down for dinner, and Lucy has stopped hoping, the intercom is ringing once more, and she extracts herself from her friends and buzzes the lobby door open.

And she waits for him.

She thought he might not come. Told herself that he wouldn't. But there he is.

There he is, with that crooked smile. Almost-imperceptible chip in his front tooth. His eyes glittering, mischievous, dark and flecked with green. He is wearing a crisp blue linen Oxford shirt. A brown messenger bag slung across his back, his arms bracing him against the door frame. His dark hair is haphazard, from where the wind outside has messed it up. A look in his eyes that is a little bit desperate, a little bit relieved, like he cannot believe that he is there, and she is here, standing in front of him. She feels her heart swell in the special way that it does only for him.

On a day not too long from now, she will be much more certain. She will take the box out from its new place behind the sofa, register how it is warm as it presses against her fingertips, and she will show it to him, knowing that he is the one person she will share this final secret with, the one person she will trust with it. Knowing that no matter what happens, he will see her for exactly who she is. Clearer, sometimes, than she sees herself.

And he will hold onto her as she slips the lid off the box and lets its contents spill across the floor.

He will say, I'm here. Tell me what you need me to do.

That will be later, though.

Now, in this moment, he fills up the threshold with the mass of his being.

And the evening light from the window beyond floods in around him.

And the two of them are sharing a secret, here on the doorstep.

Banbury, he says.

She invites him in.

Acknowledgements

Thank you to the magnificent Anwen Hooson, who is the most hard-working, supportive and nurturing agent I could ever wish for. Thank you, Anwen, for everything you do for me and my work.

I am endlessly grateful to Charlotte Mursell, for shaping this book into something coherent and honest, and for helping me to find the right words to tell this story. Charlotte, the novel is infinitely better for your input, expertise and guidance: thank you.

Thank you to the incredible team at Orion: Sanah Ahmed, Jake Alderson, Alainna Hadjigeorgiou, Helena Fouracre and Paul Stark.

Thank you to the immensely talented Amber Gadd for once again lending your voice to my words and bringing them to life.

Most of this book was written during the lockdowns of 2020 and 2021. I don't think I would have survived the process of bringing Lucy to the page, in the midst of a pandemic, without the support of David Anderson, Sarah McBride, Ryan McCuaig and Kenny Murray. You have kept me sane and accountable; long may it continue.

Thank you to Sam Bourne and Becky Collins for your feedback on the earliest snatches of the manuscript; and for the quiet hum of a person on the other end of a Discord call. Existing together at the same time, if not in the same place, has been a godsend during the loneliest parts of writing this book.

All my love and thanks go to Jordan Friend and Ruben Willis-Powell for your generosity of time and spirit; and your thoughtful advice on writing a gender non-confirming character.

Thank you to David Gudge for kindly letting me use your account of student accommodation hell-on-earth in the novel.

Thank you to Emma Jeremy, the very greatest.

Thank you to the following for teaching me everything I know about Magic: The Gathering and Dungeons and Dragons: Scott Hodges, Danny Kent, Ryan Laughton, Charlie Little, Jamie Rosser and Matt Wright.

Thank you to my family.

If you would like to know more about dog rescue and rehoming, you can visit www.dogstrust.org.uk or www.battersea.org.uk/dogs

If you would like to know more about mental health support services near you, you can visit www.nhs.uk/mental-health or www.mind.org.uk

Credits

Kirsty Capes and Orion Fiction would like to thank everyone at Orion who worked on the publication of *Love Me, Love Me Not* in the UK.

Editorial
Charlotte Mursell
Sanah Ahmed

Copyeditor
Jade Craddock

Proofreader
Linda Joyce

Audio
Paul Stark
Jake Alderson

Contracts
Anne Goddard
Humayra Ahmed
Ellie Bowker

Operations
Jo Jacobs
Sharon Willis

Editorial Management
Charlie Panayiotou
Jane Hughes
Bartley Shaw
Tamara Morriss

Finance
Jasdip Nandra
Afeera Ahmed
Elizabeth Beaumont
Sue Baker

Marketing
Helena Fouracre

Design
Micaela Alcaino
Joanna Ridley
Nick May

Production
Ruth Sharvell

Publicity
Alainna Hadjigeorgiou

Sales
Jen Wilson
Esther Waters
Victoria Laws
Rachael Hum
Anna Egelstaff
Frances Doyle
Georgina Cutler

Don't miss Kirsty Capes' poignant, searing and achingly funny debut . . .

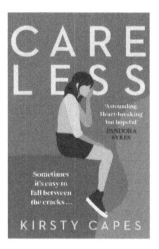

Sometimes it's easy to fall between the cracks . . .

At 3.04 p.m. on a hot, sticky day in June, Bess finds out she's pregnant.

She could tell her social worker Henry, but he's useless.

She should tell her foster mother, Lisa, but she won't understand.

She really ought to tell Boy, but she hasn't spoken to him in weeks.

Bess knows more than anyone that love doesn't come without conditions.

But this isn't a love story . . .

'The literary equivalent of gold dust' BENJAMIN ZEPHANIAH